A ROYAL AMERICAN

A New Jersey Officer in the King's Service during the Revolution

JOHN FREDERICK

© 2009 John Frederick
All Rights Reserved.

No part of this publication may be reproduced, stored in a retrieval system, or transmitted, in any form or by any means, electronic, mechanical, photocopying, recording, or otherwise, without the written permission of the author.

First published by Dog Ear Publishing
4010 W. 86th Street, Ste H
Indianapolis, IN 46268
www.dogearpublishing.net

dog ear
PUBLISHING

ISBN: 978-160844-054-2

This book is printed on acid-free paper.

Printed in the United States of America

Chapter 1

When, in April 1776, James Ricketts took the letter which Captain Hutchins, without comment, handed him, he did not realize what a contrast it would be from the other one received earlier the same day. That first letter, from his fiancée Sarah, so full of love and hope, was as he had expected it would be. She'd had her talk with her father, and apart from general misgivings about her wedding a King's officer, it had gone well enough. As a leading Whig rebel, Peter Van Brugh Livingston might well have objected strenuously but for Sarah's older sister Mary also being married to an officer in James's regiment. Her father had even suggested writing to Mary. His thought was that Mary corresponded often with Montgomerie cousins in Scotland and perhaps they would agree to allowing the wedding to be at Eglinton in Ayrshire.

Rocking gently on the porch of their quarters, a gesture of relaxation which thinly disguised James's nervousness – he had made an appointment to see his senior officer, Major Prevost - James did the only thing he could think of doing. He confided his predicament to his boyhood friend and fellow officer, Jacob Hart. The gentle Caribbean breeze, the warm sun, the exotic noises of the birds all implied a peacefulness that belied the tempest within him.

"These two letters could not be more different from each other," James blurted out.

Jacob replied vaguely, "The two letters?"

James, a lieutenant in the 2nd Battalion 60th Foot, British Army, eyed his fellow New Jersey-man, an ensign in his company, with pique. "Have you been listening to a word I have said?"

His friend answered hotly, "Of course I have, but when you finish telling me about the second letter, I have something pretty distressing to bother you with. Never mind. You tell me about the second letter, first."

James whipped the letter from his pocket as if it were hot coals, passing it to Jacob who read it:

Why did it have to be so difficult to arrange a wedding back in New Jersey? grumbled James silently. Of course the answer was obvious. What started as a skirmish over taxation had now degenerated into armed conflict in Boston and even beyond. Returning to the Province of New Jersey could prove hazardous. But he was not awaiting an interview with the battalion commander because of a letter from Sarah. The other letter breathed its own sort of fire – different from that of his fiancée. He took it from his pocket yet again, as if in hopes the impact might be softened. It read:

February the fifth, 1776

Dear James,

You will know that since you are engaged to marry my niece Sarah, I have your interest at heart and hope you will not object to my writing in an avuncular capacity, remembering that your own father is no longer alive and is, unhappily, not able to counsel you.

You must be aware of the struggle under way in which our own countrymen are determined to throw off the shackles of arbitrary domination and, as I believe they will soon openly declare, settle firmly the issue of their place amongst the independent nations of mankind. Indeed, your step-father who is to become your father-in-law as well, has been president of New York's Provincial Congress and his brother Philip is a delegate to the Continental Congress in Philadelphia. I may also mention your fianéee's uncle William Alexander, who calls himself the earl of Stirling, a most prominent Whig, amongst the eminent members of your family, now a general officer in our fledgling army. Such persons would be saddened if you were to fail to respond to your duty and perchance even place in jeopardy your rights to enjoy property and an inheritance in America.

Holding office in the military remnant of the discredited regime, you are in a position to aid your compatriots in their just strife. I trust that you will remain sensible of your obligations not only to your native province of New Jersey but also to your kinsfolk. Should you warm to the call of duty in the manner I hope of you, you may discover that inclination to me by discreetly

> *notifying the same to Mr Green at the Roundhead at Kingston in the island of Jamaica.*
>
> *I remain your Concerned and*
> *Obedient Servant*
> *William Livingston*
> *Delegate from New Jersey to the*
> *Continental Congress*

"I see what you mean," Jacob said, handing it back. "I know he's a big name in Sarah's mighty clan."

"What is worse," James went on, "is that he wants me to see some man in Kingston. I'm supposed to turn my coat and desert. Or perhaps even spy!"

Jacob felt his own moment had come. "I've had a similar letter."

"Not from William Livingston, surely!"

"No, no. From my neighbour Matthias Ogden. He returned from the expedition to Quebec and will almost certainly be offered a command in the Continental Army. Of course Livingston and Matthias know each other – they're both from Essex County - but there's no reason to think they are together in this. But my friend is determined that I shall join him in defence of our rights."

"Look here," said James, "we both have leave coming up – why not come with me to meet this fellow mentioned in the letter? I will have to tell the major what's afoot but since we both have leave coming, you could accompany me without my mentioning your feelings to Major Prevost. How you feel is your business but I hope you'll think twice before charging off in a direction you may come to regret."

"Does it not seem ironic to you – here we are, both trying to work out what is our duty, when our duty to the King seems a drab affair at best? Talk about being on the King's service, you'd imagine we had something important to do, would you not?"

Jacob smiled. "From your rueful look, I take it you are not completely consumed by the glory of your calling?"

"Glory, is it? Well, I suppose November is as good a time for wood cutting as any. Certainly there's not much else to do on this god-forsaken tropical paradise we call St Vincent," James observed.

"Why is it called St Vincent?" queried Jacob.

James could not resist exhibiting his knowledge and did not hesitate. "It was discovered by Columbus on St Vincent's Day."

Jacob, in turn, could not resist pushing the question. "But why pay attention to St Vincent? What has he got to do with us, who've always owned the island, since Europeans came, that is?"

"We know he was a fourth-century martyr of Spain," added James pompously. "I don't suppose he has much to do with us though – unless he was martyred for not cutting enough wood to please Caesar."

Jacob was diverted by the subject of wood-cutting. "I realize we need wood for housing troops but somehow I think it is mainly done to fight the infection of *ennui*," he said, keeping his end up as a sophisticate. "No doubt it's a better alternative than revelling in a rummy stupor like drunken sots. We're supposed to have two gills of rum a day but our worthy collection of soldiers from America, English gaols and German middens are resourceful at supplementing the diet. It's even more alluring than catching the pox from those mangy ladies in Kingstown."

James, safe in Sarah's love, felt himself above commenting: "I wouldn't know as much as you about that." Returning to the subject of boredom, he remarked, "Good God, they even have a Wood Call beat on the drum. This business of cutting wood is subtler than we think. Our serjeants invent architectural uses for the wood and get subalterns to think it was their own idea. Corporals consider themselves master carpenters and joiners – take Corporal Smith from Rahway, he's as ardent a carver of wood figures as any sailor is of scrimshaw."

Waiting for his interview with the battalion commander, he had time to look over what had led to his present situation. It all changed in 1771 when his widowed mother married Peter Van Brugh Livingston. He brought with him a large family including his seventeen-year-old daughter Sarah. Above all, Sarah. He also brought with him the widely-respected clout of the much larger Livingston clan, active in political and economic affairs of the provinces of New York and New Jersey. What began as a reserved acquaintanceship between James and Sarah suddenly changed. James was smitten.

His attachment to the gorgeous Sarah forced him to look hard at himself and his life. Sarah's dicomforting detachment about her family's privileged style of life enabled her to see both families from the outside, not just as an accepting insider. To James that was something new and it evoked his wonder.

Some weeks after her father's marriage to James's mother, she put her opinions to James. "What have we in our lives which hasn't been handed to us? 'Born with a silver spoon in our mouths,' do they not say? Look at the comforts we enjoy, the servants we take for granted, even the money coming in from the Jamaica plantation your family own, eked out of the sugar crop by all those poor black people who have to do it whether they would or no!" Over his mild remonstrances, she went on: "But what have we done, ourselves, to make a mark, or even to justify our smug comforts?"

Once again the idea of duty – duty to make a contribution – reared its head. Disinclined to think of fulfilling duty by running the plantation, his father's short military career offered a more attractive pattern for doing his duty.

Particularly upsetting about this elegant girl was – he knew she was right. His response disclosed another characteristic of life so far absent – the sense of adventure, even risk. He was preparing to matriculate at King's College, New York. His education, begun by the crabby family tutor, Mr Craddock, was due for completion in the city. How sensible – but not adventurous, not exciting and scarcely risky.

When he told her these feelings, she was surprised to find the two strains so clearly there: the sense of duty and the yearning for adventure. It appealed to her and she looked at him with a new interest. It also gave her a touch of apprehension despite all her bold talk. Was she falling too readily into an emotional connection? Was she ready to assume that kind of responsibility?

James could recall his idea of duty as it had unfolded in a conversation with his revered and bigoted tutor. Mr Craddock said to him: "Well, young sir, have you notions what you'd like to do in the future?"

Perhaps he had thought James would enter the ministry. Not that such a choice would have entirely pleased the Congregationalist Connecticut savant – he was sure his charge would not choose to be a proper minister but one of those papistical, dressing-up clergymen of the Church of England, thoroughly Anglican like the rest of the Ricketts family. Had they not helped found St John's in Elizabethtown and Christ Church in Brunswick? Still, he could do worse. They might be secretive papists but they weren't out-and-out ones – yet.

Craddock never seriously entertained the thought that James might want to help run the family plantation. True, most of their income came from the sugar crop. James's elder brother John was keen on doing just that. But the boys were unlike each other and James had a nagging distaste for the idea of running a plantation. He could not have organized such thoughts coherently, but it was not for him. He did, however, have an alternative path in mind.

"Oh, no, sir" James adressed his tutor, "I'm sure 'tis a good thing to take Holy Orders but I want to be an officer. You know, sir, in a red coat, like those who used to come," – he managed to swallow the lump in his throat – "when Polly was alive." Pretty Polly they'd called his sister who was admired by an unending delegation of army officer admirers out of the New York garrison - before she died at sixteen. When James matriculated at King's College, Mr Craddock no doubt had thought: a damned English-church hothouse, not some sensible place like Queen's College in Brunswick, founded by the Congrgationalists' sister church, the Presbyterians.

He also remembered Mr Craddock's words: "If you put on a red coat and are a proper King's man, what happens if our ties to England diminish? There are those who think that's going to happen. If it comes to enforcing the King's law against our people, what would you think about that?" the tutor asked, with the Stamp Act in mind.

James recalled the time when Mr Craddock learned he'd chosen the 60th or Royal American Regiment of Foot. Mr Craddock had been quite definite about that too. "Now there's a strange corps, I must say. Look here, it's first officers were Swiss and German. Now they're in the West Indies – what a hellhole! It's not that they're fanned by slaves on a plantation, the way your brother John probably is, slumped in the arms of luxury, ordering poor blacks around and fathering numerous half-breeds."

As far as blacks were concerned, James had come to look with pride on the honesty his father had shown. The records of St John's Church, Elizabethtown, showed the baptism in 1750 of "a negro child of Col. Ricketts", Francis, and the colonel's will of ten years later directed that "my Child Interr'd in Elizabeth Town be put in the same Decent Mahogenny Coffin with me". James thought Sarah would appreciate that.

James's ideas about combining duty and adventure matured. Sarah, to her surprise, did not put him down as a spoiled brat but increasingly sympathized and connived at his ambitions. They spent much time together during his college vacations. Nor were their relations entirely cerebral – particularly on one occasion in a barn when they had rough-housed themselves into an intimate embrace. It proved to be so intimate and startling – something their upbringing had not prepared them for – that they quickly came to a mutual, fully-clothed climax. In the afterglow of their mutual spending, they declared their love. Since they had no words to speak of what led to these declarations, they kept it a secret to be shared, mutely, by them alone.

For all the pleasure of Sarah's love, James was determined to pursue adventure as well as duty. Sarah would have it no other way, either. Before graduating from college, James pressed his mother to buy him a commission. She and her new husband had become aware of the attraction between the two and thought a time apart might be a good idea. So, on the sixth of January 1773, he was gazetted an ensign in the 2nd Battalion 60th (Royal American) Regiment of Foot, "vice Uniacke" – James wondered what had happened to Mr Uniacke - then in the West Indies. By then he knew enough about military and legal language to know that "vice" did not betoken some moral lapse by Mr Uniacke, but that he was appointed in the place of Uniacke. With a commitment made to duty as a soldier, another aspect of duty came to the fore and he reconsidered finishing at college, delaying his departure to Antigua until after his graduation. For whatever reason, his battalion seemed content to await his arrival, listing him continually in the muster rolls as "not yet joined".

His appointment with Major Prevost was at ten o'clock. James entered the officers' mess with an hour to spare. He stretched out in a wicker chair, comfortable in the atmosphere of the officers' mess. Differences in rank were downplayed with the officers encouraged by the 60th's colonel in chief, Jeffery Amherst, to foster comradeship and avoid boredom through games like billiards.

The clock chimed ten but the door of the major's office remained closed. At this moment, a welcome interruption occurred; someone arrived who could talk of life beyond the island – Captain Brehm.

"This is a pleasure, sir!" James said to Diedrick Brehm, maintaining the tradition of banal patter considered *de rigueur* in the mess. Captain Brehm was a Hanoverian who had thrown his lot in with the British years ago – part of that close relationship between Hanover and London built upon having a German King of England, and a German Queen too. "Oh, *ja*, not too wretched, I reckon. But I am off to London early next year, to recruit more *Deutscher-und-Schweitzer* as vee are the only corps that hass that privilege."

As Brehm had business elsewhere, the encounter was short-lived. Brehm had been captain-lieutenant of the battalion – a peculiar post. Since the Colonel's company of a battalion had to be led by someone other than the Colonel, who was usually a general far off elsewhere, the actual commander was styled "captain-lieutenant", ranking as the junior captain of the battalion. James knew, however, that being the Colonel's company, its commander would be picked by the Colonel as someone of unusual competence. At that time, "foreign" officers could advance freely in the 60th, which became a kind of foreign legion in the British regular army.

Chapter 2

What to tell the major? I've already had verbal assent to take leave, though Jamaica and New Jersey have not been specified. What do I know about him? That Mark James Prevost is in his early thirties, comes from a family long associated with the regiment in North America and the Caribbean, knows New Jersey well. He became a major two months ago and, with the absence of Lieutenant Colonel George Etherington on leave, is acting in command. Do I come out with everything I know, or do I pussy-foot about?

These thoughts were cut short when the orderly serjeant came to take him to Prevost. The small office whose proportions proclaimed it as the fruit of the serjeants' planning and the corporals' joinery, contained a desk – and Prevost, who rose and shook hands with James.

What to say when the major asks me how I came by the letter? Handed to me by Thomas Hutchins, another Jersey-man. And the current captain-lieutenant, too, appointed by our Colonel, General Sir Frederick Haldimand, a Swiss original of the 60th. Hutchins had succeeded Brehm as captain-lieutenant, and James had no wish to do him harm, even if he'd delivered a message from a rebel. But then, he did not know that Hutchins had done any more than pass along mail newly-arrived for the garrison. No, there could be nasty complications arising from any aspersions cast upon the commander of the general's own company.

"How did you come by that letter?" asked Prevost with a disconcerting directness.

James took refuge in the fact that Hutchins had made no subterfuge or hint of any trepidation. "It was handed to me, unopened, by Captain Hutchins, sir."

Prevost, somewhat to James's surprise and relief, did not pursue the matter. "James, it could be argued that you owe it to your future uncle to see the man Green, but you also owe it to me to tell me what you learn of him. Is that agreed?"

James nodded.

"I take it that means yes."

"Yes, sir," added James hastily.

"There's no problem here then. If anyone should ask you why you visited a man of doubtful loyalty, you can truthfully say you were charged to do so by me. Now, as for visiting New Jersey, your wish is at least two months too late. Rumour has it they may even arrest Governor Franklin for his loyalty to the Crown. If you go in uniform, you'll certainly be apprehended and we shall have the trouble of arranging an exchange – our authorities will not hold you guiltless in putting them to that trouble. If you are out of uniform, given the prominence of your family, it is unlikely you can escape detection and you might even be hanged as a spy. That would inconvenience not only you, but us! No, travel home is out of the question. I know the heartache this will cause you, James. May I remind you that my own family – my wife and two children – are all under house-arrest in the Jerseys, so I know what I say."

"Yes, I see, sir. I had not realized till now just how bad a state civil affairs had come to."

"To your successful leave and your return," concluded the major, pouring them both brandy.

On the first of May 1776 James Ricketts and Jacob Hart sailed for the island of Jamaica, armed with orders for Colonel Christie and his leave certificate from "the Honble. President Greathead", Commander-in-chief, Leeward Islands.

Once aboard, they found that the captain of the ketch *Bluebird*, a ruddy Englishman called Smithers, was cordial enough but said bluntly, in his north-of-England fashion: "Well now, you're both 60th Americans, are ye? What think ye of the shenanigans back home, eh?"

The skipper, sensing their unease, went on, referring to Kingston: "These merchants you'll see spread all over town are a rum lot. They're not above privateering which, if you ask me, is nothing more than licensed piracy. And they don't care much whose privateers they back, British or rebel. If you notice, the navy sailors allowed ashore are closely watched so that merchants don't entice them to their own ships. Then there's their bloody assembly, for ever begging for more guns but refusing to make provision to house the troops. No, your men here have their suspicions about the merchants, you'll not be surprised to hear. Then there's the climate – it kills more soldiers than battle does."

They soon sailed through the narrows of the entrance to Kingston harbour, past Drunken Man's Key, past the largely unmanned guns of the Apostles' Battery on the larboard side, then Fort Henderson and Musquito Point into the wide waters of the inner harbour. The harbour was busy enough so that the two men could disembark at the Wherry Wharf inconspicuously, wearing plain clothes.

Inquiries led to their finding accomodation at a tavern, the White Cross, much frequented by sea officers. Once inside, the atmosphere was convivial, the wine passable and the yam and salt beef edible. They decided to retire early.

At the same time when James and Jacob were docking in Kingston harbour, an impassioned meeting took place between a father and son in Kingston. Neither one was known to James but one of these men was to have a deep effect on James's future.

"'Their sword shall enter into their own heart, and their bows shall be broken.' Yes, father, you see why I must leave for England."

Old Cartwright looked uncomfortably at his son. "Be warned that the spirit of vengeance does not possess you and eat you up, my son, my only son."

"No fear of that. 'The righteous shall rejoice when he seeth the vengeance; he shall wash his feet in the blood of the wicked'."

Old Mr Cartwright marvelled at his son's familiarity with the psalms but did wonder if it blinded him to the subtleties and charity of christian truth.

Peter continued: "Ever since you embraced the Stuart cause back in the Forty-five, you have suffered at the hands of your adversaries."

"I cannot deny that. I was hounded from the city by the usurpers, though I suffered as much from the misguided citizens of Edinburgh who refused their rightful king because they feared a papist on the throne."

"Ah, father, 'they go astray as soon as they be born, speaking lies'. You do understand, do you not, the great chance that has come our way? If the colonists can throw off the German yoke, who knows, Ireland and Scotland may follow. I have seen Mr Green and he has lighted my path, showing me the good part I can play in the work."

"I am not sure what Mr Green's part is in all this" said the parent. "Is he not a mainlander who has lived here for some time?"

"Indeed, father. And it grieves his soul to see how some of his own countrymen play into the tyrant's hands. Mr Green acts as a messenger between our people on the mainland and our island folk. He has also encouraged me to follow my convictions and suggests I go to England to see if I may be of service later. On the mainland."

The next day, being a Monday, the two officers explored Kingston independent of one another. Jacob found his way to the Roundhead tavern, unaware that it was the abode of Mr Green of James's letter. In fact, James had explained few details to Jacob and Jacob was even unaware of the advisability of avoiding mention of his profession. Whilst there, Jacob struck up a conversation with a tall and sallow man who, when Jacob revealed he was an officer of the 60th, clumsily steered talk round to the contention between the colonists and the mother country. Apart from expressing sympathy for the rebellion, and voicing venomous hatred toward the wearer of the crown, the stranger showed little of himself, taking refuge in an extraordinary panoply of biblical-sounding phrases. He did suggest Jacob should have a word with a Mr Green.

For his part, James, wandering along King Street, saw the old parish church of Kingston, St. Thomas the Apostle's. He entered and saw the notice that Admiral Benbow was buried there. James felt an urge to absorb the quiet of the church and soon found himself repeating the prayers he had learnt at St John's, Elizabethtown. It struck him that the Church was one of the few institutions which called people together. As he leafed through his prayer-book, he saw the prayer for "thy chosen servant George, our King and Governor" - the same as that which he had prayed countless times in his own church. Not being outwardly pious, he nevertheless felt drawn to pray for angelic assistance in the words of the collect for Michaelmas, "as thy holy Angels always do thee service in heaven, so by thy appointment, they may succour and defend us on earth", even if his friends might think that a bit papish.

At six o'clock he entered the Roundhead, ordered a shandygaff and awaited the arrival of Jacob who had gone out to tour the town. The public house was, as most buildings in Kigston were, built of wood. The main room was large and smelled noticeably from the fireplace, smoke from which also tended to hamper vision. James approached the bar and asked for Mr Green. The barman looked at him sharply, saying, "Who wants to see him?"

Tell him that Mr Ricketts and Mr Hart from St Vincent would like to talk to him privately.

"Ye'll have to wait a few minutes afore I'm free to pass your message, sir." said the barkeep in a west-of-England accent. If James had thought his arrival was going to occasion scurrying feet, he was to be disappointed. About a half-hour later, the barman vanished, returning laconically after an interval. "Mr Green is engaged this evening, sir, and he suggests you enjoy a meal and come back tomorrow at seven o'clock." Since they had already eaten, they left.

On Tuesday, they arrived at seven and were shown into a small parlour where, by the fireplace, sat a middle-aged, birdlike man who rose, smiled and shook hands. "Mr Ricketts, a pleasure to see you," said Green in what sounded like a drawl from south of the Mason-Dixon line. "I gather you have some business with me, though I had not actually expected to see you in the flesh, as it were. A pleasure, for all that. But who is your friend?"

Introductions over, James mentioned the letter referring him to Mr Green.

"Aye, very good of you to come. I should make my position clear. I act as a messenger conveying news and correspondence to and from the mainland. Your uncle-to-be, is it? told me he'd written and that I might just hear from you. May I ask what you feel about his letter, and why you've come to me?"

"Mr Green, I'll be frank. I come from New Jersey, I hold the King's commission, and I regard myself as a loyal subject. However, I would be stupid not to recognize that my countrymen have legitimate grievances against England but I would feel – dishonourable – if I betrayed my commission and my military oath."

Green brightened. "I can appreciate what you say, sir. You see, I have the advantage of you. I well remember your father, the colonel, when he came for spells at Ridgeland. A fine gentleman he was, to be sure, often sitting on the magistrate's bench, even after he removed to the Jerseys. We always called him Colonel, even though his commission was not a regular one. Of course, in those days," he continued, "you could be a provincial colonel on the mainland as well as a Jamaica magistrate – no need to choose one over the other. Not like our times, eh?

He continued, "I can see we are both men of honour. Unfortunately, such civil conflicts encourage skullduggery and underhanded behaviour. I hope my part in this will be adjudged gentlemanly – respecting the dictates of conscience. If you threw your lot in with the colonists, I could help you get in touch with them. If you be unable to do so, and are principled enough not to dissemble but tell me that plainly, then I will respect your decision and do nothing to undermine you."

"Mr Green, since you speak in such a fair manner, let me explain farther. I had hoped to take my leave in Elizabethtown – for one thing to arrange my wedding to Mr Livingston's niece. As a matter of fact, she is my step-father's daughter, so her father will become my father-in-law as well as my step-father. I tell you this because I want you to realize the strong temptation to go home. But that is possible only through some subterfuge in which I pretend to be won over to your cause, and then slip away trickily later. I cannot do that. By telling you so, perhaps you'll accept me as being as candid as you've been to me."

"I respect you for that," said Green, "but what about you, Mr Hart?"

"Yes, well, as gentlemen of such opposed views are so straightforward with each other, I incline to be likewise. I had a letter like James's – only from my neighbour Matthias Ogden. I have to say the issue seems less complex to me than it does to you. From what my friend tells me, New Jersey is defending its rights and resisting tyranny which London tries to impose on us as if we were not Englishmen with the rights of Englishmen. Don't you see the force of that, James?"

"Oh, I see that well enough," replied James, "but I'm not convinced by it. I grant you, London behaves foolishly. But what nags me is – what's at stake? People say 'No taxation without representation' but who is properly represented, even in England? And are the taxes in question really crushing? That seems to me to be laughable! The government put the price of tea lower than it has ever been and the Boston merchants dumped it over the side because they wanted to charge more for it. That sounds like hypocrisy to me.

"All right," James continued, "we're treated unjustly, to be sure. But what an insular point of view we fall into, so easily. We can't put up with a bit of injustice for the sake of the empire – our family unity is to be shattered because we're asked to bear some burthens. Some of these are burthens which the British taxpayer incurred to keep the French and Indians off us. Our own regiment is the perfect example. The King himself put up money to raise it for our protection. People easily forget that. No, I'm not yet convinced that rebellion is right."

"I can see why you might think that way, James. But my neighbour Matthias went off to Canada with Aaron Burr and may well take high rank under General Washington. I cannot believe that good men like them or Benedict Arnold would serve an unjust cause. I suspect we could argue about it all day, I have to tell you that my mind is made up. I'm not going back to the regiment. I'm off to New Jersey the quickest way I can go. It's my home and I will fight for it. You always did see two sides of every quarrel whatever anybody else said, James, and I respect you for it. Earlier I had a talk with a Mr Cartwright and it helped me make up my mind."

At this, Mr Green lifted his eyebrows momentously, but said nothing. After a moment, he answered. "Gentlemen, we can see the endless debate such controversy engenders. I suspect neither of you will change the other's mind.

"But there are certain things I have to say to you. First, when Captain Hutchins dropped in here, having some slight acquaintance with him and knowing him to be from your province, Mr Ricketts, I asked him to deliver the letter. I have no reason to think he knows its contents."

"I did go out of my way to tell my commanding officer that the letter was unopened," replied James.

"That was fair and decent of you, sir," Green threw in. "As well, I admire your fairness toward your dissenting friend. James – if I may call you that – you seem to desire gentlemanly behaviour on the basis of principle, as do I.

"Third, and it pains me to say this: Jacob mentioned his talk with Cartwright. Now that man has decided views and will do whatever he thinks will aid the Jacobite cause. That means he will aid all rebels to King George. But he cares nothing about the principles. He is consumed, eaten up, devoured, not by desire for liberty, but by loathing and hatred for the Hanoverian monarchy. He is utterly without scruple. You can see that I am uneasy about him – an understatement, to be sure. If I were you, I would give him a wide berth. I say this to you hoping you will let my words go no farther – he is a very dangerous man."

Chapter 3

James penned a letter to Prevost apprising him of the gist of what had occurred and saying he was sorry that his companion had chosen another course and had gone off unannounced. He then turned his attention to Ridgeland, the family plantation. Not about to go by road to the parish of Westmoreland in which Ridgeland lay – roads were too rocky – he made inquiries at Wherry Wharf which led him to the barque *Rosehip*. Reckoning the offer of ready cash would appeal to the ship's master more than deferred payment through a travel warrant, the offer of cash also underscored his awareness that his leave had actually begun.

I must avoid making a clumsy fool of myself over the local currency, he thought. Fingering his coins, he recalled one ryal or bitt was worth seven-and-a-half English pence; ten bitts made a dollar also called a cobb, worth 6s 3d Jamaican. Thirty-eight bitts made a pistole or £ 1 3s 9d (Jamaican); sixty-two bitts made a moidore, the name of an old Spanish coin, or £1 8s 9d (again Jamaican). Finally £140 Jamaican was equal to £100 sterling. His voyage cost him thirty-two bitts, that is, he recognized, a pound Jamaican. Dinner aboard was a further four bitts and for one bitt he got a shave.

As they pulled away, the sun shone and he was about to settle down for a pleasant cruise when his peace was shattered by two shots across the bows. "What the devil is that?!" he said, flinging the words at the captain who seemed completely unperturbed by the spouts of brine rising a hundred feet ahead of them.

"Nothing to fret about, m'lad, nothing at all. Unless you're carrying some contraband the customs want to take from you. You see the old port a few points off our starboard beam, don't ye? That's Port Royal, or it used to be before the earthquake roughed it up some years back. A proper pirates' den, it used to be. I reckon the navy and the revenue keep to old ways: and the end of piracy hasn't convinced them to change. We'll just have to heave to and let them come aboard."

I wonder if my uniform will make any difference to them, James thought silently. But they were not the least impressed so familiar was the going to and fro of army officers in Jamaica. After a half-hour's cursory search and much chatter with the captain, they let the barque go.

The thirty-league trip was broken by one stop. At one in the morning not much could be seen of Bluefields. James remarked to the boatswain: "There's a story in my family that my great grandfather once commanded that fort." The boatswain's curt nod conveyed what he considered appropriate for a useless bit of information.

Around noon the next day, the barque anchored at Savanna la Mar and James found a tavern for luncheon. He soon located Joey, sent down the Cabaritto River in a small boat to pick him up. The servant's incessant use of "Massa" as a form of address, used much as a private soldier would say "Sir", was strange to his ears. He wondered what thoughts really passed through the mind of Joey. By late afternoon, they had worked their way past innumerable fields of sweet and sour oranges and woods heavy with palm and cottonwood trees. Though the island produced much cattle and wheat, the western part of Jamaica raised mainly sugar cane. A sugar plantation would also need cattle – at Ridgeland there were over a hundred head – to provide food and also manure for the fields.

He got off at the bacardier or sturdy jetty and walked up to the big house, followed by a cart with his luggage. There he was welcomed amiably enough by Arthur Jones. "A good day to you, Mr Ricketts." His ten years as overseer at Ridgeland did not disguise the Welsh voice. "Did you have a good journey?"

"Yes indeed. I found a tavern at Savanna la Mar and ate lunch."

"Oh my goodness me – what a risky undertaking!" observed Jones. "I suppose they gave you their usual clucking hen broth and pepper pot followed by tom tom plantains and fish beat together? Fit for blacks, mainly."

Though put off by this patronising display, James had to admit that Jones had, in fact, described the menu with minute accuracy. Jones pressed on: "I hope they found you something potable to drink?"

"Some Spanish red wine, actually," replied James, not knowing what torrent of denunciation that might bring down.

"Gracious to goodness, things must be looking up." "Did you happen to notice Captain Linders propping up the bar and holding forth?"

"I can't say that I did," said James, briefly.

"But I expect you are tired, Mr Ricketts. And I am wondering if you'd like to give me some idea what you want to be doing whilst you are with us."

"I'm not particularly tired. After all, it's only a dozen or so miles from the town and I am curious to know more about the life here. For one thing, how do people feel about the trouble in North America?"

"Ah well, I hear there's talk of independency up there. To tell the truth, people here are more concerned with the trade with the colonies than they are with politics. As long as they trade with us, we'll be happy. Not that there's much agitation for separation from Great Britain hereabouts. We need the Royal Navy's protection. And the troops to keep down slave rebellions, if it comes to that," he added, glancing at James's uniform.

To show he was not completely ignorant of such things, James observed: "Yet, disputes with the Lords Commissioners of Trade and Plamtations in London have been fierce at times, have they not? At least my brother has told me that."

"And of course your brother John must be right." James wasn't quite sure how that was meant. "He is often away, enjoying the fleshpots of Kingston, so he leaves the day-to-day running of the plantation to me."

"Well, I'd very much like, Mr Jones, to find out how the estate runs - whatever I can about how life goes on here," said James, adding "I must rejoin my company by mid-June, so I should be able to see quite a lot in, say, five months. I had hoped to visit my fiancée in New Jersey but I fear events in North America put that out of the question. The fact is – life here is strange to me and I do not understand, for one thing, what deportment people expect from me, especially those who work the estate."

"Oh, Master James, don't you worry your head too much about that," Jones was quick to reply, leaving James feeling patronised once more. The overseer went on, "The Negroes here, apart from an occasional freeman, are your property or more correctly you and your brother's, who inherited after the colonel died. What is wanted is that they should please you and not the other way round. Mind you, they are valuable property so we don't mistreat them, as some planters do, but we try to keep them healthy and fit and reasonably content. We don't go out of our way to encourage their resentment – no more than they already feel, nor do we allow indiscipline either. That sort of slackness never works, not for them nor for us, neither. My goodness me, no!"

In the days that followed, James was taken to see various aspects of life on the estate which at the winter season included the cutting of wood, about which he reckoned he already knew something, repairs to the wattle and thatch dwellings so as to enable them to withstand the customary stormy weather and occasional hurricanes. "Does not the wattle become cracked in the dry season?" asked James.

"Aye, we mix water, soft cow dung and wood ashes with a small bit of fire mould to make it thick for rubbing into the walls," observed Jones. James saw that some of the work, especially the digging of holes in hard soil for the planting of sugar cane was unpleasant toil indeed.

James concluded: "I suppose you could sum it up by saying that work is centred on three basic tasks: farming sugar, raising food for the servants, and growing timber for fuel and construction."

"You could put it that way," said the overseer.

One of the arduous jobs, hoeing cane and weeding, had been completed in October. Hoeing was tricky as canes were sharp and could cut those wielding the hoe. On the whole, medical care seemed to be scrupulously observed, not out of kindness so much as from the economic necessity of keeping a healthy labour force. One affliction to which the workers seemed particularly prone was crab-yaws in which painful hard patches appeared mainly on the feet and legs. This was cured by putting hog-plum tree bark in a pot and boiling it, with the addition of water till it became strong. This was placed over a gentle fire and the afflicted part kept in the pot, as hot as could be borne, for nine days and nights.

James soon discovered that overseeing the work of the slaves or "servants" was not all that white bosses expected to do. He was displeased, if not surprised, to find that their proprietary rights over the blacks extended beyond the working of the plantation. Consequently, maintaining a healthy labour force, and a healthy corps of bosses, was more difficult than he might at first have imagined. Venereal disease afflicted slaves and masters alike, since whites often seemed to feel little hesitation in exploiting the more comely wenches among the house slaves. This extension of owners' perquisites was made clear to him one evening.

A twenty-year-old mulatto girl named Hannah, having brought his evening meal, came up to him as he dined alone and stood close beside him as he sipped his coffee. His attention was caught by the mildly-perfumed scent of soap and by her long, straight black hair, caught back loosely. For the first time, James really noticed her. She smiled down at him somewhat shyly, her lips parted as she smiled at him, her unusually green eyes beautifully set off by her light brown, soft complexion. Her eyes were fixed on his face as they looked first at one eye of his, then the other, in a way he found penetrating, intimate and disquieting, all at the same time. When she spoke, it seemed like the purr of a devoted cat. "It's so pleasing to have you here with us, Massa - James." His name was subtly separated from the word before it in a way that made it almost a caress. Nor could he avoid noticing the way she held back her arms so as to emphasize her small and exquisitely rounded breasts whose nipples were undisguised by her translucent chemise.

James wondered whether young female "house-servants" were all accustomed to presenting themselves with an insouciant precocity field hands would never show. It gave him pause to see how easily he could use the opportunity she presented to him so unashamedly, and he felt cross with himself.

At this point, Jones entered the room, apparently noticing nothing unusual, even though she assumed a different, less provocative posture and picked up a plate to cover her movement toward the pantry. When she had gone, Jones's face took on an impish, presumptuous smirk, making James feel compromised and angry. Jones spelled it out to him, as if he were some particularly dense and innocent schoolboy: "Well, Mr Ricketts, it's clear you've made a great impression on Hannah. She's usually very slow to favour anyone with her attentions, but you seem to have got well under her skin." As James's breathing became shorter and more controlled, he informed James that no one would take it amiss if she were to share his bed.

Looking hard at Jones, James answered: "Is that one of the normal rights of ownership?"

Noting there was no trace of amusement in James's face, Jones was compelled to explain himself: "Nutmegging, we call it. Everybody does it in these parts." Though not putting it into so many words, Jones's meaning was clear: more fool you, not taking advantage of it. Jones soon removed himself from the awkward confrontation, leaving James alone.

James convinced himself – a bit too easily – that his relief at momentarily avoiding entanglement with Hannah was his loyalty to Sarah. But he was also aware that any such liaison was complicated by the manifest attachment to Hannah of one Sam, a creole who ardently courted her. All in all, he flattered himself by feeling virtuous. And he eschewed putting himself on Jones's level. Was he being a snob? He also felt rather lonely.

He pulled himself up short and tried a round of self-examination. What was he upset about? He needed only a short time for that point. He was attracted by Hannah and knew he wanted her. Moreover, he was certain she knew he did and, because he managed to avoid her for the next few days, guessed she was puzzled by the distance he kept. It would be easy and she was so willing. Why then resist her? True, he had heard of Sam and he did not fancy ploughing another's field.

There was no future for James and Hannah; both of them must know that. So why was Hannah available? I cannot really be irresistible to her. He fancied it must be that Hannah wanted something from him and knew no way to get it except by encouraging him to use her, putting him in her debt, encouraging him to grant her some boon. What boon? Sam?

Suddenly, he felt anger surge through him. He was aware that no need arose for such a tangled distortion of sexual relations between him and his own peers. Sarah and he had freely exchanged affection in Elizabethtown, even reaching climax but without exploitation or even penetration. The deviousness, the disguised objectives, the resort to manipulation was due to the setting of slave and master. Hannah was being obliged to win a champion who, once he had exercised his "rights" might be cajoled into taking her part. And he too was manipulated by the unsavoury system – she had sensed his lonliness and was exploiting it in the only way open to her. "I'm sure you must be lonely, massa – James," (once again, that separation of the two words). "Why not let me be your friend?" she had appealed to him on one of the few occasions he could not avoid being alone with her.

That was the trouble with this damned system: it corrupted both master and slave. He wanted to confound it, to smash it as least as far as his life was concerned.

There was only one way to do that. He would have to arrange a change in the circumstances, the status, of Hannah, Sam and himself, too. He would give them what they needed but freely, without the intermediate manipulation. Doing it that way would annoy people like Jones. That alone almost made it worth doing. The vague outlines of a plan began to form but would have to await his brother John's return before anything concrete could be done. Meanwhile, somehow, he maintained the distance between himself and Hannah.

In a few weeks, John returned to the plantation from Kingston where he had, amidst the amusements of the town, found time to negotiate the sale of sugar from Ridgeland. James felt lucky that he and Jacob had narrowly missed running into John on their trip to Kingston. The complications of dealing with his brother and Mr Green simultaneously would have been too much. He felt relief.

Of the two brothers, John had elected to live in Jamaica full time. That would not have surprised Mr Craddock. It soon became clear that John shared the opinions of the planters. James, on the other hand, grew increasingly estranged in his ideas respecting relations between master and slave. John was often away as a militia officer and, consequently, James saw little of his brother. He felt more than ever content to let John attend to estate affairs and had little yen to be involved in what was to him a disturbing imbalance in the social relations between the different races – whites, mulattos, creoles, maroons (descendants of the slaves of Spanish days who had built themselves up into a sizeable and free community), blacks: their relations with each other were all dominated by an hierarchical frame of mind.

Not that overseers were stand-offish. They entered into the social life of the slaves quite avidly, making it their business to know personal details intimately. They attended feasts of "Negro music" and though James thought such contact a good thing, he knew that control was the motivation for their interest.

One evening he was put on the spot by Hannah who approached him. "Massa James" (no separation of words, this time) "when I offered you my friendship, you turned me down and I was hurt."

"No, Hannah, I never turned down your friendship – only the way you were offering it," said James, uncharacteristically precise.

"How could you be – friendly – without opening your bed to me?" she asked.

"Are you saying, Hannah, the only way I could be a friend to you is to use you, then cast you aside?"

He could see, despite the silence that ensued, that her mind was racing. She lacked no intelligence. "You mean you could be my friend and not bed me?" she said as if the idea had never occurred before. Suddenly she made a decision and boldly acted on it. "Can I take you at your word? Can I take your meaning in a way someone like me cannot do, normally? I mean the truth is – I want to marry Sam and there is no way people like us can marry, and be free, without someone – important – to back us up."

"I see, Hannah, what you mean. You mean you wanted to win my help by making me a gift."

"Yes," she replied, smiling in a way that now contained no hint of guile or exploitation, "you could say that."

James was touched. He moved to carry out his plan to help Hannah and Sam and quickly tackled John. It was no easy thing for James to talk to him. He could not ever remember a heart-to-heart talk with him. But he seized the bull by the horns with results that quickly unfolded.

He proposed to pay John the price of their manumission, allowing them to marry and be free. This he discussed with John, who thought him a sentimental fool. James persisted and John was persuaded to accept a manumission offer of seventy-five pounds each. James was able to meet the terms and was present at the marriage in the parish church, following the baptism of Hannah and Sam. Less objection was offered than might otherwise have been the case since the two suitors were mulatto and creole, respectively.

Though his leave was for six months, James felt he'd had enough of plantation life to last him for years, so at the beginning of September he made his excuses and began his return to the battalion.

Chapter 4

Back in New York, Sarah was aware that her love for her father had clarified and deepened in the last two or three years. She recognised his loving nature and respected his commitment to the patriot cause he believed in, but she was mentally sharp and clear about his shortcomings.

Sarah's father was determined to finish some business for the province in the city. Three days after they settled in at the house used by the provincial treasurer, his secretary broached the news: "Three British ships have appeared off Sandy Hook." Two days later, the same unwelcome herald announced: "There are a hundred and thirty King's ships and probably nine thousand troops lying off Staten Island."

Everyone knew that the deceptive calm after the British evacuation of Boston would not last. Certainly the British government would not take its frustrations lying down. Enough intelligence was reaching the province to settle the conviction that the city would be a primary target for retribution. At least it seemed so to the Continental Congress and to General Washington as their troops had been pouring into the city to defend it for some weeks.

Sarah's uncle, William Alexander, who had been appointed colonel of the Continentals' 1st New Jersey Regiment in November 1775, became a brigadier the following March, taking command of the city until Washington's arrival on the thirteenth of April 1776. It seemed strange to Sarah that Uncle William, who was also in Manhattan, had an action under way in the House of Lords to claim the title of Earl of Stirling whilst commanding rebel forces.

On the second of July, General Howe landed on Staten Island unopposed and on the fourth, his brother Admiral Lord Howe arrived with one hundred and fifty ships. The arrival of another contingent from the unsuccessful assault on Charleston brought the total to over thirty-one thousand men. The threat to New York became even clearer when, at the end of August, the rebel forces in Long Island were trounced. As Sarah and her father learned to their dismay, Lord Stirling was made a prisoner of the King's German ally, General Heister.

In the Livingstons' city household, breakfast conversation revolved round the peace conference between Benjamin Franklin, John Adams and Edward Rutledge, on the one side, and Admiral Lord Howe, on the other. Those negotiations lasted two weeks and though Washington used the time to re-position his troops, the concensus was unfavourable to the city's defence. "Our commander has shuffled his men around to no purpose save to place them in the worst places," remarked the secretary.

Hours before the truce's end, a knock sounded at the front door. They opened it and found a major in blue and buff. "Good evening, sir. May I speak to Mr Livingston, please? My name is Ewing, William Ewing, aide-de-camp to General Spencer."

"I am he, major," answered Peter. "I have not had the good fortune of meeting the general."

"Would that we had time for that, sir. The general was lately in Connecticut where General Lee was raising levies to defend this city and only arrived with them in March. General Spencer is concerned lest you be taken if – perhaps I should say when – the city falls. He earnestly begs you to let us escort you to the dock so you may slip over to the Jersey shore without delay."

Occupied with plans to flee, Sarah and her father were not kept abreast of the disastrous details. They knew only that the lull was drawing to a close, and they had better leave the city which was in short order evacuated by General Washington. The next day, royal forces landed at Kip's Bay on the East River and soon crossed the island to arrive on the Hudson just in time to exchange shots with Washington's rear guard.

The journey of Sarah and her father to Basking Ridge, their new home, was carried out during the lull. Before leaving, they heard the news of her uncle William's capture on Long Island by the German General Heister's forces.

Her father remarked, "William and I were often involved in finance together. But even a dispute over a loan I made to him cannot dim his generosity in asking us all to his place at Basking Ridge. I hope he will soon be exchanged."

Having navigated the Hudson River across to Elizabethtown, Sarah and her father entered the local tavern to arrange transport to cover the twenty miles to Basking Ridge. Sarah's father had a short wait but arranged hire of a trap and driver with the innkeeper who managed a profitable sideline in providing transport. The innkeeper, a bluff and affable fellow who would talk too much and too long, could not be restrained from making observations. "Ah, Mr Livingston, is it? You're lucky to be heading inland and also *when* you are – I mean another few weeks and I reckon you'd be very lucky indeed to find a horse-and-trap anywhere in Essex County."

"Really? Why is that?" asked Livingston in all innocence.

"Well, sir, for one thing, I reckon every cart and coach will be carrying people westward as fast as they can skedaddle. And what hasn't been hired out will be taken by redcoat officers showing their ladies around." Sarah, listening in silence, could not tell if the innkeeper viewed such a prospect as a tragedy or a blessing.

Waiting for their trap to be readied, Livingston eased into conversation with the prosperous-looking man on the same bench. This man was quick to say, "It certainly looks as if the show is all over, sir, doesn't it? The rebels have had a run for their money but the game is just about up, I think. And as for people streaming to get away, I think a lot of us'll be staying just where we are and maybe glad all the commotion is finished."   "It's all very sad," Peter ventured, not indicating whether he meant the rebellion or the fall of New York, "We shall have to wait and see."

By mid-September, life at Basking Ridge had pretty well settled down. They heard news of events a few days after they happened: the New York fire on the twentieth, the gradual pushing of Washington's forces into Westchester County culminating in their defeat at White Plains at October's end – another success of Howe's after which the failure to follow up missed the chance of destroying the rebel army despite the capture of Forts Washington and Lee, forts which Uncle William had built.

In 1776, Elizabethtown was a pleasant place. Situated on the Jersey shore, it abounded in farmland and its small river afforded access to Manhattan across the wider waters. The town had a number of influential citizens but a hint of trouble lay therein. Families like the De Lanceys and Hetfields were Tory and loyal to the crown; others like the Ogdens and a number of Livingstons were Whigs and supported colonists' rights.

Elizabeth, James's mother, had married Peter Van Brugh Livingston in 1771 seventeen years after James's father's death and two years after Peter's first wife's death. The second Mrs Livingston thereby became step-mother to Peter's surviving children among whom was Sarah, now twenty years old. Elizabeth had trod carefully in winning the confidence and affection of her step-children. After the return of her husband and Sarah from New York, Mary raised the subject of Sarah's marriage with her step-daughter.

"Do you know, Sarah dear, what an – unusual – position it puts me in, you and James's wanting to marry?" she remarked.

"Yes. Not only will you be my step-mother but also my mother-in-law. Does it worry you very much, Mumsy?" answered Sarah.

"Only in wanting to retain your love. We all know how easily brides talk about their mother-in-law and I would hate to have our real friendship eclipsed by anything."

"I'm not afraid of that happening," whispered Sarah, hugging Mary.

Mary continued: "I'm so glad you went with your Papa to help him in the city. He is clearly upset at the way things are going. Politics have always been so important to him. No one knows what will happen next, but if anyone can encourage him to do what is wise, it's you."

"From what Papa says, if we find Elizabethtown too exposed and have to leave it, Uncle William has offered us refuge at Basking Ridge. I suppose it's a possibility since Uncle William is one of the generals of the Continental Army. How odd it all is – my sister Mary is married to a 60th officer, I'm planning to marry another 60th officer, and they might be attacking New York at any moment," Sarah mused.

"Thank goodness, the 60th are well out of the way in the West Indies," replied Mary.

Sarah's eighteen-year-old sister Susannah curled up at the foot of her older sister's bed. Susannah enjoyed the conspiratorial atmosphere which accompanied a private chat with Sarah. "How can Papa keep up his important position if we have to go traipsing off to Basking Ridge?"

"O, my dear Susie," Sarah sighed, "you are so impressed by influence and family position."

"Of course I care about our family's reputation," she retorted. "Why not take pride in them, and our place in polite society? Don't you like having a nice country estate and fine clothes and, er, all," petering out.

"Of course I like such things, you ninnie," agreed Sarah. "But we don't have them through any merit of ours. We happen to be born into wealth and renown. None of it is our doing – yours or mine. I mean, any credit for position belongs to our ancestors. To claim the credit and, worse, to act on it, is just snobbery."

"How can you talk about dear Papa that way?" remonstrated Susannah, somewhat illogically.

"I'm not deriding Papa. I have great respect for what he has done himself but you have to admit that a powerful clan behind him has not hurt. You talk about Papa. What about our Mama who died when you were eight? She married at seventeen and she bore Papa fifteen children, of whom only seven are still alive. Do you realize, Susie, that's a child every two years, regular as clockwork? You have to ask: our dear loving Papa – for that's what he is – was he sure-sighted in fathering so many children, and half of them sickly, which ended her life at twenty-eight years of age?"

Susannah was aghast, mainly because she had not thought of it herself. "Why...why...I don't know about all that, but he's a true patriot and foresighted when it comes to his country."

"Well, that's as may be. I would never reproach him. I say it to you only because I see you growing up and I don't want you going round with a lot of silly ideas in your head."

"When did you both fall in love?" she asked.

"I think it was at Mumsy and Papa's wedding – at least that's when James showed interest – though it took me a long time to respond," explained Sarah smugly.

"O, Sarah, do tell!" Susannah oozed skepticism.

"No, really, it is true. I found him pompous, self-important, something to do with his going to King's College, maybe. I warmed and when we came to be excited by each other – I'm talking about bodily excitement, Susie," – Sarah enjoyed shocking her sister – "then we both agreed we could not complete our desires; you know what I mean? We were forced to examine just what we did think of each other. Then he proposed to me."

Susannah had reservations about that account but let it go. Again turning abruptly to a new subject, Susannah said, "Do you think Papa can ever be happy out of politics?"

"I've been thinking on that too. Why does he think of it: giving up being president of the New York provincial congress? Perhaps the answer lies in us. Look at us, his children. Philip, loyal to the crown as can be, now in England. Catharine, married and away from home. Mary and I, both British Army wives – or soon to be. Peter a rebel. William a loyalist. You and Elizabeth both young," Sarah concluded, rather haughtily. With our family that divided, would it be any wonder if Papa decides he's done his bit?"

On the thirteenth of September 1776, James travelled by horse and trap to the small port of Savanna la Mar, ten miles away on the southwest coast of Jamaica. Making his way to the docks in uniform, he was reminded of his regiment's wide dispersal by encountering two private soldiers in Captain Phillips's company of the 60th, in red tunics with the blue facings of a royal regiment, whose salute he returned promptly. He quickly went aboard a brig bound for St Vincent.

At the same time, following Mr Green's advice, Peter Cartwright was bound for England. Unknown to one another, they passed within two cables length from each other.

The trip to St Vincent turned out to require a fortnight because of the prevailing wind and an unpleasant storm which blew them miles off course and confirmed James's feeling that he was not a bad sailor, as far as his stomach went.

Over a thousand miles to the southward, James rejoined his company. On arrival, he found a letter awaiting him from Sarah, dated Christmas 1776, which read:

> *My dearest One,*
> *Our plans fairly race along. First of all, I had it out with my father. Not a tussle really as he is so loving and understanding. After reading me once again his lecture about how difficult it might prove for me to be the wife of a King's officer, I felt he could find little to object in you, his own step-son!*

Our worst problem is how and where to meet for a wedding. You cannot come to the Jerseys or New York which fell to the King's forces three months ago and I cannot see any way to join you.. You know I have a distant cousin in Scotland who might be able to offer us protection and hospitality, and it will not do us any harm that her husband is a general in the army and might be able to bring some influence to bear in getting you to Scotland. I shall make enquiries in a general way and let you know, dearest One, of anything I learn - quick as I can..

Meanwhile, in haste and with all my love,

Your adoring
S

Chapter 5

Back in St Vincent, James's heart sank at the sound of wood-chopping. As far as his fiancée was concerned, her letter depressed his spirits while increasing his longing. It's all very well to talk of marrying in Scotland, he thought, but how can she take passage from a rebel-held port like New York?

He took refuge in the officers' mess in hopes of some distraction and ran right into the major. "Looking for a game, James? I'll play you, but first I've been hoping to talk to you. Step inside."

He continued: "Good to see you back. I've read your report on Kingston. Deep in the clutches of espionage, I see, but no for'arder, are we?"

"Only in a bad sense, I fear, sir. My taking Ensign Ogden with me exposed him to a temptation he did not feel able to refuse."

Prevost surprised James. Instead of pursuing the theme farther he seemed anxious to change the subject. "James, you know that the regiment is doubling in size but you may not yet know that our two new battalions are just beginning to train at St Augustine. Yes I know," anticipating a query, "even though the Floridas lie on the mainland, we don't consider them to be part of the north American region - they are an extension of our Caribbean holdings even though they lie just south of those pestilent provinces. I've heard about our new men – scum, a lot of them, convicts, and a lot of Germans brought over straight into the 60th by our ingenious Colonel von Scheither, who passes them on to Captain Brehm who's been grabbing them up for the Additionals in London."

"Yes, sir. I had a word with Captain Brehm when he was last here." said James.

"There's also a number of loyalists from the disaffected provinces." The major was in full flight but where was he heading? "You'll see that pounding all these varieties of spice together into something edible is going to be hard work. Our lords and masters have decided we shall offer all the help we can give and I suppose having three of our companies there, and our own John Brown in charge of the whole garrison, means there's no way we can get out of it, even if we should want to."

He paused briefly. "Isn't Major Brown married to a future sister-in-law of yours? Quite a family affair this is turning out to be."

"That's true, though I've only met him once – at their wedding in '72."

"As a matter of fact, Brown is no tyro. Went with Robert Rogers to beard the French at Detroit – commanded our grenadiers at Louisberg and Niagara." James reflected on a strange coincidence – Hutchins was with Brown's company in those days.

"If anyone can bring it off, I'm sure that canny Scot will. He's known America for over twenty years," continued Prevost. "At any rate, that connection may make what I am about to say to you more palatable. I want to send you on command" [detached service] "to help with the training. There will be a number of colonials joining up and as one of them, you know their mettle, and also what their adversaries are like."

Was this a vote of confidence in him? He had heard that Major Prevost's elder brother was to command in the Floridas; so the major would have a personal reason for helping out the troops at St Augustine. In that case, perhaps he should feel complimented in that Prevost would only send someone in whom he had confidence to help them train. Nevertheless, it was all drawing him closer to the strife in America.

At the same time, he was glad to accept the offer. He was aware that there had been no mention of just why the new companies were to be trained at St Augustine. As yet there was no threat from Spain, from which East and West Florida had been taken in 1763. To train troops at a place removed from the rebellion but close to it was probably no accident. The make-up of the expanding regiment indicated that, whatever care the government were taking to ease the consciences of a largely American corps, they were willing to accept as many loyalists as possible in its ranks. Care for uneasy consciences was bound to disappear - another sign of polarization. The government could well decide later to throw them into what was, whatever else it might be, a civil war.

"When would you want me to go to St Augustine, sir?" asked James.

"I'd like you there just as soon as you can go," replied Prevost.

In January 1777, James sailed by transport to St Augustine, entering by the north channel, passing St Anastasia Island on their larboard side, and negotiating the harbour at the mouth of the Matangas River. He found there a confusing medley of troops in various states of unreadiness. In quarters, he made a list to keep them straight:

H.M. second Battalion Sixtieth or Royal American Regiment of Foot
    Commanded by Lieutenant General James Robertson - five comps:strenght 92 out of estab. of 145; pay in arrears, much grumbling.

H.M. third Battalion Sixtieth or Royal American Regiment of Foot Commanded by General Sir John Dalling K.B - Seven comps very weak

H.M. fourth Battalion Sixtieth or Royal American Regiment of Foot
    Commanded by Brigadier General Augustine Prevost - Six comps very weak

H.M. Fourteenth Regiment of Foot Commanded by General Lord Rossmore - Five comps appalling condition, three comps fit

Of the twenty-six companies in the garrison, fourteen only were to remain after the rest had been trained and sent to West Florida. The Spanish threat was not out of mind. Though the companies' strength began to increase dramatically, each battalion comprised at first no more than 400 men. Lord Amherst, colonel-in-chief of the whole regiment, was acting energetically. He had not used the Navy Board to transport 60th recruits, but had hired transports himself. On the eighth of June the first of the new recruits for the 60th, two hundred men, arrived from England. The numbers continued to grow; the three 2nd Battalion companies reported that with the arrival of the new recruits from Europe only fifty-two men would be lacking. The supply problems diminished with the arrival of the Ordnance storeship *Springfield*.

Having settled himself in the moist quarter reserved for the battalion, kept comfortable by offshore breezes, James made his way to the temporary officers' mess in the town. No sooner had he set foot inside than he was accosted by the unmistakeable Germanic voice of an old friend.

"*Ja, ja, ja*, I knew that bad pennies turn up when you don't expect them, but you do astonish me. *Donnerwetter*, where did you come from?" the voice said, affecting multiple teutonic expressions. His friends knew that these expressions were disconcerting playthings he sported when it suited his mood. He did in fact speak and write English, French and German fluently and the pose fooled only self-important and cocky parvenues who would be embarrassed when they discovered they had been too quick in leaping to derogatory conclusions.

The voice was that of Diedrick Brehm who had appeared so briefly to entertain the officers' mess in St Vincent. Commissioned from Pennsylvania some time ago, he quickly made his mark for astuteness, judgment of his soldiers' character and a devilish wit. People liked him. He had succeeded John Brown as captain lieutenant of the battalion, preceding Thomas Hutchins, and now he was about to leave for London to handle "the Additionals", hastily raised wartime recruits from English gaols and slums and from Germany. He was worthy of promotion and command. He knew he was such a man and joked about it and everybody else knew he was, too.

James was even more astonished to see him on this side of the ocean. Brehm seldom accepted the opinions of others where his own particular responsibilities were concerned and had decided to come and see for himself how his "bunnies" were getting on.

James, quick to moan about the difficulties of training men at St Augustine, got short shrift from Brehm. "*Ach*, you think you're hard-pressed. You should see what I have to put up *mit* in London. Look! I tell you a tale that makes you think you the luckiest devil in the whole world. You have not of Imbert de Traytorrens heard?"

James owned that he had not heard of him. Brehm's reaction was "Well it iss *nicht* a surprise! I heartily wish I had never heard of him. He was one of those *Schweitzer* who were persuaded into the King's service. Why he signed his name I cannot imagine. He was with us only a few days when he announced – announced would you credit it – that he would not stay. Moreover he left with not so much as a by-your-leave for Egremont where he had money, because, he said he was *dans un Diable de pays où on m'empoison*. Why should we want to poison him – unless it was because he iss such a dribbling infant *dummkopf*?

"He even had made a confidante of the Countess of Egremont – how these *Schweitzer* worm their way into the graces of the nobility gives me *palpitations du coeur*! He put her completely into a fright by telling her that the officers of the regiment want to poison him. He even offered half a guinea to a boy, the son of the man he lodged with, if he would tell that they wanted to poison him and then he told me, to my face, that he had been poisoned by the people in the house he last lodged at. Some of our people told me that he had then gone to Portsmouth and that he had been seen along with a young French man in a hackney coach going over Westminster Bridge to Dover, they thought."

"What on earth did you do?" asked one of the other officers drawn into rapt attendance on Captain Brehm.

"Well, I thought it best to help him avoid bad company so I begged his landlord, M'sieur Bonhotes, to write to M'sieur Dejean, who was going off to Switzerland, to take him along to his parents. Then I wrote to the good General Haldimand in Quebec to say I hoped I had done right and that it might meet with his approbation – after all, while our colonel is a general far away, he always wants to know what happens in the regiment and Captain Hutcheson always writes him long letters from New York to tell him how everyone gets along. Since even our esteemed colonel-in-chief, Lord Amherst, did not know he was gone, I was sure the general would give him leave of absence until his father was acquainted with his dislike of the military life. I said that I thought that all his being poisoned and disorders were only a pretext to go to his own country. Meanwhile, I got his luggage from Portsmouth and I lodged it at M'sieur Bonhotes as I was not certain at that time if he was gone to Switzerland. Mr Rochat, one of our subalterns, agrees that Traytorrens has the *maladie du pays* as never did a young gentleman behave more oddly than he. Of course, General Haldimand did what I asked – we cannot have homesick Swiss officers being arrested as deserters the next time they forget themselves and choose to visit members of the English aristocracy!" Brehm obviously thought the 60th Regiment lucky to have weeded him out before anyone's life was the responsibility of the nincompoop.

Brehm had the confidence of General Haldimand: "*Ja*, I write often to the good general our colonel to keep him informed. He iss very interested in the goings-on in the regiment. So kind of him to give that *Dummkopf Schweizer* a way out that iss not the hangman's rope, *der Schluchzener. Ach*," he added, "if only that *touche-à-tout* bungler Germain had not exiled the general to Canada for being *ein Ausländer* and had let him run the war in America instead, it would all be over now!" The fact that his surrounding coterie of fellow-officers would see that his remarks about the Right Honourable the Secretary of State for the Colonies and Lord Commissioner of Trade and Plantations never leaked out of the room, showed the affection they felt for the *Deutscher*, and his confidence in them. Besides, James knew full well, they agreed with him.

James thought about the "nincompoop" Tratorrens. He felt a certain sympathy for him – to be a soldier when your heart was not really set on it – how awful. Luckily, despite the times of boredom, it still attracted him. Perhaps, he felt, there was the combination of duty and, at least the prospect of, adventure.

On duty, James was again reminded that training of recruits meant moulding them into a routine – how else could they be kept track of. As a subaltern who had indicated his desire for higher command, James was aware of the requirements. Their colonel had said: "A company commander ought to know the names of all his men and personal details of their families. He ought to know the location of each man at any time of the day or night. It is as vital to train officers up to that standard as it is to train the rank and file to their duty." That was why subalterns like me, thought James, received almost daily talks from their company or battalion commanders.

Encouraging individual initiative was all well and good - actively pursued by a small proportion of forward-looking officers who could see the shortcomings of Prussian-style discipline. But most officers held firmly to the ideal of teaching soldiers to obey instantly and unquestioningly. Therein lay the emphasis placed on close-order parade-ground formations. The objective was not only to have sections moving like clockwork – essential if the effect of a line of one-hundred-yard-range muskets was to be maximized – but also, parade drill inculcated that obedient mentality to prevent platoons falling to pieces during the inevitable mishaps of battle. There was to be no *sauve qui peut* stampede, such as was expected from lesser mortals like militia.

The men's background had to be taken into account. Most lacked education; many could neither read nor write and, of course, the presence of so many Germans in the 60th presented another problem since few knew English. Those who came from appalling slum conditions and those from the meanest of country hovels had little notion of hygiene. Army discipline had to do that. He recalled serjeants cajoling the men: "You will wash yourselves completely every Sunday and Wednesday, and change your shirts on those days. I don't care if none of you ever did that before you took the King's shilling, you'll do it from here on."

Most companies had two drummers, usually in their teens. The day began with the drums beating "reveille" at about six o'clock, followed by breakfast. At this time of the year, a beat called "the troop" was sounded at nine o'clock: squads assembled from their quarters under a non-commissioned officer. Each squad was dressed (aligned) by him, the roll was called and a subaltern inspected the squads, being handed the sick report by the non-commissioned officer. The officer then gave out any instructions for the day after which the squads marched to the parade ground. At St Augustine, the small garrison assembled and, except for the quarter guard of a serjeant, corporal and twelve men, remained on the ground for an hour of drill. Breezes from off-shore lessened the discomfort of drill, especially when autumn came.

On most days, subalterns took turns supervising drill on the parade ground. The piercing growl of NCOs projected some distance across the parade ground contrasted humorously with the often highpitched squeak of young subalterns. James's parade-ground voice did not have the penetrating steel of a serjeant major, but he tried to keep his pitch low and masculine. Luckily, most commands were given by drum taps of various sorts.

Practice insured that everyone knew what to do in answer to the different beats: "general" (prepare to march), "march" (move off), "assembly" (repair to the colours), "beat to arms" (stand to at the local alarm post), "troop" (parade for roll call and the reading of orders of the day). The men were jammed elbow-to-elbow when marching, kept their arms stiffly by the side; there was no arm-swinging or foot-stamping. The normal pace was seventy-three thirty-inch steps a minute though a quickstep of a hundred and eight paces would sometimes be used. In such manoeuvres as wheeling, the object being to change direction while maintaining an unbroken front, the pace was increased to a hundred and twenty per minute. On the march the rate was one and three quarters to two miles per hour, including a stop of ten minutes. Speed in movement was less important than keeping an unbroken line.

The day that began early with the "reveille" drumbeat ended at 10 p.m. when the drummers beat "tattoo". "Right, soldiers, time to go – ye won't want the cat to catch you!" - tavern keepers encouraged the swift departure of customers they viewed with a mixture of welcome and caution. The soldiers returned to quarters where the NCO called the roll. Half an hour later, a patrol checked on the taverns to see no soldier lurked behind. A final roll call was followed by the orderly serjeant making sure that all fires and candles were extinguished.

James quickly settled into this routine, having found himself posted to Major Brown's company, no doubt at Major Prevost's prompting.

Hundreds of miles to the west, while James was visiting Ridgelands, another complication emanating from New Jersey unrolled. The weather at Mobile was clammy but cooled by sea breezes. James was not the only 60th officer troubled by William Livingston's correspondence. The officer at Mobile was a captain with only a small number of men in his company, raised only a few months ago and newly-arrived after training at St Augustine. They were short of brown besses, the standard musket of the British Army, the best musket in the world, used even by the rebels. Pay was in arrears, morale in the unhealthy climate of the Mississippi delta was poor. Two of the German recruits on seeing themselves dumped in this *gottverdammt* place for God knows how long, deserted.

The captain was an experienced and valued officer from New Jersey. In 1757 he was an engineer officer of Pennsylvania troops and a skilled Indian agent. He had held the King's commission since becoming an ensign in the 60th in 1766, serving the regiment as a surveyor and engineer. He had surveyed in the Illinois country and in 1770 was at Pensacola to design the fortifications and to be in charge of public works. For years he was detached from the company he was listed under in the muster rolls, his name always appearing in the monthly returns of strength under "absent officers"; absent first from the grenadiers of the 1st Battalion, then as captain lieutenant of the 2nd Battalion, and now as captain of a company in the 4th Battalion – in all these posts he was only a name against which was written "not joined" or "absent on the King's service". His engineering skills were too valuable for him to be kept in the line. And he was a skilled map maker. Even now he worked in Pensacola, sixty miles from his nominal company at Mobile. His name was Thomas Hutchens, and he first appeared in James's life when he delivered William Livingston's letter.

He sat moodily at his desk, scarcely stirring in a wicker chair until at last, a decision taken, he reached for his quill and began to write

10th August 1776
Brigadier General William Livingston
New Jersey Militia

Respected and dear Sir,
Nine months are passed since you afforded me the honor of bearing your letter to a certain young officer whom for discretion's sake I do not name. Even though I have not seen the text, you had discovered to me the intent of that letter – that you hoped to stir up in his breast a willingness to enter that service which you have wholeheartedly espoused. You are doubtless aware, Sir, that if he acceded to your suggestion, he would render himself in the position of a King's officer aiding and abetting those

whom his sovereign has publickly declared to be his enemies.

I write not in complaint against the task you set me. I am sure that we both realized what a hazardous undertaking was being mooted. I know not what that officer's subsequent sentiments have proved to be as he has not communicated with me in any way. If he has not decided to follow your lead, I must tell you that I, at least, am much affected by your sentiments. Though I have served the King for over ten years, I have no wish to fight my fellow countrymen and will endeavor to follow a course that avoids bloodshed on my part without incurring dishonor.

I believe I will soon be ordered to England. I shall try to resign my commission in order to secure my liberty. Since a general order is in effect prohibiting the resignation of any officer of a corps serving in America, I am unsure if I shall be allowed to do so. Perhaps the technicality that my regt is not part of the forces engaged in North America but is under the command of the authorities in the West Indies – Pensacola being considered an outpost of the Caribbean – will allow me to resign. I have no assurance that such will prove to be the case, but I am anxious to apprise you of my intentions.

I am, Sir, with deep respect,
Your hmble and obdt svt,

Thomas Hutchins

Born an orphan, entrusted to the none-too-gentle mercies of an aunt and uncle, Thomas had always been dogged by a feeling of precariousness. In particular, he was always worried about money. So far, his salvation rested upon his mathematical abilities, shown early in childhood, his recognized aptitude as an Indian agent and his initiative and skills as a surveyor and map maker. He had always hoped to make his services to the Crown incomparable - to be known as the government's foremost agent in the Gulf area. Like many officers, the purchase of a captain's commission was an investment for the future. Now, however, there were the upsetting events of 1775 and '76. What would they mean – his ambition increasingly rewarded by a grateful monarch, or the collapse of his hopes in a world gone mad?

    He folded the letter and sealed it. He knew that in furthering his contact with a prominent rebel, he could be accused of pampering an unsrupulous ambition, arranging to reap benefits whatever the outcome. Certainly, he had a mixed reputation: professionally unexcelled but personally one to raise his superiors' eyebrows. He might be the best surveyor around and know the Gulf like the back of his hand, but he had three illegitimate children by three different mothers, and that would not sit well. To him it seemed hypocrisy to hold that against him; was it not commonly known that the higher one's social standing, the more that sort of thing was indulged and overlooked? He had better take what steps he could to keep his options open.

Chapter 6

The hospitality of John and Mary Brown certainly takes the edge off tedium in St Augustine, thought James. How much did he really know about the Browns? John Brown was in his early forties; despite his unmistakeably Scottish voice, he had spent almost as many years in the colonies as in Scotland. Mary was thirty-one years of age. She had not her younger sister Sarah's beauty but she had charm. He felt at home with them both. Their children Margaret, William and George scooted round the house until corralled by their nurse Heather. It reminded him of his own nursery years.

John had the knack of reducing broad matters to specifics, a fact about the commandant well known to his fellow officers. "It doesna' serve to preach your redcoats a sermon on the importance of salvo density, ye have to present 'em a real target – trees or paper – for them to shoot at so they can appreciate the destruction they can do," John advised James. A practical Presbyterian, the incongruity of coupling sermons with fusillades did not occur to the major. "That way you can show the need to fire as rapidly as possible – give 'em a four-minute spell to shatter the targets. Keep impressing on them the awful truth: if they fail to make hits fast and furious, it'll only be done to them. And remind them that the bayonet is the British soldier's friend," something I'd rather not find out, thought James.

"It's most effective when *they* are the movers. The attacker has the advantage. Ye can make this evident by bringing half the company to spring a surprise rush on the other half. Then talk to them about how being on the receiving end made them feel like victims." He ended with a stock phrase that had long ceased to provoke knowing smirks from his officers: "Make it practical, man. Make it practical!"

One evening in October, as they sprawled in front of the fireplace, John raised the matter of wedding plans. "Ye'll ken we now hold New York, so why not have Sarah under Mary's and my escort sail to Greenock whilst you make your own way thence?" asked John with the benevolent affability which helped to disarm those offended by his curiosity.

"New York?" expostulated James. "I did not know the city had fallen. So Sarah might be able to sail from there. Lord, how easy to be behind the times it is."

"Aye," Brown assured him. "My point is: you and Sarah have your parents' permission to marry and that would normally take place in the colonies. In these times, it may well be an advantage to marry in some neutral place far removed from conflict."

Mary filled in the idea: "The old Countess of Eglinton, Susannah, is the present earl's grandmother. She is in her eighties but has an active, if eccentric, mind. We are distant cousins and we correspond. The present countess, having been Lady Jean Crawford before she married the general five years ago – he's Archibald, the present earl - is also someone I write to. We've always kept close in touch and I'm sure she'd play host to the wedding – gladly so."

"Aye, 'tis a bonnie place, too, grand enough to suit the taste of even a Livingston," quipped John, casting a quick glance at his wife. "The castle is in bad shape though, having suffered in the 1600s at the hands of their enemies the Cunninghames, so they live in Auchans at nearby Dundonald – yet on the Eglinton estate. I know the place well as I was raised at Kilmarnock about ten miles away."

James observed, "You say the old countess is eccentric."

"She's that all right," said Mary. "Four years ago, Dr Samuel Johnson visited her at Auchans, so she has a pretty wit. Lady Jean tells me that when he left, she wished him 'farewell, my dear son' and virtually considered she had adopted him. Apparently he was delighted. For all her peculiarity, she is yet to be reckoned with – in fact the poet Allan Ramsay dedicated his comedy *The Gentle Sheperd* to her. She's as strong as an ox but her step-daughter-in-law, Lady Jean, is not so well. But even she is fairly peppery. She's the daughter of the Earl of Crawford and married the present earl about the time of Dr Johnson's visit."

John Brown broke in. "I should say she is pretty lively. You see, Archibald was quite a rake in his earlier days and Lady Jean said that as he was prepared to strew his attentions round and about, she – in all fairness – ought to be considered released from her conjugal restrictions! That caused quite a stir and even the old countess had a good laugh over that. But, see here, I have business at New York so I'll be there early in the new year and we could sail for Scotland, say, in February. What do ye say?"

"I don't know what to say, sir."

"Och, 'John' will do, seeing we are to be kin - except in front of the men."

After several thank-you's, James accepted some more brandy and joined heartily in more toasts than was usual, even in the exuberant Scot's parlour.

A minor hiccough occurred when young Margaret shot into the room and before she was gathered up by Heather, flung a question at James: "When do we go to beat George Wash... Wash... Washton?" Heather's intervention forestalled an answer and she was hauled off to her bath. "That's the sort of offal they pick up from the other garrison children," observed Mary.

"That's something else I've been meaning to ask ye. Suppose – just suppose – and I'm not saying I believe it'll happen – but what if the rebels throw us out? What then?" He began to open the subject more fully. "Take our family. I will be of one nation whilst Mary, or at any rate most of her family, will be of another. You have a British commission but your family will be foreigners. What would you do?"

"That is a hard question for me," said James gloomily. "I have turned it over and over every day. If I fight for the King, which is my duty, I could end as an outcast at home. If I side with the rebels, then I am a traitor."

"Mind ye, please God, it may never come to that," said Mary, feeling more perturbed than she let on.

John observed: "I must say, it seems strange that the rebels proclaim their independence just about the time they are losing their second biggest city and may well see their capital go. Still, I would-na' hoot too triumphantly just yet. I served in the colonies for years and I know how vast is the area and how completely we depend on the navy. And how long will people at home support an army over here? Already, I hear many of our merchants would like to give up the effort."

Brown expanded: "I've seen their declaration of independence. It has high-sounding words, I grant you. Aye, the rebels are masters at words. Patriotic words that distort realities and hoodwink people. To read their exaggerations, you'd think the freedom of all mankind depended on their vaunted throwing off the slavery of King George the Third. They actually call him a *tyrant* – he, the most scrupulously constitution-minded monarch we've ever had. They talk of getting out of the wicked British Empire, but what are they really after?"

James struggled: "Are you saying they make their own grab for power, trying to set up their own empire by starting a civil war."

Brown was well under way. "Can you imagine what they'll do if they succeed? All restraints on their own ambitions will be gone. Oh, they'll not use the word empire save as a term of abuse, but they'll want one all the same. They'll flood across the Appalachians, killing the Indians or kicking them off the lands they covet. And who will stop them once they see off the other claimants to North America - Britain, France, Spain - they'll go right to the Pacific Ocean, maybe farther – who knows? - all in the name of some blatant, boastful, divinely sanctioned virtue. Our gullible colonists lap up that pap about nationhood versus empire, freedom against British tyranny, but all the while their leaders are grasping power and ending restraints on their own cupidity."

James shifted to something more personal: "I can see why Sarah's father pulled back. Colonial rights was one thing, but the wider ambitions are another. It's ironic considering where their ideas on liberty come from – they come from being British. Their military forces are a copy of ours. Even their law is *English* law."

"And what do ye suppose will happen in the years ahead?" said Brown. "Who can tell?" he continued. "Despite all the talk of liberty, it doesn't seem to cover anyone who disagrees. No, it's tars and feathers for such as them. They think nought of taking away the rights of loyal people. If they are unrestrained in the exercise of their power, real tyranny could flourish. And then there is the world beyond America. With an ocean between themselves and the outside, they'll not care what happens elsewhere. I've heard the preachers: Americans are the redeemed remnant, the 'lamp set on a hill'. They will have ruined the prospect of a united English-speaking community able to restrain the real tyrants. Why even the princes of India invite us in, preferring law to anarchy. It may not always be thus, but it is thus at the moment. And while they say British rule makes them slaves, they maintain an institution of slavery in their midst without parallel. Their insularity leads them into hypocrisy; they are determined not to be challenged by the thoughts of others outside who share the same language and traditions."

Mary observed: "How can they maintain the whole of America is striving to throw off British rule? If that were true, there'd be no peaceful Canada, nor any people like us, indeed. If the colonies were really united against the King, our troops would be swept away in a week."

"You mentioned the people they call Tories," said James. "Doesn't that rather prove the point? Even their own leaders admit most Americans are cool to the notion of independence. Loyalists are an embarrassment to them. Their leaders are so busy promoting the idea that they are a nation in arms against foreign rule, they find loyalists an unbearable witness to the truth."

Brown intervened: " No wonder they treat them so unspeakably. Och well, we shall see." As always, Brown the realist wanted to turn to practical matters. "I do feel for you, James – before very long Mary and I retire to Scotland – to Knockmarloch in Riccarton Parish - but you will be just choosing where you are to live, and you may have to face the question of whether people will allow you to live where you want. Meanwhile, we rejoice in the wedding that lies ahead. If you write to Sarah and her parents, we'll settle the Scottish end of the matter."

After six months at St Augustine, James secured six months leave for the trip to Scotland. A few days before sailing, John Brown called him aside and James took the opportunity to tell him of the William Livingston letter. Brown's eyebrows shot up.

"That is extraordinary, indeed! You mention Hutchins delivering the letter to you. Now I have a delicate matter to put to you. Mark Prevost has given me his own thoughts about Captain Hutchins, if only in outline. Quite apart from Hutchins's role as a messenger, he has reasons of his own to cause him to worry. Mark has sent you a letter enclosed in one to me with strict instructions that I pass it to you right away. So, here it is. It may have something to do with what you've just told me. Let me know if I can help in any way."

James retreated to his rooms and tore it open. It read
December 16th, 1776

My dear James,
Major Brown has been kind enough to bring this letter to you, which I write in confidence.

Our colleague Hutchins recently wrote to the rebel Governor of New Jersey in friendly terms and, in the course of that letter, indicated that he had conveyed a letter to one of his fellow officers (something we both know about). Hutchins intimated that on arriving at his posting in Europe, he may seek to resign his commission and wonders what he can do to be useful to Livingston. As Hutchins is in London, and will be encouraged to stay at the Belle Savage in Ludgate Hill, I ask that you meet him if you can, being on your guard. It would be helpful to us if you could gather an impression of what he really thinks. I ask this; I cannot command it.

His letter to Mr Livingston was intercepted accidentally by government agents who were then instructed to let it be delivered, as they do not wish to act precipitously in hopes that even more news may be obtained. I realize that enquiries may be fruitless since you will be unable to reveal that you have learnt this from me or that his letter has been seen. You may feel such a task ill accords with the straightforward candour one officer should always show to another and in that case I shall honour your decision.

Kindly inform me, at your earliest convenience, what you intend doing.

Ever Yr Obdt Svt,

Mark Prevost

James thought hard. Major Prevost places a lot of confidence in me. Also, from my point of view, seeing Hutchins may help me clarify my own thinking. Certainly, there is nothing to be gained from refusing his request. I don't like duplicity but I ought to consider Brown's advice – "be practical, man, be practical". Obeying Mark's request is not ideal but it is the best I can do.

James conferred with John Brown, who commented: "I'm sure all this shows just how seriously the rebellion is being taken. Our people have set up some sort of clandestine service so that correspondence between Livingston and Hutchins, and – dare we say it?

– between Livingston and you will not pass unread by us. In my opinion, it also reveals the extent to which loyal Americans are involved in passing us information – who else could get their hands on letters like these?"

On the twenty-seventh of January, James set sail in a small despatch vessel. Two days out of St Augustine, on a clear and windy Thursday, the crow's nest shouted urgently: "Deck there, sail on the larboard beam!" Hurried discussion amongst the captain and his officers concluded the vessel could be a privateer – French or Yankee – bent on boarding them. She did not have the weather gauge and that resulted in a decision to make a dash for it which enabled them gradually to give the slip. Precautions were, however, taken. Gunners prepared the two small swivel-guns for action, cutlasses and pistols were readied and all despatches of value were weighted down ready to be tossed overboard if necessary. The pursuer, as now it seemed certain it was, fell behind and the next morning she was gone.

Their voyage continued without mishap but took longer than James preferred, heaving to at Gibraltar to deliver despatches before resuming a northward course. Eventually, they passed a hundred miles off Porto, then Cape Finisterre off the starboard beam. They passed Lough Swilly and Lough Foyle and so on to the Firth of Clyde and Greenock, when a quiet sigh of relief passed through the ship, especially amongst landsmen like James.

Before leaving the town, James made use of his first trip to Scotland to walk about, visiting the Old North Kirk. He mused that John and Mary Brown and their three children must have made their way to New York in time for Christmas with Sarah who had made her way to the city escorted by her brother Will. They all felt that in prevailing conditions it would be safer for her father to stay out of what was now the main British army base on the continent. For over two months the port had been open to British ships so they got passage in a supply vessel bound for Greenock, arriving without mishap despite the bitter winter weather.

James reached Greenock about a fortnight before the wedding day. Greenock was the nearest available port to the Eglinton estates. Its west harbour was only completed in 1710, James learned. He wondered what route to follow south. Shivering from time to time in the sea air, he noticed Jamaica Street, bearing witness to an active trade with the West Indies.

"Can I have a trap to drive straight south toward Ayr?" he asked innocently.

"Och, I'm afraid not, sir. I wouldna' let one of my carts wander 'cross those hills and moors. Why ye could be set upon by robbers and none the wiser. If ye broke down, there'd be nary a soul to help ye – not many live in that desolate part" came the reply from the local hirer of horses.

James had seen too much of the hilly landscape to argue with that. "How may I go then?"

"Ye'll have to take the coast road through Largs – it's the on'y way unless you wish to go by Kilmacolm and Johnstone, but that's a rough ride and a wee bit longer too. In fact, only a few days ago I gave the same advice to a group of four adults and three children who needed a much larger carriage to make the same journey."

In the end, James went by the west coast road and managed to arrive in fair condition after a forty-three-mile journey, taking two-and-a-half days to do so. Apart from the characteristic terrain, he knew he was truly in Scotland when he stopped for some refreshment and heard the sound of a lone piper over the rise. He said to the maid serving him: "What's that?"

"Och, it's the doctor" she replied, looking at him, a silly man not to know that.

"Is he practising?" continued James, hoping to boost his reputation with her.

At this, she looked really shocked. "Oh, no! He can play!" she answered.

On arrival at Auchans House, he was impressed by the sturdy grandeur of the four-storey turreted building – in fact it seemed more comfortable and grand than Eglinton Castle, a few miles away near Irvine – that was now a ruin. Despite the fortress-like appearance of the house, he was instantly heartened by the friendliness of the Montgomeries. He passed his first day there chatting with his new friends, riding over the rolling countryside with Sarah, keeping himself under such emotional control as was necessary till they should be married and finding that more difficult than he had expected. He presented himself, too, to the old countess but found conversation with her hard to keep up. She was very canny and he looked at her with a sense of awe. It was rumoured that on occasion she invited the rats which inhabited the house to dine with her – had actually trained them to take dinner with her. James was gratified that he had no personal evidence of this.

Mainly, he spent his time with Sarah who shared his elfish sense of humour. "I suppose one of the things that make us different is that I tend to theorize about things like a sense of humour. A sense of proportion seems the necessary foundation of humour – humour meaning the ability to recognize incongruity and and hence demanding a sense of proportion. Perhaps that has enabled you to keep your head above water in the surrounding sea of oppressively moralistic Presbyterian uprightness."

"And if you plan to kiss me, do you intend to preface it with such an analysis?" she answered. He took the cue and ended the conversation.

Since arriving, James had not had much chance to talk to his host, the earl. One evening after dinner the earl said: "Join me for a brandy, James?"

"Thank you, sir."

"I know your country well," the general remarked, pouring them both a generous glass of brandy. "I commanded Fraser's Highlanders in Canada in the French war – the 78th we were then. If I do say so, we did rather well." James wondered if the Scots shared the English taste for understatement, or was it *de rigueur* in his class? "When Pitt raised Highland regiments for the war, he got onto something really worthwhile." The general was a Scot but his English bore not a trace of a Scots accent; his speech was as good a king's English as George III's and a good deal better than George II's, James realized. "General Wolfe called us the most manly lot of officers he had ever seen. Louisburg, Montmorenci, Quebec – we were up to the gills in all of them. We even took Newfoundland back from the French before we were disbanded. Most of my men settled in Canada."

"Those must have been stirring times, my lord," replied James tentatively, though from Eglinton's bearing, he did not think the general cared two hoots about such forms.

"Yes, indeed they were. Fraser was a remarkable man. He'd fought for Prince Charlie in the Forty-five – some of my family then supported the Stuarts – was tossed into prison for that but received a royal pardon, and then set about raising the regiment. And then, bless me, he did it all over again two years ago; they're the 71st now, but still Fraser's."

"I hear they're in North America, sir," ventured James.

"Yes, but it pains me to see that only half the 1st Battalion was at the capture of New York since a privateer nabbed the other half's transport. And then there's the poor lads of the 2nd Battalion: sailed right into Boston harbour, they did, after Tommy Gage had gone, worse luck. But they're raising again, and there's even a third battalion coming along."

"That was very hard on them, sir," replied James, having decided that 'my lord' was a bit too obsequious - perhaps "sir" was about right. How Sarah would laugh at these hair-splitting concerns, he reflected.

"Ah, but you see, my boy, the Scots always take things the hard way. If the English like to play cool – never better than in defence under adversity – the Scots balance them nicely by rushing forward, often unwisely. You've heard of Flora McDonald!" Here, the general did not even pause as it was inconceivable that anyone would be ignorant of the woman who had had helped the Pretender. "Well, she raised over a thousand Highlanders in the Carolinas and they marched with broadswords, kilts, tartans and screaming pipes to rush the rebels at Moore's Creek Bridge. Slaughtered or captured they were by the rebels who were forewarned. Those Scots had no strategy, no finesse, they just roared and clambered toward their enemies – typical! I cannot understand why the rebels are always talking of "the English". What about the Scots? There's James Paterson, adjutant general in America, John Campbell of the 37th, and Allan MacLean who stopped Montgomery in his tracks at Quebec, or James Robertson commanding in New York, and James Grant who trounced Washington at Long Island, to say nothing of McArthur, Campbell and MacLeod of the 71st or Pattie Ferguson and his new rifle."

James wondered if a phenomenal memory for names was a prerequisite for being a general.

"Take Ferguson," continued the earl. "He invented a breech-loading rifle, the first such, to my knowledge. As you doubtless know, rifles are in disfavour with our people because the muzzle-loaders take forever to reload and a charge by bayonets does in the riflemen. But his rifle could get off several rounds a minute and hit a target two hundred yards away. I saw it demonstrated before the King, who was ecstatic. I believe Ferguson's got permission to form a corps of a hundred men for Howe's army, armed with the new rifle."

"That would be devastating, wouldn't it, general?" asked James.

"Yes, but don't forget what I said about the English character. Introducing the rifle would change all the rule books. Tactics would be altered beyond belief and the idea that we could suddenly switch everything over in the middle of a campaign is scarcely credible. I wouldn't be surprised if Ferguson's corps ends up disbanded, with the rifles put in store. As you must have seen, our army is a very conservative affair, whatever His Majesty's enthusiasms may be."

Eglinton expanded on the virtues of comparative English cunning and its limitations. "If only Gage – Honest Tom they call him, the very best sort of English officer, with all the good and bad points – if only he'd used his wits and his courage and fortified Dorchester Heights at Boston, he'd still be there, cock o' hoop. But that's Honest Tom and your English professional soldier all over – he was splendid as an administrator but not much of a tactician, for all his success in the French war. A nicer man you could never find, but...oh dear; I don't suppose you've met him?"

"I'm afraid not, sir, but then you see I've been in the Caribbean three years."

"Of course not," continued the general, "but perhaps you know Major Stephen Kemble? He's from the Jerseys, too – Gage's protégé – hoped to become adjutant general, he did, Tommy being wedded to his sister. But after Boston, that sort of career looks nipped in the bud, I should think."

"I have heard of him, of course," answered James, "his home is only twenty miles from mine."

I hope America will follow Scotland's lead" said Eglinton, changing tack.

"How so, General?" James asked, puzzled.

"I suppose I can say it to you, not being Scots yourself. I mean Scotland fought England tooth and nail at times, but in the end we were beaten by the English, not without a good deal of Scottish help, I can tell you. But we've joined them in a union now which is almost seventy-five years old. Many Scots resented losing our parliament and having to send people to Westminster, and not being able to smuggle legally, but in the long run we've all benefitted. Scotland's been dragged out of the ditch of penury and, if anything, we've got more representation in Parliament than our numbers warrant. As they say, it's the Scots who run the British Empire. If the Americans remain with us, they'll end up running the British Empire." He paused for a sip, punched the log in the fireplace with his foot, and resumed: "I've not always been a peer, you know. For eight years I sat for Ayrshire in the Commons. If my cantankerous brother Alexander hadn't got himself killed by a poacher, I'd probably still be there. Of course, when I came to the title, I was, er, booted upstairs, into the House of Lords, which normally rather hampers any political influence. But now I'm political again, a Representative Peer, they call me."

Returning to the subject they had skirted, James spoke from the heart: "It is grievous to me, sir, seeing that I come from America and may have to fight my own kin."

"I wondered how you felt about it, James, and I do sympathize. If it's any help, I could point out that ofttimes Scots had to what they thought right and been damned from here to hell and back by their neighbours," replied the old soldier. "But I have no doubt you'll do your duty. That way you may not find it easy to live with your neighbours, but at least you'll be able to live with yourself," he concluded.

James felt strongly comforted and knew that he had a friend – perhaps the old 78th had felt something of the same.

With the day of the wedding coming closer, the countess had arranged for James and John Brown, his best man, to use a cottage near the castle while Sarah and John's wife Mary, acting as best maid, stayed in the lodge that was used in place of the damaged castle. On the eve of the wedding, Brown took himself off to join the bride and her party at the castle for a festive meal. The best maid, on her own, was escorted by two subalterns of the 51st Foot in scarlet tunics with grass green facings and gold lace, white small-clothes, white stockings and breeches and tricorne hats – the earl had been the 51st's colonel for fifteen years, retaining his regimental rank as he rose to the rank of Major General, as was the common practice.

Meanwhile, James was also attended to. Upon coming to the cottage, according to the Scottish custom, the bridegroom's shoes and stockings were removed and the "feet-washing" took place in which his feet were immersed in a tub of red wine. A ring was thrown into the tub, the first of James's groomsmen to find the ring shouting in triumph in the firm assurance that he would be the first of that group to be married subsequently.

Early the next morning, Sarah was dressed by a maid. Custom dictated that the clothes could not be fitted on but had to be made to fit in some other way, somehow. Fortunately everything fitted well, Sarah's weight having been easy to keep down owing to the rough sea passage. Her attire consisted of a brown velvet habit and a large hat with a white plume. Her bridesmaids wore whatever fine clothing they could muster; they did not wear the same design nor did they wear white. Since they were to ride sidesaddle, the bridesmaids were all dressed in a variety of riding-habits. Sarah managed to save a pair of green garters for her older sister else, all averred, bad luck would befall the new couple. The bride and her party ate a breakfast of oatmeal porridge made with milk, sugar, curds and cream. There was even some dancing till the time of departure, accompanied by fiddlers – being a lowland village, they furnished the music rather than pipers. Two men of James's party, called the sens, went to Sarah's to fetch the bride and her attendants, receiving for their trouble a dram of whisky each.

That morning, being a Monday, the twenty-fourth of March, was a crisp but sunny day. The women in the bride's party all put on Josephs, surtouts made of duffel for warmth over their habits which they called Brunswicks. They mounted on horseback and left at an arranged time for Riccarton parish church where they arrived, as expected, just before James's party, also mounted. Josephs were removed and piled at the back of the church awaiting the return journey. Sarah was supported on either side by the sens. She had been cautioned by those wise in such matters not ever to look behind her lest she bring misfortune upon her marriage. She was escorted into church by her two attendants and shown to her pew, the bride stool, by the pompous little beadle in uniform, bearing his staff of office. Hot on her heels arrived the bridegroom's party. James, supported on each side by two comely lasses, went to the pew and sat on Sarah's right hand, giving her hand an unscripted squeeze, then paying the beadle with a sixpenny bit. James wore the customary uniform of his regiment, the red tunic with buttons marked '60', white smallclothes and white stockings with his breeches – he had gone to some pains to keep the stockings clean during the ride to church by donning black gaiters over them.

Apparently the original church had been built in the thirteenth century as a chapel of the monastic community at Dundonald and had subsequently been under the parish of Paisley, having been a parish church only since the Reformation. Sometime around 1725 it was rebuilt and, as that had not been an efficient undertaking, had been remodelled only five years before the wedding. Even so, it was a grim sight – dilapidated and ill cared-for. James thought one part of the roof looked dubious and the rest of the structure did not look too safe.

The news of the wedding had got around and the church was full. Many of the attenders were known to the bride and groom or to the Eglintons but there were also some who came from outside the immediate community. Among these were a tall, dark-complexioned man who disappeared immediately after the service.

As the minister entered from the vestry - more a ramshackle alcove than a proper room - to face the congregation, James and Sarah took their places in front of him – Sarah to James's left – so he would be free to draw his sword in her defence if conditions so warranted, and the best maid and best man stood outside the bride and bridegroom, respectively. When all others, including the members of the principals' parties were in their pews, the service began. The minister, it struck James, differed in appearance from what he knew at Anglican weddings in that he was sombrely dressed in a black preaching gown with Geneva preaching bands, all without any white surplice. But as the rite progressed it seemed to differ little from the English rite except that there was no giving away of the bride.

"Dearly beloved brethren," began the minister from the John Knox service in the Book of Common Order, "we are here gathered together in the sight of God and in the face of this congregation to knit and join these parties together." The rite continued with the normal Scottish, to James exceedingly lengthy, prologue setting forth every conceivable text supporting marriage, eschewing no earthy reason for that institution, until the minister read the charge: "I require and charge you..." There being no objection to the marriage, the answer given by James to the question about whether they agreed to marry, seemed to him charmingly worded: "Even so I take her, before God, and in the presence of this congregation". Sarah's reply, in turn, was also firm: "Even so I take him, before God, and in the presence of this congregation." All then joined in the singing of the old Scottish paraphrase of the Hundred Twenty-eighth Psalm:

Bless'd is each one that fears the Lord
and walketh in his ways.
For of thy labour thou shalt eat,
and happy be always.
Thy wife shall as a fruitful vine
by thy house' sides be found:
Thy children like to olive-plants
about thy table round.
Behold, the man that fears the Lord,
thus blessed shall he be.
The Lord shall out of Sion give
his blessing unto thee.
Thou shalt Jerus'lem's good behold
whilst thou on earth dost dwell.
Thou shalt thy children's children see
and peace on Israel.

James then kissed the bride and a kiss followed from the minister with no chance of her escape from it. Having signed the register placed on a table by the side, the party formed up for the procession. First came the earl, wearing his red-coated Major General's uniform. He alone would have commanded the respectful awe of the well-wishing onlookers: in addition to commanding Fraser's Highlanders which, to hear Scots talk, were responsible for just about all Wolfe's victories in Canada. He was accompanied by a colonel of the Ayr and Renfrew Miliotia acting for Sarah's father. The two went first, then the bridal pair followed in turn by the best man and best maid, walking together, then the other members of the party forming couples. The minister followed on with members of the congregation, it being believed that his invitation to the wedding festivities must be the last to be extended. Proceeding a few yards to their horses, they all mounted and rode in stately manner in the same order all the way back to the hunting lodge. The countess, being unwell, came to and fro in a carriage. With her in the carriage was Grandmama Susannah, the widow of the ninth Earl who, at ninety-one years of age, had been a widow for over half her life and whose eccentricities had been discussed by James and the Browns before leaving St Augustine.

Dismounting, the bride was carried over the threshold. Once inside the banqueting hall, a sieve was placed over Sarah's head in which shortcake was put, the bride then being whisked smartly from underneath to avoid the cake spilling on her. The cake was distributed to all - portions were meant to be kept by the guests for some time. A broom was then proffered to Sarah and she swept the hearth.

Jollity ensued: dancing and frivolity galore, well past midnight. With what was meant to look like modesty, Sarah absented herself to go to her bedchamber. But the Scottish custom does not give the bride up to her own devices so easily, and the bridesmaids rushed off after her, hallooing and squealing with gallumphing bravura. They were engaged in the ceremony known as "bedding". They assisted Sarah to undress for bed, in reward for which each received a dram, bread and cheese. Finally, she was joined by her husband, suitably attired. The attendants finally left and what happened then no one can relate as an eyewitness. Thoughts of intrigue were far from their minds.

Chapter 7

London beckoned and the newly-weds prepared to leave. There was little point in observing the American custom of 'seeing company': entertaining a flock of callers, since they knew so few people about who were not already members of the wedding party. Instead, they decided to leave soon after the wedding day so they could have a leisurely journey.

The evening before their departure, the general drew James and Sarah into his study. As he shut the door, he said to them: "I'm sure you realize that what began as simple hospitality to some relations has grown into something much more satisfying to us here. You've become part of our family. I only regret that the times are so uneasy."

The general reiterated his offer of the use of an ample coach and team of four horses, complete with a coachman and postillion, and would brook no demur on their part. He even had the foresight to arrange for a large trunk, containing mainly Sarah's clothing, to be sent on by sea from Greenock to the pool of London and from thence to the inn where they were expected in about a fortnight's time.

"Besides, I have a favour to ask of you. I am going to give you a despatch for you to deliver."

At this point, the general suddenly frowned and said: "Did you hear something?" He quickly thrust the door open. All that could be seen was a footman carrying a tray past the room, who started at the door's sudden opening. However, he continued at a deliberate pace, balancing objects on the tray.

The door shut again, James asked: "You were about to say, sir, where the papers are to be delivered, I believe."

"Yes, to be sure. There will be no address on them, but they are to go to Mr Marlin at the War Office. It is a confidential letter – a sheaf of papers, in fact. At some point someone may try to take it from you. There is much more to tell you, but you may hate the whole idea of this, in which case I need not go on."

"We'll do whatever you want, sir," said James. Sarah's just dying to be involved in something like this, he thought.

"Let me explain: we have reason to believe our enemies know these papers will go from here, but they will consider you to be amateurs, so they will not expect neither aptitude nor resistance. At the same time, four of you and a coach, stopping frequently, would be hard to tackle without causing general alarum, so that sort of behaviour is unlikely. In any case, if someone tries to relieve you of the packet, I must insist that you comply meekly – I cannot countenance your putting yourself in unnecessary danger. So, no heroics, do you understand?"

They nodded agreement.

"Now as to defensive measures: I will also give you another packet which from the outside looks much the same. Only this one will contain an enticing batch of nonsense. It will look like the real one but it will contain pages needing careful scrutiny before anyone reading them realizes what they are. They will contain both text in plain English and also groups of numbers like code. That packet you can give up with all appearance of confusion, reluctance and dismay. Am I clear so far?" asked the earl.

James saw one difficulty: "What if the thief discovers our ruse after a day or so? Could he not double back and intercept us farther along the London road?"

They discussed a plan for getting over this possibility. Sarah fairly glowed with pleasure at the thought of such intrigue.

"Are you sure your ready agreement is not glib?" asked the general.

"We are happy to do it," they said in chorus.
"You have not mentioned it and it is one reason I say your ready agreement may be glib, but surely you must wonder why I do not simply send the papers under military escort in a usual manner."

"Indeed, I did wonder, sir, but knowing you I assume you have reasons for not doing so."

"Your confidence humbles me, James," said the earl with a hint of a smile. "The truth is that I have little choice in the matter since my superiors feel that you may well bring our enemies out into the open which is what a troop of dragoons would not do."

"I assume they will know I carry the papers?" queried James.

"It is likely, I'm afraid. One or two incidents lead us to believe that if you carry my papers, they will know it. I wonder if you remember a lanky, dark man at your wedding?

"We didn't notice much except each other," replied Sarah, causing James to groan inwardly.

"In all modesty, my experiences have produced a keen eye and it did not escape my notice," the earl remarked honestly. "In this case the man was more interested in marking James in his mind than the bride." Sarah assumed a mock-rueful expression. "No, they may not know who the papers are intended for, but they will probably know you have them. That point is important since it will allow you to hand them false papers bound for some place other than London. Unlike the real papers, the false ones will have a remote address on the outside, to add to the confusion."

"Before I say a final yea or nay, I have to ask you two questions, general. Have I been picked out for this task purely as a matter of obvious convenience, or is there some other reason I've been chosen?" asked James. "The second is – would it be possible to tell me anything about the papers?"

The general weighed his words with care. "Yes, you are specifically mentioned in my instructions. I can only imagine someone in authority wants to test you. From what I was told, they have no reason to doubt you and they may want simply to test your capacity to cope with subterfuge. They give no hint as to why they are interested in that. They are not, however, any of the usual military authorities, so none of the soldiers you deal with day by day has any part in this. Perhaps that is some small comfort. Especially as I am not allowed to say who is interested in you. In fact, they would probably be annoyed with me for telling this much. I would, myself, tend to resent unusual tests, especially when they seem to be designed to elicit skills other than an infantry officer's normal professional aptitudes. Perhaps it means they have some unusual work in mind for you but need to know you better than they do. I don't know what their devious minds harbour.

"As for the second question: the papers have to do with the raising of additional Highland troops for America – something a spy would clearly go to some lengths to obtain."

He continued: "In light of the – unusual – impositions of the matter, I think you have every right to refuse the mission, in which case I will happily tell them their plan is unwise, is inconsiderate to a most satisfactory officer and – in short – is unworthy and they can go to the devil!"

As James and Sarah took their leave and went to bed, the general drew a letter from a drawer. Frowning, he read it for the third time:

> Horse Guards
>
> 3rd February 1777
>
> My Lord,
>
> Lord Germain, Secretary of State for the Colonies, has directed me to apprise you of the following and to request your assistance. There is an officer of the 60th Regiment, Lieutenant James Ricketts, who, he is given to understand, will shortly come under your Lordship's hospitality and protection. Sir John Dalling, C.B., Commander in chief of the Leeward Island &c, &c, places every confidence in the loyalty and discretion of that officer but there are two reasons for making sure that confidence is well placed, viz. he is to marry the daughter of a notorious rebel and he has received correspondence from her uncle who is also notorious and in a position of importance amongst them.
>
> Mr Ricketts went on leave to The island of Jamaica with everything properly arranged and after consulting his commanding officer as required but, with the situation in the colonies being so precarious and the stakes so high, it becomes necessary to take unusual steps, even ungentlemanly steps, to confirm loyalties to his Majesty's interests.
>
> Therefore you are directed to entrust the enclosed papers to Ricketts's care for delivery to the War Office in the knowledge that nefarious and villainous intriguers may well try to take the documents from his person. His Lordship has complete confidence that you will be able to arrange with Ricketts that, if he be intercepted in his journey to Westminster, he will be able to retain the papers through some subterfuge.
>
> By this means, his Lordship will know for certain the degree of confidence to be placed in Ricketts and will also

ascertain the extent and effectiveness of those who work clandestinely to harm his Majesty's interests.
I am your Lordship's humbl & obdt. Servant,
Nigel Smithers
Captain, H.M. 2nd Troop of Life Guards
Military Assistant the Rt Honble the
Secretary of State for the Colonies

Damn them for their impudence, thought the general. That scoundrel Germain has manipulated us both into doing dirty-work for him. Germain! Sacked for incompetence in India – now look at him. If we lose the loyalty of the Americans, it'll be because we deserve to!

Before leaving the estate, James and Sarah poured out their gratitude to the Browns for all that they had done for them. James asked what their plans were.

John Brown replied: "Well, my retirement is not so far off so I am loth to cross the Atlantic again only to come back shortly. Fortunately, the War Office feel the same way so I shall be employed on staff and recruiting duties in the south of Scotland."

Mary moved away to have her own talk with Sarah. "John feels very bitter about the war. He feels he's put so much of himself into America – he feels betrayed. So many friends who've died or been invalided out of the service by their time in America – he feels they've been let down, not just by stupid policies of a stupid London government, but by the Americans as well.

"I've spent some time with John in Scotland. I know we're a privileged group but, even making allowances for that, it's true that most people here feel they have freedom. It's not perfect freedom, I grant, but relatively speaking I've always felt that people here feel themselves free. They may not always hoot about it, or write long tracts about it as if they'd just discovered it, but they feel it nonetheless. The biggest threat to my freedom is wondering - will I ever see Papa again, or my family? Will I have to think of myself as a foreigner if I should be fortunate enough to visit America?" Mary paused. "I don't think I'd better go on this way. But I want you to know that we love you both – let nothing ever stand between us, please God!"

"Amen!" echoed Sarah with a catch in her voice, as they enfolded each other in their arms. They smiled wanly and left each other for the night.

"'His mischief shall return upon his own head, and his violent dealing shall come down upon his own pate' says the psalmist. Let that be a warning to you, you thick-headed Irishman," proclaimed Cartwright. "You needn't look so ill-used, Healy, just because I called you a thick-headed son of Hibernia," he added for good measure.

I don't care tuppence if you call me thick-headed," answered Healy, "but I'll be damned if you'll call me Irish – I'm Scots?"

"With a name like Healy? Well, I am buggered. Never mind. What I cannot understand is why now, with all that is at stake, you should choose to pick a fight in a tavern – calling attention to yourself. If I hadn't paid off the landlord, you'd probably be behind bars."

Healy continued to look glum, having some time ago given up the struggle to match words with his colleague.

"Here we are at Kilmarnock, a stone's throw from Eglinton, on the verge of uncovering matters of vital interest to our side, and you draw attention to yourself."

"What is so all-fired important about Eglinton and why take so much interest in a mere lieutenant?"

"Really, my friend! 'So foolish was I, and ignorant: I was as a beast before thee', you might as well admit. Eglinton is notable since the earl is a general and, from what our friend tells us there, is intimately concerned with raising troops for use against our friends in America. Ricketts may just be our chance to secure those plans. Have you forgot, our friend says the general is asking Ricketts to carry papers on the very subject."

"Thus, we are to shadow him and grab them?" volunteered Healy, with all the excitement of one who just seen the light.

"Aye, but we are not to be caught – and certainly not through our own foolishness, so we must take especial care," said Cartwright, glaring at Healy.

"What I canna' understand is what an English gentleman like you is doing working with a lot of twang-nosed provincials."

"Do not be deceived, my good Scots Healy. My father was hounded from this land for his views but before we went, he made provision that I should have the best education obtainable. By the bye, you take umbrage at being called Irish; I might do the same at being called English. True, I went to the most famous school in England, so I speak English like the gentleman I am, but I'm as Scots as you are. My father believed 'the fool and the brutish person perish', so he saw to it that no one could be ignorant that I am a gentleman." He stirred abruptly. "Enough of this. We have work to do."

Chapter 8

April the first, All Fools' day, might seem to the superstitious a poor day to leave behind the solid comfort of the Eglinton estate. The Rickettses did not think themselves subject to rustic superstition. They were proud of the reputation of American observers of the natural world such as Benjamin Franklin, whatever one might think of his politics.

Having finished dinner at one o'clock, they congratulated themselves with the optimistic self-regarding benevolence newly-weds exhibit and they kept their meal unusually light in an effort to endure without distress the motions of a carriage on rough roads.

All was ready. Two sturdy portmanteaux were on the coach and the travellers issued from the front door of the house amid a flurry of good wishes, immanent tears and scurrying. Waiting by the handsome coach with the Eglinton arms on its doors were two smiling servants. These were introduced to the couple – the coachman Donald and Iain the postillion. The former would ride high and important on the crossbar above the vehicle's front behind the second pair of horses – the wheelers – the latter to ride astride the nearside horse of the front pair – the leaders.

As if all the attention and affection were not enough to cement their feelings of well-being, the general had even detailed an escort of six jocular officers of his regiment. Though serving in Minorca, there was a recruiting party in England and there were always a number of other officers on leave who enjoyed their colonel's hospitality. They were enough to give any highwayman pause, garbed in red tunics bearing the olive green facings and bastion lace with a green stripe, recognizable as the uniform of the 51st of Foot, of which the earl had been colonel for a decade. To protect their white leggings while riding, the officers wore black leggings and the effect was imposing, even menacing. The escort viewed their colonel with genuine affection, delighted to perform such a pleasant task. The coach finally jolted into motion and uttered an initial squeal as it rumbled away, throwing up a dust cloud which gradually hit the phalanx of waving hands and kerchiefs.

The younger servant, Iain the postillion, imagined he looked quite splendid. In his amply-cut grey coat and fancy three-cornered hat, his slender, upright bearing did, indeed, cut a dash. A youth of eighteen, conscious of his exalted employment and determined to make the most of it, Iain was an impressive lad. Moreover, he had something of a reputation. Observant fathers on the Eglinton estate kept a wary eye on their daughters when Iain was about. Local swains, on several occasions, had felt called upon to leap to their enamorata's defence in affairs that impartial watchers could admit, it was not entirely certain that the women were as unfriendly to his presence, or even intentions, as their protectors might wish.

Donald, the coachman, held his own opinions of Iain. He's what they call a flash-man, Donald mused privately. Mixed with envy of a style of life he could no longer observe was the conviction of being in charge. Iain was to be kept in hand. I musna' let the wee laddie get oot o' hand, he warned himself.

By contrast, Donald was impressive in a different way. Attired also in keeping with his employer's standing, his bearing had not the devil-may-care insouciance of the postillion. What impressed people was Donald's professional capability; his stolid, large frame exuded strength, not comeliness. He resembled an overgrown, muscular bulldog. Of early middle age, he was as certain of his abilities as was Iain, only they were different skills and his confidence arose out of experience, not aspiration. He was wise enough in village ways to be well aware of his postillion's abilities with horses as well as his youthful mischief. He regarded his position, enjoying as he did the Montgomerie family's indulgent regard, as one of efficient oversight of all that might come within his ken.

The coach rumbled along at between five and eight miles an hour so as not to tax the horses too much nor make the two passengers uncomfortable. Besides they wished to conserve their horses, coaching inns not being so frequent in Scotland as farther south. They wheeled through Dundonald village, the main street of which was thinly lined with well-wishers and the merely curious, enjoying the spectacle of a mounted escort. Passing March Bridge and Tarbolton Loch, they made their way through Fairford on the Ayr road to Mauchline and descended the hill to Cumnock. There they stopped after doing nineteen miles, finding themselves at the New or Heid Inn. There was still some daylight so the first day's journey was deemed a success. No one paid attention to two horsemen, cloaked against the April wind, who observed the escorted party from a hill. Shortly thereafter, their escort saluted with drawn swords, gave three cheers and returned toward Eglinton. The pair of cloaked watchers had gone.

Cumnock was not far from the vast Eglinton estate, and well within the home stamping-grounds of so enterprising an opportunist as their postillion. As Donald was not surprised to discover, Iain had slipped off down Glaisnock Street round about midnight to seek the company of one of his favourite lasses. Unfortunately for him, the girl's father was a light sleeper and appeared, whip in hand, effectively ending the escapade. The postillion was not one to be downhearted by the occasional check, however, and was in good spirits come the dawn. The coachman even felt a twinge of regret that he could not, himself, burn the candle at both ends as Iain could do.

The next day they left at eight o'clock, the newly-weds having eaten the light breakfast they cautiously limited themselves to. They covered the thirteen miles to the New Inn at Sanquhar in Dumfriesshire, where they changed the horses they had secured at Cumnock. They were unaware of the postillion's falling sound asleep mid-morning, though he was a good enough horseman to remain mounted until being summoned to wakefulness after twenty minutes by Donald's whip straying from its usual inerrant path to flick Iain's arm.

That afternoon saw them at Thornhill, crossing the fertile valley of the river Nith and passing Halfmark Hill on their left. Thornhill boasted (or was it endured?) a tall column surmounted by a winged horse, the emblem of the Queensberry family. It was a sign that Scotland was still largely feudal. The emblem was also in sharp contrast to the capabilities of the hired nags who seemed to resent leaving Cumnock. The travellers were not sorry to find refuge in the Royal Oak, an ample coaching inn built some sixty years before.

So their journey continued without mishap. On the Thursday, after going fourteen miles, they changed horses at mid-day at the King's Arms, the coaching inn at one side of the spacious square of Dumfries. The town still showed signs of hard usage by Prince

Charles Edward in the pretender's rebellion of the Forty-five. From Dumfries they went eastward sixteen miles through the village of Mousewald, spending the third night at the Queensberry Arms in Annan. On the Friday, they made an easy day of it, doing the eighteen miles to Carlisle during the morning, changing horses at Gretna Hall in the famous wedding village of Gretna Green and crossing into England over the Sark Bridge.

In order to have a quiet place to stay and yet be able to visit Carlisle, they decided to put up four miles east of the city at the Queen's Arms Hotel at Warwick-on-Eden. Running the horses under the arches of the L-shaped wing on the east side of the small but comfortable inn, they were ensconced by mid-day, taking in some of the sights of Carlisle, the border citadel which had been the scene of countless battles between the English and Scots.

"I can just imagine Bonnie Prince Charlie entering the city on a white charger preceded by a hundred pipers," said Sarah.

"Yes, and apparently 'twas the first time the city had ever surrendered to invaders from the north," interjected a scholarly-looking man who overheard her. "But 'twas not long before the prince limped back north, dispirited after his retreat from Derby," he added.

It was just as well they had allocated a stay longer than usual since Donald discovered a wheel was about to come off.

On the next day, they travelled the nineteen miles to Penrith, lunching and changing horses at the Crown Inn, which had been built only seven years earlier. Their progress was slowed by the market, it being a Saturday. Eventually they wended their way through the milling crowd which, though quite friendly, were not about to scamper left and right for the sake of travellers who impinged on their primary rights of possession on market day. Another fourteen miles saw them arrived at the Tufton Arms, a sixteenth-century coaching inn at Appleby-in-Westmoreland for the fifth night of their journey.

That morning, the first Sunday after Easter, known in England as Low Sunday, the couple went to the ancient church of St Lawrence and found that they were celebrating Holy Communion, following the still unusual 'high church' practice of celebrating the eucharist on the first Sunday of the month. This was their first chance to receive the sacrament as Anglicans, a practice they were to carry out faithfully whenever they could for the next four decades. James knew that Sarah had, of course, been brought up in her family's Presbyterian church but she had secretly cherished a love of the ordered ceremonial of the Church of England, particularly valuing the freedom from long and arbitrary ministerial harangues where, it seemed to her, the congregation did little save listen, attentively on occasion. Her first encounter with Anglican worship had been at the age of seventeen, when her father had married James's mother. It had struck her aesthetic side long before she noticed a different theology. She confided to James about her family's Presbyterianism: "It was so dour; the English service allowed everybody a part, to do other things than sit still and listen to long sermons."

After going nine miles and changing horses at the George at Brough, found immediately on the right-hand side of the road on entering the town, they joined the Great North Road in the North Riding of Yorkshire, making the King's Head in Barnard Castle for their sixth night and wandering round the castle ruins before driving on to Catterick Bridge for a change of horses at the George and Dragon. The inn was attractive enough, right by the river Swale, but one of the procured horses soon huffed and puffed in a most alarming manner and everyone, the coachman, postillion, James and Sarah breathed more easily themselves when, after eight miles, they pulled into the New Inn at Leeming Lane. Changing horses, with relief, another ten miles saw them just two miles north of the Crown Inn at Boroughbridge.

Traffic was very light on the road which was bordered by flat fields with woods occasionally reaching down to the road. They were startled by a horseman galloping past them, who disappeared ahead of them. They talked of their good fortune in being able to enjoy the relatively comfortable ride the earl's coach afforded, especially considering the rough state of the Great North Road which had degenerated over the last mile or so. Travelling on a singularly bumpy stretch, Donald slowed the coach, then stopped dead. Alighting, he came to the nearside window.

"What's wrong? Why have we stopped?" inquired James.

"I'm sorry, sir, but there is a man lying on the side of the road next to an overturned trap. I'll just go forward and have a closer look."

James did not hesitate but alighted and walked up to the man who appeared dazed and, with Donald's aid, was sitting on the verge of the road. To questions like "Are you hurt? Is anything broke?" he did not answer but felt himself over ruefully. Finally, he shook his head slowly, saying hesitantly: "I think not. I must have been knocked out – I don't know for how long."

Donald surmised it was only shortly before their arrival else other traffic would have come upon him. Examination of the trap showed a wheel had come off, though the hub and axle seemed unscarred. Odd, thought Donald.

"Where are you bound, sir?" asked James. "You may have broken nothing but I imagine you are a good deal shaken. We could take you on to our next stop for the night. You could resume your journey on the morrow,"

"Most kind, most kind, to be sure," the tall, heavily-eyebrowed man managed to utter, managing his approach to their coach gingerly as if testing his limbs.

"Iain can bring your bag aboard and, as the pony seems unhurt, we can attach her to the back of the coach."

As James and the stranger entered the coach, the two servants took up their usual positions and they set off, the stranger wincing once or twice as the coach negotiated bumps. James introduced him to Sarah and, until reaching the inn, they engaged in desultory conversation. Sarah commiserated with the stranger but on the whole they forebore intruding on the periods of silence which the man seemed to need in getting over his shock. In fact, not much information was gained from him saving his name, Peter Cartwright, and his speech revealed him to be a gentleman. He did gradually warm up in response to Sarah's encouragement and seemed to appreciate her charm and beauty, examining her with his eyes in a way she found disquieting.

James's mind raced. He does not realize his name is already familiar to me. Perhaps he thinks Jacob Hart never mentioned him – believable since Jacob was about to desert. Nor will he know that I was pointedly warned about him as a dangerous man, by Mr Green. Was he the person at the wedding whom the earl noticed? I cannot answer any of these questions at the moment satisfactorily.

Dusk was settling as they reached the inn at which Donald and Iain unloaded the luggage. Cartwright saw to it that he took charge of his belongings himself. The ostler, all bustle and welcome, descended upon them with assurances of his capable hospitality. "Aye, sir, ye' can have the blue room for a night. It has a sitting-room just off a very nice bedroom. I'm sure ye'll be right comfortable, indeed."

The inn was very grand. A site of importance from the early middle ages, it became an inn around 1600, James learned. It was ideally sited in the angle between two major roads and was spacious, being essentially divided netween two residential sections, with stables at the back,

Before supper, Cartwright appeared in the taproom and approached James and Sarah, asking: "Would a brandy suit you, Mr Ricketts – perhaps your lady would prefer a glass of wine?"

Conversation developed well as they found they got along passably together and soon Cartwright was persuaded to join them for supper in a small room off the bar. "You are both so kind to take me under your wing the way you have," said their guest, with a diffident and suddenly warm smile. "I feel I'd like to tell you more about my journey and," – here he paused to find words – "to tell you of the plight I find myself in. I don't like to intrude into your privacy but I feel I owe you something by way of explanation."

James made no immediate reply but Sarah, sensing his awkward diffidence, came to the rescue: "Oh, you don't have to tell us more than you really want to but we should be pleased to do anything we can to alleviate any distress you may be under."

"I am grateful, truly grateful, ma'am. The truth is I am engaged to marry." He smiled demurely, which struck James as theatrical in one who was no spring chicken and, indeed, seemed to be fairly experienced in the ways of the world. "However, my suit is hampered by one obstacle: my fiancée's father, whose opinion she defers to in every respect. He is suspicious of my sincerity and my worthiness in seeking her hand. He has insisted that I meet him tomorrow at lunch in Wetherby, a dozen miles to the south. I fear he will stop our marriage, if I fail to be there. The point is that I have no way of reaching there and if I do not keep our appointment, I fear the worst."

Sarah, whose sympathy could not remain dormant in the face of such a romantic tale, volunteered a solution: "Nothing could be simpler. We go by way of Wetherby and could put you down there on our way."

With surprising agility for one whose part in the conversation had hitherto been reserved, James broke in: "Of course, we veer eastward to Market Weighton after Wetherby, but we could certainly do as Sarah suggests." Sarah forebore darting at James a look of surprise. The meal concluded, the couple took their leave after agreeing to re-assemble for breakfast.

"My dearest," blurted Sarah the moment they arrived at the privacy of their chambers, "Why ever did you tell him that nonsense about going on to Market what's-it?"

"If you are going to delve into clandestine activities, my love, you had better develop a bit of suspicion about your fellow men. What do we know about him? I don't like some things I see. We find him dazed after a fall at speed from his carriage but no bones are broken, he has no cuts or marks on him, nor are his clothes torn. Most wheels breaking off a cart shoot on ahead but this one was sitting right beside the cart. The wheel and axle looked undamaged and it seemed as if the wheel might simply have been unattached while motionless. Cartwright did not have a travelling case as you might expect to take in a carriage but only saddlebags designed for a mount, and which, you may have noticed, were quickly taken off the coach by him so no one could have a close look." Sarah, who had noticed none of these things, was mute with astonishment.

James continued to expound: "The name Cartwright will mean nothing to you, my sweet. But it's the name of that dangerous cove Mr Green in Kingston warned me about."

"James. That horseman who raced by us just before we ran across Cartwright – do you think he bolted ahead to set up the so-called accident?" offered Sarah, spurred into mobilizing her critical faculties.

"That could very well be. If so, that fellow is lying low, but, if so, we have not seen the last of him, I'll warrant. Last of all, when he came over to us to invite us for a drink, he fair leered at you, his eyes up and down like a lecher."

Sarah had actually noticed that and her eyes lit up with delight. "My darling, I do believe you are jealous!"

"Yes, of course I am" James replied smugly. "And I don't want him knowing our route. Thank you for not giving it away."

"Of course, sir," she said, happily.

Chapter 9

Elsewhere, Donald and Iain found congenial company and were not ready to retire. The setback suffered in his amorous escapade at Cumnor did not dissuade Iain from applying himself on this occasion. His attention was drawn toward a plump, dark-haired chambermaid called Emily who attended the servants amusing themselves in the small bar where were assembled Donald and Iain, deep in reminiscences with those who, like themselves, looked after their masters' needs. If Donald's attention was thoroughly engaged in conversation and games of shove ha' penny, Iain's was not.

He was involved in bouts of pregnant eye-contact with Emily. Her tantalizing, delicious bosom and fetching eyes revealed a disposition toward pleasure to Iain, who had eyes to see. He managed with the artful wiles he had honed in sundry encounters with susceptible wenches, to rivet Emily's interest. Initial probes in her direction, by means of humorous remarks and soulful glances were well received and his insinuations found their mark.

He succeeded in cultivating her flattered sensibilities to the point where he felt he could exploit his advantage by gaining information essential to the conquest he envisioned with growing anticipation. "Now, lassie, we Scots have a sharp eye for appraising when we see someone of such incomparable charm as..." her eyes widened, "as...yourself'"

"Oooh, ye do talk nice," said the chambermaid, revealing that whatever she might lack in intellect, she more than made up for by her responsiveness. "You're enough to turn a gal's head, you are, and that's no mistake" was the encouraging rejoinder.

"Your comeliness, lassie, is too much for me to bear with tranquillity," pursued he, seeing he was making distinct progress as he sidled up to her so. "Would you torture a poor lad with flirting? Come now, my sweeting, how can I come to you – to show you real proof how much you've stolen my heart?"

"Ooh, you're a sly fox, you are!" she declared and, as if it were an afterthought, added helpfully: "If I told you I'm in the room on the right at the top of yon stairs, why – you might pop up like a jack-in-the-box, to catch a gal all defenceless, you might, an hour after midnight, perhaps!" Iain digested this intelligence as she slipped away, all businesslike and bustling to fetch pints for the other guests.

When the village clock struck one o'clock, after what seemed to the postillion hours of delay, he groped his way along the upstairs passage to her room. Noiselessly he opened the door. "Hello, who's there?" she whispered tremulously. She was holding up to her soft neck a coarse sheet which made her skin look downy soft by comparison. It utterly failed to disguise the desirability of his quest.

"It's me, smitten by your charms and all afired to worship at your feet," he replied with inward embarrassment at the thought of what his friends might say to him had they overheard him. She seemed to take it as a sufficiently passionate declaration. It was enough to remove the last vestige of her resistance and, in the dim light of a single sputtering candle, she opened the way to the prizes she had in store.

In about ten minutes time, at the other end of the inn, a different sort of nocturnal operation was unfolding. Someone slipped into the sitting-room adjoining James and Sarah's bedroom and was examining its contents with a hooded lamp. At this very moment, the innkeeper, jolted into a resentful wakefulness by tell-tale grunts and sighs in the room at the end of the hallway, made his way, half asleep, toward the energetic sounds, growling "Who's there, what's afoot?"

Iain's armoury contained measures for evasion. In a trice he was out of Emily's chamber and round the corner before the ostler gained the door to Emily's room. Iain, having narrowly escaped detection, took refuge in James and Sarah's sitting-room. The result was that Iain careened into their intruder, neither one recognizing the other in the dark. The intruder suspended his search and just managing to retain his hold on the hooded lamp, put it out and bolted past Iain who, a moment later, left the sitting-room to regain his own accomodation.

Called to account by the ostler, now aware only that her room was quiet and her bed disorderly, but that something in the room had made noise, he heard Emily explain the din by saying it must have been one of her nightmares. Apparently she had had similar misfortunes before and she had developed a convincing technique to complain of her affliction. However implausible her account, the ostler felt some unease even though he said no more and left her in peace. Emily thought to herself – I wonder if he has similar plans himself and needs to avoid offending me.

James had been wakened by the scuffle in the sitting-room. My pistol, he thought, reaching for the nearest drawer to the bed. He cautiously opened the door to the adjoining room. The room had just become empty though the door was ajar. Failing to find anyone, he rejoined Sarah in the bedroom; she was now thoroughly awake and in a state of some alarm. They discussed the possible intrusion, decided not to raise an alarm and tried to imagine just what had happened.

"Nothing seems to have been taken," said Sarah, though neither was in doubt about the point of the entry. James had buried the genuine despatch deep inside his portmanteau and placed the false one in the blue civilian jacket he wore on the journey. They then took what sleep they could find.

At breakfast they were approached by an affable Cartwright. After breakfast, with everything loaded, they all set off, James had first apprised Donald and Iain that they were likely to be stopped on the road but that all was foreseen and they were on no account to offer anything but meek submission to anyone stopping them.

At first Cartwright was brimming over with gushy thanks. The first few miles passed agreeably enough, when Cartwright inquired again what route they were planning to take after he left them. James felt qualms, fearing that his previous intervention on just this point might not have been believed. Sarah came to the rescue. Seeming to be on the verge of tears, she blurted out: " Oh dear! Alas, my poor aunt at Market Weighton. I only hope we will not be too late – she is much loved and near death, I fear."

Cartwright expressed his condolence in a somewhat perfunctory manner and his tone began perceptibly to alter. "I'm afraid I have another favour to ask of you. In about ten minutes we shall come to a crossroads where a companion of mine will be waiting. You will be in extreme danger if you do not stop there on my orders. I must also ask that you hand over a packet from Lord Eglinton which I know you carry."

The couple huddled together in agitation and looked aghast at the pistol pointed menacingly. James took the papers from his inside pocket and, after suitable cringing and craven posturing, handed them to Cartwright. He opened the seal and had a quick peak at the contents, not daring to give much attention to them as he had to keep the couple at bay. James could see that if Cartwright perused the papers he had handed over, their nonsense might become apparent and all would be lost. He felt it imperative either to shorten the examination or else to distract the reader. Had the manner of handing them over been too easy? A show of reluctance was called for.

"Do you really think you can get away with this?" asked James, mortified by the use of such a cliché. He tried to give it plausibility by peering angrily at Cartwright. The man's eyes narrowed as he raised them to look at James. He peers at me as if I were some inconvenient insect, noticed James. Cartwright's grip on the pistol tightened.

"I wouldn't worry over that if I was you," was his equally conventional riposte.

James, determined even at some risk to avoid discovery of their hoax, did not relent but tried to engage Cartwright's attention more completely. "What are the papers to you, anyway? Private papers to which you have absolutely no right whatsoever!" James even contrived to shift himself a bit, looking fixedly at a point just over Cartwright's left shoulder.

"Found your tongue, have you, you Hanoverian lackey!" James was anxious not to overdo it but he was glad to have evidence that all this had to do with politics. That discovery was worth a bit of risk, certainly. Cartwright fell back on his favourite idiom, looking smug, "'I have pursued my enemies and overtaken them'".

At this point Sarah intervened. "You may be our enemy but surely you have some gentlemanly instincts. We did everything we could to help you yesterday. Can you not cease threatening us? Just take the papers and go." She appeared to be on the verge of tears.

Cartwright liked to balance two personae – the gentleman which by upbringing he fancied he was, and the ruthless conspirator which he was by choice. "Don't let yourself become too agitated," he said, as if that satisfied both roles. "All this wasn't arranged in two minutes. You may not have noticed our watching you just after you left Kilmarnock, but you had an armed escort then. Pity we missed seeing them scuttle back to Auchans when they did, or our meeting might have been earlier."

Then he actually smiled. He almost relaxed, basking in his control but the crossroads were fast approaching. "Enough. You will see me no more when I leave you, and you will be free to travel to your aunt's, unmolested," said Cartwright, condescendingly falling back on his role as gentleman.

At the crossroads at Allerton, seven miles from Wetherby, the coach duly halted when confronted by what looked like a highwayman. As instructed, the servants answered with unalloyed timidity. Their demeanour seemed to convince the two spies that they had their quarry just where they wanted them. Cartwright and his companion rode off. James complimented Donald and Iain who admitted their feelings of relief that the dangerous affair was now over.

Pushing on at rapid speed for seven miles to the Angel at Wetherby, James sought out the local magistrate who offered every assistance when he learned they were come from Lord Eglinton whom he knew in his soldiering days. On the assumption that the villains would, when they discovered they had been deceived, make for Market Weighton to overtake the carriage, the magistrate sent off a troop of dragoons, one half along the Rufforth road to try and intercept the horsemen before they reached York, the other half-troop along the Bishopthorpe road to catch them should the villains' progress prove too swift for the first half-troop.

"It will go hard with those two if they are caught, though I must admit I'd give a lot to see their faces when they find they've been foxed," said James. "Even if they're not caught, they will still think the general has some need to communicate with the commandant of Colchester garrison, as the cover reads – they won't even know their true destination."

Sarah giggled maliciously. "Can you imagine the commandant's face if the packet ever does reach him?"

"I suppose that's unlikely, unless he is one of them," was all that James could think of saying.

Chapter 10

Upon seizing the papers, Cartwright and his companion set off eastward on the Rufforth road. Trotting swiftly, they passed through the southern part of the ancient city of York, along Paragon-street just outside the old city wall, entering the Market Weighton road opposite Walmgate Bar. In three hours they had reached the small inn at Barmby Moor, deciding to stop the night there rather than go on to Pocklington, which was larger and better-known. After a quick meal, they retired to their plain room to examine the papers they had stolen.

"Come, Healy, let us see what we have here – what 'songs of deliverance we can sing,'" invited Cartwright, almost rubbing his hands together. He crooned: "'Mine eye shall see my desire on mine enemies.'" Then he spread out some of the pages on the oak table. The first few pages contained extremely untidy text in bad penmanship, interspersed with occasional passages of four-digit number groups.

"It must be in code," observed Healy. Cartwright's eyes showed how unnecessary he thought that remark was. Healy was a sandy-haired lumpy man whose blue eyes were set in a nondescript face. Good in a fight, but not much else, thought Cartwright. Healy appeared to have some difficulty reading as his squint became pronounced. Cartwright suspected he was illiterate.

"Yes, well, let us see," The last pages were taken up with troop lists, sites where Scottish regiments were to be raised for the American war, and dates of projected embarcations. In all, Cartwright spotted fifteen regiments of foot. When he looked at their titles, he blanched. "This is nonsense! Just look at those regimental numbers." Healy tried to oblige but the extent of his ambition was to read the numbers, not interpret them. Cartwright continued: "175th Foot, 215th Foot, 223rd Fusiliers – Good God! Why, the army don't have a regimental number above 71. And look at the subtitles some of them have – the Duke of Wick's Own, the Earl of Inchnadamph's, Lord Corgaff's. Shit!" he pronounced solemnly. Healy did not remember ever hearing Cartwright use the word. For one thing, was it in the Bible? he wondered.

"And just look at those places where they are supposed to recruit: Kirkton of Glenbuchat, Braemar, Ladhar Bheinn – isn't that a mountain peak near the Kyle of Lochalsh? Who would take the King's shilling there? Three shepherds and ten mountain goats, I should think. Where is this nonsense supposed to go?" Looking for some indication, he found it at the bottom of the second page as well as on the cover *–To the commandant of Colchester garrison.* Cartwright exploded in a torrent of frustrated fury. "'The mouth of the deceitful are opened against me: they have spoken with a lying tongue.' We've been buggered, well and truly buggered!"

Healy didn't know what to say so he made a few indeterminate sympathetic mutterings of a distinctly gaelic flavour. Cartwright could not be placated. "Hell and damnation – this is utterly useless. 'False witnesses are risen up against me.' Let me think, let me think," something Healy was quite prepared to allow so long as he didn't have to join in. "They said they were off to Market Weighton to see a sick aunt. What a performance. I suppose we could go there and try to pick up a lead but it's almost certainly a wild goose chase. London is more likely. We'd better get a good night's sleep and be off early for the south." Cartwright pulled out a flask of whisky which he offered to Healy, having had a long pull on it first.

In the morning they woke up early and were about to descend for breakfast when there was a clatter of hoof-beats outside the inn. The ostler was accosted by a dusty officer in red tunic and metal helmet with a ridge of fur fore-and-aft, who could not be more than seventeen years old. "Have you see two men on horseback come this way?"

"Who wants to know and what are they like?" replied the innkeeper, never one to waste words.

The two conspirators remained immobile just long enough to hear "Cornet Robinson of the 22nd Light Dragoons, from Wetherby..." They clambered down the stairs to where they had readied their horses for departure. In a flash they were off across the field, keeping the inn between them and the dragoons. When about three hundred yards away, the ostler spotted them. "I think your villains be there – and they ain't paid!"

The chase was on and, fortunately for the companions, the terrain was wooded and flat and their horses were rested while those of the dragoons were not. Before long they had put some distance between themselves and the pursuers. "Let me draw them off while you go on to Market Weighton," suggested Healy, rather breathlessly.

Cartwright, whom the chase had pitched into a cavalier, hunting mode, answered "That's good of you, ol' boy. But these papers ain't worth delivering to anyone, so I suggest we make our separate ways to the Great George in Southwark. I have a letter from the Governor to deliver to Captain Hutchins."

With a burst of intellectual acumen, Healy asked: "How will ye find him?"

"More to the point – are you capable of finding the Great George without compromising our whole enterprise?" After Healy's long-suffering response, Cartwright went on: "I do not know where Hutchins lodges, but I know the mapping office where he works and I can trace him to his abode. At least there we can make plans without fear of further interruption. By God, if I ever catch up with Ricketts, he'll rue the day he met me." On this note, the two companions split up.

Resuming their route, the newly-weds followed the Great North Road for seven miles to a change of horses at the Swan, Abberford before putting up for the night at the Swan at Ferry Bridge. There they found welcome glasses of port waiting in their bedroom. The rest of the journey, they stayed in varying degrees of comfort at the Crown at Bawtry and the Angel at Grantham which claimed to be the oldest inn in England. The next overnight stop was Buckden in Cambridgeshire.

"This town is very interesting," observed Sarah. "Because it lies at the intersection of the Great North Road and a main east-west road, it boasts two inns – the George where we stay and the Lamb, a very grand place, right across the road from us."

"To say nothing of the Bishop of Lincoln's palace built seven hiundred years ago, where Henry VIII's first wife, Catherine of Aragon, was imprisoned. We find this happens in England: out-of-the-way places turn out to be full of romance and mystery," observed James.

The next stop, Hatfield in Hertfordshire, proved to be another such place; the Salisbury Arms was not far from where Henry III's children spent much of their time. It took a week and, after a fortnight on the road, everyone was glad to arrive at the Bell Savage in the City of London on Monday, the fourteenth day of April, 1777. James and Sarah were equally glad to find the rest of their baggage awaiting them. Heartfelt farewells were made to Donald and Iain. Mention of their courageous aptitude as secret agents made them chuckle unrestrainedly. James rewarded them with a purse and the suggestion that they take a couple of days to see the capital before returning to Dundonald where, he had little doubt, the earl would hear their account with interest. Besides, he added, Iain probably had other matters to interest him, causing the postillion to redden.

Chapter 11

Three months earlier (January 1777), Thomas Hutchins had received his orders for London. That was where the Additionals had their headquarters. He had expected to have to work with them in the depôt company of the 60th Regiment for the receiving of recruits. He was pleased to learn, instead, that he was to work on maps. He was to place his surveying and mapping expertise at the disposal of the military authorities. His skills were much needed since it became apparent that the rebels were using better maps than the King's troops had. Making himself available in this way ensured regular captain's pay, and he was removed from the struggle in North America.

He was also able to find employment in a private capacity and had correspondence with clients as far afield as France. Eventually he dealt with American merchants in that country. By February, two months before the arrival of the Ricketts couple, he was well settled into a cheap inn at Shoreditch. That was an arrangement which did not long suit some other persons.

It seemed to him a simple coincidence when he fell in with a Guards major at the tavern to which he frequently repaired. Standing at the bar, the major happened to stand next to him. He turned and smiled. "I find this house very pleasant and convenient, you know. The beer and brandy are passable and the pork pie edible. I could not help overhearing you a moment ago – American, are you not? Apart from that, I noticed your regimentals: Royal Americans. Have I got it right?"

"Quite so, major," answered Hutchins, puzzled by the tentative nature of his observations since his buttons clearly bore a "60" on them. But then, he reflected, English gentlemen were often circumspect when introducing themselves, assuming a tentativeness as a courtesy which was unfamiliar to many colonials. An officer in the Guards should prove very much a gentleman.

"I see you are an officer of the 2nd Foot Guards," ventured Hutchins.

"My dear fellow – certainly not!" replied the officer, looking offended. "There's no such regiment, sir. We rank after the 1st Foot

Guards but our motto is *Nulli Secundus* and from the Restoration of 1660 we've been the Coldstream Regiment of Foot Guards, or the Coldstream, or the Coldstreamers, but never, never the Coldstreams and decidedly never the Second. Such mistakes have been the subject of duels, I'd have you know, sir."

Hutchins was beginning to understand how regimental pride was the backbone of the British Army. In the course of conversation, they agreed to dine at the inn on the morrow and, when the time came, the major was accompanied by a good-looking wench and by a plump friend called Sophie who soon attached herself to Hutchins with a proprietary air.

"Where do you lodge, Thomas?" asked Sophie. When he supplied the name of his indifferent establishment, the major cut in: "Oh, my dear fellow, you must not let 'em fob you off with such a place. 'Pon my soul, Thomas, I'll see you in to the Belle Savage if it kills me. It's so much better and in the heart of the city."

Hutchins was glad to accept the suggestion and was surprised that the major even took the trouble the next day to walk him there, having a private word first on Hutchins's behalf with the innkeeper.

After moving in to the Belle Savage, the American received a letter which had been delivered by someone who did not stay to make himself known. It was from William Livingston, Governor of New Jersey (if one discounted Benjamin Franklin's loyalist son William, effectively deposed). The letter was dated in December 1776, four months ago, Hutchins reckoned, and confirmed the receipt of Hutchins's letter to him. It applauded his determination to resign and suggested that the deliverer of this letter, who must remain anonymous, might be able to assist him "to be of service to his country" once he had resigned "with honour". The letter ended with a note about his nephew by marriage, James Ricketts, with whom the governor knew Hutchins to be already acquainted. The governor was anxious to convince young James where his true obligations lay and, since James, his wife and Hutchins were to be in London at the same time, the governor would be obliged for any salutary influence Captain Hutchins might bring to bear. The governor regretted he had not had the courtesy of a reply from James "in contrast to the thoughtful letter received from you."

Hutchins was uneasy. How did the unseen messenger know he was at the Belle Savage? He'd only been there two days after starting his mapping assignment. Did the major who steered him here, and who would not take No for an answer, have anything to do with it? Not the major – surely not. That was too far-fetched. Perhaps he was being watched by the governor's unknown agent? How did they know Ricketts would be in London? It was more than he could fathom and, alas, the key to the puzzle, the agent, was not showing himself. At any rate, London was huge – how would he set about finding Ricketts?

Stepping onto the staircase, he was astounded to see none other than Ricketts and, presumably, his wife enter the hall followed by two servants with luggage. He shrank back. I've heard of coincidence, he said to himself, but this is too much! Still, he could not see why it should be to anyone's advantage to arrange their close proximity, unless it was Livingston's and his agent's. If it was not coincidence, then the major must be acting for Livingston. That he did not believe.

His meeting with James was not going to be difficult to arrange. He would write James, congratulating him on his marriage and hoping they might meet as fellow guests at the inn.

The couple were no sooner ensconced in their chambers, sampling the Madeira which the innkeeper had left for them – such was the style one expected in the capital and occasionally found in the provinces – than James began turning over in his mind how best to carry out Mark Prevost's request to take a look at Hutchins. The subject was made urgent when a note was slid under the sitting-room door.

James was thunderstruck. It was a friendly missive suggesting that as they were all staying at the same inn, they might enjoy meeting. In fact, the writer was all agog to make the acquaintance of Mrs Ricketts, about whom he'd had such glowing reports.

James said to her: "Here were we, thinking we'd need to track down our quarry. Now I suddenly feel I'm the quarry. I don't know, my darling."

"It begins to look that way, doesn't it?" replied Sarah, according to James's lights not very helpfully.

James became more intense. "You give me a strange feeling, you know."

"My darling," responded Sarah, ready to move towards him amorously.

"No, no, my sweetest, I mean it. Look, I've travelled more than you. I'm older. I've seen more of the world than you, yet sometimes I know you're way ahead of me in subtle things and I'm a babe following after."

"If you were as devious as you make me sound, I shouldn't love you at all," was the reply which rendered him speechless. "It's not that hard, I think. Whether he wants to see us desperately or not, is neither here nor there. It's surprising, but it doesn't alter anything. We come upon him, not by accident, but by his invitation – the three of us – quite naturally."

"My love, if you don't mind and it, er, doesn't discommode you – all right. You are so artful you can seem artless," said he, thinking that he was paying her another compliment. She loved him well enough to avoid setting him right.

Instead, she half-smiled. Knowing he needed to be settled down amidst all the confusion and intrigue, she applied the remedy she had learned in their short time together was unfailing: "Come to bed, I have the greatest need of you."

They got into bed. Neither remembered the fatiguing day of sightseeing but James could not drop Hutchins from his mind. She whispered to him: "I'm sure life has all sorts of entanglements. We must not be ruled by this particular one."

A few moments later she seemed to be in a perplexity of her own. "Good heavens, talking of entanglements - I'm all tangled up in this sheet."

Her protector's thoughts finally switched from Hutchins to something indescribably more pleasurable. He rose to her rescue gallantly: "Oh, my love, you must never, ever, let yourself be entangled *that* way – why there's no telling where that might lead!" A short spate of inane and suppressed giggling was followed, after a significant interval, by sighs and murmurings.

That same evening, at Southwark, Cartwright and Healy conferred on their own. Cartwright boasted: "As I told you I would, I tracked Hutchins down and gave him the governor's letter. He didn't see me. I take pains to keep my contacts as few as I can in this affair. As the psalmist says: 'he will guide his affairs with discretion'."

Healy cut in, fearing additional scriptural citations: "What is the letter about?"

Good heavens, fellow. A gentleman doesn't read another's letters – certainly not Governor Livingston's."

Healy had one ace up his sleeve. "I watched the Belle Savage, as you bade me, and guess who I saw going in? A picture of beauty, she was."

"Oh, the German whore herself, no doubt" responded the spy, laconically, feeling sure that even Healy would recognize he meant Charlotte of Mecklenberg-Streliz, wife of George III.

"Not quite, but someone you know better - Sarah Livingston."

For once, Cartwright had no reply at hand.

"That's right" added his accomplice. "A wee bit later, I saw her husband at the inn, too."

The spy suppressed a hoop of joy. "Healy, for once, you've come up trumps. 'The testimony of the Lord is sure, making wise the simple.'"

Healy was uncertain if he was being complimented.

"If Ricketts has not already delivered those papers – possibly to the War Office – you must catch him like 'a lion that is greedy of his prey'. Seize the papers and make off like the desert wind. Begone now, make haste for the papers! 'Let thy wrathful anger take hold of them.'"

The next morning after breakfast James walked to the War Office in Whitehall, not far distant, to deliver the earl's papers and to see about passage back to St Augustine. Administrative arrangements between the various government departments concerned with army officers' movements, the Navy Board and the Admiralty, and the relations between them were usually in a state of baffling confusion. However, at last passage was set for them on the armed Ordnance storeship *Earl of Bathurst* which plied its way frequently across the Atlantic, ferrying troops for the Caribbean and the Floridas. In a fortnight's time, she would carry recruits for St Augustine. This time there would be no question of having to deal with some irritating privateer. There would be a convoy made up, including a third-rate ship-of-the-line of seventy-four guns, and a frigate fresh out of Gibraltar accompanying them, bound for Admiral Richard Howe. Sightseeing by the young couple would have to cease near the end of April, since their departure from Dover was set for the tenth of May.

Whilst at the War Office, James could at last deliver the papers entrusted to him and Sarah. It would be a relief to be rid of them. As he approached the mounted Blues in sentry boxes on each side of the main entrance, his mind was on sightseeing prospects and he failed to notice that the guard was about to be relieved inside the courtyard. At the last moment, he realized it was no time to be entering by that yard. Two ranks of horsemen were drawn up therein – the old guard, found by the Royal Horse Guards Blue, dressed in blue tunics – as their title implied – white small-clothes and black polished high boots. Facing them the new guard was found by the 2nd Troop of Life Guards wearing similar uniform except for red tunics; each corps wore the full tricorne hat with gold lace but the polished cuirass, familiar in earlier and later times, was not worn.

As James moved to his left, out of the way, a non-descript, scruffily-dressed man grabbed the despatch case he had slung over his shoulder and was in the process of making off when the relieved mounted sentry in the near box moved forward out of his box in order to make room for his relief who was taking the place he had just left. The thief colllided with the front leg of the trooper's horse and took a spill. James grabbed back the case but failed to apprehend the thief who was able to escape through the crowd that always attended the changing at Horse Guards.

The guard mounting finished, a thoroughly-agitated James crossed the courtyard and entered the building where a dismounted Life Guardsman gave him a sweeping sword salute. Inside, he stopped at the porter's desk to ask the way to Mr Marlin, as the earl had instructed him to do. The civil servant seated at the desk looked James over with care before answering him. "May I ask your name, sir?" When told, he reached across into a drawer and drew forth a sheaf of papers, consulted them and said: "Of course, Mr Ricketts. The gentleman's chamber is on the second floor. You will also find his name on a door near the staircase."

James walked down the corridor as directed. Thank goodness, he thought, soldiers indoors are uncovered, so cannot return salutes, or I would be here all day. The Horse Guards seem to swarm with officers of higher rank than me - saluting would be an infernal nuisance. On reaching the landing on the first floor, he stood aside to allow passage for a sixty-year-old man exuding an air of authority; he must be either a secretary of state or a general or both, perhaps, mused James.

He was tall and thin with an aquiline nose. The man peered at James's uniform facings, then at his buttons and addressed him in what Sarah would have called a "gargley" voice: "I say there, young man, to which battalion of Royal Americans do you belong?" James saw that the man had not only spotted the correct regiment and knew that it had more than one battalion. The venerable man persevered: "Look here, can you spare a moment? I'd like to hear something about your service."

James followed him to a large office and sat down as bidden. Answering queries about his service, James thought it might be good to reciprocate with some of his own: "Do you know the 60th, sir?"

Looking amused, the man barked: "Know the Royal Americans! Why you young pup, what do they teach you these days?" he said sharply but his tone was not unkind – as if enjoying a private joke. "I'm your colonel. Not your battalion colonel-commandant, but your colonel-in-chief. You have no way of knowing that, I realize. Amherst is my name," he said as he held out his hand.

"Good heavens, sir, er, General, er, my Lord, I had no idea," stammered James, painfully wrong-footed.

"I am glad to see you offer no excuses, my lad. Very glad – a good officer gives basic reasons for his errors, not excuses for them. Unlike Gage and Howe and some others I might name. Never mind, I'm delighted to meet someone from the 60th, somebody from America. Before James could reply, Lieutenant General Jeffery, Lord Amherst continued: "You're clearly new round here, young man, but there are two things you ought to learn. One is – at Horse Guards you are liable to meet anybody, even the King, or the Prince of Wales – he's always coming up with some fetching change in uniforms to suggest - so be alert. The second thing is – I know it must be hard for you coming from a rebellious province – not everybody will think of that. Some will take their amusement at your expense. Offered me the command in America, they did, just as happened twenty years ago. I told them I would in no wise agree to fight Americans. Doesn't mean I think the rebels are right; I don't!

But I'm too old, for one thing. Still, I do what I can to see my regiment is looked after." He concluded by asking: "Where are you off to now?" On being told, he remarked, "Marlin, no less. You do move in mysterious circles. Watch what you say to him – he's nobody's fool. My compliments to him. Don't let him put your nose out of joint. And remember, if you want to see your colonel-in-chief, you have only to ask. I'm usually here or at my place in Kent. I'll let you know if it is not convenient."

James's head spun. He made as coherent a farewell as he could. Going one more flight upstairs, he found a door with MR MARLIN in carefully executed white paint on a black background, rather like the solicitors' nameplates he had seen at the Inner Temple. Knocking, he was greeted by a grunt which he took to be a summons to enter. He explained his mission and gave an account of the attempt to steal the papers on their journey, which brought more grunts at various places. When he related the incident outside the building, the grunt had a questioning lilt to it. Finally he conveyed Lord Amhert's compliments and received another grunt. James was about to turn on his heels to exit when Mr Marlin spoke: "I reckon you know not what these are, eh?"

"Not really, sir. I have only a general notion of their subject matter."

"You do, eh? But you deliver them notwithstanding."

That seemed a strange remark but he doubted it would be explained to his satisfaction.

"That is the lot of His Majesty's servants. We do what we are told and are none the wiser," prosed Marlin piously.

"Well, sir, the fact is, I was not *told* to do this, I was asked."

"You say Lord Eglinton *asked* you to do it. Do you think he would distinguish his asking you from giving you order?"

"Yes, I do. He also told me I could turn it down if I did not think it...honourable."

"Very interesting. Very interesting," Marlin said, putting his fingertips together - like Mr Craddock. "That is to your credit. You didn't have to, but you did. Second, Lord Eglinton himself thinks highly enough of you to give you a choice in the matter. Very interesting. Perhaps you don't realize what a compliment he paid you?"

James had the feeling he was in front of one of his judges - the unseen grey men who pull the strings. "Certainly, Mr Marlin, it was all of that, whatever else it was."

Marlin looked up sharply as if aware that this mere subaltern was not run-of-the-mill. And as if he realized James seemed to be aware that other reasons lay behind the affair than had been mentioned so far. He paused before continuing: "I trust you find your inn convenient as well as comfortable. I see another 60th officer, Captain Hutchins, is staying there. I wonder if you know him?"

"We are acquainted, sir, but I cannot say I know him well."

Marlin indicated an unexpected concern for that officer. "It must be lonely for him in a place so far from home. He also comes from New Jersey, I believe."

James was uneasy at all the things Mr Marlin seemed to know.

As if he knew what James was thinking, he added: "Not much takes place at the Belle Savage which I don't know about, Mr Ricketts. It was our Major O'Shaughnessy who took Hutchins there and made sure he was welcomed."

Mr Marlin stood up to bow from his side of the desk. He did not actually shake hands but then, James knew, the English do not shake hands as readily as do the Europeans, or Americans. He came away with the conviction that he had met one of those people Lord Amherst had warned him about – those who had their amusement at his expense. Yet, there was no malevolence in Marlin's face. He was both impressively direct and uncommonly devious, all at one time. James thought to himself: an odd thing, the English sense of humour. Quite engaging, if you don't weaken. The English can be oppressive, but they like you for standing up to them, he believed.

He departed and could not be aware of Mr Marlin's next action – he took up the papers James had presented after such effort, looked at them nonchalantly, smiled, and then chucked them carelessly on the smouldering fireplace where they flared up, turning to ashes. "He'll do, he'll do," he muttered to himself.

Chapter 12

It seemed to James that things happened fast that evening. Deciding not to pen a reply to Hutchins's note, he and Sarah strolled into the taproom to find that officer in the company of a dark-haired, full-bosomed woman. Too much paint on her face, was Sarah's reaction, plus a strangely-placed beauty mark and a dress too tight to satisfy a competent couturier. James was reminded of Hutchins's reputation as a lady's man. As they entered, Hutchins quickly rose, an eyebrow raised, and exclaimed in surprise: "'Pon my word, I do believe, Sophie, I spy Mr Ricketts – how very nice!"

"What a surprise, indeed, to receive your nice letter; we thought it less complicated simply to find you rather than write, though it was kind of you to do so," replied James. "My dearest, may I present Captain Hutchins of my regiment?" Sophie's langorous eye was reserved for other characteristics than regimental identifications. Hutchins introduced her as his friend.

"How charming," added Sarah, "to think we meet another Royal American so far from home." She added with an impeccable hint of intimacy: "I do feel it's far from home; do you feel it too, Captain?"

"Indeed, ma'am, it's a rare treat meeting a Jersey woman in this place," he said. "The whole regiment knows that the gallant lieutenant was off to wed Miss Livingston. I fear there are few secrets in an officers' mess, ma'am." He went on ruefully, "The Americans whom I see are such a gloomy, dispirited lot, I fear, refugees bemoaning their exile and mostly hard put for money."

"I hope you'll not find us too dreary company," James answered. "We are on our wedding trip and we sail soon for the Caribbean."

"Ah, the Caribbean may have its attractions but lovely ladies from the Jerseys is not commonly one of them," Hutchins gallantly observed. Sophie was, it seemed, hard pressed to make any reasonable contribution to the conversation. After a laboured half-hour, the party engaged to meet again the next evening, parting with expressions of mutual esteem, except for Sophie whose eyes had glazed over.

"He seemed nice enough," said Sarah when they had reached their bedroom. "I think he was genuinely pleased to see you, though I'm not sure what Sophie thought."

"I know what Sophie thought," James said, wanting to reassure Sarah that, in his eyes, none of his attentions paid to her in any way signalled admiration. She saw through him easily and put his mind at rest deftly: "Come and kiss me, my one and only." Nothing more was needed.

The next evening, after a day at the Tower of London, James and Sarah went back to the taproom. They found Hutchins on his own in a small sitting-room reading a newspaper. Sophie apparently had another engagement, something which did not seem to bother the captain much, and he rose to greet them. After recounting where they'd been, Sarah admitted: "I feel quite exhausted after today's sightseeing so I hope you'll not think me rude if I leave you both to talk." Hutchins thought to himself: I doubt if it's sightseeing has really tired her. Lovely filly.

They bid her a good night and Hutchins turned to the brandy bottle which a servant had just produced.

"Have you heard any news, Thomas?"

"Only that after Mr Washington was sent packing from New York and White Plains, he crossed to the Jerseys. Howe and Cornwallis pushed him southwards to the Delaware. I would have thought him finished there but Cornwallis was too slow and the fox managed to slip across to Pennsylvania. Now that's a strange thing, James. He came back over the river and completely smashed that overconfident German, Rall, at Trenton – destroying his entire brigade. Then Cornwallis thought he had him again but the rebels spurted round him to Princeton where he caused havoc, even storming the big hall and rousting out the 40th Regiment. As far as I know, he's safe at Morristown while Howe sits in New York. And so the whole wretched thing goes on with no end in sight. I suppose Philadelphia is next on Howe's list."

"Is there no chance of peace, then?" said James glumly. "What makes them carry on, I wonder."

"Well, they always felt strongly about being taxed. 'No taxation without representation' is the catch-phrase."

"Yes, but that phrase is pretty hollow, surely," said James, who proceeded to tick off the familiar arguments why ungrateful colonists should not rebel. If anything might flush out Hutchins's true sympathies, putting things that strongly might do the trick, thought James.

Hutchins was not a transparent man and did not reply immediately. He paused to pour more brandy into both glasses and worked to get his long pipe going. Clearly, James was no fence-sitter waiting for one side or the other to predominate. "People can see things different ways, my friend," he replied. "You recall that letter I delivered to you from Governor – I suppose we should call him 'Governor' now – Livingston? We never had a chance to talk about it, but I've wondered how it feels to have your family so committed to the other side. Would you welcome fighting Americans, James?"

"No, I would not want it, but I wonder how far your sympathies for the rebels would lead you to go."

"I suppose it's not surprising you should wonder that. Nor are you alone in wondering. I had a strange visit the other day from someone called Cartwright. As far as I could tell, he was fishing to see if I might betray my commission – pass information, that kind of thing."

"Cartwright. That man is everywhere! I had my own run-in with him and I did not enjoy it," said James. "I could not help wondering if there is any connection between William Livingston's letter to me and Mr Cartwright. At any rate, he is as was described to me – a dangerous man."

"I suppose that might be, but I don't really know. Knowing Livingston's position, I would imagine his letter tried to swing you to his side but I didn't read his letter. I suppose you told Mark Prevost about the letter?"

"Actually, I did but I was careful to say it had not been opened."

"Surely, he must have been interested in my delivering the letter? It would seem a pretty obvious matter to look at," observed Hutchins.

"Oddly enough, he never raised the matter."

Hutchins is no fool, thought James.

That impression was reinforced by Hutchins's next words: "That means one of two things. Either Prevost had independent information on that score and didn't need to ask you, or he is a slipshod fool who didn't see the question lying in front of his nose. The latter I simply don't believe. In any case, James, I much appreciate the way you talked to him."

"To be honest, Thomas, I did not think it was part of my job to involve a fellow officer on such uncertain grounds, certainly not when the consequences for you could be serious."

"Hmm!" rejoined Hutchins, searching James's face carefully. "I'll play you no games, James. If I had no other obligations, I'd help the rebels. I think their demand for independence is just. But, as I told Cartwright, I'm no weazel. As long as I have the King's commission, I'll not act in anything devious. I rather resented his attempt to suborn my duty. In any case, how would I know he is not an *agent provocateur*, working for British intelligence?"

"Take it from me, that's not likely," said James with feeling. "I'm glad you told me how you see it, Thomas. I respect you for it."

"Thank you, James. To be candid, however, you cannot know if I'm telling the truth, can you? If I were a traitor, I'd hardly slip you the wink, would I?"

"No, that's true. But I do believe you. I hope you'll consider me not only as not your enemy, but as a friend. If I may say so, sir, without being presumptuous, I hope things work out – honourably."

Hutchins looked hard at his fellow officer. "Handsomely said, James. I'll remember that. I hope as the war unfolds, you won't have memories later that distress you."

James took Thomas's proffered hand and they adjourned, each man feeling pleased that they had talked.

Chapter 13

The Belle Savage coaching inn lay at the bottom of Ludgate Hill. James and Sarah learned that the name Lud belonged to a mythical ancient-Briton king. Ludgate Hill was next to the Fleet prison, named after the small stream flowing by – not the navy. It was used for those charged with contempt of court and for debtors.

One who was under indictment for contempt of court had been spokesman for a large party of east-enders, aggrieved over some injustice about which James was unclear. The man had been shabbily treated, or so his supporters alleged. They felt this so strongly that a great crowd had assembled and was, minute by minute, becoming angrier. Not possessing an armed police force, it was customary for the authorities to call upon the military for help. That was one reason for public ambivalence about a standing army. In fact, the suspicion took an odd legal form: each year parliament had to reconstitute the British Army anew.

Two battalions of the 1st and the Coldstream Regiments of Foot Guards were drawn up, precisely in ordered ranks. The mob grew ever more noisy and shouts of "The Fleet, down with the place! Burn the prison!" were heard. James and Sarah were reminded of what happened in 1770 when, on a much smaller scale, the so-called Boston massacre had occurred. The scale of this was much larger and there was danger of considerable bloodshed.

The troops extended themselves by meticulously performed manoeuvres across the streets giving onto the prison. Their show of force continued with that awesome ritual, the fixing of bayonets, done in a measured, deliberate time and accompanied by drum signals amid the over-arching shouts of the non-commissioned officers.

The gaudy official representing the Lord Mayor undertook to read the Riot Act. They were within the bounds of the City of London, a square mile with its own rights and privileges where even the sovereign had to ask permission to enter. He intoned gravely:

"Our Sovereign Lord the King chargeth and commandeth all persons being assembled immediately to disperse themselves, and peaceably to depart to their habitations or to their lawful business, upon the pains contained in the act made in the first year of King George for preventing tumultuous and riotous assemblies. GOD SAVE THE KING."

"Guards...(long pause)...by the centre...(another pause)...advance in slow time...ad...vance!" came the command, the troops then moving toward the mob, drummers beating with their sticks raised in unison to the nose to form a line of white drumsticks crashing down with intricate precision on the sidedrums, bayonets held menacingly to the front, gleaming in the sunlight, moving inexorably at the peculiarly slow pace used by the Foot Guards. When only a dozen yards from the multitude, the inescapable danger became crystal-clear to the dullest-witted. First, a few people began to break, then more turned to scamper away as the gap lessened between them and the bayonets. Future generations may have seen the tall bearskin hats as the most distinctive feature of the Guards' array but this was still the time of the tricornered hat and what impressed that crowd was, without doubt, the bayonets. In a flash, the whole mob took flight.

The area behind the mob was carefully left clear of obstructions and the mob took the available route, encouraged by sheriff's officers who grabbed some of the least mobile offenders to examine their part in causing the affray. A dragoon officer who was staying at the inn, standing next to James and looking out of the window at the scene, turned and commented: "Just like the way we always deal with insurrections, isn't it? Push 'em from one side but always give them room to make away. Never, never leave 'em without a way of escape."

James saw more than that. "More than that – that's just how the authorities see the war in America, ain't it? They cannot take it in that it's a real war, so they treat it like a mob scene."

"Whatever do you mean, sir?"

"Well, look at Howe – he sent up his grenadiers at Breed's Hill just like some parade ground 'advance in review order'. Up the hill they go but the enemy's rear is left open, not by oversight, but in hopes they'll disperse for good, just like that mob, with as few casualties as possible to both sides.

"Only in war the enemy don't act like some mob. Or what about the battle in New York? Move against them but leave an exit to the north so the...mob...can get away. Only they aren't a mob. They are soldiers, green soldiers to be sure, but still soldiers with officers over them. So they escape, but it's a withdrawal – they're still intact as troops and they reckon to fight another day.

"Yes, sir, if we lose that war it'll be because our people don't see it as a serious war. They think they're dealing with a rabble, as you see here today."

The young officer was a cornet in the 16th Light Dragoons, about to go to America, so he paid attention to James. He had not thought of it that way.

Chapter 14

Earl of Bathurst was a grandiose name for a 385-ton merchant vessel hired by the Ordnance Board, a separate government department under the Master General of the Ordnance, responsible for furnishing the army and navy with guns, ammunition and related supplies. The ship was also used as a transport to oversea stations. The number of soldiers she carried was limited by the space needed for such stores, particularly on this trip when a large number of heavy siege guns for the defences of Antigua and Barbados and large amounts of equipment for the garrisons of East Florida took up much space. The army families were fortunate to be allocated small cabins aft, near the ship's officers' quarters but far enough away from them that the unpredictable voices of young children would not be too disruptive of their comfort, or so the sailors devoutly hoped. There were actually no infants this trip. The ship was manned by a merchant crew of eighteen men and four boys under the skipper and, in this case, the army officers and their families were doubly fortunate in that the ship's captain took care to see that they sailed in relative comfort.

Late the morning of sailing, James and Sarah's three portmanteaux were manhandled aboard to their small cabin. "Here y'are, sir, madam, though how you're to move about once we put 'em in here, I couldn't say," opined the seaman in charge of the working party, taking pleasure in thinking a landlubber officer was now faced with an unexpected difficulty.

"Never mind, bo'sun," James replied to the surprise of the seaman whose rank had been correctly assessed. James's next remark jolted him even more: "We knew space would be limited so we can make do with just the one case – this one – the other two can go into the hold or wherever you'd like, boatswain." The boatswain, disappointed that James was not the helpless soul he had supposed him to be, was also chagrined that the four seamen with him had witnessed his gaffe. They wore suppressed smirks on their faces which were turned in apparent fascination toward the woodwork above them.

The peace of the latter part of the morning was rudely terminated by the thundering sound of clumping coming first from the side of the ship nearest the wharf and then from the whole of the ship. The craning of heads out of the portholes and various hatches revealed that about a hundred and fifty recruits were arriving. Packs on their backs, they clobbered their way aboard, grunting, spitting over the side of the gangway. They were undisciplined men and their voices bore various accents: a melange of raucous, gutteral German, high-pitched Scottish, singsong Welsh and the unmistakeable vowels of gutter-Cockney. They were a rough bunch except for the occasional scrawny, bony recruit who could only have passed the medical officer's scrutiny by some sort of military miracle. Certainly the sailors, whose conditions of service were better than the average for tars in a King's ship – owing to the ship being hired – were heard to make choice contemptuous comments on what was the army coming to?

The army officers and their families had been allotted the best berths available. A long table was set up lengthwise down what in a ship-of-the-line would have been called the wardoom and small cabins were found on both sides, set back from the table at which the families were to have their meals. At one o'clock, the officers' party had their first chance to meet as a group. There were eight officers and four wives: a stout, short, cocky major of the 16th with his dumpy wife, two captains of the same regiment with their wives, a captain of the Royal Engineers, a lieutenant of the Royal Artillery, a lieutenant and an ensign of the Royal Americans, as well as James and Sarah. The wives of the 16th's lieutenants were oddly matched – one extremely plain, the other wearing a constant come-hither look. They sought refuge in their slight acquaintance but betrayed their inexperience by exposing their misgivings before strangers. They set about quizzing one another in over-strained voices: "Do you think we will have a calm passage, Hilda?" said the ravishing one.

"Oh, my dear Melissa, I do hope so – I scarcely know what I shall do if it's rough," replied the plain one.

The major seized the opportunity of asserting his rank in the presence of the two husbands who were to be under him, speaking curtly from the lofty heights of his experience: "Bound to be rough at times, m'dears. Spring showers, westerlies, sharp trade-winds, don't ye know?" On this note, and with the half of the group that belonged to the 16th suitably subdued, a thoughtful silence dominated the party for the rest of the meal.

However, apart from a few improvised deck games, cards and reading, there was not much for them to do except talk. They did so. One evening the major, as the highest-ranking officer, secured some quite good claret from the purser and, after dinner, the ladies having withdrawn on deck in deference to a general but unspoken feeling that standards ought to be kept up, the officers discussed the war. That subject was taboo during the meal itself and especially in the presence of the ladies.

"Well, gentlemen, do you think this trouble will last long enough for us to see it?" said the major, hoping to provoke discussion.

"Even if it does go on another year, I can't see my sappers and miners having any part in it," ventured the engineer captain. "Where we're stationed, we're likely to be well out of it."

"Yes but they need troops and I can't see keeping two thousand of them sitting about doing nothing," said the 60th ensign.

"Aren't you forgetting the froggies, Evans?" asked the 60th lieutenant. "I mean, we have to guard the Floridas for the sake of the Caribbean, whatever happens farther north, so London might not consider sitting in St Augustine to be a waste of time, after all."

The Royal Artillery officer startled them by the note of authority in his voice: "Why not let the Americans go their way? The Caribbean – places like Jamaica – they're what count. Besides, the less we antagonize the rebels with bloody campaigning, the more willing they may be to drift back into some sort of partnership with us."

"Assuming we want a partnership with that bloody lot!" volunteered Evans.

"Come now," said the gunner, "policies are not followed to satisfy our emotions. They arise from our *interests*, not because we like somebody or hate them. Today's enemy is tomorrow's friend."

"According to that view, our glorious winning of Canada was a bad policy because it allowed the Americans to feel they don't need us," said the major, as if he had disposed of the gunner's argument.

"That's quite right, sir. We fight the Americans because of a previous successful policy which may not turn out to be in our best interest," agreed the gunner. "But I go back to my premise: the Caribbean is what counts; our efforts could profitably be directed there rather than against the rebels farther north."

James could stay out of it no longer. "Are you saying that a policy of interests means we have no enemies to hate, nor friends to cherish?"

"Precisely," answered the gunner; "not in matters of state policy."

James pressed his point. "In that case why have soldiers kill anyone? If the enemy pursues evil policies, are we not right to hate him. How else can we kill?"

"We do such things, not because he is evil – in most cases he is not bad nor are we good – we do these things because we serve our country's interests. It is our duty. If I have to, I shall lay my gunsights as well as I can to destroy the enemy, not because the enemy is evil but because it is my duty."

The direction the conversation was taking displeased the major. "Well, I say damn the rebels! Confusion to the King's enemies! First let's teach the rebels a good lesson, then we can get back to the French."

James thought that the major's view was not very different from the gunner's. They believed their duty was to serve the national interest. The difference was that the major needed to hate the enemy while the gunner did not. Was the gunner being cynical? James felt a deep sympathy with the gunner and, if he could not dissect his reasons with clinical efficiency, he yet trusted his warmth toward the gunner as a trustworthy sign that the gunner was no cynic.

The gunner did not let the conversation end with the major's appeal to patriotism. "It's all very well saying 'Teach them a lesson', but that may not be so easy. Look at the sheer size of the colonies. Look at the failure to bag the rebels in New York or the Jerseys. And now I hear, Cornwallis has let them slip round him out of Trenton and set upon Princeton. They were supposed to be beat yet in a month everything has been stood on its head, and now their army has suddenly grown and sits glaring at Howe in New York." He sat back and drained his glass moodily.

None of the others knew much about Trenton and Princeton and they were sobered by the news. How did he know all this? As if in answer to that question, he remarked: "Mind you, I wasn't there myself but I hear that Mawhood's regiment lost half its men – the 17th, that is – and the rebel guns were well served."

"You seem remarkably well informed on what none of us has yet heard. How on earth do you know that the American guns were well handled?" blurted out the major, feeling upstaged.

"My brother was there in the Royal Artillery," the gunner informed them, "and I had a letter from him before I left England."

"Perhaps he can keep us informed better than the war office," was the enigmatic reply of the major.

"I'm afraid not, sir," the gunner replied icily. "He was killed in the following week."

After a depressed silence, the major rallied the company: "I'm so sorry to hear that. Now I think we'd best join the ladies, gentlemen," he said. His fellow-officers did not expect him to say anything else.

If the comments of the ladies were not to be heard at their husbands' table, they still had plenty to say on their own. Melissa began: "I do hope St Augustine is no complete wilderness. I've been told that the officers put on quite acceptable balls."

Hilda added; "All work and no play makes Jack a dull boy, certainly. But I hear that the climate is beastly – simply horrid. And are there not alligators or crocodiles – I never know the difference – and mosquitos and swamps and awful things like that?

"I'm sure that wherever the drum goes we shall follow faithfully," said the woman who was fast acquiring in Sarah's mind the name 'Mrs Major'. The two other lieutenants' wives were not inspired or even reassured by Mrs Major's observation.

"You come from that country, do you not?" Hilda asked Sarah. "It must be like coming home for you, isn't it?"

"Indeed no!" shot back Sarah. "That is to say I do come from America but hardly Florida which I'm sure most Americans will always regard as an undesirable place to live. It must be a thousand miles from St Augustine to my home, as far as from London to North Africa." She noted the look of glazed astonishment appearing on the three faces – she had noted before the difficulty in coping with the difference of scale between the old world and the new. She then launched out on another tack: "Why don't we all make a point of keeping in touch at St Augustine?"

"Yes, indeed, what a splendid idea," said Mrs Major who was the one woman of the four the other three were least interested in meeting again.

By mid-June the small convoy had reached its first port of call, Barbados in the Windward Islands. The British felt it imperative that this island be defended but it lay southeast of the French island of St Lucia and of the larger main French base at Martinique. It was a constant source of worry to Britain. Because there were no regular gunners on Barbados, the militia would play a big part in any action and the *Earl of Bathurst* had some guns to deliver. The only harbour was at Carlisle Bay on the southeast coast, unsuitable for any but shallow-draught boats. It was with difficulty that the guns were man-handled into such craft and got ashore, together with the Royal Artillery lieutenant who had, by now, become a valued friend of even the major and, Sarah noted particularly, of the beautiful Melissa.

Sarah was relieved to see him disembark. They had been either discreet or innocent but Melissa's husband was noticeably unpleasant toward the gunner during the last week he was aboard. Sarah wondered if the ravishing Melissa were a classic flirt – loving to excite a man in dangerous circumstances but a chicken at heart, beating a frightened retreat when the chips were down. It was no good conjecturing with James, who seemed in this affair unobservant, nor did she wish to mention it to any of the other women who would only magnify the issue regardless of consequences.

The next stop was St Vincent, seventy-eight miles due west of Barbados and an easy voyage in the prevailing easterly wind. Here a part of James's battalion remained as during his first posting here, but now under Lieutenant Colonel George Etherington who had returned to the island. That officer's lot was not a happy one. He had asked not to be sent to St Vincent but London sent him anyway, aware of his reputation for making friends with the native Caribs. He also was at loggerheads with the pompous governor of the island, Valli Morris. There a number of 60th recruits had to be dropped off. James showed no interest in looking at the island from the ship's rails, in contrast to his shipmates.

Then the convoy headed north to Antigua, four hundred miles away, passing between Guadaloupe and Montserrat. The last lap of that journey was the roughest of the entire trip since they had to tack against very strong winds. Happily, they reached Antigua and dropped anchor in the splendid natural refuge of English Harbour. Antigua was the headquarters of James's battalion though at present only three of its companies were there. The naval escort stayed at English Harbour so the *Earl of Bathurst* was henceforth on her own, except for the brig *Oedipus* which, bound for St Augustine, joined them.

A brig was not an impressive fighting ship nor was she fast or manoeuvrable. With two square-rigged masts, she weighed one hundred and eighty tons but was armed with fourteen 24-pounder carronades. In the oddities of naval culture, carronades were not reckoned when a ship's guns were counted. They were ugly, pot-bellied mortars whose balls could cause frightful damage when lobbed at short range. Though not introduced into the Royal Navy for another year or so, *Oedipus* was trying them out for the first time. They were later known as 'smashers' – not for nothing. As the naval lieutenant in command remarked, "God help those who are at the wrong end of these demons."

Though his passengers were not told by him, the skipper knew the eighteen hundred miles from Antigua to St Augustine would be the most fraught of the entire trip. He did not fear the weather – the hurricane season was still some weeks, perhaps months, away – but he knew that privateers could endanger his ship during the next ten days. He hoped that the strong wind would continue but that it would not be strong enough to blow the two ships apart from one another. Passage could be perilously unpredictable between the Bahamas and Bermuda.

Rebel privateers had been active. It was known that spies reported every movement of men and ships in the Caribbean and though the rebels had nothing to compare with the Royal Navy, their privateers found a surprising amount of sympathy in certain places, particularly Bermuda, many of whose colonists had relations in Virginia.

When about eight hundred miles off their destination, there came the first hint of trouble. "Deck there" shouted the seaman in the crow's nest, "sail on the starboard beam."

In three or four hours, the ship sighted proved to be a two-masted sloop with perhaps ten 9-pounder guns. It could be American. *Oedipus* adjusted her pace to keep just astern of *Earl of Bathurst* so that she could move to either side of the larger ship or, if it seemed advisable, cut to the nearer side of the sloop should that ship come too close to the transport.

The skipper of the sloop was being cagey. "What is he up to?" was the general reaction.

The naval skipper surmised: "He could be taking a good look at us before deciding whether to engage. He no doubt knows a transport when he sees one but he can also see we are armed, and that we are accompanied by a brig. The brig will never impress him with its sailing qualities, and I wonder if he's aware she's got those new-fangled mortar-type smashers he may just have heard about. The rebels seem to know most things about us."

Despite the prudent assumption that the privateer knew about smashers, their captain, to everybody's amazement, decided to brave the brig's armament. The brig's captain concluded that the American – if that's what she was – might not, after all, know about the smashers, incredible though it seemed. He was certainly acting as if he were unaware.

The sloop broke out her proper ensign: a flag of thirteen red stripes on white with the British Union in the canton, in use despite the declaration of independence. As the sloop moved in quickly to pick off the brig before tackling the ordnance ship, her 9-pounders peppered the brig. Screams echoed as splinters took their toll and the privateer was quick to move in for the kill.

She had not prevented the brig arming six of the seven starboard smashers and when the moment came, the deafening roar and billowing smoke proclaimed carnage aboard the attacker. Five of the balls had crashed into the sloop, dropping like mortar-shells from such a vertical angle that she was dismasted and helpless.

The brig then clumsily turned about and was preparing to fire off her larboard battery when the sloop's ensign came rattling down – her captain yielded rather than suffer another round of smashers. Officers and their wives were among those who watched in awe as a boat put out from *Oedipus* with a prize crew to take what was left of her in charge. The surviving privateers were taken aboard both *Oedipus* and the ordnance ship and safely locked up. Five days later, without further mishap, the small convoy docked at St Augustine.

The town presented an unusual sight. Very Spanish in its buildings and streets, its civil population, a hodge-podge of nationalities and races, was dominated by the British military who seemed to be everywhere. Set to one side of the town was the grim and menacing fortress of San Marco, guarding the harbour and serving as a refuge to which inhabitants had in the past fled for defence. Soldiers mingled on the docks and in the streets with seamen of the Royal Navy, squads of redcoated sentries could be seen marching to relieve others on guard duty at the fortress, the Union flag floated over the main tower.

James was soon advised where in the old town he and Sarah could be billetted - glad to be ashore out of the wet, though times would come when they yearned for more rain to allay the oppressive moist heat. There was a breeze from the sea, but not much of one. They felt uncomfortably sticky, along with everyone else in the town except for a few strange Latin folk who might like such a climate.

On arrival, James and Sarah found that Major Mark Prevost was now there too and had been promoted to a 'local' lieutenant colonel. He would still be carried in the Army List as a major, but would have the pay and authority of the higher rank when in the East Florida region. Lieutenant Colonel Lewis Valentine Fuser was commandant at St Augustine, having replaced John Brown when that officer went to Scotland. Because Fuser was also in command of East Florida operations, the actual command of the town passed to Lieutenant Colonel Prevost.

Prevost's house was the scene of an extraordinary event. In the large parlour at seven o'clock one evening were seated all the nearly fifty officers of the garrison. Not only was such a gathering unusual but this was to be a briefing. The colonel rapped his stick for order as the clock struck the hour. Everyone was seated, knowing that the colonel's reputation for punctuality would embarrass anyone who was a minute late.

"Gentlemen: I take the uncommon, some may say, eccentric step of calling you together to apprise you of the state of affairs on this side of the ocean. In my opinion, ignorance of strategy amongst officers means ignorance amongst the rank-and-file and I think neither can be tolerated." That was quite an opening and everyone knew it was – ignorance in the lower ranks was assumed to be the normal thing and no cause of undue concern. Something was emerging which was not what they had thought to hear.

"We are small in number. Our companies are very under-strength. Therefore each of you is to instil in your men that he is counted upon to do his work and to know the significance of it. I expect you to show that candour and intelligence are qualities we expect from everyone. Frankly, I have heard such fantastical ideas bruited about that I am convinced of the need to impress upon you that our soldiers must be professionally trained and informed.

"First, what has happened? Beginning in April two years past, an armed insurrection has grown from small beginnings. It could have been snuffed out several times but it wasn't – I'll not go into that further. We lost New England last year but rebounded with a large force from Europe by way of Halifax to retake New York – the city, that is, not the province. Mr Washington was chased to Philadelphia which as yet remains in hostile hands and is the seat of the congress. They have declared for independency. An attempt was made last year to capture Charleston in the Carolinas, a hundred and fifty miles to our north, which failed. At present, General Howe sits in New York and General Burgoyne is setting out with General St Leger in a two-pronged offensive from Canada – aiming to split the colonies in two.

"As I see it, General Howe has four choices. He can move up the Hudson to join hands with the troops from Canada. Secondly, he can retake Boston with the navy's help. In truth, I have to say, very little can be done in this fight without the navy! Thirdly, he can strike at Philadelphia by sea. Some people, thinking in European terms, believe that by taking their capital, the rebellion will end. That seems to fall in disastrously with the notion that seizing land is the way to win a war. I do not believe that. The only way to end this war is to beat the enemy, and that has not happened. Fourthly, General Howe can try again to reduce Charleston. Even if successful, it remains a flattering diversion – and this is the crux – the enemy is not there.

"Now a word about the enemy. It has always been a singular conceit of our regular officers to underrate the enemy because his parade-ground appearance is ludicrous. In my view, that is one of our greatest weaknesses. For one thing, the rabble he started off with is rapidly becoming an army. Their undependable militia is being stiffened with what they call their 'continentals', and those are less like a rabble with every passing day.

"There is another important factor: the French. They smart with hopes of revenge for the defeats we gave them in Canada. At this point, no one can say what they will do. But if the rebels achieve any notable successes, the French may very well join in. If that happens, it could widen the field of operations from the Caribbean to Quebec. It will place you and me in the thick of it.

"I will hold future meetings like this one, to keep track of developments. But meanwhile, I expect each of you to see that your people understand what is afoot. Now, gentlemen, have you questions? You may speak freely."

James felt that here was someone at last who does not despise the enemy, someone who understands that a pompous show of force will not answer, as if the foe were only an oversize mob. If only London saw it as he sees it, if only the army higher commanders saw it too, the day might be ours. What a pity that vigorous and far-sighted men like their former colonel, General Haldimand, were left to moulder in Quebec.

Not many questions were put. The abrupt disowning of patronising, self-serving over-confidence was a well-delivered shock. Sensible questions would come later; for the moment, sober reflection was the order of the day. Training continued with a new sense of purpose.

One matter that came to the fore in subsequent meetings was: what could be expected of loyalists. Prevost pointed out that the provincials, as such soldiers were called, were risking everything in holding to the old flag but that the slaughter of the Highlanders at Moore's Creek Bridge had shown what happened to ill-prepared and premature risings. He felt that there were many loyalists but we could not expect them to act without a good chance of success – they had too much to lose. They were being armed and trained but kept back, particularly on Long Island outside New York. Instead of being an asset, at present they were more of a burden - New York overcrowded with them and large numbers pouring into East Florida where they were a drain on accomodations and a drain on supplies.

Chapter 15

Sarah yearned for feminine company, fidgeting at the domesticated style of inactivity some officers' wives cultivated. Thinking she might be acting foolishly, she set off to call on the woman she had dubbed Mrs Major. I had better watch my step or I shall call her that one day, she thought. Her name is Hannah, let me think of her that way.

In mid-afternoon of an oppressively sultry day, she found that Hannah was not at home but the door was opened by a young and lissom black maid who offered to convey any message Sarah might choose to leave. "That's kind of you. I...I'm afraid I don't know your name," Sarah remarked.

"Juno, Ma'am."

Sarah wrote out a short note for Hannah, thanked Juno and left. When on the next day Juno arrived at Sarah's doorstep with a reply, Sarah let her in. "A cup of tea, Juno? Even today I find it refreshing".

"Oh, thank you, ma'am, if you say so, I'd like to try it," replied Juno with a grin. Juno had never tasted tea, owing to its cost.

"Well, I'll show you just how I like it best, Juno – with a little milk and one lump of sugar. The sugar will give you a spurt of energy and it will soften the flavour, which may seem to you a little bitter if you're not used to it. The next time you come, I'll show you how I make it, though I suspect you know that the whole secret is in having boiling water".

Hannah's note expressed regret at missing Sarah's call, and she hoped Sarah would try again the next day at four o'clock. Accordingly, Sarah arrived at the Whites'. She was welcomed by Hannah herself. Seated in a small library, Hannah admitted: "I've not been an officer's wife very long, you know." This surprised Sarah who tended to think Hannah had never been anything else. "I feel it would be easy to sit in this house doing nothing useful while the world slips by, don't you know?" Hannah confessed.

Hannah's speech was marked by certain arbitrary ways of speech and action, certain graces, knowledge and – presence, was that the right word? By now, all temptation to think of her as Mrs

Major evaporated as Hannah revealed herself - a worried woman lacking the self-confidence her peers put forward. Sarah had heard of similar circumstances before – women who married "above themselves" and then found themselves struggling either to gain the poise they lacked, or to conceal their social disadvantages.

Sarah attacked the matter head-on. "Hannah, I have to confess that I have no patience with the snobbery so common in the army. There are always those who think their standing as officers and gentlemen entitles them to behave as if they were not gentlemen – the same applies to their wives, too. I don't know if I'm in any position to be helpful but if I can do anything you regard as useful, please Hannah, don't hesitate to - to (she hesitated to use a perhaps patronising word like 'ask') talk to me."

"I knew there was something – special - about you when we were on the ship. Then, yesterday, Juno told me how you treated her when she went to see you – you were so kind to her – no side, no condescension. You just talked to her natural-like. I knew then I could talk to you," said Hannah.

"I'm so glad we are friends", Sarah managed to say, giving Hannah's hand a squeeze. "Do you know, I'm thinking about what you said – about us not having enough to do. It's absolutely true. But I have noticed that the town is being filled up with refugees. They're such an unhappy lot – so uprooted, not knowing what they're going to do if the rebellion is not ended. Do you think there's anything we could do about them?"

"Perhaps we could," answered Hannah slowly. "But you're the one person in our set who has the ability to organize; I can see it clearly. I would like to talk to my husband about it."

"That would be splendid," Sarah agreed. "Some of these people have so little; they live from hand to mouth, and they are so friendless."

"Quite so. Why don't we talk again soon? Now, what about some tea?" On cue, Juno appeared with a tray. For the first time Hannah had requested Juno to prepare the indispensable beverage.

At dinner, Sarah apprised James of developments. When dinner was cleared away, they were able to talk privately. James observed: "He's a strange bird, our Major White. When you say Hannah has married above herself, I'm not sure about that. I've watched him. He's a well-meaning cove really, but he comes from humbler beginnings than he lets on. It's as if he's less at ease with the other officers than he'd like people to think. He got his promotions, you know, not by purchase, so somebody must think he has unusual qualities though I don't know him well enough to know what they may be. Perhaps that will become clearer should he take his wife's suggestions seriously. In any case, my sweeting, she will need your guidance, though you'll have to be tactful or you might put her husband's back up."

The next time Hannah invited Sarah to tea, Major White, who by now admitted he bore the baptismal name of Horace, joined them. "Hannah has been talking to me. Have you specific ideas?"

"Well, Major, it seems to me that the refugees have two outstanding needs," Sarah replied.

"Yes?"

"Well, they need shelter and many of them are short of food and clothing," she replied.

"As far as that goes," said he, "the army authorities have a bit they could help with, but food and clothing could certainly be augmented by some volunteer, er, recruiting activity, I think. What else do they need?"

"It's the less tangible matter of morale I'm thinking of. They need to develop trust in each other, and in the garrison. We might organize some sort of town-meeting, as they say in New England, so they can say what they need and discover what resources they have to help themselves," explained Sarah.

Hannah said to her husband: "Sarah has such good ideas and she seems to believe that we might be the people who could put them in train."

"Oh, I do know that without sensitive people like you two, little can be done," Sarah said quickly. "Why is it that authority often seems to be arrogant? I feel that you both would not fall into that trap – somehow I just know it." I hope I haven't gone too far, thought Sarah.

"We feel encouraged by your confidence, Sarah. Bless you, my dear," the major remarked to Sarah's astonishment. "May I suggest that I have a word with the chaplains? There is no English parish church here, what with the strong Spanish influence, but there are three army chaplains I know of. If they felt like it, I'm sure they could make a big difference – giving the men something more to think about than home and the miseries of East Florida."

"What a good idea!" said Sarah.

The first 'town meeting' took place on a sticky and hot Monday, the first of September, in a large hall in the town centre. To everyone's surprise, the hall was filled to overflowing. Word had got round to the two thousand or so refugees within reach, a number that by the end of the next year would reach seven thousand. By this time the commandant of the garrison, Mark Prevost, had been approached by Major White and approval was given for the three chaplains to encourage the interest of the rank-and-file in the undertaking. The six 4th-Battalion companies, with their large element of thoroughly homesick Germans, had taken the lead in providing volunteers to manhandle supplies and sort items of clothing being collected by civilians who had come under the chaplains' influence, the four clergymen being the only "non papist" clergy in the town.

Collection of supplies and keeping track of the refugees and their particular circumstances was a time-consuming task. It was shared out amongst a number of committees containing a mix of civilian, military and even the occasional naval members. It was decided by the general committee to have a monthly town meeting but the number of refugees grew so fast, with people pouring in from the Carolinas and Georgia, that it was decided to have two meetings a month: families whose names began with A-to-L would be welcome at the meeting near the beginning of the month whilst those whose names began M-to-Z, and newcomers who missed the first meeting, would convene at the mid-month meeting. Almost all the garrison women took part in some way or other and the number of officers and men who were in attendance at the various functions was considerable. Hannah White, at Sarah's insistence, took the chair at most of the town meetings though occasionally Sarah sat in for her. The support of the acting commandant and the chaplains was decisive and it was soon understood that the snide title of the Ladies' Brigade, which some wag had attached to the project, was to be considered a label of honour.

The ladies included Hilda and Melissa who seemed to blossom in having a task that demanded something of them and undercut their boredom. But the couple who most flowered among all were Horace and Hannah White. Hannah found an authority based on good intentions and sound thinking rather than social standing – she was superb at her new role and everybody knew it. The major found that his views had gravitas with his fellows and especially with Mark Prevost who had noticed the sensitive support Horace had given his wife while encouraging her to make decisions. Even Juno, hampered because she was unable to read, proved to have a phenomenal memory for detail and could remember the circumstances of each refugee family in a way that the subalterns envied.

Chapter 16

By New Year's 1778, operations of the Ladies' Brigade, at first a condescending term which soon became respectful, had more or less settled down to a routine and the committees turned their attention to fine-tuning. One evening at dinner alone with James, Sarah mentioned that she should soon have to cut back her activity. "James, my dearest, you are going to be a father and I am going to be a mother." James was unable to say anything for the moment. "Is that not good, my sweet?" asked Sarah, somewhat subdued by his silence.

Suddenly, he leapt from the table, overturning his chair, and gathered her up in his arms, tears rolling down his face as he hugged her mercilessly to himself. "Of course, of course, of course," he poured out with an untypical abandonment of reserve, "Oh. Lord yes, of course!" They got back on an even keel by bursting into peels of laughter. "When is it to be?" he asked, more composed.

"I saw the surgeon today and he figures it to be June." "I see, I see," said James, appearing to be in danger of relapsing into the idiotic repetition of phrases she had just endured.

Sarah managed to forestall that event by cutting in: "It's all right, James, really, there's nothing to worry about."

James, who knew full well there is always something to worry about, said: "Of course, my sweet, of course."

"James – if you say 'of course' again, I'll thump you on the noggin".

Sobered, he leapt to the officers' reaction to any good news: "What about a brandy? This calls for a toast!"

"Not for me, I think, James, but please, you toast me."

"Of course, er, yes indeed," was his more thoughtful reply as he dove for the decanter. "Your best health, indeed, your best health," as she wondered if this inclination to repetitive phrases was to become a permanent affliction.

"What on earth is that?" exclaimed the master of the house, examining a singular pile of rectangular-shaped cloths.

"They're known as napkins and they're used to catch all the mess that babies make and which you would rather not know about. Fancy not knowing what they are!"

"It's actually been some time since I sported such attire; I imagine my memory must be slipping," was the only comment he could muster.

"Excuse me, ma'am, there's a lady to see you," interrupted the servant.

It was Melissa who had turned out to be one of the stalwarts of the Ladies' Brigade. "Sarah, James, I thought you might be able to use this. Just something I got up in odd moments."

Peering at her keenly, Sarah observed "Excuse my presumption, but you wouldn't happen to be in the same condition as me?"

Melissa actually blushed and said: "Well, yes, but about a month before you."

"How splendid!!" She unwrapped the gift, drawing forth an exquisite smocked garment. "With all you have to think about, you still found time to do this?"

"Go on with you!" Melissa uttered, feigning annoyance.

There were other tokens of affection from a number of people whom Sarah had, in one way or another, taken trouble to please. The months passed, too slowly for Sarah, but on the fifth of June, a boy was born. Juno, too, came to see the baby saying: "June the fifth – that's St Boniface's day."

"How very nice," said James, "the apostle to the Germans" he added, not wishing to be thought totally heathen. "But how did you know that, Juno?"

"I'm a-learning to read, sir, but just to be sure I asked Father Xavier – he's our parish priest – and he said I was right."

In August, a humid unpleasant month, the infant seemed off-colour. In that month a lot of people were not at their best but, to be safe, Sarah swept him off to the regimental surgeon. He examined the child painstakingly, then asked her: "This is your first child, is it not, Mrs Ricketts?" She acknowledged it was, searching his face for any significant hint.

"Sarah, there are all sorts of things going round in this climate. He's picked up something nasty. I wish I could tell you what it is, but, to be candid, I can't. It could be from a mosquito bite, even malaria, I simply don't know." Seeing that Sarah's reaction was what he thought it might be, he tried to forestall it: "Sarah, a mosquito is very small and no one can erect foolproof defences – besides, we don't know if that is the cause. I can find no bite mark on his body but that means little. He has a high fever, so keep him well wrapped. We'll pray he can sweat it out."

At home, both parents took turns sitting with him. Sarah confided to James: "What really hurts is that he won't take my milk. I have so much to give him but he just will not take it. It breaks my heart."

James was devastated. *How can I comfort her?* Visitors kept arriving but mercifully forebore uttering platitudes. They and their friends were not raised to verbalize their feelings, but they all knew that about each other and all understood one another. The longing was silently expressed and care bestowed. The surgeon came daily as did the chaplain.

The third evening, Sarah took James's hand in hers. "Oh dear, he's so ill. Can you baptize him, please, please?" pleaded Sarah. James, hating the thought that they had to act in such haste, agreed. "Do it now, James, now – I implore you." James fetched a bowl of water, remembering the words in the prayer book. He held his son tenderly, pouring water over his fevered brow, saying "James Livingston, I baptize thee in the name of the Father, and of the Son, and of the Holy Ghost. Amen."

The following morning, the fourth morning, the child was cold. The hours that followed seemed an eternity of confusion and misery. The regimental chaplain buried the child in a shroud in the plot marked out for soldiers of the garrison. The couple were hazily conscious of the friends coming to offer sympathy after the interment.

James went to see Major Prevost. "Sir, I must get Sarah away. A change will help her, I'm sure of it. I want to take her to Ridgeland where she can rest. It would be a complete change – could I take leave for a while?"

Prevost, shortly to leave St Augustine for operations along the St Mary's River on the Georgia border, had some things he wanted to say. "I don't think I ever told you but I had a twin brother who died of pneumonia when only a few weeks old. I can imagine how devastated my parents felt. I know you are a believer, James, as am I. It's not something we talk about but it's something we share. I think we believe even when we can't make any sense of it – at a time like this. You know what I'm trying to say, I'm sure."

"Thank you, Mark." It was all he could manage but he meant it.

Knowing James wanted to nurse Sarah, Mark granted him the leave he needed to do just that.

Intruding on her isolated misery came a timid knock on the bedroom door. Melissa came to her side one rainy day. Sarah's first thought was, oh no, I don't want to see her; I can't talk to her. Melissa did not say much at first, a few words of condolence only. Then she leaned forward earnestly, taking Sarah's hands in hers. Oh dear, thought Sarah, I'm not up to listening to her troubles, not just now.

Melissa opened herself to Sarah: "You remember on our trip. The gunner officer who got off at Barbados, before we reached here? I'm sure you do. Actually, he made quite a play for me and turned my head. I had the feeling you saw that, if no one else seemed to. The truth is – I think I would have gone with him, had he asked me.

"He did try to get in touch with me again, just a few days ago, but by then...." She struggled to find words. "You'd had your baby and lost him, and, well – I know it sounds odd – but it made me realize what I was throwing away, and I told him No."

"Dear Melissa, I am glad for you. Especially now, that you are to have a baby."

"Sarah, my dear Sarah, I'm not making myself clear at all. Don't you see – it's because of you, and James. Your loss shook me awake. Your pain made me think. Really think. You, and your baby, you are what saved my marriage. I had to tell you that, Sarah. You think of it as your loss – perhaps nothing else. How else could you think of it? But I want you to know there's more than that. I'm glad I got up the nerve to tell you," she said.

"So am I, Melissa, darling. So am I." More followed and it left the mother strangely comforted. How strange it was, she thought, comfort comes when least expected.

Chapter 17

It took the first week of July to sail from St Augustine to Savanna la Mar in a despatch boat bound for Kingston. It dropped them off at the small port near the plantation. From thence they went to Ridgeland in a coach sent from the plantation which a previous letter had arranged. On the way north, the coachman related how their letters to Mr Jones, the overseer, had alerted the estate to their coming. On the estate's edge the coachman halted at a cottage from which emerged a couple.

"It is none other than Sam and Hannah whom I manumitted," he told Sarah.

They had with them a little girl of sixteen months – their first-born, Josie. After greetings and introductions, Sarah asked: "May we come and see your house?" Surprised though they were, they admitted them to the sparsely-furnished dwelling.

"How are you getting on, Sam?" James inquired.

"I'm all right, Mister James, but I have to tell you there's trouble up at the big house. I feel I can say this to you, being a free man odd-jobbing for himself, thanks to you, and my not being part of the estate itself the way the, er, servants are. The trouble is that Mr Jones has become harder and harder on them. It ain't just and they don't like it."

"But we didn't stop you here to tell you that," said Hannah, "we just wanted to say hello and meet your charming missus," beaming. Sarah studied the child Josie, bit her lip but gained control of herself once again.

They resumed their way along the rough-hewn road and alighted at the noble door of the plantation house. After a light refreshment, James packed Sarah off to bed and went downstairs to the study, where lamps had just been lit in the gloaming. He no sooner immersed himself in a book than he was startled to hear a shriek of pain from an outbuilding a hundred yards away, followed by an unmistakeable whip-sound and another wail of pain. He was torn between investigating the corporal punishment – as he believed it was - and keeping out of it. Jones, if that was who was involved, was overseer and it was hardly wise to undercut his authority. Several more strokes followed before the woman's voice dissolved into prolonged sobbing. He only hoped that Sarah had not heard it.

The next morning, while Sarah lay abed late and breakfasted from a tray, James went out on the verandah below, encountering Jones coming round the corner. "Good morning, sir" Jones greeted him airily.

"Good morning, Mr Jones. Could I have a word with you?"

"All right," answered Jones, eyeing him with suspicion.

"Mr Jones, I would not normally interfere in the way you conduct affairs on the plantation, but in this case I must do so."

"And why is that, sir?" said Jones, whose smirk struck James as bordering on insolence.

"Two reasons, Mr Jones: first, I am part-owner of Ridgeland; secondly, because the horrible sound of last night's beating was so intrusive and so unpleasant that I cannot let it pass, especially in view of my wife's condition."

"Tildy got what she deserved and you surely know that strict discipline has to be maintained on a plantation."

"I'm well aware of that, Mr Jones, but what can possibly be so bad as to bring a whipping like that, where we are forced to hear the screams?"

"Ah, if that's your worry we can arrange to have such things elsewhere."

"No, that is not my only worry. I believe I am entitled to know the reason for such extraordinary behaviour."

"If you must know, Tildy is our house servant. She stole a necklace and I had to chastise her."

"Did you recover the necklace?" asked James. It appeared the necklace was not found, Jones explaining that it belonged to his particular friend Mrs Treacher from a neighbouring plantation. She had stayed at Jones's house last week. James thought of sending for Tildy then and there but decided against it for the moment.

One of the luxuries Sarah basked in was breakfast in bed. A couple of days after the whipping incident, Tildy brought Sarah her breakfast. James had told his wife what little he knew of the affair, as much to occupy her mind on a new topic as anything else. Sarah was agog to uncover more. "Do sit with me, Tildy – lying here is relaxing but a bit lonely. Have you had your own breakfast?"

Tildy sat down gingerly. Sarah noticed that she did not sit back in the chair. She was very careful of her back. "Tell me all about yourself, Tildy dear – about where you come from, your family, what you do in the house." As the conversation progressed, Tildy's words became less disjointed, more polysyllabic and relaxed, though she never sat back in the chair. "Does your back hurt you, Tildy?" asked Sarah, gambling that Tildy would not withdraw defensively. "I notice you are careful not to rest it against the chair."

"It hurts powerful," she admitted, and then quickly removed her shirt and turned her back to Sarah. The welts were healing but they still looked forbidding and angry. Her tight, smoothly-formed little breasts were a sharp contrast to the scoured back.

"Oh," said Sarah, shocked, "you poor dear. Whoever did that to you? Come over here and fetch me that balm from the dressing table. If you let me use some, it will really help the healing." While Sarah applied the ointment with utmost care, Tildy began to confide in her. "Nobody did that to me before, never. I never was so...taken down."

Sarah's verbal probing was as gentle as her fingers were. Tildy was coming to trust her words as her trust in Sarah's soothing fingers grew. "Massa Jones – he did it to me. He knows I seen him steal the necklace from Mrs Treacher. I'm awful scared – if he knows I talk to you, he kill me for certain."

"My husband told me Mr Jones said you stole it," said Sarah but by now Tildy's yearning to confide was both convincing and beyond arrest.

"I never did – I never touched it. I saw him take it himself. He just eyed me – didn't say nothin' – not then. That evening when he whupped me, he just grabbed me and told me if I ever said I seen 'im take the beads, he'd hurt me real bad. Then he took his whip, just so's I'd know what'd happen if I opened my mouth. Oh, Missy Sarah, I'm so scared. If he knows..."

"Tildy, tell me about Mrs Treacher. Is she really Mr Jones's girl?"

"Not really, I don't think so, no more. They had bad words between 'em when she visited here last time. She had a good friend, Captain Linders in Savanna and she told me the necklace come from him. She talked like she loved that necklace and was so sorry when it went. I don't know if she suspicioned Massa Jones, but she sure was sad and it was 'cause Captain Linders gave it her."

Sarah made mental notes of all this and decided to delay further discussion, as she did not want Jones to suspect they had been talking. "Listen to me, Tildy. I will talk to my husband but no one else will know you spoke to me – no one. And you must not say either. Do you think you can do that?"

"Oh, I won't, I won't," she promised, seizing Sarah's hands and kissing them. Sarah cradled her head on her breast, like a little child.

Captain Linders had cropped up several times in Tildy's talk with Sarah and James and Sarah both thought he might be worth looking into. James sought out Sam and asked him about Captain Linders. Linders was described as a "no-account militia officer" who liked to be known by his rank, was pleasant enough to meet but was a brawler and inveterate gambler. He could usually be found at the Crown in Savanna la Mar. James drove himself there and with no difficulty found the captain propping up the bar but apparently sober. Since James was in uniform, the captain was flattered by the attention of a regular officer.

"Have a drink, dear fellow, what'll it be? A pint of stout or a brandy? No? Well, what *can* I do for you?"

"What I tell you is a mite disorganized, but a man like you will have no trouble putting my meanderings into working order," James said. "Our house servant, Tildy, has been punished by the overseer at Ridgeland. He accuses her of stealing a necklace from Mrs Treacher."

"Jones says that? That Tildy stole the necklace? Why the rotten scoundrel, the lying wretch – he brought it to me himself to pay off his gambling debt to me. The absolute bounder – it makes me fair boil to think on it. First, he pries Jenny away from me who really loves her, then he steals her necklace. Then he has the cheek to present it to me to pay his debt. It must be that way. You call him on it, just call him on it, old cock, and while you're at it see if he hasn't beat Tildy for some other reason – not thieving. Maybe she knows something and he wants her silence. If you don't do it, I've got a good mind to call him out myself, the thieving bastard! First my woman, then her property – and then beating poor Tildy who never hurt a flea."

At this point James reckoned he owed Linders a drink. The offer was readily accepted.

Captain Linders was excitable and persistent. The more he thought about Jones, the angrier he waxed. Fury at Jones's treachery was compounded by resentment at the stealing of his dear Jenny. He was certain the villain had wickedly enticed her away from him. At last, he could bear it no longer and set off at a gallop to seek out Jones at Ridgeland and challenge him to a duel. He covered the six miles to Ridgeland in just over twenty minutes.

He rode into the estate near Jones's house, calling out "Jones, Jones, you thief, you miserable excuse for a human being, come out, come out, wherever you are," reminding observers of the child's game of hide-and-seek. People knew an exciting melodrama when they heard one and this had the hallmarks of the real thing. Faces, black, brown and white, appeared from every conceivable niche.

Tildy was no exception to those alerted by Linders' shouting but she did not show herself. Discretion came to the fore as she peeped cautiously from behind a curtain in the big house. The object of Linders' search was not long in making his own appearance. Disturbed by the bellowing, Jones appeared round the corner, confronted the captain, and glared angrily. "What do you want, you drunken sot?" he spat out.

"I call you out, you unprincipled mangel wurzel. You steal my gift to Mrs Treacher. You cruelly mistreat a slave. You hoodwink a good woman into leaving her true man. And all the world knows what a cruel, nasty master you are over people who have no defence but their overseers' fairmindedness – which in your case is absent." He threw a glove at Jones's feet, saying "I call you out, you swine – name the date and weapon."

"Tomorrow will do, at noon, in Belsize wood." Jones failed to refer to producing a second – just as well; most people who knew him felt he might have trouble finding one. Linders was under no such difficulty and said he'd send someone that evening to confirm arrangements. Linders was about to turn on his heels when Jones blurted at him: "Where did you hear that cock-and-bull story about my being a thief?"

"I didn't have to hear it – you brought me the necklace yourself" said the captain, wisely failing to implicate Tildy who had suffered too much already. As he turned about, to regain his mount, Jones pulled out a pistol and cocked it. Fortunately, James had just come round the corner and witnessed the confrontation. Jones had just cocked his pistol and was about to bring it down to bear on his target, to the astonishment of the onlookers who gasped, frozen in their places by the malevolence of the scene, when James intervened. In fact, James was comparatively unarmed, having neither the time nor the foresight to prime a pistol, but he had grabbed his sword as he flew from his room. Trusting to that weapon and giving no thought to what might happen if the pistol-bearing Jones had called his bluff, and relying also on whatever authority he might have as one of the plantation family, he yelled out: "Drop your pistol, or you are a dead man!" Linders wheeled about, taking in the situation at a glance.

"I'm obliged to you, Mr Ricketts," said the captain, looking in scorn at Jones and spitting on the ground in front of him.

At noon on the appointed day, the two duellists followed the customary observances, walking ten paces apart before turning to fire. They fired simultaneously and both were hit. However, Linders was only grazed at his left shoulder while Jones was more seriously damaged in the leg, rolling on the ground and groaning as his hands clasped the injured limb. "Come, Smithers, we'll be off now," said Linders as he rode off with his second. An attendant surgeon directed the moving of Jones to his cottage where he continued to minister to him.

Duelling was not only frowned on, but was illegal. Yet it still was a surprise to Linders when two magistrate's officers appeared at his door in two days. Looking sheepish, one of these officers put the question to which he already knew the answer: "Are you Captain Linders?"

The captain's eyes narrowed as he peered at Johnson, whom he knew well, saying: "Of course it's me, you blockhead. Who'd you think it was?"

Not to be easily turned aside from what he knew to be his solemn duty – in fact the only chance he'd had in five years to manifest his authority – Johnson replied: "Now, sir, let's not be difficult, sir. I have a warrant for your apprehension from the magistrate and it's my duty to take you into custody – sir." This response, enough to warm the heart of every policeman throughout the British Empire, elicited strong approval from the other officer who silently nodded his head up and down twice, showing how completely he was giving way to overpowering emotion. He was escorted to the small local jail. Asking why, he was deferentially told that a complaint was laid against him for engaging in an illegal act with murderous intent.

After two more days, he was arraigned before the magistrate who addressed him in the court-room: "Captain Linders, a charge is brought against you of engaging in a duel and attempting to take the life of one Arthur Jones. If that be true, it is a serious enough offence; fortunately for you, there will be no charge of murder. How do you plead?"

"Not guilty, your Worship," called the defendant.

"Who represents you in this court?" asked the magistrate.

"I stand in my own defence, your Worship."

"Very well, the clerk will read out the charge." That was duly done, it appearing that the charge was brought in answer to a complaint by none other than the injured party, Arthur Jones, who was not in attendance. The lawyer representing the Crown called four witnesses in all. A very curious thing happened. Having been sworn, the first witness was asked what he had seen take place at Ridgeland.

"I seen the cap'n arrive all dishevelled-like, a-bellowin' fit-to-bust."

"A-what?" said the magistrate, determined to maintain the court's dignity.

"A-bellowin' like thunder for Jones to come out and face him."

"And then?" prompted the lawyer hopefully.

"Well, they had words, you might say, and then the cap'n and Mr Jones left."

"What about the occurrences in Belsize wood?" asked the barrister, driving to the heart of the matter.

"O-cur-rences?" repeated the witness as if a new word had been introduced to his vocabulary.

"The duel, man, the shooting," prompted the lawyer, in an exasperated tone.

To everyone's surprise, Linders sprang up to his own defence, saying "I object, your Worship. That's leading the witness."

"True, true" grudgingly allowed the magistrate, "I cannot allow that."

"What happened in Belsize wood?" repeated the prosecutor, menacingly, at a pedantical pace.

A look of disarming, innocent bewilderment suffused the visage of the witness who drawled out slowly: "Happened? You mean an oc-cur-rence? Why nothin' happened that I can recall – sir."

Three other witnesses behaved much in the same manner and the crowded courtroom began to exhibit distinct signs of boredom. Even Captain Linders was seen to stifle a yawn, at which the spetators tittered.

The magistrate harrumphed, called for order amongst the crowd, pursed his fingers solemnly and addressed the court: "I am as well aware as anybody that duelling has a long, if not entirely honourable, history, but it is outlawed in this realm of our sovereign Lord the King. None of the witnesses has seen fit to say what everyone here must know to be the truth, so I can only conclude that the force of the tradition is strong enough to flout the rule of law in this case. I cannot officially condone so flagrant a breach of justice but in the absence of conclusive evidence, I have no alternative save to declare the defendant acquitted."

He did not add that the witnesses' silence showed how widely the unsavoury reputation of Jones had spread. As the courtroom murmured in a self-satisfied vein, the judge made a final remark which they never forgot: "The King's justice is, however, not to be mocked, so I find the four witnesses guilty of perjury and contempt of court. They may of course appeal for a trial in front of a jury of their peers, and I give them leave to do so, but they will have to set that possible course of action over against the sentence which I now pronounce: one week in jail."

The clerk called out: "Be upstanding. This court is now adjourned. God save the King, and this honourable court!"

The court did adjourn but consequences followed in short order. The captain's reputation as a hero was firmly settled in his lady-love's mind. Her necklace was her's again, and she agreed to tie her fortunes permanently to the good captain whose damaged arm she tenderly nursed. Arthur Jones, his reputation in tatters, was discharged not by James's acting on his own but by his elder brother

John. He had returned home from militia exercises and been apprised by James and Sarah.

Tildy's wounds healed and she attached herself firmly to her new mistress Sarah, to the comfort of both. Sarah continued to mend from the terrible nightmare she had lived through and began to occupy herself with the welfare of those unfortunates euphemistically termed 'servants'. James rejoiced in his wife's recovery and her new pastoral activity and accompanied his brother, absorbing knowledge of the inner workings of the plantation, while thinking up ways to circumvent the economic handicaps imposed by the American war on the entire island.

At the beginning of October, a corporal of the Royal Americans arrived bearing a sealed envelope for James. It was a letter from the present commandant, Fuser. James knew that Fuser was one of the Swiss originals commissioned into the 60th in 1757 and must now be in his mid-forties. Pretty robust character, he felt.

14th September, 1778

Dear Mr Ricketts,
You will understand that I can go into no details in a letter, but I will have to ask you to cut short your leave as there is important duty we need you for. I think you would probably do best to leave your wife in Jamaica where she will enjoy a healthier climate, to say nothing of pleasanter conditions than she would find in coming back with you.

I am sorry to be cryptic but you will know that sometimes the exigencies of the service demand it. We have not met but I look forward to having you under my command. Major Prevost at present is farther north along the border so I am now commandant.

Do not reply unless there is a grave difficulty which makes your return impossible.
Yr obdt servant,

Lewis Valentine Fuser
Lieutenant Colonel, 4th Batt. 60thRegt.
St Augustine Garrison, East Florida

Haste was demanded. He hated to leave Sarah but he was a little ashamed to admit that his curiosity was well and truly roused. Giving himself two days to make arrangements, he set out on what was now becoming the familiar path between Ridgeland and St Augustine.

Chapter 18

Sam once again obliged him by driving James and his luggage to Savanna la Mar. There had been no time to make arrangements, so James sought out the headquarters of Captain Phillips's company of Royal Americans, to arrange passage for St Augustine. The company's lieutenant was in command because Captain Phillips had been taken by a privateer and was now a prisoner of the rebels. He was informed that in a week's time a despatch boat would call in on the way from Kingston to St Augustine and he could hitch a ride. That gave him a brief respite and he was able to drive with Sarah to the small chapel at Savanna la Mar for Sunday morning service.

As they arrived a good hour before the service, James had a talk with the Anglican priest who, on learning that he was leaving shortly, possibly on hazardous duty, suggested that he would celebrate the eucharist in full so that the couple and others present might receive Holy Communion. Seeing this welcomed, he further called James's attention to the exhortation in the Communion Service of the Prayer Book urging private confession "that by the ministry of God's holy Word he may receive the benefit of absolution, together with ghostly counsel and advice, to the quieting of his conscience, and avoiding of all scruple and doubtfulness." James's Anglicanism was of a straightforward and uncomplicated sort. He had never made a confession before but accepted that now was a sensible time to do so. He took a few minutes to search his memory, knelt at the rail and made his confession after which he was absolved in the ancient words which, despite the efforts of reformers, had survived in the English church. It being the seventeenth Sunday after Trinity, the gospel was from Luke 14 and contained a text he would have occasion to remember later – "Friend, go up higher".

They rode home largely in silence; something about the visit to church was at once both mellow and unsettling. Sarah rigorously suppressed the panicky idea that having lost her first child, was she now to lose her husband, too?

Without words, they went to their room, drew close to each other and studied each other's eyes, then took each other in their arms, savouring each moment to its utmost and every slightest movement. It was their first coming together since the child-birth. Their love-making expanded with nearly motionless deliberateness. Mutual absorption grew almost imperceptibly more and more encompassing. After what felt like half the sultry day, their passion was fulfilled in the stormy emptying of love-making's completion. Bound tightly by breath and sweat, they knew in each fold and cranny of their being the paradoxical giving-and-receiving, the violent tenderness which the mind does not fathom but their experience affirmed.

When James had finally left Sarah and Ridgeland behind and been dropped off at the small harbour of Savanna la Mar, he found a subaltern and three civilians also awaiting passage. They boarded the despatch vessel and repaired to their cramped quarters. The despatch boat was of more ample proportions than he had expected, a two-masted sloop, a stroke of good fortune which its supernumeraries, as the muster roll had listed them, rejoiced over. They set off in balmy weather which, being landlubbers at heart, they appreciated. Making round the west coast of Jamaica and then northeastward, they negotiated the Windward Passage and headed northwest toward the Floridas. Even such landsmen as they remarked how the sky darkened, though the sun was well up. The darkness increased as the breeze stiffened and rapidly became a formidable gale. At first the westerly winds drove them in the right direction at breakneck speed as they ran before the wind.

Blustery wind was only the first hazard. What began as a refreshing downpour of rain did not disperse like a squall, as they expected. Instead the rain burgeoned into torrents dousing every nook and cranny of the ship. After three hours of battering, the skipper turned all hands to reefing the sheets. The danger they realized as immanent was terrifyingly brought home. One of the crew aloft missed his footing in the shrouds and fell into the sea, his despairing cry briefly heard before he plunged into the hungry water. No chance of rescue existed for him as the boiling ferment swallowed him. Even should he know how to swim, which most sailors did not, he could not survive.

One sail was unreefed, flapping madly before it was torn to shreds. The mainmast cracked and came crashing down, bringing the foremast with it and pitching the whole spiky tangle into the sea. It trailed briefly along the starboard side before being cut loose. All pretence of navigation was now abandoned as the sloop was now dismasted. The most ignorant landlubber aboard knew there could be no recourse to boats in that boiling sea.

The sole hope was to keep the sloop afloat. To this end all efforts were bent. They ran with the wind wherever it took them, the helmsmen stretching every limb and muscle to keep the wind astern. They must not be swamped.

Just as all appeared to be hopeless, the rain did ease and the wind softened. Then it virtually stopped. They lay tossing about but at least the dreadful battering ceased. The sky lightened and they found themselves in a kind of doldrums where they bobbed up and down but made no headway. James, whose experience of storms had been limited largely to land, recognized the eerie grey-green of the sky and failed to share his companions' sense of relief. He believed they were in the eye of a hurricane and looked ahead apprehensively to renewed torment when the eye passed them by. After an appreciable interval – no one thought to reckon just how long – the winds strengthened once more and the treacherous truce ended abruptly.

They were about to be plunged into the revived hellish maelstrom. Only this time, as if some gigantic mirror had descended from on high, the winds blew from the opposite direction, the southwest. Survival depended on reversing direction so as to present the stern to the changed winds. The skipper had fortunately foreseen this and a boat was lowered to drag the bows around a hundred and eighty degrees, with a cable joining the boat and sloop in a tedious operation known as warping. Since the storm's resurgence made this manoeuvre increasingly dangerous to the small boat, they completed their work in a hurry, returned to the ship and clambered aboard just ahead of a turbulence which would have doomed them to a seething, watery grave.

Battened down below the secured hatches, James's party could only hope and pray. The sloop was buffeted and driven relentlessly to the northeast. They all took turns manning the pumps, an endless purgatory, especially for the civilians who were in poorer physical shape than the rest. As the hurricane eventually propelled them outside its most virulent reach and moved off to the west, the sky's hideous gloom lightened in time for them to see their ship, broadsides, approaching land rapidly. Their view clarified as they came to the shore until at last, with crunching, scraping and juddering they came to rest, keeled over at an uncomfortably sharp angle on a beach. Finally becalmed, everyone helped wade supplies and belongings ashore.

Night was falling. The sailors gathered what wood they could find, lighting a fire for warmth against the bitter air. After a night of exhausted twitching and turning, dawn came. They looked ruefully out at what remained of the sloop: the bruised hull stripped of its superstructure. Breakfast was readied and all set to it hungrily. For a while they felt alone, as if on a deserted isle. The unceasing din of the offshore breeze plunged them into a timeless void where nothing seemed to change.

However, after a couple of hours, a party of men was observed coming toward them from inland. As they came nearer, it was seen that these men were armed. Any resistance, should that be called for, was out of the question since dry powder was unavailable for the few muskets they had brought ashore. The leader of the advancing group came gingerly into their camp, smiling as he looked at their desolation.

"Well, I declare, you are in a right old mess!" said the man whose voice bore the unmistakeable traits of a scrod, a seaman from Boston. "Captain Moore, of the United States privateer *Franklin*, at your service, gentlemen," he announced in an incongruously courtly manner, sweeping off his hat. "I don't aim to increase your misery, but you are my prisoners. I see here a shipwrecked crew, all right, but do I also spy some passengers as well?" It was obvious to James, at least, that they had been under observation from at least their arrival.

James, as the senior military officer present and not one of the crew, made known the passengers' identities and disclosed St Augustine as their destination. "But where are we, and what are you doing here and what do you intend doing with us?"

"Well, three questions, just like that, quick as a cracker," replied Moore. "I guess I can answer them. First, you have come ashore at John Smith's Bay on the southeast shore of Bermuda. Second, you may not be aware that American vessels bearing letters of marque often use Bermuda for refuge. It has any number of nice little creeks and as yet no soldiers to prevent it. In fact, we're right well-disposed to the Bermudians – they gave us powder back in '75 and most of our ships are Bermuda-built. As for question number three: I confess your plight awakens a responsive chord in my bosom. For I was one of six seamen, as were three of my mates here, who were wrecked on a Caribbean island some time ago when we were discovered by a young officer called Thornbrough, of your navy. You could rightly say that the tables are now neatly turned, yes siree."

"How does this bear on our case?" asked James ungraciously curt, as he was beginning to lose patience and had not yet been told their fate.

"Just hold your horses a moment, young man. I'm coming to that. This Thornbrough I'll never forget. He was wounded at Bunker Hill trying to take our men in the rear but he held no ill will against us, for all that. He turned out to be a really nice fellow. You'll find it hard to credit, he didn't clap us in irons and send us off to Dartmoor or some stinking hulk in the Thames. No sir, he had the real feeling of one seaman for another and he picked us up, treated us with great hospitality and damned if he didn't sail into Boston harbour under a flag of truce and drop us off, well fed and all. I've never forgotten that kindness. We may be rebels but we ain't barbarians, if you take my meaning. I always reckoned we owed him for that and I'm not one to forget debts. It's a kind of obligation. Sailed right into Boston, he did, so we unfortunates could return to our families, all comfy, as you might say. Well, you ain't sailors exactly, but no matter. You'll do to settle an obligation. So I reckon we'll drop you off near your destination. You might actually think the better of us for it."

After a pause, James said; "I'm astonished, sir. I don't know what to say."

"Of course," Moore added, as much to remove his embarrassment as for any other reason, "I don't imagine your people would let us sail right in to St Augustine – that wouldn't impress the garrison with what scoundrels we all are. But we could put you off as near as dammit. Oh," he added almost as an afterthought, "the crew can go free to find help, provided they give their word to wait twenty-four hours before raising any alarm."

James was not the only man on the move. In London, Cartwright was wrapping things up. There was little more he could do there and his superiors had instructed him to travel to Charleston. He might be needed there in the south – the war might well move there, either with an enemy push north from Florida or the Caribbean, or south from New York. Command of the sea gave the King's forces many options.

When he mentioned it to Healy, the reaction was instantaneous. "Move from here to America? I'll not be doing it. No, I'll not! I wasn't saved from trans – trans..."

"Transportation?" interjected Cartwright.

"Aye, trans-port-ation to New South Wales just to be kicked to America. Why, it's thousands of miles away."

"Oh?" said the spy. "Who was it who rescued you from your sentence? Who risked life and limb to give you comfort and employment so you could get back at your oppressors? I. I did, you ungrateful wretch."

"Nothing you can say will persuade me. Nothing."

"Is that really so? After all the dangers we've endured together, you will leave me indeed? Am I 'brought to desolation in a moment'?" After an interval of some moments when he appeared to be thinking hard while glowering at Healy, he appeared to relent.

He reached behind him for a bottle of brandy and two glasses. "Well, I suppose you know your own mind. There's nothing to be done. But let us part as friends and drink on it. Just give me a moment to clean this glass."

He soon returned, turning away to fill the glasses on the shelf behind him. He held out one to Healy and said: "No hard feelings, eh. And to each of us, prosperity, and our just deserts."

A few minutes later, Healy's dead body slumped to the floor and Cartwright vanished.

A week later, a small boat slid onto the beach five miles south of St Augustine. It could easily be taken for a party of fishermen returning late as they crunched their way inland. The party from the wrecked sloop trudged wearily. Even their luggage, strapped to a small trolley, was put ashore with them. What will the contents look like after these adventures, wondered James.

They reached the outlying houses of St Augustine. Shorttly they were challenged by an outpost which took them in charge. Discovering who they were, and especially as the group contained an officer of the 60th, their escort swiftly conveyed them up the main street to the town headquarters.

Once surprise over their manner of arrival had died down, an account was given them of the damage suffered ashore from the hurricane. James could not help but notice that the atmosphere in the garrison had changed markedly since he was last there.

At headquarters, James did not find Colonel Fuser, who was operating somewhere near the Georgia border. Colonel Augustine Prevost, elder brother of Mark, had been in command of operations in East Florida since the start of hostilities but most of his time, too, was spent outside the town - working on the efficiency of the new provincial regiment, the East Florida Rangers, and conducting occasional raids into Georgia or defending the border between East Florida and Georgia. His younger brother was active outside the town, in his place. He also was away from town.

Instead, Major Beamsley Glasier was in command – a Massachusetts man, one of the 60th's originals. James's interview with Glasier made clear that his return from leave was most welcome. No details were provided by the major but he could not hide his excitement. Meanwhile, James was to be posted to the grenadier company of his regiment's 2nd Battalion.

He found that the company, while understrength like all the rest, was not nearly so weak as most and its officers and men were conspicuously above average in experience and capability. Furthermore, the company had begun to function in common with the grenadiers of the 3rd and 4th Battalions. Such a configuration in the order of battle usually meant active service since it was common practice to group the grenadiers from different battalions into one battalion for operations. In early December, the commandant called one of those staff meetings for all officers of the garrison that had been such a feature of Mark Prevost's tenure. The commandant ran the meeting.

He first sketched the general situation. "Gentlemen, I thank you for coming together so promptly. In the summer of last year, Major Prevost mentioned that General Howe had four options following his seizure of New York. He could have headed up the Hudson to meet General Burgoyne's offensive from Canada, which he did not do, with the result that Burgoyne capitulated at Saratoga in October 1777 and the French were encouraged to come out openly against us. He could have moved against Boston thus denying the French fleet the use of both Boston and Newport, which he did not do. He could have had another try for Charleston, which he did not attempt.

"He chose instead to invest Philadelphia which he took in September of that year – not that it did us any good. In May, Sir Henry Clinton took command and left Philadelphia, not by sea, but overland for New York a month later – thus he had to fight the inconclusive but costly action at Monmouth.

"Our only significant success so far has been the enemy's failure to take Newport, Rhode Island three months ago, owing mainly to the incompetence of their General Sullivan. Naturally they blamed it on d'Estaing's fleet leaving them in the lurch, with the result that their confidence in the French has reached an all-time low." The sixty-four year-old officer from Ipswich, Massachusetts, who addressed them, had a distinguished career going back to the Louisburg expedition of Sir William Pepperrell in the year '45 and had been an officer of the Royal Americans since almost its formation. He spoke with authority and had the full attention of his hearers, despite his advanced age.

"I have three bits of news that you will not have heard. At the end of last month, Lieutenant Colonel Archibald Campbell sailed from New York to invade Georgia." A sudden murmur burst throughout the room.

"The second item has to do with us. Lieutenant Colonel Fuser has been creating mischief for the rebels along the Georgia border – three weeks ago he almost took Savannah but pulled back with the prospect of a larger rebel force breathing down his neck.

"Lastly, another push will be made by... you!. Colonel Prevost will be gathering up every man he can lay his hands on and plans to set out two days before Christmas. We will probably be known as the Florida Brigade and the force will include East Florida and Carolina Royalists. That does not give us much time so I expect each of you – in keeping with Major Prevost's principles – to exert every effort to prepare his men, and to inform them where they fit in. I have had to weigh the advantage of secrecy against that of having the troops know what they are about and I have concluded that so little time exists before we move that we can risk explaining the plans."

The commandant paused to let all this sink in. No one could think of a question he ought to ask, perhaps because they all had too many questions. Finally, one subaltern's hand was cautiously raised and a question followed: "Sir, will Major Prevost be coming along?"

"Yes" answered Glasier, "I am happy to tell you that Major Prevost will be second-in-command under his brother, and I shall lead our grenadiers. Now I have a number of promotions approved by the King to announce, to take effect from the beginning of the campaign. Colonel Prevost is to be a Brigadier General, Major Mark Prevost is a Lieutenant Colonel, Captain-Lieutenant Benjamin Wickham is to join the 2nd Battalion's grenadiers as an attached captain, Lieutenant James Ricketts to be Captain-Lieutenant of this battalion vice Wickham but will serve with the grenadiers under Captain Muller."

James's promotion meant that he was to be the captain commanding the Colonel's company of the 2nd Battalion since the colonel, Brigadier General Gabriel Christie was never expected to be with his company. Christie was thought to be on his way back from London to the West Indies. James's mind went back to the gospel reading when he and Sarah received communion, about the guest at the banquet who sat down in the lowest seat – "whosoever exalteth himself shall be abased, and he that humbleth himself shall be exalted." He blushed inwardly at the absurdly vain and inappropriate ascription of such a passage to himself. He wondered if there were any connection between his new appointment and his "testing" in England.

Though James's quarters seemed sadly quiet without Sarah, he had little time to think about it, such were the many preparations to be made. In no time at all, the twenty-third of the month had arrived and the pace accelerated.

Chapter 19

On the twenty-third of December 1778, some two thousand troops boarded flat boats to navigate the inland passage from St Augustine to Georgia. James found the first part of the journey relatively easy since the St John's River was one of the few in North America to flow north, but after Yellow Bluff Point the going was harder and the passages more difficult to navigate. Officers took turns with their men at the oars or at pulling from the occasional towpath. James found his hands hardening to the task after the initial plague of blisters and sores.

Three battalions of Royal Americans between them furnished four hundred and twenty-five officers and men for the expedition, leaving a hundred and eighty-four men behind as part of the garrison - there was a general feeling that anything, almost anything, was better than stewing in the East Florida garrison. The 16th Regiment, Skinner's New Jersey Volunteers, the South Carolina Royalists, Georgia Rangers, the East Florida Rangers and a detachment of sixteen men from Captain Johnston's Company, 4th Battalion Royal Artillery were also in the brigade. Brigadier General Prevost worried about the shortage of officers, particularly in the regiment's 3rd Battalion which found only seven officers in their six companies.

Despite the gentle winters of East Florida and Georgia, travel in that season always had its hazards, the primary one being shortage of food since the trip took longer than hoped.

The troops were compelled to use their wits to supplement the meagre rations and when oysters were found to be in abundance, this supply of food was fallen upon with alacrity. "God help any poor women who come our way" observed one of the randier subalterns, "they would not stand a chance in this potent crowd."

"Pity we brought no saltpetre with us" returned one wiseacre.

A fortnight later, the troops bivouacked seven miles from the important port of Sunbury in Georgia, glad to be off the water. Even so, the mid-winter frost and mist dampened all their clothing. Fires were lit after a sufficient response to the drums beating 'wood call' to give warmth and dry the tents before nightfall. As James and his grenadiers had laid out their tents in impeccably neat rows, posted sentries and done all the things they should do properly, they were affronted by the arrival of a scruffy lot from Fuser's 4th Battalion, 60th. These troops had been at Sunbury more than a month previously. Hoping to take Fort Morris but unable to do so, owing to the the unwelcome arrival of the North Carolina militia general, Ashe, they had fallen back to await Prevost's force from the south. Since this motley crowd had been campaigning in Georgia's swamps and forests all this time, their clothing was dirty and they stank. The grenadiers were shamed into taking a less hoity-toity attitude when they realized why Fuser's men were so unkempt.

Captain Robertson, who accompanied Fuser, chatted to the grenadiers, among whom were James and the dependable Bert Smith, now a serjeant. They talked about Fuser's previous attempt on Sunbury. "Do you see that disreputable-looking civilian there?" Robertson asked, nodding toward a bearded man with an ugly scar just under his eyes who was swigging from the jug of whiskey he shared with the black man beside him – his 'man' no doubt.

"Yes, he's not in uniform. What about him?" asked a subaltern in a superior tone.

"He may not look like much but you won't find a braver man in His Majesty's army, I reckon. He's Rory McIntosh - was with Oglethorpe's Highlanders during the War of Jenkins' Ear almost forty years ago. Anyway, we got to Sunbury on Christmas Day and found no nice presents waiting for us. Heathen lot, those rebels! What we did find was Colonel John McIntosh and his Georgia Continentals. Maybe the two were kinsfolk, I don't know, but *our* McIntosh rushes up to the fort brandishing his claymore, his man tugging at his sleeve the whole time. McIntosh cries out 'Surrender, you miscreants; how dare you presume to resist His Majesty's arms?' Funny formal words to use, I guess, but I hear he's given to pompous gestures. Maybe he practised it before. *Their* McIntosh seemed to know *our* McIntosh because their people were told not to fire on him. In fact they threw open the gate and said 'Walk in, Mr McIntosh, and take possession.'

"'No' says Rory. 'I will not trust myself among such vermin, but I order you to surrender.' Then someone fires at him, hence the wound you see. At least he got back to our lines."

"He must be sixty-five at least" said a corporal.

"How did you fare for food after that rebuff?" asked someone.

"Oh, we had no trouble finding oysters" answered the captain while his hearers groaned understandingly."

"Don't talk to me about oysters!" was Captain Muller's contribution. "I can't think what someone does who gets sick on shellfish," he added.

"Since we begin our attack tomorrow, let's hope they have some better victuals awaiting us," observed Major Glasier who had strolled over some time ago to visit his grenadiers.

"Amen," someone murmured.

"This time the other McIntosh has gone north with Howe's troops – *their* general Robert Howe, I mean to say, not *our* general Howe. Bless me if I don't think people with the same names on both sides is confusing. He's left a Major Lane in charge – anybody know a British officer called Lane?" asked Glasier.

The next morning, the sixth of January 1779, the troops were roused by fifes and drums parading around the bivouac playing *The Three Camps*. Rolls were called before the sun was up and as it rose the troops breakfasted on hard tack, cheese and grog while the mist, mingled with the pungent smell of wood smoke, cleared. In an hour they moved to just out of musket range of the fort and set about the tedious digging of shallow trenches angled toward Fort Morris. Their movement was impeded by two galleys and an armed schooner in the river behind them which fired at them in a desultory fashion. James's company extended itself cautiously round the fort out of range of the fort itself. By nightfall on the eighth they had met no enemy outside the fort and had encircled it, establishing defensive positions to forestall any relief getting through or defenders getting away.

That night, under cover of darkness, the New Jersey Volunteers' contingent of a hundred men, joined with over two hundred and sixty South Carolina Royalists, had succeeded in bringing up an 8-inch howitzer and two small mortars by the Newport River. At sunup, that artillery was in position, well dug in by the exertions of the provincials and a dozen regular gunners. The morning was taken up with surrender negotiations under flags of truce and in the afternoon, a deadline having expired, the demand for capitulation was reinforced by bombardment from the three pieces of embedded artillery. The fort's defence was plainly untenable and in the forenoon the enemy schooner suddenly sailed away while a white flag broke from the fort. The two galleys could not run the gamut of musketry from the shore, scuttled, and their crews were captured.

General Prevost was able to report to London that twenty-one pieces of artillery, two pairs of colours and two hundred and twelve prisoners were taken. A captain and two rank-and-file of the enemy were dead and six wounded while the attackers had suffered one soldier killed and three wounded. The battle had not been so fierce as to create bitter hatred so the surrender was a gentlemanly affair. Everyone, including Captain Lane, realized that his force could hardly have resisted five times their number. They were allowed the honours of war – to march out with colours flying (two only were available), drums beating (two only) as they passed between two ranks of King's soldiers with arms at the present - redcoated regulars and provincials whose green tunics had mostly by now been replaced by red. They then handed over their weapons at the end of the dolorous procession. Lane, having no sword, was allowed to keep his pistol. The fort was promptly re-named Fort George.

On the twelfth day of January, General Prevost entered Savannah. In James's eyes, the town was a delight to see with its gardens and spacious squares, luscious even in winter. The Georgia Rangers, about one hundred and fifty mounted men, and South Carolina Royalists led the force in a triumphal procession. Colonel Campbell with his force from New York had been in possession of Savannah for more than a fortnight, Augustine Prevost now assumed direction of operations in Georgia. Prevost and Campbell knew that the rebel general Robert Howe was nearby so they set about readying Savannah's defences against him. Since the major element in Campbell's force was the 71st (Fraser's) Highlanders, of whom the Earl of Eglinton had spoken so lyrically to James, it seemed fitting that Prevost's entry to the town should be greeted by forty pipers whose skirling music was now, for better or worse, a familiar sound to the Germans and Americans who comprised the rest of his command. On the nineteenth, news of his promotion to a 'local' Major General was received. Meanwhile, rebel troops were moving energetically to recover the lost parts of Georgia.

Howe was a soldier of some experience. Coming from wealthy planter stock, he was schooled in Europe and became wealthy in his own right. He joined forces with General Lincoln and handed over command to him. The rebel troops were concentrated at Purysburg, South Carolina, right across the Savannah River from Prevost in Georgia .

Howe's successor Lincoln was different from his predecessor in many ways. Not rich, he was the son of a Massachusetts tradesman. He attracted the favourable attention of Washington who made him a major general in the Continental Army.

While the main British force was at Ebenezer, they still took the precaution of strengthening the defences of Savannah itself. Large 18-pounder guns from the ordnance ship in the harbour were placed in the lines on the twenty-third of January. A garrison of two Hessian regiments and three of the five loyalist battalions of Campbell's force was detailed to remain behind at Savannah.

Opposite Purysburg at Ebenezer, Prevost reorganized his army of three thousand regulars and royalist irregulars against Lincoln with his Continentals and militia. All Prevost's men except the Savannah garrison were shepherded by Lieutenant Clark of the navy in boats upriver twenty miles to Ebenezer. Before embarking in the boats, the troops paraded and the 60th's three grenadier companies, styled in orders as the Division of Grenadiers of the Florida Brigade, took the right of the line next to the small detachment of Royal Artillery under Captain-Lieutenant Fairlamb. The leading boats carried the advance guard, the 2nd Battalion of De Lancey's New York Brigade.

On arrival at Ebenezer, quarters were allocated - field officers had two rooms and a kitchen, captains one room, two subalterns were to share a room and staff officers had a room each. Each regiment had a messroom and kitchen; each company had a place where they were allowed to cook and soldiers used barns and outhouses to dwell in. At least, thought James, we're under cover.

A fortnight earlier, as the major part of the army settled down at Ebenezer, Colonel Archibald Campbell was sent northwest along the Savannah River toward Augusta with about eight hundred regulars. Campbell met so little resistance that on the twenty-ninth of January he took Augusta, almost a hundred miles from Ebenezer.

The battle for Georgia had become a series of movements and feints between three points of a triangle – Savannah, Augusta and Charleston.

The North Carolina militia general John Ashe was sent to join the twelve hundred South Carolina rebel militia opposite Augusta, This was an event of importance, as James would discover.

Soldiers were aware how prominent the Prevost family were in the army's arrangements: Augustine Prevost, now a major general, commanded in Georgia, Captain Augustine Prevost of the 3rd Battalion 60th had been Brigade Major of General Prevost's 1st Brigade and was the new Deputy Adjutant General to the army, Lieutenant Colonel Mark Prevost, whom James knew well, now commanded the 2nd Battalion 71st Highlanders.

It was a temporary appointment – the nominal commander was Patrick Ferguson whom the Earl of Eglinton had mentioned as the inventor of a marvellous rifle. I wonder where those rifles are now, thought James. Since Ferguson had been wounded at Brandywine in September of '77, the Scotsman's experimental corps of riflemen had been disbanded and, he imagined, the rifles put in storage as the earl had surmised would happen.

James was entertained to see that Mark Prevost had his work cut out for him looking after his new Highland battalion – General Orders were published cautioning the men of that battalion to behave well, like the other battalions. The weather continued to be unseasonably warm, so much so that salt was issued to accompany the eating of fresh meat.

On the second day of February the funeral of one Captain Munrow of the Georgia Loyalists took place. No one seemed to know why he had died. James felt that the army authorities were paying exceptional attention to the details of the funeral in order to make it clear to all that the services of loyalists were highly valued.

There followed an order subjecting anyone who destroyed fences to severe punishment. The army was anxious to convince the civilian population that it was a benefit to have the King's troops in charge. Further indiscipline amongst the Highlanders was noticed: "mean villains" were said to have plundered the commissary and attempted to "plunder a Negro" in front of the headquarters before several officers who witnessed it. Despite the high regard for the Highlanders as fighters, this sort of treatment of civilians was not going to be tolerated; a reward of one guinea was offered to any soldier who could identify the miscreants. James wondered what Lord Eglinton would have to say about that. Besides, mistreatment of blacks was no way to win over their loyalty, as the army wished to do.

Work continued on securing the defences of Ebenezer – parties of troops were ordered to collect fascines, dry brushwood useful in such matters, the party to assemble for directions from the post engineer at eight o'clock the next morning.

The heat continued to be a problem and orders were issued that meat killed in the morning was to be served to the troops by the same evening. The daily rum ration was reduced to a gill per man till further notice. James was never much for rum, so it didn't bother him. Four days later the troops were told they would march at daybreak the following day.

On the twelfth, Colonel Mark Prevost called a council of war back at Ebenezer for the officers of the 2/71st and the 60th's grenadiers. "Come in, gentlemen, we are open for business! You've doubtless heard rumours – now I give you facts. Ashe is coming up with militia, mostly. The general wants us to upset the enemy trailing Campbell as he pulls back from Augusta. They must be kept away from Ebenezer. So, tomorrow we march north to Brier Creek about fifty miles upriver. I plan to be there on the sixteenth."

Captain Muller had a question: "Suppose we meet an enemy force coming south? I realize they are probably not that near yet, but what do we do in that case?"

"In case of alarm, the grenadiers will line the wood on the road. They will lie in ambuscade whilst the enemy are allowed to pursue our troops as far as the end of our ambuscade. They will then charge with the bayonet – not a shot to be fired. Is that clear?

"The battalion of the 71st will draw up on its own ground, detaching one company to guard the artillery and baggage, but they will not move an inch till ordered. I want to be sure that the fires of picquets and guards are to be put out by nine o'clock, not to be rekindled till daybreak.

"Now, as for tomorrow: when the 'assembly' beats, the troops will be ready for the march and horses will be in their carriages. The 'long roll' will be the signal to fall in. At repeated 'long rolls', the troops will set out. Picquets will head the column. Captain Johnston of the Rangers will ride at the head of the column. Small parties will go ahead to search every thicket and report all dwellings of significance to Johnston. The Carolina loyalists will flank the column at a distance of a hundred and fifty yards with the customary five paces between each man."

They reached Brier Creek on the sixteenth of February. Battalion orders for the 2/71st brought a smile to many faces as it was reported that Lieutenant Hugh Campbell had lost a silver watch on the road for which a reward of a half-guinea was tendered. The things we have time for, thought James. I suppose it all goes along with promoting the idea that ours is just an ordinary profession.

A couple of days later, Archibald Campbell's force, moving south with Ashe shadowing him, reached Brier Creek and it was decided that all the troops there would move south nineteen miles to Hudson's Ferry. There was a pause at that place, during which Colonel Campbell thanked the Carolina loyalists for their services and took the opportunity to scotch rumours, started by what mischief-makers no one knew, that their two corps were to be disbanded and the men distributed throughout the rest of the army.

On the twenty-third, picquets and guards were called in at four in the morning while the troops fell in at half past four and marched off at five o'clock. The Highlanders were ordered to replace the kilt with white trousers, the whole force to make as little noise as possible. The next day found them at Two Sisters, a few miles north of Hudson's Ferry. Campbell now abandoned Hudson's Ferry as he resumed his southbound course, going in the opposite direction from Prevost's detachment.

Some miles to the north, Ashe crossed the river into Georgia on the twenty-fifth and two days later reached Brier Creek. He found Campbell had demolished the bridge. At that point, he decided to stop rather than proceed farther south against forces of whose location and strength he was uncertain.

The next day, Mark Prevost called another council of war. "As you know, my brother wants us to discommode the enemy. The time for that is nigh. Colonel Campbell has left the 1st Battalion of Fraser's Highlanders along the south bank of Brier Creek, to amuse Ashe. I propose that we make a wide westward circuit of the enemy, in all about fifty miles, and hit him from the north where he least expects it. I would like to reach him in five days. That should mean we won't be too tired when we do. What do you think?"

"Of course we can, colonel. We're not grenadiers for nothing," offered Wickham, ever the enthusiast. "Och, aye, what aboout us Hie'landers, even if we're in trews?" said one of the Scottish captains, another McIntosh, it turned out.

"There will be plenty for you to do, I warrant," answered Prevost.

"How many effectives will we have, sir?" asked Muller.

"Besides the three companies of grenadiers, we have the 2nd Fraser's, Baird's light infantry and the mounted loyalists – perhaps eight or nine hundred men," was the answer.

"What's the enemy force like, sir?" asked a subaltern.

They have a militia brigade, a battalion of light troops, a hundred Continentals – about fifteen hundred in all".

"With odds of two-to-one against us, is there a problem?" remarked Glasier.

The force moved off very early on the twenty-seventh, the day after the council of war. Colonel Prevost felt he could risk his entire military career in one big play, saying to the Highlanders' pipe-major: "Mind you, Pipe Major, no music till we actually charge them." The incredulous grumbling amongst the Scots was audible if surprisingly subdued.

For three days they marched through a wilderness of swamp and woods but avoided any settlements. On the third day of the sweep around Ashe, the pace quickened. A mounted Georgia light dragoon who had been sent by Captain Johnston at the column's head, bent low in his saddle and called out: "Captain Ricketts, there's a plantation on the left about three hundred yards ahead". Notwithstanding the dearth of good maps – despite Hutchins's work in London which James knew about– they had not expected to run across dwellings as they forged ahead. "Captain Johnston's compliments, and he wonders if you could take a look, sir."

"Please thank the captain and tell him I shall come directly," replied James, who was on duty at the point of the main body. "Serjeant Smith, bring six men – we're going to look at the house." The reconnaissance party hurried along and fanned out around the building to prevent access or egress. James knocked loudly at the front door of the large white wooden farmhouse, waited, then knocked again. A tremulous female voice inquired from within: "Who's there?"

"Captain Ricketts of His Majesty's 60th Regiment. We do not wish to startle you but we must talk to you, ma'am," he demanded. Bolts were drawn and slowly the door opened. A pale, wide-eyed face ringed with curly brown hair looked at them, peering, frightened.

The young woman was thin, clothed in a cotton house-dress and wore no cap. She wore shabby but once expensively fashionable shoes. "What is it you want, sir?" she said, her eyes narrowing as she took in his uniform and accoutrements.

"Our troops are passing by your house, ma'am, and we must be sure that there is no danger to them from this house," James explained.

"Does it look like it? Am I a threat to His Majesty's troops?" she came back to him sarcastically, fixing him with her enormous eyes which seemed to have calmed down rapidly.

"I confess, ma'am, you seem to be no bigger threat than the army can handle. I realize the presence of troops always upsets people, but I assure you we mean you no harm. We do have to be satisfied that the house contains no enemy troops. I'm afraid I must ask you to allow my men to make a quick search."

"As you see, I am powerless to deter you," – he was captivated by the way she pronounced 'ah'm pahless ta detah ya' and he figured that, delightful though it might be to deepen their acquaintance, time pressed and he must get on. Before he could summon his men, she quietly added: "My young boy is sick upstairs – I beg you, be considerate."

"Perhaps, ma'am, if you allow, I can have our surgeon look at him. We have little time so it will be a quick peek but he might be able to suggest something," James said helpfully. She was intelligent and could see the veiled fist behind the velvet glove but, even so, there appeared to be a struggle in her mind between the dislike of intruding redcoats and the reasonableness of accepting advice.

Presently, she answered in a low but plaintive tone: "That would be kind of you, sir."

"Harris: run back and find the surgeon at the double," James instructed a private soldier who ran out of the house nearly colliding with the men entering to do a search. By the time the search was ended and they had found nothing amiss, the surgeon appeared and examined the boy. While his cool professionalism was reassuring to everyone, he said not a word about the boy's condition. Nor did he offer any advice or treatment. To the anxious mother's look he replied only "keep him wrapt up, he could probably use some sleep." He then turned about and, as he strode from the room, remarked to James: "I'll see you outside, sir."

The rest of the group of soldiers then departed, leaving the mother and child to themselves. James thought they must all be glad to avoid the danger of infection. Just before leaving, James found her name to be Amy Temple. He felt that she had shown a burgeoning confidence in the kind officer when she admitted that her husband was with the enemy artillery. He had escaped the clutches of Colonel Campbell at Savannah's fall and had joined the 'good general' Ashe.

As they left the house, the surgeon took James's arm. "That boy is no sicker than I am!"

"What!" exclaimed James, shocked.

"You wouldn't be the first person to be hoodwinked by southern charm," Henderson attested. "Coming from Maryland I'm southern enough to recognize it when I see it, and northern enough to suspect it. My suspicion is that she daubed the boy with a red tincture to make him look well-fixed, but she's a mind to get on that horse in the field yonder and scamper off. She'd as soon warn Ashe as look at you. I said nothing at the time because I thought things might be complicated further if she realized we were on to her."

"Mr Henderson, you astound me. My God, what a true babe in the woods I am," James candidly admitted. "Just to be on the safe side, I think we'll take that horse with us. We can always release him in ten miles – he'll probably find his way back too late to help Ashe."

The surgeon bestowed more of his wisdom: "Of course, vanity is the weak point. It always is with these southern belles. She couldn't resist crowing over her man and giving away he's a rebel. At any rate, what good it does I don't know, but she may just think that we are less villainous than she thought before. Of course, when she goes for the horse she'll think we're less foolish than she thought before." Henderson, as was his reputation, summed it up neatly.

James took post with the main force near the front of the column at the rear of the grenadiers and the head of the Scottish battalion. Colonel Prevost trotted up to James – both were mounted now - saying "We may encounter the enemy any time, James. You will have to see that the 71st does not rush into the fray in full fury, ahead of the grenadiers. I love my 71st lads dearly but I have no illusions about their strategic sense. My hope is that we take Ashe by surprise. Two days ago, some of their horse picked up our movement but – thank God – I believe their messenger was taken. Yet he must know something's afoot. He's faced by a deep swamp three miles wide and the bridge down. If that's not enough, Macpherson's battalion will discourage his advance, sitting on the far bank of the creek as they do. If I was he, I'd dig in madly, set traps, prepare ambuscades, but I can't see that he's done any of that!"

A report arrived from the head of the column to the effect that an outpost of Ashe's had been met and had taken flight. In two hours, the advance party saw what Ashe had really done - and not done. He had formed his troops in column with Elbert's hundred Continentals in front. Quickly, the British deployed their troops at a hundred and fifty yards from the enemy, changing from a column to two extended ranks, grenadiers to the right, Highlanders to the left.

James, now dismounted, and Serjeant Smith were in the middle of the front rank of the long line, at the point where the grenadiers and the Highlanders met. Ahead of them were the Continentals who were in good order and, firing with precise timing, got off two rounds of musket fire. The serjeant remarked: "Those fellows in front fire like professionals, Captain, but at this range they must know they can't hit anything."

"Look at that, serjeant!" said James. "They're moving to our right in front of that group coming towards us. Good Lord, they've actually blocked the muskets behind them." At the same time, the right wing of the militia unaccountably veered off toward the 71st's left flank, opening a gap between the two concentrations of militia. Unlike most soldiers in battle, occupied with details near them and unaware of the bigger scene, James and his men could see the significance: the Continentals shifting towards the British right were completely nullifying the might of the New Bern regiment – they dared not fire else they would hit the Continentals. Simultaneously, the Edenton regiment of the same brigade had lost its way, opening the gap even wider.

The Highlanders also took in the picture and with characteristic wild excitement were hopping about, straining to rush forward. Repeated shouts, threats and abuse were hurled by James and his nearby officers and NCOs to hold the Scots back. Thankfully, drum rolls from the grenadiers to their right flank soon sent the whole mass cascading into the gap with blood-curdling shouts – a cacophony of shrieking voices aided by the skirling of twenty pipers freed at last from Colonel Prevost's monstrous restriction. Yet, strangely, no British musketry was heard. It was a bayonet charge. As the rest of the enemy militia, the Halifax regiment, saw threatening mayhem sweeping toward them at an alarming pace, they fled without firing a shot. In a matter of seconds, panic had permeated the whole of Ashe's fourteen hundred men. Even the Continentals, who held on for a moment, broke and joined the rout. General Ashe was soon captured.

As the smashed infantry, light troops and mounted rangers dashed pell mell into the swamps and rivers, many were drowned though some escaped on rafts or by swimming. James and his serjeant swept forward in the rush where they came upon three small field guns beside which only two men in blue uniforms still remained. "Yield in the King's name!" shouted James at which one of the two raised a pistol toward him. But the bayonet charge was too swift for him and he fell to a grenadier's thrust.

The other artillerist, an officer, heeded James's challenge and raised his hands just as a Highlander, wild with blood-lust, rushed at him. James leapt and crashed into the side of the onrushing soldier. A big man, he was still sufficiently deflected by James to be knocked down. James picked himself up and yelled at the Highlander who had by now turned his attention wholly to James, and said "You forget yourself, man. We do not kill prisoners!" These words and the proximity of other cooler heads sobered the attacker.

Presently, James was able to talk to the prisoner. "That was a brave thing to do – to stand by your gun in all this panic. But, alas for you, brave or not, you are my prisoner. Perhaps you'd be kind enough to tell me your name."

The captive replied: "That was brave of *you*, sir, to save my life from that ruffian. You could easily have looked the other way but you stepped in at no little risk to yourself. I'm obliged to you, sir – I recognize chivalry when I see it. You're a true christian gentleman." Holding out his hand, he added: "My name is Temple, Lieutenant John Temple of the 2d Company, Georgia Artillery."

"What!" James exploded. At this Temple, who feared he had inadvertently caused offence, somehow or other, he could not imagine how, began to drop his hand. But James seized it warmly, blurting out: "I simply do not believe it! I had the pleasure of meeting your wife at your house a few miles away. What a truly charming lady and, if I may say so, a resourceful one."

Temple looked a bit perplexed and James did not explain. He was also aware that he had no time to idle away. "I have no doubt, you will be exchanged one day and when you get home, kindly convey my compliments to your charming wife. Tell her I hope she got her horse back and that I expect your son recovered from his chicken pox miraculously fast!"

The Georgia gunner looked puzzled. He had not heard about his son having chicken pox. "Hmm," he observed. In a few moments, he was led away with the other prisoners.

In all, Colonel Prevost had lost five killed and eleven wounded. Ashe had suffered nearly two hundred killed and over a hundred and seventy men taken captive. Of those who escaped, no more than four hundred and fifty rejoined their army; the rest went home, reconciled to the return of the province of Georgia to the Crown, if that's the way things would go. It was an astonishing victory.

Chapter 20

Brier Creek destroyed the rebels' hopes of regaining the Province of Georgia in 1779. The British thought so. The rebels thought so. Everybody thought so – except Benjamin Lincoln who set out on the reconquest of Georgia. Undeterred by Brier Creek, he decided to go on the offensive.

By mid-March 1779, Mark Prevost's troops were back at Ebenezer camp. Campbell continued downstream along the Savannah until he too reached Ebenezer. Leaving his troops in the main camp, he went all the way to Savannah to command the garrison there and to ready everything for the return of the governor, Sir James Wright.

In April, Lincoln decided to return the abandoned post of Augusta to his fold; the village was one of those three points of the to-and-fro manoeuvres. Leaving the resourceful Moultrie with a thousand men at Purysburg, opposite Ebenezer, and at Black Swamp farther north, he led the remaining four thousand up the east bank of the river towards Augusta. If his progress had continued uninterrupted, he would have found Augusta almost a sitting duck save for a hundred men of the East Florida Rangers, who held on to the town.

General Prevost countered Lincoln's threat to Augusta by driving through Moultrie's small force and lunging eastward to threaten Charleston. Notified of this move, Lincoln rightly assumed it was a feint to discourage his northward progress. But in dismissing Prevost's feint, he was as shocked, as Prevost was surprised, to find how little opposition the King's forces met in approaching Charleston. On the eleventh of May he was in the outskirts of that jewel of the south. His virtually unopposed advance was as significant a showing of the people's lukewarm attachment to independence as was the successful recruiting of loyalists.

Many poor farmers on the frontier of the day loathed the eastern establishment. They regarded the revolution as a rich landowners' conspiracy to seize control of affairs against the real interests of the common man. Nowhere was that sentiment stronger than in the hinterlands of Georgia where many waited for the return of Sir James Wright, though they would not say so openly.

What eventually crippled loyalist recruiting was the defeat at Kettle Creek on the fourteenth of February. Prevost and Campbell were certainly disappointed at the failure of loyalists to mobilize but that probably indicated little more than their unwillingness to suffer for an uncertain cause rather than any ardour for independence. Their failure to fight for the crown did not mean love for the rebels, as Prevost's unimpeded movement showed.

The 60th's grenadiers, including James Ricketts now captain-lieutenant of the 2nd Battalion 60th Regiment, detached from his colonel's company, were part of Prevost's threat to Charleston. The seventy miles were covered quite quickly but care was taken not to overtax the troops. In early May, James and his men made camp in a ramshackle hamlet which, to him, seemed to have all the least attractive attributes of Georgia cracker life. Tattily-dressed children ran around and the men looked like throat-slitters when they were sober enough to carry out such a task. One of the toughest men sauntered up to James, clearly furious about something, a fact which did not escape Serjeant Smith who cast a wary eye on the cracker and slowly moved closer to rescue James if need be. If ever there was a revolutionary, a man with hatred for the rich, someone who would spit at the idea of authority, here he was. The man intended to be heard. What would he spit out in his transparent anger? Could James and his men even understand him with his impenetrable variety of backwoods English? James braced himself for the encounter.

"Wherefo' y'all act in this goddam stoopid way? What y'all thinkin' of? Ya let all these town-folks a-rahde o'er us – you don't seem to ca-yuh!"

James was searching for a reply when the man went on: "H'yar we is, God-fearin' loyal subjects of His Grac-ee-ous Majesty King Giawge, and do we git help from the lahkes o' you? No siree. What's the matter with y'all? Why don' ya give us arms? We're good people. We could slay the King's enemies – 'confound his enemies, frustrate their knavish tricks' – that's what ma hymn book says, don' it? We could do the wo'k befo' yo' powdered Dutchmen get off their boats, we could!"

James and his men were astonished. It seemed the man was furious, as indeed were most of his fellow villagers. Only, he was angry because they had not been given arms with which to slay the King's enemies. His natural enemy was not the King but the King's richer subjects. He found little to say to the cracker, but it impressed him with how wrong assumptions could be.

The unanticipated easy path to Charleston tempted General Prevost more than he cared to admit. To seize such a prize as that city would change the whole course of the war. It would cover him and his men with glory. If he let his imagination run wild, he saw himself praised by coming generations of Americans as the saviour of his country, the audacious general who insured the defeat of the rebellious faction of self-seeking planters and merchants trying to deprive America of her rightful place in the British family.

But Prevost was also an able officer who knew that with three thousand troops and how many fair-weather converts to the royal cause no one could know, he was unlikely to smash Lincoln and his six and a half thousand men. There was also the unknown factor of Washington's forces farther north. With a sigh of reluctance, he pushed these daydreams aside. He would pull back along the coast to Savannah with Commodore Parker's ships assisting him. He must be satisfied with having forced Lincoln to dash back to Charleston in a panic. Besides, he was too old for this sort of thing, as he had candidly told the authorities in London.

Meanwhile he got the troops to John's Island, less than ten miles from Charleston, and from there pulled back farther to Port Royal. On the sixteenth day of June, hearing of "commotions" round Purysburg, he sent his brother Mark into Georgia to pacify the area. That force included the grenadiers of the Florida brigade. The rest of his force, including twelve companies of the Royal Americans, made Port Royal on the seventeenth, reaching Stono Ferry the next day. There he left the eight-hundred-man rear guard in the hands of Lietenant Colonel the Hon. John Maitland, who had assumed command of the 1st Battalion, 71st Highlanders from Major Macpherson. His battalion was well aware he bore the title "the Honourable" because he was the son of the Earl of Lauderdale.

The Stono Ferry troops were the rear guard of Prevost's army and were subjected to sporadic musket fire daily, mainly directed at their sentinels. At seven o'clock the morning of the twentieth, similar popping alerted sentinels and Maitland sensed an attack was coming. In fact, Lincoln had decided personally to conduct an assault by twelve hundred men. The assault was badly planned and cost Lincoln over three hundred casualties including a hundred and fifty-five missing, most of whom deserted to Prevost. Prevost's loss was about a hundred and thirty. The British pursued for about two miles before giving up the chase.

On June the twenty-third, Maitland withdrew to John's Island without interference. Using ships under Captain Elphinstone of the navy, they finally arrived at Beaufort on the eighth after negotiating shoals and strong currents.

The general left the force on that day and reached Savannah on the twelfth while Maitland dug in over the next two days. Prevost hoped fervently that the summer would not see active campaigning. In a letter to Sir Henry Clinton in New York, he foresaw extreme difficulties with everyone in his command falling victim to the unhealthy climate by the end of August. In particular, the camp at Ebenezer returned two-thirds of its soldiers sick in each weekly return in spite of exemptions from arduous duties. The temperature had once reached 108 degrees. Thankfully, he had reason to believe that the enemy was as sick of campaigning in summer as were the King's troops.

James knew that despite grenadiers being more apt to complete full numbers than other troops, the 60th's grenadiers were short of officers – only three besides himself instead of the nine allotted. "How do we keep effective control with so few officers?" James asked Captain John Muller, acting commander of his company. As he had known Muller since their time together in St Vincent almost five years before and James's respect for the German-American had blossomed during their duty at St Augustine, where Muller's fluent German had helped win the confidence of many of the recruits being trained by him, James could approach him with an ease he felt for few of his superiors. Muller had an innate awareness of life's difficulties for men a long way from home, immersed in a culture not imbibed with their mother's milk. Yet, for all his sympathy with them, his basic loyalties were with the King, the regiment and British North

America, in that order. He was a professional officer with the common touch.

"Yes, James, we are short but we have almost our full establishment of serjeants and corporals. We can rely on them. And they're good! The kind of fighting we're involved in is very risky. Very little parade ground action. So we encourage them, get them to depend on their judgment. That's risky. But there's no intelligent initiative without risk. We need them to take risks, so we have to take risks too."

James always remembered two things about John Muller: he believed in taking risks and trusting his NCOs. Muller came from the wilds of Pennsylvania and he kept a copy of Tacitus, in latin, by his cot.

The grenadiers who left John's Island for Purysburg four days before Lincoln's had not thereby escaped fighting. On the twentieth they engaged in a nasty little action against backcountrymen who took advantage of Prevost's absence from the province. About fifty men were detailed to watch the fords across the Ogeechee swamps. They were therefore not in contact with the main friendly forces. James was in the detachment at the river.

He turned to his companion, Serjeant Smith: "I don't like this one bit, Smith, not one bit. Our people are under cover but where is the captain?"

"Before I joined you, Captain, he told me he was going to cross the river," replied the serjeant who was, as he had often proved, a good soldier and knew something of what a wise soldier does and does not do. "He has gone ahead, almost on his own, not knowing what's in front. It's not right, sir, not at all."

The crows on the far side of the Savannah had been screeching in their usual ugly fashion for at least two minutes. "Listen to those damned birds. That must be a sound campaigners on this continent will remember – those bloody birds."

As if the noise of the birds were an evil omen, their crowing suddenly intensified as a fusilade of shots across the water erupted, where he could not see. James could bear it no longer. He called to his men near at hand: "Quick, across the ford in two columns, one on each side of the trail. If the rebels are there, I want them flushed out." The company rose from concealment and dashed helter-skelter across the ford, splashing noisily. As they worked their way into the woods on either side of the path, a number of men were flushed like grouse and rushed away farther into the wilderness. They had been lying in ambush and their dirtywork done, they scattered to safety by undisguised flight. On the narrow path leading away from the river lay a body. It was discovered to be Captain Muller, killed by the murderous fire with five of his men. James and the serjeant examined the bodies which had been hit several times by musketry.

"Back to the other bank!" called out James as they picked up the bodies and wended their sad way back. "I feel sick. Why did he do it? So reckless, such a fine officer." J.F.K. Muller took care of his men like a nurse her children, so much so that two of them at least had tears on their faces. James wondered if his own death would be similar – a needless mistake in some God-forsaken unhealthy corner of a troubled empire.

On the South Carolina side of the river they buried Muller and his five companions. Then they stood for a moment in silence, their mitred grenadier caps off, some doubtless praying for the repose of the souls of their comrades. General Prevost learned of Muller's death while he was at Beaufort almost three weeks later. He too grieved, in silence. Benjamin Wickham, a close friend of the slain officer, though from the English home counties, assumed command at a place which most Americans, and few in the home counties, had ever heard of.

Chapter 21

Peter Cartwright felt he had come a long way since his Jacobite hatred had been unleashed in the increasingly violent and desparate setting of the war in America. In England, where he'd gone at the suggestion of Mr Green of Jamaica, he found a niche in the small group of undercover agents seeking to discover and disrupt government plans to raise more troops to fight the rebels. He was painfully aware he had not been a success.

That Scottish escapade, in which that infernal Ricketts pair thwarted him, stuck ever in his craw. In thinking let them beware if our paths ever cross again, he was secretly determined to see they would cross, if possible.

With the war shifting to the southern provinces, his coterie of agents decided he could best serve in that theatre. Besides, they felt uncomfortable in the face of his venom. Also, with the increasing importance of the French playing a role, it made sense to have someone there who was fluent in their language. Unencumbering himself of a reluctant and increasingly useless colleague, Healy – he'd shown how inept he was in the fiasco at the War Office – he made haste to cross the Atlantic on a French ship.

Once arrived, he operated in Savannah. When that city fell to Colonel Campbell – "the Hanoverian enemy" in his eyes – at the end of December 1778, he remained hidden in the city, arranging espionage as best he could. In particular, he took pride in pressing into service a belle dame of Savannah, rendered vulnerable to a sort of blackmail through the indiscretions of her brother, an officer of Washington's army. Cartwright's spirits were lifted not only by the prospect of, for once, successful spying but also by the thought of revenge on the accursed James Ricketts, whom he knew was in the force assigned to garrison the city. He had taken the trouble to keep track of James's movements. By the time James arrived, Cartwright had been set up for over six months.

August was hot and steamy. It all started with languorous inactivity. A lull had settled over the campaign. The tedium of garrison life in Savannah was, for officers, alleviated by parties to which they repaired as to oases in a desert. At one dinner party, a particularly elegant affair for which guests donned the nearest approach to full dress they could conjure up, James found himself seated next to a dark-eyed beauty, Mrs Bainbridge.

She did not speak in the witless way southern belles sometimes took on to intrigue gentlemen with their helplessness. She exuded self-assurance. She confidently assumed everyone would take her to be what she had no need to claim: a loyal subject and a member of Savannah society content to patronize her defenders for their amusement.

James wondered if she descended from cavaliers who ran from Cromwell to settle in the Carolinas. On the other hand, she might have come from convicts transported to the province. The way she lowered her large eyes and lifted them again to delve longingly into her dinner partner's eyes, either descent was plausible. Cavalier or convict, James saw her as a danger whose good regard was yet desirable. Her eyes moved in such a way as to hint at availability and spoke of the possibility of pleasurable indiscretions.

He was startled by the readiness with which he responded – she was powerfully alluring and disconcerting. He realized his danger because she seemed able to anaesthetize him against caring about that danger. She allowed him no time to organize a defence, to think, pause and reflect as she moved rapidly from one arresting innuendo to another. He felt a thrill at just watching her artfulness, like a cat convincing a mouse that it was about to become a cherished playmate.

Her power lay partly in her directness. "Tomorrow evening I dine at home. Will you favour me with your company, Captain? Allow us the chance to become more...intimately acquainted" she explained, more a statement than a question. She smiled softly and raised her ruby-red glass to him.

"You're most kind, ma'am; I'm truly flattered," James replied, his interest in her thoroughly aroused - more than he would have admitted, if he had had the mental space to consider his reaction and its propriety. In a trice, it was arranged that he would return tomorrow evening for a light refreshment with her and, it was hinted, another couple. She did mention another couple, didn't she? – later on he wasn't sure if she had.

After the party broke up, he looked in at the officers' mess. He fell into conversation with Muller's successor Captain Wickham who was also at the dinner party. "Come and have a brandy with me, James," invited Wickham.

"By all means, Captain," wondering if there was a particular reason or whether it was simply in line with a company commander's duty to know his men. They had seen each other about but had previously exchanged words in a rather perfunctory way. They chatted easily about this and that until Wickham broached the topic which was on his mind.

"I don't want to be thought unreasonably intrusive, if I mention a certain matter, James. Hear me out and perhaps you will be glad of it. I could not help but notice that you got on like a house afire with that engaging Mrs Bainbridge."

"Indeed she is, as you say, a most agreeable dinner partner and, more than that, I should think something of a *femme fatale*," James observed, wondering what was coming next.

"Yes, she certainly is that!" agreed Wickham, searching out his words with care. "But there is something else - something you ought to know. They say forewarned is forearmed."

"That does sound intriguing, sir. What is it, I wonder?" James asked.

"Your reply leads me to feel you view her with the distanced detachment of a true man of the world, James. I do not know you well enough to know whether that is really your character, or not. I hope in one way, it is. In another way, I should like you the more if it is not. What I'm saying, and saying badly, is this - Glasier, you know, is an American, like you. He knows a bit about her and says she is a widow – or at least that's what she manages to convey. She never actually says it in so many words. More to the point, Glasier says she has a brother. They used to be acquainted but he is now an officer in the rebel army."

"I can imagine she might well not mention that. She certainly never hinted it to me."

"No, I'm sure she did not," replied Wickham. "The fact is, she has arranged several *tête-à-têtes* with officers before you met her. No harm in that to be sure – whatever her brother's views - she clearly has a mind of her own. However - and what I tell you may seem odd. In two such instances, she complained to their commanding officers the following day about their behaviour. It was as if she wanted to undermine confidence in them."

"How do you mean? Had they made advances of which she complained?" asked James, puzzled.

"No. It's not so simple as that. She wasn't complaining about that, so much. She implied, rather worse from our point of view, that they talked too much. They gabbled in fact, freely, of military matters. They bragged. They disclosed information she felt she had no right to hear, nor they any right to divulge."

"How very puzzling!"

"Oh, I grant you that. But when these officers were summoned to give account, they both separately said that she pursued them. Each in his own words said that she came on vigorously – I think that was one of the terms used – and when each officer reached a critical point, if you take my meaning, she played the frightened flirt. She cooled off in no time and they were, not to put too fine a point on it, dismissed with a flea in the ear. It makes one think, does it not?" concluded Wickham, hoping it would in the case of Captain-Lieutenant Ricketts.

"Indeed, that sounds like a true flirt, through-and-through. More than that, in trying to damage the officers' reputation, having led them on, she sounds a proper bitch. But there must be a motive for it unless, of course, she simply hates our people - or is mad."

"In no way do I think her mad. In my view, and I am one with Glasier on this, the officers involved were both inexperienced - guileless, in fact - naïve, and could well have spilled a few beans in addition to hoping to spill their seed. It was as if the moment they did the former, they were forestalled from doing the latter. It sounds as if she turned cool when they began to spill information – if, that is, they did give her information. Once they started to talk unwisely, she ceased to be interested amorously. Why should she tell us about it, though? If she is a spy, that seems the last thing she'd do, unless she's sacrificing lesser fish in hopes of catching bigger prizes by impressing us with how worthy of our confidence she really is – just to mix metaphors."

He continued: "We will, naturally, watch her to see if she does make contact with the enemy but, whether she does or no, none of this seems quite that straightforward. Caution must be the word in any case, don't you agree? To be blunt, James, I should hate to see you embarrassed by her."

"What can I do? Write a letter calling off the meeting on some pretext?" He was alarmed when he realized he hoped the answer to that would be No.

"Perhaps you could play a more useful part than that. If you simply back out, she may have at you again and nobody will be any the wiser. Instead, why not play up to the courtesan element in her, and only later shock her with a bit of false intelligence? You might pass on some startling but erroneous news – such important news that, *if* she is unreliable, she would insist on conveying. If she is engaged in mischief of that sort," said Wickham rather incoherently, trying to do justice to the complexities of the matter.

"You want me to be an *agent provocateur*?"

"I suppose you could put it that way. Of course, it must be done with the full connivance of the colonel. That way you'll be covered. It could just clarify the truth."

He turned to the question of how to do it. "What in heaven's name could I tell her?"

"Let's see – you could tell her that General Prevost is so ill that his brother is going to take over. As a matter of fact, he has been confined to his house for a week – he would be apprised of the scheme, of course. And you could lay it on even thicker: you could say that in the middle of next month, all available troops are to go by ship to Charleston for a surprise attack. That would be something worth passing on."

"This is all very unsavoury, I declare," James could not help himself moaning. He was interested in Mrs Bainbridge sufficiently to hope she was not complicitous, but he knew his duty, especially, he mused, when it slaps me in the face.

"Unsavoury, I agree. It is. But if our suspicions are right, she plays no innocent game, James. If we are right, she would scarcely hesitate sending thousands of our men to disaster. And, if our suspicions are wrong, she will do nothing – apart from thinking you are mad and she had best avoid you like the plague."

"All right, I agree," said James, reluctantly.

The next evening at the appointed time, he pulled the doorbell and was escorted into a drawing room, where he was joined shortly by his hostess. In her late twenties, her charms were ripe. She was dressed to manifest them for his appreciation. Nor was there was any sign of another guest, an omission she did not deign to explain. He felt that she knew he was as pleased as she, that such was the situation.

At the 'light meal' of ham and salad, wine flowed into his large glass. She topped it up whenever it seemed the least bit down and James was cautious to empty it partially into a vase when she was absent to fetch and carry food. There was no servant to oversee the two.

After dinner, they betook themselves to a divan where she sat so close it almost required care not to acknowledge her scent by coughing. Her hand closed on his and her eyes caressed him. "Tell me about yourself, dear James. Do you see yourself mouldering in this provincial town? Or do you see yourself playing some gallant, courageous role." A slight pause ensued – not enough to allow him to reply. "I suspect the latter. I knew the first moment I saw you that you could do great things."

She must think me truly under the table, James thought. She placed her cheek softly against his, moving his hand to a place moist and warm, hypnotizing him by her audacity. Somehow, he managed to ease himself into his planned boastful discourse, gradually opening out into the secrets he had prepared for betrayal. The more lucid his description of the general's impotence, in love as in military affairs, the more intense her interest in his words. She did not seem to be cooled off towards him by his indiscretions. The more he indulged himself in flights of boastful imagination over his part in forthcoming breathtaking subterfuges, the more credulous and appreciative became her open admiration of him. Yet he could not rid himself of the feeling that the question of who was playing the fool was still open.

"Tell me, dear James, what great deed would you perform, in your heart of hearts, if you could do anything you want to – anything?" she put to him as she looked into his eyes and pressed his hand to her bosom.

"I know not quite how to answer. Do you mean – how shall I put it – what would I do to you, had I *carte blanche* on a field of - linen?

Or do you mean what deed would I accomplish as a soldier, on a field of battle?"

"Oh, you bold one. You take my breath away - I'm dazzled, truly." Even with his senses a mite dulled by alcohol, it sounded to him like a kitchen drama. She pressed herself tightly against his loins and what she detected there caused her to smile in mock-triumph as she moved her head in front of his, where she could look into his eyes, saying: "Even at the peak of your yearning – yes, I can feel you yearning" she confided in a whisper as if they shared a secret.

"But even though your yearning presses me hard, I can see your brain ticks away, measuring logical options precisely. How can you be so – integrated? Each part of you alive in its own way. I think that's why you excite me so." She caressed his nose with hers but kept her lips an inch from his. "Tell me first your deed of *military* derring-do and then we'll – expose - the other."

James was just enough in command of himself to realize the opportunity was at hand to slip in that nonsense about a ship-borne expedition against Charleston. He hoped he managed it convincingly. He had no way of guessing whether he had jumped that hurdle satisfactorily, and if he had, whether he would be dismissed like his predecessors, suffering excruciating indignity.

Her next words gave him an answer: "I'll tell you some time what I think of *that* act of daring. Now, dearest James, show me that act of daring on the other field you mentioned."

Two hours later, her taut body had ceased its urgent movements and moaning and she gave way to sleep. Breathing deeply and unself-consciously beneath his chin, her whole bearing showed he had played his part to the bitter end - if that was the word for it. His daring had received its reward. He quietly dressed and took his leave. He had come as intimately close to her as possible yet her motives remained a mystery.

There remained a price to pay for his conquest: as anyone who knew him well could have told him, his conscience would not let him alone. A saloon-theatre refrain occurred to him: "the things I do for England". But the attempt to shield himself from himself with the objectivity of humorous detachment, did not lure him into a feeling of comfort. Inevitably he thought of Sarah. He wondered about her reaction – if she were told. He also knew he neither hated nor despised Daphne Bainbridge. He was deeply unsettled.

A week passed. If anything, the mystery of Mrs Bainbridge deepened. Wickham and Glasier revealed that she had passed no news at all to the enemy, as far as they could tell. Nor had she complained of his behaviour to anyone. James reluctantly voiced the conclusion: "As far as she goes, we are no for'arder. Not for want of trying, I can tell you." His companions looked at him thoughtfully, wondering how James really felt about it.

"Would you think me mad if I say I'd like to come clean with her? I mean, tell her there are suspicions about her? If I talk to her straight, we might learn something," added James.

"I can't see any harm in it – we are getting nowhere at present" answered Glasier. Wickham agreed. The next morning James wrote her a letter, signed with his initials only. It said plainly "I must see you." Her reply came forthwith by hand: "This afternoon at five."

At five o'clock precisely, she opened her front door to him. She was dressed comparatively primly in a flowered frock closed at the neck. It did not lessen her loveliness. Indeed, the domesticity, the ordinariness of her attire was more threatening to his composure than if she were dressed for a sultan's harem – it turned his mind to what she must be like, on a day-to-day basis, in unspectacular settings. She seemed to be completely plausible, even utterly believable in a role he had not been privy to beforehand. That touched him and he knew she was more of a danger to him that way, than as a siren. In this case, her Martha meant more to him than her Bathsheba.

She might be the housewife but she could never look plain. The painful part was that her beauty had lost all theatricality. That touched him. She closed the door, smiled at him, and put her cheek against his briefly, holding his hands.

"Mrs – er, really! I can't go on calling you that" he admiited ruefully.

"Daphne" she obliged.

"Daphne. We must talk."

"Yes. Let's do, by all means," she agreed but looked apprehensive.

"First of all, hear me out, to the very end, I beg you. This is not going to be easy for me."

"Say on, James. I promise, I'll be very patient. But first, let's sit."

"Daphne, when I came to you last week, I had been warned that you might either try to get information for the enemy, or that you might entice officers into behaviour which you could then use to embarrass them. That did not prove to be the case, but that is what I was told."

Daphne lifted her hand to her face in a gesture which she converted to pushing stray hair out of the way.

"Let me continue; there is more. When I told you of military plans, you did not pass them on. And when I made love to you, you took no advantage of that either. So I am puzzled. You accused me of using logic when it seemed unusual. I cannot help that, I suppose. What I mean is: I thought *about* you while I made love *to* you – both at the same time. Logically – there it is again," as he noticed her wistful look, "logically, I cannot see why you gave yourself to me but made no use of the things I told you."

She took a long moment to reply, composing herself. "You ask, dear James, why I give myself to you without using you?" Her use of the present tense did not pass him by and it touched him. Before he could reply, she put her finger to his lips. "We are both quick to see things, are we not? One reason I feel as I do. First, I must ask *you* something. Why are you telling me all this? Is it because you are under orders to satisfy your superiors? Or is it, rather, because *you* want to know my motives, for your own reasons?"

James took a moment. She did not rush him. "Daphne, what my superiors want to know amounts to two things: do you pass on information and why you tried to injure two officers' reputations. They are relieved about one thing: you did not use what I told you. The truth is, they admire you and would be delighted if you were in the clear. On the other hand, they still don't know why you accused two officers."

James went on: "So much for them. Now me. For my part, I hope you don't pass information because I care what happens to you. Such a thing could ruin you, as you must know. And I have to say I am puzzled by the two young officers - why reject them but accept me?"

He continued: "But, I cannot ask you to be candid without being so myself. You ask why *I* want to know. It's certainly not just because I'm an officer. The truth is, I'm in love with you. I find you – how can I put it? Exciting, lovely, tender – I confess it - irresistible. Even though I am married and I love my wife and I don't want to ruin my marriage, even so - I want you. Can you believe that? And if you believe it, can you possibly respect me for saying it?"

She intervened. "You ask why I didn't use your information, and why I cooled off the two young officers? Have you heard of Occam's razor? The doctrine that of various explanations, the simplest is to be preferred?"

She looked into his eyes long and searchingly. Her eyes were not being used to charm or excite; on the contrary they were being used to understand and, above all, to speak of affectionate acceptance. "Yes, of course I believe you. And I respect you too. You cannot turn affection, love, on and off like some tap, to suit convenience or even appropriateness. At least, I cannot, and I don't think you can either, my sweet. Now, I have things to tell you. Occam's razor. Yes. The simple explanation is that I turned the officers off because I did not want to hear their secrets. And I did not betray you because I love you. But I have to tell you more. The "more" does not contradict what I have said, but it goes farther. Can you listen patiently, too?"

Daphne Bainbridge told a story the like of which James had not heard. It was, for all that, believable. Her brother in the rebel army in Virginia, had committed a serious indiscretion – exactly what it was, was neither here nor there, she explained - but he was being blackmailed. Or rather, she was being blackmailed to keep him from disgrace or worse. To save his reputation, she was being pressed to discover secrets from British officers. She did not want to spy on anyone. She did not care which side won the war – her friendships in the last few months had given the lie to the cruder sort of propaganda and she did not accept the freedom-versus-tyranny hypothesis.

About ten years ago she married a man who mistreated her and from whom she ran off after a year. There had been no contact since then and she did not believe he really cared any more; she thought he was also with the rebels somewhere up north, but didn't know or care.

The blackmailer would not leave her alone. If she did not produce something useful, her brother would be hurt. As for undermining the two young officers – she knew that they were susceptible to her and would volunteer information she did not want to hear. "What could I do? I was desperate. The only thing I could do was to turn them away in such a way that others would not follow their course. Perhaps it was foolish. It may have created more problems than it solved. I don't know. I hope not." She paused, looking him full in the face, saying: "Oh James, James, I knew from the first I would tell you these things. Has it made you wary of me, or even hate me?"

Assured by him, she went on: "I was fully as indiscreet as you, and I don't regret it one bit. I could never complain about you. There was nothing to complain about, my sweet. Women are not the only vain creatures in this world.

"You would like to think your influence has brought me to throw off my spying duplicity, wouldn't you? That I kept sensitive information to myself and protected your reputation because of my love.

"Dear James: honestly! Besides not wanting to play the spy, there was another reason I could not pass on what you told me. All that military misinformation you poured out to me. I did not believe a word of it. It was too transparent. I did not know why you were telling me such things, until now, that is."

James was in a pickle. Her words had just re-opened the possibility of her continuing to be a spy. If she did not pass on what she learned *because she knew it to be false*, her path as a spy was still open. Why, though, had she told him that?

She was quick to help him. "James, had I believed your stories, I would still not have passed them on. You have, of course, no way of knowing that for certain. But just imagine: if that is not the truth, why do I confide in you? Tell me that!" she finished in a whisper.

"Daphne, my brain and my heart are confused."

"So, my sweet, you see: your brain and your heart are inseparable after all. Yes, you see, I trust you, even if you did pass me a bag of tripe about army affairs. More than that - I love you, don't you see? You see so much – can you fail to see that?" She paused and saw him look – beleaguered, was it? "Don't feel embarrassed by it or see it as a trap or a threat – but the truth is: I *am* in love with you."

James folded her in his arms and, as she knew it would, his mind raced. Had he used her, carnally, simply to gratify his lust and pamper his self-esteem? He was not guilty of that, because he not only wanted her but he cared for her future and her wellbeing. And he had the hideous added spur of being under orders. He was in love with her - enough to see that Daphne would not suffer from any action of his. Also, he wanted to do anything he could to help her in the predicament caused by her brother, and the enemy. He was determined to help her.

"Tell me, who is your blackmailer? Let me do something about him?"

"You'd have to be even more wonderful than you are, my darling, to do that. He is English or perhaps Scottish, a Whig who wants to do the Tories down. He is obsessed by the monarchy being Hanoverian. Doing them down is his richest motive, not American independence."

"What is his name, Daphne? Tell me his name."

"Cartwright. Peter Cartwright" she breathed, barely audible, with a sudden flush of hatred.

In the officers' mess the next evening, James again joined Wickham and Glasier. With permission from Daphne, James told them what he had learned. He also told them what he knew of Cartwright and the story of their run-ins. He could not instantly tell if they were sympathetic, or annoyed by all the complication. They seemed cross.

However, he discovered that what they resented was Cartwright, especially as he was not an American and in their eyes had no business to be meddling. They also saw that by protecting Mrs Bainbridge, they might further the King's cause by overturning Cartwright and his ilk.

"Of course, all this sort of thing is really the province of the Adjutant General and his people. I can have a word with him. He may feel it's useful to feed her certain information to pass on, just to keep her credible to them. He might even suggest we could arrest her to make her safe, if that is called for in the future. Perhaps you could keep her informed, James? For better or worse, you and this wretch Cartwright seem to be yoked together; perhaps you are destined to be his undoing?"

James's thoughts turned to Daphne. He had the uncomfortable feeling that he still needed to show her he had not simply used her.

Giving way to his wanting of her, joining with her body, did not fulfil the requirements of love. Perhaps in freeing her of Cartwright, he would act in a purer, less selfish, manner. That intention became firmly lodged in his mind. "If I can down Cartwright, I will certainly do so," he concluded, surprising them by his angry tone.

Other bits of regimental gossip drifted into the three officers' conversation. A major item of bad news was that St Vincent, with many from the battalion, had been taken by the French in June. By the end of next January all the officers and men were expected to be at Antigua, awaiting exchange with French prisoners on parole. With the French committed to the war, and the Spanish, the world, like his private affairs, was becoming ever more complex, and unsatisfactory.

Chapter 22

Between July and September 1779, James had less and less time for pursuits of his own. For just over a year, the French had been allies of the rebels and it was beginning to make a difference. Savannah was now threatened by attack and all efforts were being directed under General Prevost to prepare a defence.

Prevost with his engineer, a New Jersey man named Moncrieff, decided on plans to fortify Savannah. They erected fortifications swinging in an arc a mile-and-a-half southwards from the docks, outside the town. On the west, in front of the Yamacraw Swamp, were to be guns manned by sailors backed up by the frigate *Germain* in the harbour. The other end of the arc was to be in front of Wright's Plantation to the east. Redoubts were built along the arc. One of these was at Spring Hill at the Ebenezer road junction and at first was manned by provincials. Later, the 60th's three grenadier companies, including James, replaced them, with a contingent of marines helping.

"That seems just the place an enemy would want to come up," mused Prevost. "It is a broad bit of flatland over which regular troops would choose to act."

"Then, sir, we'll need to cover the two furlongs between the sailors' battery and Spring Hill, say two redoubts and another battery."

"That will take up most of my artillery," observed Prevost sardonically. "I have no more than ten heavy pieces in all."

At the end of their planning conference, the general referred to the arrival of the governor, returning after his initial flight two years earlier: "Sir James Wright arrived from England on Tuesday. I must summon a council of war, to include the governor, 'ere we are committed to such a plan."

In two days the governor had made his weight felt. Among high-ranking officers in Savannah, two schools of thought emerged: one in favour of defending Savannah, the other favouring an extended foray into the backcountry to arm loyal subjects. Sir James cast the deciding vote.

"Gentlemen, there are four reasons why I vote the way I do. First, we cannot abandon the many loyalists in this town to who knows what retribution. Secondly, if we give up Savannah, few people will risk joining us openly. Thirdly, to go galloping off on a jaunt into the backcountry, far from the navy, is to encourage defeat – Burgoyne taught us that. Fourthly, we do not know what the French are doing. D'Estaing may come our way and cut us off in the interior. We should be in a pitiable plight. I vote: we stay and fight." The die was cast.

Another conference important to the fate of Savannah took place just after the arrival of the French. Major General Benjamin Lincoln, commanding in Charleston, Colonel Lachmer McIntosh, uncle of the McIntosh who had been at Sunbury, Brigadier General William Moultrie, Lieutenant Colonel John Laurens, Brigadier General Isaac Huger and Colonel Francis Marion met at noon prior to their meeting the French admiral who, having landed his brigade at Beaulieu south of Savannah, was planning for the assault.

These six rebels knew each other well. None of them except Lincoln knew the tall, dark and gaunt stranger in civilian clothes who was introduced by General Lincoln. The civilian was newly arrived from London and, the way Lincoln talked of him, must be a rare one – a successful undercover agent. And an English gentleman, from the sound of his voice. They noted a certain arrogance. He did not demur at any of the extravagant attributes Lincoln attached to him. His name, Lincoln announced, as if they ought to have heard it before, was Cartwright.

When Lincoln disclosed that Cartwright would be invaluable since he had an agent behind enemy lines inside the city, curiosity was aroused, to be dampened by Cartwright's words: "Let me amend that, General. I *had* an agent but after I got in touch with, er...him" changing the gender of the spy, thinking it would go down better, "as I say, after getting in touch to alert him to his moment of destiny, he was seized by the British. Why, I am not sure. We are always vulnerable to the wiles of our enemies. 'The wicked deviseth mischief upon his bed'," he interjected – somewhat irrelevantly, they felt. "He is locked up where I cannot reach him. He did manage, however, to get a message out to me, just before being apprehended, saying that the British defences at Spring Hill were very weak despite the carefully-engineered attempt to make them look otherwise.

"Further than that, I have no information. It would be useful, though, if you could let me be a fly on the wall at your forthcoming conference with the French, for my own edification if not for your's."

"Well, gentlemen, I think we'd better concert ourselves before we talk to the French. So far, they've not been much help."

"That's putting it mildly," said Laurens.

Lincoln continued: "I have to agree with you there. Their fleet left Toulon in April last year but was so slow – eighty-four days, was it? – that they missed bottling up the enemy fleet in Chesapeake Bay. Then they let down General Washington in his hopes of taking New York. Then they smeared their reputation by letting us down at Newport. As if that wasn't bad enough, they put forward a fatuous and irrelevant plan for attacking Nova Scotia and Newfoundland and when that – thank the Lord – was dropped, they weighed anchor for the Caribbean, leaving us in the lurch."

Moultrie had noticed Cartwright's habit of quoting from the psalms and was not to be outdone: "Like the daughters of Zion 'they walk with stretched-forth necks and wanton eyes, walking and mincing as they go,' – Isaiah three," he said, glaring at the spy.

Laurens added: "Their Admiral d'Estaing said he'd return last May but he didn't. Now, finally, he's here."

"Well anyway, they've now come ashore with a brigade under a sort of Irishman in their service," said Lincoln, referring to the *Brigade Dillon*, then fourteen miles south of Savannah.

"I was curious to note," said Moultrie, "that one of his four regiments is the *Royal Roussillon* which surrendered at Quebec twenty years ago – I wonder what d'Estaing thinks of that?" The others chuckled.

By the way, how many of you can speak French?" Lincoln asked. McIntosh, with Scottish reverence for learning behind him and easy familiarity with Georgia society – he was reckoned the handsomest man in the province – put up his hand confidently. Moultrie, Laurens and Huger also followed suit, less confidently.

Marion, whom the others thought illiterate, shook his head: "Not a word of the Frenchie tongue do I speak, Benjamin," thereby indicating at one stroke that he was uneducated but was still completely comfortable in the society of generals, anyway. They would discover that, uneducated he might be, but they had a genius at guerrilla warfare on their hands. Lincoln, wishing no embarrassment among his staff, added: "My French is pretty schoolboy-like; I doubt if I can follow what they say."

Marion interjected: "Have you heard the frog...er, French sent Prevost a surrender demand?"

"What, all on their own?" exclaimed McIntosh.

"I fear so," admitted Lincoln.

"And what's that I hear about them telling our boys to stay clear of their camp – that they ain't real soldiers and must stay out of the way?" added Huger.

Lincoln's brow clouded. "I fear we'll have to put up with more of their arrogance for the sake of this alliance, *mes amis*."

"Well, if we can get them varmints to attack right away, it might just be worth it, Monseers," said Marion archly.

Lincoln added: "I agree with you, *messieurs*, and he must be pressed to do so. Perhaps, Lachmer, you could make a point of it? Till this afternoon then." They took their leave.

At three, they entered a grandiose, spanking-clean white tent, more like a marquee in their eyes. White-coated sentries stood outside and presented arms as they entered. They found a cloth-covered table behind which sat Charles Hector Théodat, *Comte d'Estaing, Amiral-général* of His Most Christian Majesty's service, fifty years old, looking more like a soldier than a seaman. Beside him were two aides, *Capitaine de vaisseau* Armand Duprés and *Lieutenant* Gargnier-Croisé; all rose on the entrance of the Americans. *"Messieurs, je vous prie de m'accorder l'honneur de vous présenter mes aides-de-camp..."* d'Estaing said, naming them.

The Americans stumbled a bit over acknowledging these aides-de-camp, Marion even reproducing his solecism *Monseer* to the hidden embarrassment of his colleagues. Cartwright, who had been viewed askance since he entered the tent – they knew not who he was nor why a civilian should be there anyway – by contrast, bowed deeply. His colleagues had not done that and some felt a degree of distaste over such exotic extravagance. He added to the rebels' discomposure by saying, in rapid French: *Enchanté, messieurs, de faire votre connaissance. J'étais donné le grand plaisir de comprendre le grandeur fin des forces armées de Sa Plus Chrétienne Majesté il y a plusieurs années quand je voyage en votre bel pays. Enchanté, absolument enchanté.*" ("Delighted, gentlemen, to make your acquaintance. I was given the great pleasure of understanding the artful grandeur of His Most Christian Majesty's armed forces several years ago upon travelling in your beautiful country. Delighted, absolutely delighted.")

To give him his due, d'Estaing sized him up for a vain fellow and immediately switched to impeccable English – better English than most of his American allies, in fact, though he noted that Laurens, the diplomat's son, having been educated in England, was better at it.

After a few well-meant remarks by the Americans, the admiral looked at Huger, saying: "Do I perceive from your name, General, that you are of French blood?"

Huger smiled. "Well, sir, my name, which in this country is pronounced 'YOU-gee' is from Huguenot stock."

"Yes, I see," said d'Estaing drawling his inquiry to an end. A practising catholic, he had no wish to explore heretical origins further.

Laurens then began to urge d'Estaing on the need for an immediate attack, beating McIntosh to the punch.

"But, alas, Colonel, I'm afraid that is out of the question. My compatriots have been fighting the English for a long time – much longer than you have, I dare say – and we would not dream of an assault without regular approaches, parallel lines and all the apparatus so familiar to professional engineers...and soldiers." At that *mot juste* his aides nodded like approving schoolmasters confirming the head's pronouncement. Further discussion was useless, clearly.

One of the American officers lifted his eyebrows.

Cartwright was moved to utter: "'Yea, the Lord our God shall cut them off'."

The admiral thought to himself, *mon dieu*, what have we here? An Huguenot, and an Anglo-saxon Jansenist!"

The Americans had the impression they were dealing with a man of culture and mediocrity. They noted that, whatever his limitations, he harboured a hatred of England at odds with his urbanity. It was a loathing exceeding anything that they ever felt. It embarrassed them.

D'Estaing went on to say that on the twenty-third, he would begin digging parallel trenches north of the French camp which, by then, would have moved to a point about two miles south of the town. He planned to open a bombardment some ten days after that. He proposed meeting on the eighth of October to agree final plans. The Americans said nothing, looked at each other, got up and left. Departing, one of them muttered "just like that, eh?"

For his part, when they had left, d'Estaing turned to his aides, reverting to French: "So untutored, so inexperienced, these colonials. And do you realize that half of the English army is made up of colonials too, who will be as naive as their enemies, our comrades-in-arms? Mind you, gentlemen, much as I despise the English bandits who stole Canada from us, I sometimes wonder what we think we are doing helping English subjects to renounce their lawful sovereign. How can we do that without encouraging the same ideas in French heads? We do well to keep this rabble out of our camp. We have to discourage any contagion."

In the British camp, Colonel Maitland provided an example of courage and resourcefulness. Ordered back from Port Royal Island on the twelfth, he extricated his eight hundred men by land just before the first of Lincoln's troops left the city toward their rendezvous with d'Estaing. Maitland had no help from the navy in the face of a sizeable French fleet, so his withdrawal had to be by land. Not only did he manage to bring out his men, avoiding all unfriendly patrols, sloshing through unhealthy swamps, but he fought the ague fits he had contracted and kept his head clear enough to guide them despite his overwhelming fever. On the sixteenth, as the rebels surrounded the town and reached out to the French, he made it into town. That was the very day d'Estaing sent his surrender demand to Prevost that the British – the English he always called them – surrender to the arms of the King of France - no mention of the Americans. Prevost, playing for time, had secured a twenty-four hour delay; his gamble worked and Maitland was home. The two battalions of Fraser's Highlanders, especially, were a large and welcome addition to the defences. They had got in just before Lincoln closed the gaps and the twenty-four hours were up. Prevost then rejected the demand for surrender.

As expected, French troops started digging approaches a week later. It seemed to Laurens and McIntosh that, for all d'Estaing's yearnings to be off, he was amazingly slow. On the third of October, the hot weather moderated. The French artillery bombardment began from the south while their ships fired across Hutchinson's Island from the sea. The cannon did damage to some of the four hundred and fifty houses but defence works were not hit. The minds of the civilians were concentrated while the works they slaved at with renewed vigour were unhurt. That was to prove a singular advantage in the days ahead.

Five days later, a council of war met at d'Estaing's bidding – 'council of war' proved a somewhat inaccurate term since it consisted largely of the rebels learning what the French had decided. A battalion of the *Brigade Dillon* would begin attacking with a feint before dawn toward the Sailors' Battery, pushing ahead if possible, whilst Huger's five hundred militia would make a second feint pushing up the southerly road into the centre of the perimeter.

The main attack would begin with three columns of French assaulting the Spring Hill redoubt. Simultaneously, two American columns would attack to the left of the French, coming in at the redoubt from the west. The latter thrust would engage Laurens's 2d South Carolina Continentals and 1st Battalion, Charleston Militia to be followed by a second echelon: 1st and 5th South Carolina Continentals under McIntosh. The foot troops were to be preceded by Pulaski's cavalry moving to the left in front of the redoubt until the first echelon breached the abatis and allowed the horsemen to exploit the breakthrough. It seemed a straight-forward enough plan but timing was vital. The council broke up.

When General Prevost and Captain Moncrieff felt that an attack was imminent, they changed the disposition of their forces. Charged with matters of intelligence, the British Adjutant General's section in Savannah had indeed managed to implant an idea in the enemy's minds that Spring Hill would be a weak point in the defensive system. At the last minute, the loyalists at the redoubt were replaced by the 60th's grenadiers, amongst whom was James.

As dawn began to break, he and his companions heard firing from their right. The musketry was accompanied by the distinctive squeak and splatter of the swivel guns the sailors had set up and which fired a mixture of nuts, bolts and anything else which was handy and lethal. The French had sent a battalion along the riverfront to make a diversionary attack which, owing to darkness and the thick fog, was at first undetected. They groped forward toward the sailors' battery, stumbling and splashing about on the wet ground and at first light were subjected to murderous fire from the entrenched tars and marines. As if that weren't bad enough, HMS *Germain* in the river became aware of the troops moving along the shore, adding their firepower. Soon the French veered off toward the south, moving away to James's right, all thought of advancing toward the town abandoned. Apart from hearing the firing from his right, James and his men had no idea what was afoot.

More noise from their left caught their attention. Again, they could only guess what was taking place. In fact, Huger's advance toward the Cruger redoubt was brought abruptly to a halt by the two de Lancey battalions and the New Jersey Volunteers. That particular bout of fighting did not last long because Huger's men were militia and militia never reckoned to make a sustained assault under heavy, effective fire. These militia were not about to start a new trend. A few found cover, most scampered off.

James had Serjeant Smith with him once again. "So, we heard a sharp action to the right which died down, then firing to our left, eh, serjeant?"

"Yes, sir. I imagine as it gets light, the fog near the river on our flanks is clearing and people can see enough to try and kill each other. It's like a nightmare, ain't it, sir? I mean who knows what is out there in our front? Thank God we had time to build up an abatis" observed Smith, referring to the sharpened poles the enemy would confront after climbing the steep earthwork behind which the grenadiers waited. Such was the place Cartwright expected to be a weak point.

The grenadiers' thoughts of what lay ahead of them were well-founded. Moving eastwards a half mile, three French columns deployed along the edge of a wood, ready to advance across five hundred yards of open ground toward the redoubt. Their assault was meant for five o'clock when American columns would be attacking from the west. But the French were late and the whole allied force of forty-five hundred began to move in one long column toward their objective. Without waiting for the troops to deploy into five columns, d'Estaing led his leading column across the open field.

The leading attack column advanced as they had been commanded, hearing the admiral's familiar voice urging them on but most of them not seeing him nor knowing for certain whence the voice came which called so confidently *vive le roi* and *boutez en avant*. Nothing lasts for ever, however, and the purgatory of blindness and disembodied sounds gave way to a hell of violent noise. The last sight many of the column saw was the horrid ditch behind which stood high the even more horrid abatis.

James and his soldiers heard the French voices to their front but, afflicted by the same blindness and inability to fix the range of sounds, could only wait for something – anything – concrete to consent to being measured by their bewildered senses. They had not long to wait. The French suddenly materialized out of the thinning fog. Each side saw the other for the first time, not more than twenty yards apart. The result was predictable. All was shouting and explosion as the French hurled themselves yelling into the ditch and up the other side, struggling to reach the malevolent forest of felled trees which blocked their way on the parapet. At the instant they began to rush into the ditch, the defenders opened fire. D'Estaing was wounded but bravely urged on his soldiers. As the first column was shattered, the remnants moved to their left, more in a daze than with any clear intention. The other French columns coming behind them had been swept by grapeshot as the gunners became alert to what was advancing against them, even if they could not see the enemy, and poured onto them fire which at least the leading column had not had to endure. The second and third columns had also to reckon with the wall of musketry and also the unnerving sight of what had befallen those in front of them, wandering about the ditch aimlessly or laid out dead on the slope to the abatis.

James was completely occupied in adding to the musketry pouring from his nearby soldiers. He could not see what was happening to his right and was too busy to care about it if he had seen it, but another chapter of the terrible drama was there unfolding. The cavalry of Pulaski's Legion had shifted to their left, as instructed, and were waitng under heavy fire for the infantry to breach the abatis. Marion's South Carolinians and the Charleston militia were met by the same sort of heavy fire as James's men had administered and were further decimated by a foe not before encountered – enfilade fire from both the redoubt to their right and the Sailors' Battery to their far left. The Carolinians nevertheless succeeded in hacking their way through the abatis, planting on the parapet a flag with a crescent in the canton, the regimental colour of the 2d South Carolina, with the fleur-de-lys flag of France next to it. They got no farther. The three officers carrying the colours, one of them Lieutenant Garnier-Croisé of the admiral's staff, went down. Another American officer re-planted the colours but he too went down. A third time the colours went up, this time put in place by an American non-commissioned officer with a well-known and courageous record, but he too went down, mortally wounded.

James, Serjeant Smith, Major Glasier, Captain Wickham and the three grenadier companies had been firing into the attacking troops. When the crescent flag dropped to the ground for the third time, Beamsley Glasier, seeing the attack was faltering like a wave at the tide's turning, seized the opportunity. "Now! Grenadiers, Now!" he screamed and the soldiers, joined by sailors and marines from the battery and redoubts on the right, charged furiously into the stymied enemy before them. James discharged one of his two pistols at a Frenchman who seemed to slide off to the left out of his vision. It felt like slow motion. With his sword he parried a bayonet thrust and struck at the enemy soldier who crumpled as the blade took him in the chest. Suddenly, the path ahead of him was choked with bodies, only the bodies were either inert in death or were calling for quarter. As the fog had lifted sporadically during the hour-long battle, other troops, being able to see more than James's men could, had joined in from left and right. The view that emerged was one of bloody chaos.

Meanwhile, Pulaski's horsemen had tried to force a way between the redoubt and the defences farther to the west. The result was a textbook one: unsuited for an assault against an unbreached abatis, they were hopelessly mauled. Pulaski, in a surge of futile gallantry, tried to rally his men but they knew their hope of survival lay in flight. Pulaski was fatally hurt and Major Horry, whose mother had made the crescent colour, took over. There was no changing the outcome as the horsemen fled to their rear.

McIntosh arrived with his column, the 1st and 5th South Carolina Regiments, but his front was swept up by the remnants of the first column of Americans who were stumbling their way into the Yamacraw Swamp where, to add to the misery, they came under fire from HMS *Germain*. There they floundered as the firing died down. When it was reported to him that no one was left standing on the parapet, McIntosh ordered his column to retreat. The magnitude of the debacle was prevented from being even more crushing by the fog which was still heavy enough in places to discourage pursuit.

James, winded, and with no one in front he could see to pursue, looked back to take in the scene of the slaughter. A tally showed later about eighty enemy dead in the ditch and a further ninety-three between the ditch and the abatis behind it. The British loss was sixteen dead and thirty-nine wounded. The French lost six hundred and fifty men, a higher percentage of their soldiers than the rebels who lost about five hundred and fifty. At ten o'clock in the morning, the enemy requested a truce.

When the dead had been buried, General Lincoln retired to Charleston to lick his wounds. He now had the dispiriting task of piecing together what had gone wrong. He conferred with the familiar officers he had talked to before the attack, less Colonel Marion who had gone to the west of Charleston. Their mutual dislike of the French allies made Lincoln's task easier at first. "Goddamn frogs. They looked down on us like some kind of offal the whole time, didn't they?" he asked of his companions, most of whom nodded in agreement. Resentment was written all over their faces, even when they didn't speak it.

Moultrie voiced what they felt: "Off to the Caribbean to avoid meeting the Royal Navy – gone in eleven days, they were."

"Then there was that insolent demand for the city's surrender to the King of France," added Laurens.

However it was Huger who presented a more balanced attitude. "Oh, I don't know about that. Look at it from their point of view – they furnished more infantry than we did and practically all the artillery, and the sappers. They suffered all but a fifth of the eight hundred casualties, too. I grant you, d'Estaing led an incompetent attack but he was damned brave for all that. No doubt it's a comfort for us to put the blame elsewhere but we made mistakes too. What about sending in poor old Pulaski to prance about in front of the entrenchments, an impossible job for cavalry, if ever there was one?"

After that post-mortem, Lincoln still had one niggling thought: the fiasco at Spring Hill. He called in Cartwright. There was some difficulty in locating him but at last he was found emerging from a brothel. "Why the mess at the Spring Hill redoubt?" the general asked the intelligence agent. "It wasn't lightly defended. It was very strongly held and very competently too. It's ironic that while we were beat by a regular regiment, it was one raised in the colonies!"

"You do realize, general," replied Cartwright, thinking a haughty tone his best protection, "that intelligence about enemy dispositions is never a sure thing. My source was quite correct about the arrangement of troops at the time the report was rendered to me. We could not help it if there was a last-minute switch."

Lincoln did not pursue it farther, but Cartwright was not so self-assured as he appeared. Why was the alteration made? Would a mere switch of troops account for the extent of the fortification? Presumably they were like that before the last moment. Am I faced with some sort of collusion between Mrs Bainbridge and the British? He did not know the answer to any of this, but he wondered, and would not let it rest.

The battle had one curious epitaph. The tune of *The British Grenadiers* had for long been a march heard round the world, the epitome of British military music. Drummers beat the well-known rhythm when the fifes became inaudible on the field of conflict. It was used, not just by grenadier companies, but by the Royal Regiment of Artillery. In the nineteenth century it was adopted for the 1st Foot Guards when they became the Grenadier Guards. The origins of the tune and the drum-beating are not known but the words, known to British and other schoolchildren over the world, and considered to be the most British of British marches, were first sung on the seventeenth of January 1780 at Covent Garden by Charles Frederick Reinhold. It is ironic that the words (attributed to Charles

Dibden) and so British in reputation, should have been composed in honour of the grenadiers of the 60th or Royal American Regiment of Foot. The good news of Savannah was published in the London Gazette on Christmas Day, 1779. A fortnight earlier a Royal Proclamation had commanded a day of fasting and humiliation. The words sung on the stage quickly became well-known:

> *Some talk of Alexander,*
> *And some of Hercules*
> *Of Hector and Lysander,*
> *And such great names as these.*
> *But of all the world's great heroes, There's none that can compare*
> *With a tow, row, row, row, row, row,*
> *To the British Grenadier.*

Chapter 23

What would be the next steps in the campaign and what part would he play in them? November provided him no answer. That month saw very little military activity. There were few dinner parties for officers to attend; the siege had done damage and social life had scarcely resumed. Governor Wright settled down and resumed many of his contacts of four years ago. One fine day, James was strolling in the town centre chatting to a few people he had come to know. He was bundled up against the cold breeze off the ocean as he walked. Rounding a corner, he came face-to-face with the one woman he yearned and dreaded to meet – one who had not attended any of the few dinner parties he had – Daphne Bainbridge.

He knew of her part in the Spring Hill affair – in fact his own life might well be owed to her. He also knew of her arrest "for her own good" and, indeed, her being wined and dined in a most comfortable fashion in the headquarters where she had been incarcerated. Released a few days after the siege, she should be quite safe at home, released as far as people knew "for lack of sufficient evidence". He also knew that, for her credibility with Cartwright, still at large, no public display of friendship could be allowed.

He was nagged by the desire to do something for her, something really good like getting her off Cartwright's hook forever. He knew that she sometimes sat at the governor's table and that his enemy would do what he could to make use of that.

"Why, I declare, Captain Ricketts, I am surprised and," she added in a whisper "I am really glad to see you."

It was frustrating, speaking words on one level for public to note but trying to communicate on another level. As if they sensed it was safer to commune wordlessly, they walked side by side, silently, with each conscious of the other's rhythmical movement. Arm in arm they walked together in concert, saying nothing at all to each other as old friends who had no need for speech. In ten minutes or so they reached her front door and paused, neither knowing what steps to take next. He could only guess – perhaps each thought their communication could find other media to use than words.

But she made no sign to invite him in. They knew many of the faces they saw around them. Some were companions in arms. They would notice if he went inside with her. Many of the people she recognized would have doubts about her and some would earnestly believe that she was a slut and traitor who evaded British justice.

The moment passed. They adjourned – what other word was there for it. James pressed her arm gently, doffed his hat and took his leave.

She knew all the reasons he and she had acted as they had. Inside her house, she covered her face with her hands, heaved a few deep breaths, and dissolved into a shuddering flood of tears.

At December's beginning, General Prevost called together his officers. The rain fell gently as they gathered in his Bay Street house. After wine was served, he addressed them: "Welcome, gentlemen. We come to one of the moments in life people call a parting of the ways. I will shortly be sailing for England. I can hardly call it home because for twenty-two years I have served in America and the Caribbean, but it is where I will retire. I really meant to go before this but my replacement was taken prisoner by the French fleet in September, and I had the unexpected privilege of being amongst you during the siege we have just endured. Nay, more than endured – you have done your duty gallantly and while I always had the highest regard for the army, the events of the last few weeks have made me aware, even more than before, of the great honour it is to live amongst, serve and command you, my friends.

"We have all been so busy here that some of you may have lost count of what is going forward in other places. For example, so many of you are Royal Americans that you will be anxious to know what is happening to the regiment elsewhere. I can tell you this. The 1st Battalion remains in Jamaica though they have a fifty-man detachment at Pensacola where are also found four companies of the 3rd Battalion, four of the 4th Battalion as well as some of the 16th Regiment – I realize full well there are 16th here, and a splendid contribution you have made. Getting back to the 60th – The French took our seven companies of the regiment under Lieutenant Colonel Etherington when they captured the island of St Vincent last June. No more popular wood-cutting there, I'm afraid (a few chuckles in the group). The companies were parolled to Antigua by way of Martinique; three of the companies arrived in August and the others are expected in Antigua shortly.

"We have some final figures from the siege which I know you will want. Two lieutenants of Fraser's were the only officers killed, along with eight men of the same regiment as well as four men of the 60th with two marines and two seamen at the Spring Hill redoubt. The provincials lost four officers killed and thirteen others while the Germans lost five men killed. In all, four officers were wounded and fifty-nine men. Four men are still missing and forty-six deserted to the enemy. That may surprise you. Of these forty-six, all but ten were from provincial corps – I don't suppose, to be realistic, that should surprise us. I yield to no one in my admiration for the splendid work of the provincials, as Colonel Campbell said, but there are unavoidably some men who can claim service with both sides.

"Now, some business. Spain, as you are all aware, has joined France against us. She will want to wrest the Floridas back from us because we took them from her sixteen years ago. We have won a signal triumph in holding Georgia, but the affair is far from finished. I am concerned now by the situation in the Floridas. It is vital to His Majesty's interests that we strengthen our position there as best we can. Already our Mississippi River posts under Lieutenant Colonel Dickson of the 16th had to surrender to General Galvez in June. Therefore, I am sending the Florida brigade back to St Augustine. The forces here will have to do without them, and I am sure they will do very well. Archibald Campbell, who is promoted to full Colonel, will assume command in this province under Sir James Wright, the governor, and Lieutenant Colonel Prevost continues as lieutenant governor."

James saw this information as a shaft of light filling a murky room. He had had his fill of shooting at fellow Americans and, besides, he did not relish being stationed in Georgia indefinitely. The summer climate was appalling. Sickness was everywhere. St Augustine would be closer to Sarah and, to tell the truth, leaving Savannah would – simplify, yes that was the very word – simplify the nagging question of Daphne Bainbridge, a woman whose look, scent and voice he could not shake off. He wondered if they would meet again – probably not.

Two days before Christmas, all of the 60th still left in Georgia were to set out under Major Glasier for St Augustine. By now, James and the other officers of the Florida brigade had come to know Beamsley Glasier better. They admired him for having filled the shoes of Mark Prevost who had left the brigade to take up the lieutenant governorship. His stock had grown enormously with his decisive, courageous action at just the right moment at the Spring Hill redoubt during the siege, and all this in his sixty-sixth year. The Massachusetts soldier's career went all the way back to Sir William Pepperrell's expedition against Louisburg. Forty men had then agreed to form a forlorn hope, a spearhead of volunteers in an attack where most of them would probably be wiped out; the forty men had agreed to volunteer but only if he would lead them. Despite disputes with other provincial officers he became a lieutenant colonel in a New York regiment and then a colonel in 1756. In March he joined the 60th as a subaltern and in the 1760s was a principal founder of the New Englanders' outpost that became the province of New Brunswick; it was the beginning of a long history of land speculation. He was a man in whom the men placed confidence.

Colonel Fuser, whose health was worn down by campaigning and heavy responsibilities under General Prevost, suffered deteriorating health and was in no state to command the trip to Florida so Glasier took charge. As Prevost's two-brigade configuration of troops was no longer needed, with the end of the siege, Captains Kelly and Barrow were able to join the journey as were Lieutenant Walker of James's battalion, four lieutenants of the 4th Battalion and three ensigns of the 3rd Battalion, bringing the total of officers to twelve to oversee 278 men. Prevost had written his superiors of his desire to reinforce St Augustine – that they were "not of that force it ought to be in case of a formidable Attack – but such as we could Spare for the present".

James remembered well the journey north just a year ago. That had not been easy despite uncommonly warm weather and the often northerly flow of currents. He joined in the tasks of the two days before embarkation: allocating men to the boats and storing luggage aboard. Major Glasier explained his reasoning to James and the other officers: "I've rounded up eleven Durham-type flatboats in the fortnight before. Each boat is sixty-five feet long with a maximum beam of eight feet. In ten boats are placed nine planks a foot deep with four feet between each, to serve as benches. The first bench is ten feet behind the bows, providing space for tents and provisions, and ten feet separates the rearmost bench from the stern where a twenty-two foot sweep or tiller is placed. The after ten-foot section of each boat has a rude cabin with a gap in the aft bulkhead kept free for the tiller. Certain items of luggage and gear will be put in the cabin because of its protective roofing."

"Is there any provision for a sail?" asked one of the subalterns who fancied he had some nautical experience.

"I gather you think the wind will be something other than our implacable foe. Well, I hope you're right," answered the major. " Just aft of midships is a placement for the thirty-foot mast which can be erected to take a triangular sail if conditions suit. Thus the first ten boats will carry twenty-seven men, three abreast. Three of the outboard men on each beam will row eight-foot oars while one more man on each side will help by using a setting pole or punt, walking the wide gunwhales. The boat captain handles the sweep. The tasks will be assigned by rota so as to distribute labour fairly, officers taking turns as well. The eleventh or luggage boat has four benches and will be rowed by four oarsmen; it also has two punters, a boat captain and a comfortable seat for Colonel Fuser. All oarsmen are to be relieved each half-hour – an awkward arrangement for the eleventh boat since each ninety minutes it has to be drawn up close to a boat in front to relieve its oarsmen. These are very hardy boats and they have to be – each boat has to carry up to four tons yet draw no more than three or four inches when moving slowly. If running swiftly with the wind – something that still remains a hope – they may draw up to a foot."

The last day of loading was unpleasant; severe cold descended and freezing rain made everything slippery. Several soldiers manhandling luggage had mild frostbite and Colonel Fuser, though ill, was not too sick to reprimand the officers in charge for letting their men work without proper looking after. One unfortunate officer to trigger his wrath was Lieutenant Lockell whom Fuser had reason to know.

"You gentlemen ought to know better," he expostulated with the eight uncomfortable subalterns whom he had called to attention in front of him, out of hearing of the men. "You, Mr Walker, you have the excuse of being newly-commissioned and I understand Captain Duffield's is your first company. But you, Mr Lockell, this is not the first time we've had words, is it?" Lockell looked as if he would gladly volunteer for an expedition to Hades – anywhere to escape the colonel's beady and rheumy eye. He'd been on the mat and threatened with court martial only two months before, for lingering at the billiard table rather than look to the needs of his men. Eventually, the subalterns thought their ordeal was over and were about to disperse but Fuser had one more arrow in his quiver.

"What provision have you made to feed your men, eh? I mean apart from the food and rum rations they'd expect, and rightly so. We could lose food overboard, or run out – has any of you thought of fishing gear, and do you know how to use it?" Most of them looked as if they'd never seen fishing gear, let alone knew its use. "Gentlemen, let this be a lesson to you. Do not sit around exchanging gossip about your conquests among the ladies of the town. Instead, use your wits, such as they may be, to think ahead – how to meet awkward circumstances before they happen and before some higher officer has to come and tell you what to do, eh, eh, eh? To your posts."

Early the morning of Thursday the twenty-third they pushed off. Normally, transports would move them south but with a French fleet to worry about, the navy would not entertain that idea of making their lives as pleasant as possible. These two hundred and fifty men might be important in His Majesty's affairs but they weren't that important. The men hoped that the wind would do a lot of their work for them but it turned motionless or squally by turns; it would have taken better sailors than they were to have used a sail in such conditions. Reliance was placed on the oars which was tedious and sometimes backbreaking toil. As long as the passage was a wide one and river ice had no chance to surplant water, oars sufficed but when the oars encountered only ice, it was impossible to make headway. The first day, they set off with few hints of the difficulties to come and the rota was working smoothly even though the current against them was, at that time, slight. They moved eastward from Savannah harbour, going with the current of the Savannah River as it flowed to the sea, waving to the docks where friends had gathered.

As they sailed by, not far from shore, James, in the fourth boat, saw Mrs Bainbridge. He waved and she blew him a kiss. Soon the little flotilla turned south into the aptly named Augustine Creek, leaving Whitmarsh and Tybee Islands off to their left side or, as James thought he should call it, the larboard beam. The wind was cold on the water and hands dipped in the water felt chilled but at least the reprimanded subalterns had seen to it that sufficient gloves were on hand. The next day they reached Osabaw Island on their left and entered narrower waters.

The third day saw an ice storm which halted all progress while the troops took shelter on land. When dawn of the next day broke the storm had ceased but the weather turned even colder and the oars skidded and skipped over the ice. After an hour of fruitless activity, they gave up and retreated to the shore. The freezing weather had its positive side – the swampy ground was solid enough so that they didn't have to slosh about.

"My God, what hellish weather," remarked Glasier to no one in particular. He turned to James: "It seems to me that rowing our way is no good but if we camp here waiting for warmer times, we'll be here for weeks."

"By your leave, sir, what about towing from the shore?" offered Serjeant Smith.

"You're probably right. It looks the only way."

Before nightfall, stout ropes were attached to all the boats and after breakfast the camp was broken up. Everybody pulled on them as if they were on a tow-path by a canal, except that the icy ground made them slip and slide. Also, there was no tow-path. Soldiers had to go ahead slashing to cut a way through the underbrush wide enough for the haulers to use. Over the next two days the waterway showed little sign of melting and the tedious and slow procedure continued. They became reconciled to making no more than two-and-a-half miles a day. It was essential not to tire the men too much.

The British Army was usually meticulous about personal cleanliness. Because the water, though plentiful, was cold, only the hardiest viewed bathing with much joy. Men were allowed to grow facial hair though Glasier insisted the officers remain clean-shaven. "If any officer grows a beard here, I'll see to it that he keeps it at St Augustine," he threatened. No one tried to see if he was joking.

They also had to find food. The daily fishing competition with a prize of an extra gill of rum to the winning boat was a popular sport though the ice on the water made the catch unimpressive for the most part. Enthusiasm for eating fish, if not for fishing, waned dramatically for a few days when the catch rendered almost everybody sick and trotting. It was decided to abandon eating fish for the time being.

The officers consulted and decided that every third day would be spent in camp with parties sent out to shoot game. Provision was made for the third day being very good for progress by water, in which case the camp day might be delayed a day or two. Fortunately, the subalterns had secured some fowling pieces and some traps as well as fishing gear. Their stock rose perceptibly with Colonel Fuser. Rations of the food they had brought with them were halved. This was no hardship when replaced by fresh game but rum was a different story.

Serjeant Smith spoke for many: "Has anyone discovered any rum-birds? What, none? None? I'll give half-a-crown to the first man to shoot one!" This attempt at humour did not go over well in the face of a reduction of the rum ration to one gill per day. The extent to which everyone felt himself to be part of a team was revealed in that, with the rum curtailment, no one talked of "them" being responsible; comments were mostly good-natured. Partly this was due to all fit officers sharing in all tasks, a point not missed by the fast-learning subalterns. The colonel spoke of it, just in case they'd missed it. As if these difficulties were not ample, Fuser's condition worried them all. Every effort was made to see that he was warmly wrapped up and kept dry.

In two weeks they reckoned to have covered only fifty miles. They came to St Catherine's Inlet which was a wide body of water, a river entering into the sea from their right. The wind was harsh and the progress so slow they needed the better part of the day negotiating the inlet. On St Simon's Island to their left – the string of islands forming one side of the Inland Passage was always on the left – they passed the ruins of Fort Frederica which, in Oglethorpe's time, had helped to put paid to the Spanish threat to Georgia by commanding the Inland Passage. Compared to this journey, last year's had been a picnic outing.

However, in a remarkably short time, precautions that would have seemed too much to expect before the trip became standard procedure. No one going to or from a boat should mistake an alligator for a log and it became an instinctive drill that a companion kept watch when such a manoeuvre was attempted, or when any soldier went into the brush to relieve himself. It was, all would admit and remember the rest of their lives, a nightmare which none had before experienced, but it was also a time when they learned how to take care of themselves, and of one another. They discovered to what extraordinary lengths they could depend on most of their fellows and how quickly the undependable few revealed themselves.

On one occasion they camped near some friendly Indians who had secretly followed their progress. The Indians had been set upon in the summer by a party of troops dressed in hunting shirts. They had lost some of their people to these barbarians who seemed to have no motive other than inflicting cruelty and they had heard that these attackers were enemies of the men in redcoats. Quite simply, they assumed that the redcoats, being enemies of their enemies, would prove to be friends. That hope was strengthened when they cautiously revealed themselves to the men in red – one of the redcoats had raised his musket at first but then lowered it while his companion made a sign of peace.

James had just returned from a "nature-trip" into the bushes when he was startled to behold a dark, painted face in front of him, fixed intently upon him. Several of the Americans in the party knew some sign language – enough to cement good will with the Indians and to prevent the English or German soldiers, frightened by their first contact with "savages" from behaving badly. Fortunately, one of these knowledgeable soldiers was near James and intervened with sign language.

Captain Kelly, a New Yorker with considerable knowledge of Indians, even undertook to instruct the head man that the men in hunting shirts must never be allowed to win against the great Father across the ocean or the lives of these people would be made miserable and probably short. They stayed with the Indians two days and were amply fed with game, in exchange for which they gave tobacco, trinkets and some rugs. Until they got near St Augustine, these were the only human beings they saw, though they might well have been seen by others whose survival usually depended on seeing others first.

The worst mishap that afflicted them was when it started, during the fifth week, to get warmer. They were by then in a fairly broad stretch of water, having negotiated some extremely rocky rapids with a number of unusually large rocks. Since the current was fast and the jutting rocks might well shatter the oars, they pulled into the side, left the boats and resorted to the tow-path technique. It worked well and they arrived in rapidly clouding weather at what looked like an ideal place to camp. They tied up the boats to trees on Jekyl Island and settled down for the night.

Just after midnight, the wind began to howl and rain started bucketing down. Soldiers could hear trees they thought looked so firm crashing down and were fortunate that none collapsed on a tent. But at first light, when the storm was past, examination showed that a few tents had been blown down, their occupants seeking shelter in other tents. Worse, all the boats but one were filled with large amounts of water, so there would be a lot of bailing before setting out. Worse than that was the one boat not filled with water; it was the luggage boat, nowhere to be seen.

The tree to which it had been secured, and which was thought to be reliable, had come down across the water, breaking up in such a way that the mooring slipped or was obliterated and the boat swept off with the current. A party of soldiers was formed which found the remains of the boat, shattered and strewn about a half mile down river. Once it got loose, the boat had rammed onto the rocks and been gutted by the rapids. As for luggage, only a few items could be found washed ashore; the rest had been carried farther downstream and had eventually become waterlogged enough to sink.

"Damn it, I can't even *find* my luggage," bemoaned James.

An officer near him replied: "I've found my case but it's been so shattered that few of the contents will be usable again."

In contrast, their pasage by Cumberland Island and Fort St Andrew's ruins was a bit easier. It was a relief when they passed Fort Prince William at the entrance to the St Mary's River heading west, and then into the St John's River to go south again, despite the adverse flow of the current.

It was another week before, on the second of February 1780, they finally pulled their ten boats into the dock at St Augustine. No doubt they now smelled every bit as much as those soldiers of Fuser's had just before the taking of Sunbury but the garrison turned out to welcome them with cheering, rum, scrubbing baths, fresh uniforms and a slap-up dinner before bedding them down in clean and dry barracks. No officer thought about securing the sort of accomodation that his rank warranted, but fell into bed in the same barrackroom as his men, their proximity now rendered palatable to the olfactory nerves by soap, with the heavenly knowledge that there would be no duties tomorrow and they could rise when they wished if, that is to say, they could sleep through the usual reveille circuit of fifes and drums. Colonel Fuser, railing against his escort right and left, was placed in the hospital with a fever.

Major Glasier's fame as the epitome of the British Grenadiers had reached the garrison and this son of Massachusetts was toasted and congratulated wherever he ventured. Before resuming his duties as commandant, he sought out those whom he best loved: his wife Ana and their son and daughter.

He then prepared his report for Lord Cornwallis. In it he recounted the horrible journey: "the extreme Cold, & Boisterousness of the Weather (which was never known before in these parts) it was the 2d of february before we arrived here, - the Officers as well as the men lost almost all their Baggage, and our Provisions and Rum falling short by twelve days, we suffered more than during the whole of the Summer Campaign."

His letter ended with a pathetic appeal for consideration to be shown him and his men: "I mention this circumstance to your Lordship in hopes of removing every objection to our receiving the Batt & Forage" – allocation of horses for transport and their food – " with the rest of the Army – The Vouchers for Contingent Account I have kept by me as directed by Major General Prevost. I never had any Publick moneys in my hands but have been obliged to advance my own without which the King's Service could not have been carried on."

There was sadness, too. Colonel Lewis Valentine Fuser had made it back to St Augustine but his exertions proved too demanding and he died only hours after arriving. He was only in his forties but his exertions in the Florida climate had done for him.

There was other regimental news and gossip that Glasier passed on to James. Before leaving for England, General Prevost had written to Sir Henry Clinton in New York complaining that the 60th were being treated like a provincial corps; in other words, officers were not finding promotions within the regiment. Instead, officers were being posted in from other regiments bypassing the 60th's own. It was as if London had decided that their officers were outside the mainstream, and they resented that. Soldiers expected to hear the sound of battle, but not to risk all while being treated unfairly.

Chapter 24

When the men were seen to and routine returned, James sought out his friends at St Augustine. The Major and Mrs White - Horace and Hannah he called them alliteratively - and the husbands of Hilda and Melissa were still at Savannah; Melissa's time was taken up in caring for her healthy baby girl. Both women were proudly talkative about their husbands who had been posted to Major Colin Graham's Georgia Light Infantry patrolling the area round Savannah.

James waited anxiously for an opportunity to talk to Beamsley Glasier who had taken up the reins as commandant. He found him at home.

"Come in, James, a pleasure, as always."

"Thank you, sir. I wonder if I could have a word with you about the future?"

"Of course."

"You may know I was one of those officers who indicated in early '75 that I would be willing to buy a company. Of course that was before the troubles started and perhaps captaincies were easier to get. Well, I've grown attached to the grenadiers and I'm torn."

"How so?"

"I don't know which alternative to try for - my own company or staying a grenadier even though it doesn't mean promotion. Above all, I am anxious to get back to Sarah in Jamaica. I've not seen her for fifteen months." Glasier noticed the exact reckoning and, remembering Mrs Bainbridge, was glad to hear evidence of James's settled affections. "Is our part in the southern campaign over?" asked James.

"I expect so. Your coming is fortuitous, James. Having a company and staying a grenadier are not mutually exclusive. I've followed your career with interest – I suppose because you are an American like me, really. You seem to have some friends in high places – influence, people call it. Normally, that's something to be resented by others but in your case, you've not been known to toady for favour. So it must be someone who is aware of your doing your duty. Someone, apparently, who wants you in New York.

"I know few details, except that they want you to report to army headquarters for use at the Adjutant General's office. They do jobs which we don't hear about in any detail, if they are doing things properly, that is. It seems they feel you are suited to their sort of work. When you arrive, you will see what I mean. Your papers will say that you are posted to staff duty, or maybe that you are indefinite leave so that anyone seeing the orders can assume you are simply a northern patrician with the King's commission, but who is more interested in feathering his own nest and looking after his own affairs. I'd be glad to have you up there because we need a voice – someone who knows what it's like down here. You could even keep an eye on our small detachment there. They are mostly concerned with forwarding pay and clothing and how welcome your eagle eye would be I couldn't say."

"When I say staff duties, I don't mean copying out bathing arrangements or lists of officer accomodations, though you may be expected to talk as if that were the job. You've gained familiarity over the past year with the work of the adjutant general. The AG of our army in the colonies is a fancy dandy named John André. You would be working for him, though probably under a subordinate of his. Now, don't make the mistake of writing him off as a fop. He is very artistic, musical, imaginative, witty and well-liked and, what's more to the point, as sharp as a needle. It was he who arranged that famous tribute to Howe before he left Philadelphia, the *Miscianza* – perhaps you've heard of it?"

"Certainly. I gather it was also a protest of sorts, as much as army officers ever get to make, against Howe's removal. Also, if I remember correctly, the New Yorker Oliver de Lancey had a hand in it."

"It seems you know more about it than I do!" expostulated Glasier. "At any rate, your work with Mrs Bainbridge in Savannah, and your knowledge of Cartwright, slim as it is, gives you a certain cachet in intelligence circles, so you'll be suited for AG work – which covers intelligence as much as administration."

James was taken aback. "Go up higher" was always the hope but he hadn't thought it would mean New York. "Nothing like that crossed my mind," he said tritely.

"Really? That's just as well. If you were a weazelly rascal always currying influence, I'd not be happy agreeing to their request.

Look at the alternatives: there is no company, certainly not one of grenadiers, to put you in charge of down here. Benjamin Wickham has made the grenadiers of his battalion in Jamaica his home and it suits him and them very well. Taylor Croker was captain-lieutenant of the 4th Battalion and he was to have taken their grenadiers, but he died and Harry Burrard now has them. That leaves the 3rd Battalion grenadiers. When Johnny Muller died, Captain Carlyon Hughes of the Royal Fusiliers agreed to take the company, but as he's not one of our own officers, the arrangement has to be regarded as temporary, unless he joins us which somehow I doubt he'll do. Which leaves the nominal captaincy of the company open to you. Hughes would lead them but being their captain will give you some added weight in New York, in your staff appointment."

"That would suit very well. I know the climate would suit Sarah better than down here," added James. "And your confidence in me means a great deal – a great deal."

"There's a sloop making for Kingston shortly. You could find passage there to Savanna la Mar, I'm sure. Shall I arrange your passage?"

"I'd be obliged, sir."

Since most of his belongings were lost on the Inland Passage, he hastened to replace what he needed and was amused to discover how many former essentials he did not need. The Whites put on a party for him and friends bade him farewell.

The sloop took ten days. When the captain found that James was a hero of Brier Creek – was there anyone who had not heard exaggerated tales of that accursed place? – he offered to drop off James at Savanna la Mar, making an unscheduled stop. James found it easy to accept, despite the fleeting temptation to drop in to the Roundhead and see if Mr Green was pursuing his dark games. At Savannah la Mar, James sent off a message to Sam to come and fetch him – Sam had been alerted by a messenger but was expecting James to come by way of Kingston so James had a wait before Sam arrived all in a flurry with horse and trap.

Whisked up to Ridgeland, he pounded on the big front door and was welcomed by Tildy who almost threw her arms round him but restricted herself to pulling his arm up and down. He grabbed her hand, turned it outside up and, bowing slightly, gave it a quick kiss which reduced Tildy to uncontrollable hoots. Tildy flourished at Ridgeland under kinder treatment than she had ever known.

As he stepped into the hall, a peel of delight burst from the top of the stairs and Sarah came rushing down to throw her arms round him, sobbing in joy. The next hour or two were quickly exhausted by rapid talk. Each had so much to say to the other; she overflowed with news and gossip whilst he related the more acceptable bits of his past year.

"Yesterday I had a visit from Captain and Mrs Linders, as she always calls herself. They are getting on very well. She's settled down – become a real distaff type and he's lost much of his boastfulness, I'm happy to tell you," she gabbled as she grabbed his hand and kissed its palm fervently.

James told her about his friends amongst the grenadiers and had her unalloyed attention as he told her of old McIntosh at Sunbury Fort and of how the downwind melifluence of Fuser's troops had almost bowled them over. He talked of his conversation with Beamsley Glasier and of the posting at New York. She asked about the refugees at St Augustine.

"I knew you'd want to know about them," he replied, giving her a detailed account.

As dusk fell, Sarah gave him her mischievous look and, leading him by the hand to the staircase, said she had "a few things to show" him.

The following morning, later than her usual hour of rising, she introduced the new overseer, David Glyn, and his wife Elinud to her husband. After he left them, Sarah remarked "My goodness me, how very Welsh they are. Are all overseers Welsh? He's not a bad sort really. It's all because he has a nice wife. It does help, doesn't it?" she added *sotto voce*, using her eyes in the way he had come to expect whenever she had some barbed double-meaning to impart.

On the first of March, St David's day in the year of our Lord 1780, the Glyns having made sure the Rickettses knew it was the day of Wales's patron saint, James and Sarah set off after farewells and, because Major Glasier had made thoughtful arrangements – "kind Major Glasier" said she – a frigate heading to New York made a special stop to pick them up. It appeared that the navy's West Indies station all knew of the feat of the grenadiers at Brier Creek.

Captain Arkwright of HMS *Ferret* was solicitous, considering it an honour to furnish them the best accomodation he could. James was required to rehearse the details of Brier Creek more than once at dinner in the wardroom while the ship's officers quizzed him about every detail. After a splendid dinner of freshly-caught fish and plum duff pudding, washed down by excellent hock, the Captain and his first lieutenant brought out their musical instruments, after a modest show of resistance, and played them some Locatelli and Handel.

Though the weather cooled as they sailed north along the coast, it was calm. James was glad of this, as was Sarah. Unlike smaller vessels like brigs and sloops, the frigate made no attempt to follow an evasive course since, once free of the Caribbean, the French proffered no hazard and no privateer was foolhardy enough to challenge their thirty-two 18-pounder guns. Indeed, the ship's officers would have welcomed such an attempt. It was splendid, thought James, to sail in such a safe and self-confident vessel.

In a fortnight they passed near the Jersey shore by Sandy Hook, then up the East River to dock. As they moved up the river, they fired the customary salute of guns, causing Sarah to clap her hands to her ears, and they received a like compliment. They docked amid the shriek of bo'sun's pipes much as would happen in any British naval harbour like Portsmouth or the Great Nore. The thirty-man complement of marines in scarlet tunics and white clay-piped crossbelts lined the way to the gangplank, fifteen a side making James feel like an admiral going ashore. They would miss the rhythmic chanting of sailors as they holystoned the decks. The creaks and bumps of a ship gave way to to the chaotic bustle and din of the dockside as James and "his lady wife" went ashore followed by seamen lugging their three portmanteaux.

That evening they put up at a modest inn. The next day, James went along to the Commander-in-Chief's Secretary's office at No. 3, Broadway. As he passed through the front door, two sentries saluted while he made his way to the front desk to report. The atmosphere was that of a miniature Horse Guards, but with fewer high-ranking officers in the corridor or on the stairs.

No Lord Amherst called him into his office, nor even a Sir Henry Clinton. There were more blue uniforms than would be found at Horse Guards – belonging to German officers, doubtless. A few green tunics of loyalist corps like the British Legion were in evidence; he assumed they were worn by provincials who still wore the uniforms furnished them by the treasury department until, finally, redcoats from the commissary replaced them.

He inquired at the desk in the room to which he was directed, addressing a dragoon captain behind the desk. His uniform was the usual long, red tunic and with prominent white facings edged with black-edged white lace. On each side of the tunic sat ten silver regimental buttons. On his left shoulder was an epaulette, the sign of his rank. Tied round his neck was a silver half-moon-shaped gorget, held up in front of the throat by a white cord. Smallclothes and boot stockings were white and his boots were polished like mirrors.

"Let's see. Captain Ricketts, you say. Ah yes, Captain-Lieutenant James Ricketts of the 2nd Battalion 60th Regiment. Interesting corps that," he said patronizingly. "Largest in the British Army – Royal *American* – " he pronounced it as "Amedikin", "doesn't even have a British name." Before James could rebut this insular cheekiness, the officer continued: "Well, more battalions than any other, anyway – more battalions than men, eh? Anyway, jolly good show, Brier Creek and all that," he added, partly relenting. "Let's see, the Barrack-Master has got you in a house at No. 70, Broadway – that's on the west side of the city," as if James, who'd known the city since his youth, needed to be told. "It's a Friday today. Why don't you settle in and come back on Monday at eight o'clock and we'll see where you go from there? Did you bring any servants with you – a slave or two, perhaps?"

The question struck James as ludicrous. Has this popinjay any idea how the army does things in the Caribbean? I am no coddled civilian lolling about on other people's labour in Jamaica. But I suppose this fellow wouldn't know that.

James replied, "No. Any servants we have will have to hired locally. Campaigning in nasty southern climes is not alleviated by slaves serving rum punch, you know – at least not in my regiment," he said coldly, looking at the dragoon's uniform, trying to determine what corps he belonged to.

"No, I suppose not, old man," said the dragoon almost sleepilly. "No offence. You'll find helpful information on such things in the room next door, though," said the captain, "we are apt to forget, up here in the big town, what it's like campaigning in the far reaches of the empire." He smiled, hopefully.

"Never mind," said James, suddenly indulgent. "May I know your name, sir?

"St Simon," which he pronounced as "Sissimun", rising and proffering his hand, "Richard St Simon of the 17th Light Dragoons and Sir Henry Clinton's Adjutant General's department, at you service."

Cartwright was in a bad temper. Those Rickettses had made a fool of him on their way to London. Despite his efforts to convince Hutchins of his duty, Ricketts had reinforced Hutchins's yearning to behave "honourably". Then that fool Healy bungled the affair at the Horse Guards. To top it all, his work in Savannah had been soured by the planting of false intelligence on him over the Spring Hill Redoubt. Savannah was lost and the confounded Ricketts had probably even turned Mrs Bainbridge from her duty.

There was no point hanging round Savannah. Action seemed to be brewing up north, as General Sir Henry Clinton was now back in the city. He decided to go to that city, British headquarters in North America. There was some comfort in the thought that Ricketts was being posted to New York and he longed to get another crack at him. If I believed in God, he thought, I might even find the appropriate psalm.

How ill he had felt in 1780 when the fast French packet-boat docked bumpily at the small port of Greenwich near the Delaware's mouth on the Jersey south shore. Greenwich had been a promising commercial town studded with ample frame houses – a pleasant enough place, thought Cartwright, until the British naval blockade ruined it.

Loyalists roaming the countryside and frequent naval raids made life dangerous - he was lucky to get ashore safely. He was always lucky in sneaking through blockades. The first place he made for was not far from Elizabethtown. It required some careful cross-country riding through little-used byways since there was no telling when he might meet a loyalist patrol. Best to take paths through woods. It was slower but surer, at least until he got into north Jersey which was more completely under patriot control.

Time passed as James became accustomed to his new place of work and Sarah to the changed residential and social setting. As they took an early breakfast in their small garden, they were content. Their house, No.70, was near to St Paul's Church and was near the top of Broadway where the road became Great George Street. Since Broadway alone possessed sufficient length to have such a number as 70, most people simply omitted the name of the road when giving the address. Leading off their part of the road was the pleasant vista of Chatham Row; their area lay just to the east of and outside the area devastated by the fire of '76.

Much of Broadway was taken up by military and civil officials' residences – the farther down Broadway, the more important the dwellings. At the bottom of the road dwelt the Commander-in-Chief, Sir Henry Clinton, at No. 24 was the Royal Artillery Hospital. Though at the heart of activity, the garden behind the house afforded privacy and they used the site to eat breakfast on warm weekends.

Sarah interrupted the munching peacefulness: "Sweeting, do you realize we have been here two months?"

"I suppose we have," replied James who was now alerted that his wife had something more important on her mind.

"Yes, the first weeks passed so quickly, what with finding Laurie to help us," Laurie being the wife of a serjeant of the Black Watch who thus qualified for St Simon's safe list; "but it is becoming a wee bit dull for me, I must confess."

James knew that she was not making a general observation on the inactivity of officers' wives; he suspected something more demanding would appear, by and by. "Have you anything in mind?" he asked.

"I've been thinking how long it is since I saw Papa and your mother, or my sisters – any of the family?"

"That's true, love, but you know how hard it is to cross the lines into New Jersey. Very hazardous," he answered.

She smiled in apparent assent but added: "I know, James, but when has danger ever stopped us? You placed yourself in peril a year ago when it was your duty. Why should I not run some slight risk through my duty, which is to keep in touch with kith and kin?"

"I would never oppose you in that, or in any thing you really want, unless it cannot be – but you know that, don't you? Have you heard from them?"

"As a matter of fact, I did have a letter from Aunt Alida – you know, Mrs Hoffman - saying how much they miss us."

"Look here," said James, "there's no problem getting you out of the city and back in again – I can arrange that – but you might land yourself in all sorts of trouble in New Jersey. Why they might even try to get at me through you. Why not write to your uncle William – after all, they regard him as their governor – and ask him for a pass – or, better yet, have some of the family write him?"

The necessary letters were prepared and entrusted to those who routinely delivered mail despite bans on such traffic.

James was coming to see the Adjutant General's department was a unique place for hearing gossip and genuine news. In its role as an intelligence centre, the AGs felt it was their right to keep tabs on what was going on. They were a curious lot – they put their noses into everything and everybody put up with it because they knew it was their duty and they could be a useful thorn. To function, they chose some peculiar people - eccentric types like André, Richard and James. He wondered at that.

Life in the AG department was proving to be more varied than he expected. One of his tasks was to advise on the reliability of men who came claiming to be loyal to the crown. Sometimes that involved people thousands of miles away.

Richard St Simon put some papers before him one morning. "See what you make of these." On top was a copy of a letter from Major General Gabriel Christie in London where he had charge of sending European recruits for the regiment to America and the Caribbean.

"I see it has to do with one Louis or Lewis Mattay, commissioned ensign in '75." Riffling through the papers beneath the letter, he commented: "The latest muster rolls we have say he never joined. Ah, I see, an explanation follows in General Christie's letter to Mr Morse – whoever he may be – probably someone keeping Mattay in charge.

"Mattay's story is, um, he says that travelling from Choleur Bay – I take it he means, or rather the general means Chaleurs, in Nova Scotia, presumably to New York to join his regiment, he was seized by a rebel vessel and taken to Maryland. There he remained, he says, a prisoner for two years and – mark this – he never disclosed he was a British officer. But why, then, was he held prisoner?"

Richard interjected: "How odd! If he was travelling on official business, which he would be if he was joining his company, why was he not in uniform? Did he have no luggage? If the rebels were suspicious enough of him to keep him captive, would they not have searched his luggage?"

James continued: "He claims that he reached New York and then embarked again. Why not declare himself to headquarters here before sailing again? Having left for the Floridas or the Caribbean, he was again seized – how unlikely! – this time by a French ship bound for Martinique.

"Judging by his name and coming from Nova Scotia, he is almost certainly of French stock, maybe a protestant, but otherwise he has little reason to love us well. Anyway, he says he escaped and got on a French ship bound for France – that's plausible in that he probably speaks good French and maybe that's the only destination he could find a ship bound for. But they didn't make it to France because one of our frigates seized the ship, and him, and he ended up in the *Conquestador* – what's that, a prison hulk in the Thames, possibly?"

"Quite," said Richard. "I see the Admiralty released him on General Christie's application and the general wonders what Amherst would like done with him. What do you think?"

"I think the entire story sounds suspect. At worst, I see it like this: he had a pleasant captivity in Maryland and there is no indication why he was kept there, or even that he was, forcibly. Then there's nothing about reporting at New York. Do we know which ship he boarded here and where it was bound? He says not. I note Christie says he can get no sense out of him. I may be doing him an injustice but I would say Lord Amherst would be well advised to ask for his resignation. Even if he is completely innocent, he does not strike me as officer material. We'd best be rid of him. That's my view."

"I concur," said Richard.

Two months later, a hastily-scrawled note arrived for James from Lord Amherst: "I remember our meeting at the Horse Guards and am glad you are proving useful. In the Mattay affair – I had myself concluded the simplest, most just and least expensive and troublesome way was to insist he resign, and I discovered later that was your suggestion too. – Amherst".

James was stunned. Not so much by Lord Amherst remembering him, as by the implication that Amherst was concerned with his usefulness. James saw it as more evidence that higher authority had unusual ideas for him. Thinking about Amherst's remarks, James's unease arose from recognizing that he was likely to be drawn more and more into unusual work which might place him in danger. He was used to the idea of danger in the military life but this was different – the danger was murky, unknown, and therefore frightening. It could involve working specifically against his fellow-countrymen. It could even involve his family. Had he known what was happening across the river, his sense of danger would have become even sharper.

Occasionally, news of the 60th came his way. The office received a rather pathetic letter. Three 60th officers had written that their three companies had been kept apart from the rest of the battalion for five years and that they boasted only thirty-six men between them all. They wished to rejoin the battalion at Antigua rather than be left longer to rot at St Augustine. Their letter was forwarded to Lord Cornwallis who ruled that the request was reasonable and should be expedited. They were down to only four officers, eight serjeants and six drummers.

Though weekends often found them both at home, sometimes James was unexpectedly tied up at headquarters at short notice.

One Sunday when he was absent, Sarah made her own way round the corner to St Paul's Church to hear Mattins, Litany and Ante-communion. She liked the Book of Common Prayer and by now was familiar with its intricacies. On the whole, she preferred the Holy Communion, not from any theological knowledge, but because it was so much easier to follow in the Prayer Book than was Matins - or was it 'mattins'? she could never decide - with all its intricate jumping about between psalms, canticles, collects and prayers.

On entering the half-filled church, she spied a young black lad huddled in the back pew. He looked forlorn, alert but apprehensive. The sight affected her and her imagination roamed at points in the service as to why he was there. Why should he not be here, she thought? Is this not God's house – is he not a child of God too? She was uncomfortably jolted by particular moments in the service. The psalms and readings of the prayer-book office seemed on this day to be picked particularly to startle her. The lesson from Acts 4 was about how to treat the destitute: "neither was there any among them that lacked", for example. She had no sooner got over arguing with herself that the world was filled with the poor and she could not solve that problem, than a selection from Acts 11 was read and the words stung her: "the disciples, every man according to his ability, determined to send relief". That was it – she was not expected to solve the world's problems any more than her husband was expected to end this war – but she had ability to do *something*. She was further struck by the gospel for the day from John 15: "ye have not chosen me, but I have chosen you."

Sarah was not superstitious but she had an intense and deeply practical, uncomplicated faith. She had been brought up to believe that God had particular, personal plans which on occasion would be tipped to you. This, she suspected, was one of those times. She had ceased to believe in the calvinist sort of plan where you were headed in a certain direction and there was little you could do about it. She now believed that grace presented opportunities, as if a kindly God offered you something to do, and waited benevolently for you to do it.

As she walked to the door at the end of the sevice, she looked again at the misery-laden face of the boy and the words of the fifty-sixth psalm, "that appointed for the eleventh morning", came to mind as she complained inwardly: No, it's hardly fair, God, it's hardly fair of you. The words reinforced her conviction that she was expected to do something: "put my tears into thy bottle: are not these things noted in thy book?"

He looked pitiable; his clothing was dirty and tattered. Her mind was made up, so she paused until the church was nearly empty, then leaned over to talk to him. She wished him a good morning, not knowing what else to do. It seemed inadequate to the occasion. Then her faith nudged her; God had got her into this and he would jolly well have to get her out. She followed by a general enquiry about whether he was "all right" and whether he was feeling the cold since it was a damp day following the previous day's heavy rain.

During this patter, at which she was quite adept, she saw the look of helpless surprise abate. But he still said nothing.

She was about to give it up when he did utter an almost inaudible "thank you, ma'am, thank you".

"May I ask your name?" she continued, encouraged by this reply. Perhaps because she did not address him as "boy" or perhaps because she showed good will, he replied: "Cyrus, ma'am, Cyrus". Hearing that it was "just Cyrus", she knew he had been raised in bondage. She redoubled her patient efforts. She saw no clergyman on the horizon coming to assist, confirming her prejudice that if God left his doings in clerical hands, he was making a mistake. Gradually, the boy relaxed sufficiently to tell his tale.

He had seen a recruiting poster for a provincial regiment but was unable to read it. When he discovered what it said, he seized his chance of escaping servitude in the risky borderland of Westchester – the no-man's land between the two armies plagued by irregulars of both sides. He had run away and placed his mark on a paper presented by a recruiting serjeant and drummer boy outside the tavern. The serjeant, hard-pressed to find men for the West Chester Refugees, had enlisted him with no questions asked. Sarah gradually coaxed it all out of him.

However, the commander of his company, learning of the boy's age of fifteen and not having a drummer's place open, had been nonplussed about what to do with him. He summarily dismissed him from the service, saying he had no place for him. Cyrus then made his way into the lower part of town, begging food as he went. People he encountered were anxious to be rid of him, giving him food and encouraging him to go elsewhere. At length, he found himself at the church.

Sarah wished she could talk first to James but knew that delay was impossible, so she trusted to her own judgment. "My husband and I live nearby and I have an idea, Cyrus. We need a servant to help us and you could be he. Only I dislike slavery and you would not be our slave. For work, we pay. If you work for us, we will pay you weekly. You will be free in our eyes, and if you decide to leave us, you will be free to do so whenever you wish."

This unlooked-for boon took him by surprise almost as much as it did her. His face dissolved into a flood of tears. When it subsided, he accepted the offer and accompanied her home.

James was not expected for some hours so the next and vital step was to secure the support of her maid Laurie. Together, they decided that, before anything, he must be cleaned up. They set about this task and managed between them to find clean garb for him, burning his old clothes in the garden.

In the late afternoon, Sarah slipped off to evensong. Though she listened carefully to the readings from Nahum and Acts 14, she detected no further instructions.

When James returned home, it was usually time for the maid to return to her Black Watch husband except that today his regiment was on the move and she could not be with him. Laurie would stay with them until her husband's return in, it turned out, a fortnight.

James was astonished at what had transpired but, to Sarah's relief, replied: "You are simply amazing! Well, I never! Oh well, why not give it a try? I wish I was in such close touch with the divine will. Who am I to question your instructions from on high?" She then elbowed him sharply in the ribs.

Ten days later, the news of Charleston's fall to royal forces reached New York. On the twelfth of May, General Lincoln had surrendered. His troops marched out to be held until exchanged but officers were to keep their servants, arms and luggage. Militia were to go home and would be protected as long as they honoured their parole. French and Spanish residents were to be prisoners but unmolested. The booty had been enormous: seven generals, two hundred and ninety other officers and over five thousand men were taken, including about three thousand Continentals, along with fifteen stand of regimental colours. It was a disaster for the King's enemies – a third of the Continental Army was captured.

Chapter 25

Sir Henry Clinton was away at Charleston and his deputy, General Knyphausen, was in command. He was busy. Seldom had a German general been entrusted with the command of so many King's troops, and in such an important place. He wanted to make his mark before Sir Henry's return. As St Simon remarked to James: "When the cat's away, the mice will play."

Shortly after, St Simon, James and a civilian commissioner, Ambrose Searle, discussed the ominous rumblings from "Nippy's" room next door. "Gad, I do believe the general is minded to do something spectacular," said Richard; his left eyebrow uplifted.

"I tried to tell him," said James. "I tried to tell him his idea of walking through the Jerseys like some ripe orchard is over-ambitious."

"Oh? And why precisely did you say that?" asked Richard. "I would think a raid in strength by the general quite a good notion."

"Forgive me, Richard, but I doubt I'd be earning my keep if I let that stand. We receive a certain amount of news from friends and relations across the North River and I have no reason to disbelieve them. They've never forgotten the cruelty and wantonness of the Hessians working their way toward Philadelphia in the year '76. "Nippy" seems to imagine they will all cower in terror, doffing their rustic caps, mouthing cringeing declarations of loyalty and thanks for deliverance."

"That's more or less what he's been told by our American allies," agreed Richard. "You're saying their attitude toward the Germans has ditched that?"

The commissioner, who had been secretary to General Howe at Philadelphia, intervened: "Hessians are more infamous and cruel than any. It is a misfortune we ever had such a dirty, cowardly set of contemptible miscreants."

"Ambrose, really! What about their storming of Fort Washington when they climbed a cliff and did what nobody reckoned on? 'Nippy' and his men did a magnificent job." protested Richard.

"What about Trenton? Not so wonderful there, I fear," James could not resist parrying him. "No, 'Nippy' is in for a surprise if he thinks Elizabethtown will simply roll over for him."

"I know he believes," said Searle "that he may entice Washington out of Morristown by making faces from Elizabethtown, but I do not think he will succeed. I have to say, I tend to agree with James. This idea of a raid is ill-advised."

"At any rate, my friends, I'll play fair with you. I'll reiterate your views to him, but I doubt it will slow him down," Richard commented.

"Good. For myself, I will wait to see how long it is before he is bogged down. I do not think we have long to wait; he goes off in two days," said Searle.

On the sixth of June, General Knyphausen ferried his five thousand troops, half the New York garrison, across the river.

Two days later, New Jersey Continentals jumped the 22nd Regiment out front to halt their advance.

Richard remarked: "From what I hear next door, 'Nippy' has been complaining that loyalist support has not materialized."

Searle almost smirked. "What did I tell you?"

"What has 'Nippy' done about it?" asked James.

Richard, basking in his fount-of-all-knowledge role, answered: "Oh, he's retreated and dug in nearer the river. Did he run into Wayne, I wonder? He lost his advantage the eighth of June – you were right, James," admitted Richard.

"Not quite. He did not lose it on the eighth of June, Richard. He lost it when he first appeared in the Jerseys, in the autumn of '76," summed up James.

At Elizabethtown, back in rebel hands, Daniel Marsh took his work seriously. Ardent for independence, he was appointed a commissioner under the Court of Oyer and Terminer of the State of New Jersey. He was to arrange, in concert with like commissioners, hearings to inquire into the loyalty of residents and landowners. If found to be loyalists, he would recommend their attainder; they would become legal non-persons, losing civil rights, their property grabbed and auctioned.

This process had come into prominence during Henry VIII's time as a convenient way of acquiring the wealth of real or potential enemies without worrying about due process of law. It also meant "corruption of the blood": inability to inherit or to bequeath. There were many victims of this.

The harshness of treatment of loyalists varied in direct proportion to the danger they were considered to present to the revolution in each state; New Jersey, rampant with loyalists, enacted harsh laws.

Daniel had no scruples about depriving such persons of basic rights. Had not Great Washington, as the song set to the tune *God Save the King* called him, himself said that only a knave would object to tarring and feathering a "Tory" and riding him out of town on a rail? No, Daniel had no time for such legalistic nitpicking. Living at Elizabethtown, he was, however, obliged to act with another commissioner, John Clawson, which he regarded as an inconvenience.

He was not sure about Clawson. He was a bit too familiar with the social élite like the Livingstons, of whom Daniel was suspicious. However, his instructions were clear; there was no way round it. He conferred with Clawson and together they drew up a notice of a hearing to be held on the twenty-second day of July 1780. Jurors and a magistrate were to meet "at the house of John Remmington, inn-keeper in Rahway, to enquire and make inquisition of and concerning George Ross, John Nurman, Philip Boasher, William McGound and James Hetfield Jnr...which have absented themselves from this County, and as is supposed taken refuge with the Enemies of America, Contrary to the form of their Allegiance to this State and against the Laws of the same, at which time and place one Justice of the Peace and the Commissioners will attend and proceed against the above named Delinquents."

Afterwards, Daniel discussed this with his wife. She had her own views: "If you ask me, there's some that ought to be there as ain't. Take James Ricketts, for one. He's wed to one of those high-an'-mighty Livingstons – even has a King's commission, I hear."

"Sadie, as usual, you're probably right. I'll just put down his name too."

When it came to the day of the hearing, two unforseen events had occurred. First, Essex County was in confusion. The main cause of the upset was a series of British raids launched from the entrenched Elizabethtown bridgehead that Knyphausen had set up. Not knowing if a serious assault was under way, people avoided such places as Remmington's tavern.

Second, a curious engagement took place about eighteen miles northeast of Rahway, where the hearing was to be held. It was not connected to what was going on at Elizabethtown but no one was to know that at Rahway. A loyalist, Colonel Cuyler, had raised a small corps called the Loyal Refugee Volunteers, comprising men in New York and New Jersey whom the rebels had turned out of their homes.

Embittered civilians on both sides behaved with a ferocity most regulars would eschew – the civilians who accompanied Lord Stirling's Staten Island raid of January had burned and pillaged; ten days later Elizabethtown's courthouse and meeting-house were burnt in reprisal. Refugees had a habit of doing the same when their turn came. At Bull's Ferry on the west bank of the Hudson, ten miles north of Hoboken, a two-storey blockhouse was built by the small corps of loyalists.

To the rebels, this structure was merely an irritation since it was manned by only seventy refugees and was used for little more than a place of safety for loyalists to come in to and somewhere to store wood. Someone thought it would be a good idea to remove it. General Wayne, to whom the task fell, was nervous. Not only did he not know what was happening with Knyphausen but Clinton had just got back from Charleston and no one knew his plans.

General "Mad Anthony" Wayne led his two Pennsylvania brigades north, accompanied by some dragoons and artillery. At ten o'clock, the guns opened up at a range of a hundred and sixty yards, repeatedly puncturing the blockhouse. The bombardment ceased after an hour-and-a-half and was followed by an infantry assault. The defence was conducted with skill and bravery and it was a complete surprise to the assailants. With six men killed and fifteen wounded, the defenders routed the attackers with the bayonet. Captain Ward of the refugees pursued the Pennsylvanians for four miles and retook twenty head of cattle, killed one soldier and took prisoner two men, one of whom was Wayne's personal servant. How a pitifully small force of seventy had routed two brigades supported by cavalry and artillery was a mystery and an embarrassment. To the AGs in New York it only reinforced what they knew of the ferocity of men deprived of their homes.

One consequence which passed everybody by at the time was that Wayne's troops clogged the roads and repeated rumours of large British forces to the north, probably to justify their retreat. Few turned up at the tavern, not even enough for a jury. The two commissioners were there, though, but when one discovered that the other, in adding James's name, had altered the document he had signed, he was furious and declared the whole proceeding invalid.

The justice of the peace looked at the one name he recognized – Ricketts – and realized that it was the name of someone who owned no seizable property in Elizabethtown. It was owned by the wife of a highly respected Livingston. He felt that he had little choice but to declare the hearing adjourned *sine die*. He did not like the greedy gobbling up of other people's land, all in the name of a much-heralded, one-sided liberty that applied only to those who shared the grabbers' views. He did not relish participating in what he felt was disgraceful greed. Everybody went home. James did not know it at the time but it was a close thing for him.

When Knyphausen finally gave it up and left New Jersey on the twenty-third of July, there was an opportunity for a staff meeting when James was first able to see Sir Henry, General Knyphausen, Captain the Earl of Bassett (in such company, Richard sported his title) and several principle commanders assembled. Sir Henry was flushed with triumph over Charleston but disappointed with the failure of Knyphausen's venture. Sir Henry was dismayed and angry that his plans for the Jerseys had gone awry.

The Commander-in-Chief had planned, on arriving from Charleston, to throw the troops he brought with him into New Jersey, farther north than Knyphausen, to form a pincer movement, catching Washington entirely by surprise. Instead the loyalists had got at the German general accusing him of shameful inaction. The royal governor of New Jersey, William Franklin, had been recently appointed as head of the Associated Loyalists and he threw his weight behind Knyphausen attacking right away, with the result of throwing off the timing of the Clinton plan. The German had allowed himself to be catapulted into action by the bad advice of William Franklin and his Associated Loyalists.

What was bad news for the crown was good news for James – the short-lived fear of a British pincer movement was enough to throw off the hearing.

Cyrus hummed gently to himself as he made his way to the woodpile near the small outhouse at the rear of the garden. The woodpile was along the shed's side and Cyrus approached the pile through a bower formed by branches, a path which allowed his imagination to convert his chore into a stalking game in which the woodpile was a dangerous beast. On the Tuesday morning, his daydream was interrupted by a tall man leaning against the back of the shed who startled the lad: "Hello boy. You belong here?" In answer to Cryus's suspicious glance, the stranger proffered a sweet. "D'ya like licorish? Go on, don't be a-feared. Take it. It's good." It was good and Cyrus's enjoyment emboldened the stranger to press on.

The man sounds English, Cyrus thought, though his experience was limited; he suspected the stranger was a-puttin' on a right country talk for this black boy's benefit. His accent was a bit like Sarah's but she never insulted his intelligence by such a put-on.

Cyrus's assumption that the stranger thought him a slave was confirmed: "Don't you ever hanker after freedom, boy?"

Cyrus replied, quite honestly: "I always want freedom."

"I could help ya' git away. 'As a bird out of the snare of the fowler' you could be. But first you must do me a favour."

Cyrus was about to reveal more about his situation but the odd-sounding words put him on his guard. He sniffed deceit and decided to talk to his mistress before revealing more.

"I got to go now," he said, cradling logs.

"That's all right. I'll be here tomorrow – same time."

Cyrus lost no time in seeking out his mistress who saw at once that he was upset. He relayed what had been said to him which prompted her to ask: "Do you want to go away?"

"No, ma'am," was his instant reply.

The next morning, armed with her words, he again saw the stranger behind the shed. He was offered another sweet which he saw no reason to refuse, then heard the stranger say: "I can help you to get away – you'd like to see freedom, would you not? But you must return me a favour." An explanation followed: the stranger was from the people wanting freedom from the wicked rulers who wanted to make all Americans into slaves. He could help him escape from this wicked city to the land of the free but Cyrus would have to help him. His people needed *information* and Captain Ricketts worked where they had just that. If Mrs Ricketts, the woman who held Cyrus in bondage, were held by the stranger and his friends, they would get information out of her husband soon enough.

"We want you to be a hero of freedom, Cyrus, 'like a bird out of the snare of the fowler,'" he said again, savouring the aptness of the quote. "First, tell me when Mrs Ricketts will be alone. Then, in a few days, you can deliver a message for us. You'll be a hero of the Revolution and a free man. What say you?" asked the stranger, offering another sweet.

Cyrus knew that the more he said, the more likely he was to get in a tangle with the enigmatic schemer. So he said: "I reckon so."

Reporting all this to the couple, he told the man's name: "You best call me Peter, just Peter," were the man's words.

The day following his last meeting with the stranger, being a Thursday, Cyrus knew he could slip away without hindrance so he picked up his scant belongings and made off, as worked out in concert with James and Sarah. It was decided that Thursday was a good day for him to slip off, being the maid Laurie's day off – to minimize the chance of disclosure they did not tell the maid of the goings-on. The boy joined the stranger who conducted him to a ramshackle house on the west side near some docks. The house had been damaged by the great fire of four years ago and had not been repaired.

On the Saturday an advertisement appeared in the *Royal Gazette*, Rivington's New York newspaper: "James Ricketts, No. 70, near St Paul's Church, New York, offers reward for recovery of runaway Negro, aged ca. 15."

Two days later, Sarah stepped out of the house and was promptly confronted by a scruffy man holding a short pistol pointed at her breast. He demanded that she accompany him, assuring her no harm would befall her if she did what she was told and, above all, did not cry out. Down the street, a waiting carriage with blinds drawn, opened a door and she was hustled inside. They arrived in a few minutes at the dilapidated house. "Why have I been brought here in this outrageous way?" she expostulated.

To her horror, Cartwright appeared at the door of the house. At least her question was answered. "We meet again, madam." To her disgruntled exclamation, he answered, "Oh, puff-puff, madam. We know enough about you and your husband to take you seriously. My compliments, by the bye, from one professional to another."

Sarah thought to herself, if I were really professional, I would try to find out everything I can – but then I probably would anyway. Her captor seemed to enjoy enlightening her. He was elated to be looked upon as a master intriguer, a man of mystery and sinister knowledge. He revealed that James was to be forced to reveal details of how Sir Henry Clinton might be safely captured. She was to be the lever to move her husband. After Sir Henry's capture, he told her, she would be released. "Your slave boy will be free, too."

"What about Cyrus?" she asked, her brow furrowed with a concern she hoped he would put down to fear of losing a slave.

"Yes, indeed. He'll be off like a partridge, enjoying his freedom like some Mahometan in the ha-reem of paradise" said he mixing his similes. He did not tell her that Cyrus was in an upper room. "Now, you will please to write your husband exactly as I tell you."

As instructed by the kidnappers, Cyrus slipped down the back stairs, picking up the letter he had been waiting for. He was expected to drop the letter through the slot in the front door at No. 70, ring the bell and skitter away off into the dusk. Instead, he entered the back door with his key, arriving out of breath but triumphantly at the room where James and others were waiting anxiously: St Simon, two other officers in redcoats, and two dark-coated civilians.

"Good work, Cyrus. I hope everything is all right. You can find the way back, I hope." Cyrus nodded. "You must be hungry. Help yourself to ham in the kitchen," said James.

"Please, sir, can I see what's to happen to Missy Sarah? Please, sir."

"I guess you've earned the right, Cyrus. You can make sure we get to the right place, too. One of these gentlemen did some stalking but it's just as well to make sure."

The seven took two carriages to a place a block away from the spies' house and surrounded it. All except Cyrus were armed. Since it was essential to keep him out of sight, he was detailed to remain in a carriage.

In the dark, the rescue party approached the house with care. Lights were visible within. Glancing first at his companions to see if they were ready, one of the civilians abruptly kicked the shabby door open; it practically fell off its hinges.

Those inside looked like a *tableau vivant* in their shock. A second later all was confusion. One reached for a pistol on the mantelpiece but was struck with the flat of Richard's sword. Another grabbed at Sarah to use her as a shield but James crashed into him, unbalancing the man. James brought his pistol down on the man's head and he groaned, slipping unconscious to the floor. Another tried to aid his comrade and skewer James with a knife pulled from his belt. He was brought down by a pistol shot from one of the civilians, being hit in the arm which he grasped as he rolled in pain on the floor.

"Sarah, move behind me, quick!" shouted James as Cartwright, at the very least, was not yet accounted for.

The two civilians then moved, rapidly and professionally it seemed to James, through the house, searching. Doors could be heard banging as they were thrust open and closed. In no time at all they were back in the sitting room.

Cartwright was nowhere to be found. His colleagues said they did not know where he was. In a few moments, James led Sarah into the carriage where Cyrus waited for them and, leaving the others to remove the prisoners, made off to No. 70.

A couple of hours later, the rescuers, with Sarah amongst them, gathered. Brandy and talk reigned. Though young, Cyrus was allowed to listen in his role as butler.

"When Sarah first told me of the stranger's approach to Cyrus last Tuesday, I was dead set against her involvement," said James.

"The trouble, sir," said one of the civilians, "is that unless we took the bull by the horns and smoked out that nest, they would just keep on and you'd never be rid of them." His rich Kerry voice was vibrant with feeling: "You are one lucky man to have so plucky a wife, sir."

"That's kind of you, I'm sure," said Sarah archly, pleased as could be and affecting a mock-curtsey. "But we ought to give credit where it's due - Cyrus. First, it was a godsend he did not disclose his already being free. Then he came to me because he was worried, not for himself, but for us – his family, he calls us. Of course, I suggested he call himself our 'boy' because I knew the stranger would assume he was a slave."

Richard took up the account. "The next day you told me, James, what Sarah had learnt from Cyrus about the purpose of their plan. And, I must say, your notice in the *Royal Gazette* about a slave having run made it seem authentic - it established Cyrus's credentials."

"To tie it up properly, since we cannot forget Cartwright is at large and we don't want him thinking ill of Cyrus, we'll put another one in the journal on the twenty-sixth, to say he's been returned," added James.

"A creditable day's work, what?" summed up Richard. He continued: "I think you two want a reward which certainly cannot be advertised for what it is. So, I propose that you both come with me to a guest night and dine in with my regiment's officers. What about it? As I'm not a man of unlimited means, I fear I cannot take on the rest of you so I wonder how you can be rewarded?"

The four others demurred, muttering phrases like "all in a day's work, sir," and "it's what we're here for".

"Well what about our real hero, Cyrus" asked Richard. "We can't leave him out."

Sarah had a solution. "As you know, Cyrus is scoffing up ham in the kitchen like fury. He's keen on smoked ham. You could provide him a ham with some beer, Richard, and James and I could give him a new suit of footman's clothing to celebrate."

Later, James told Cyrus that he was the real hero of the adventure and that they were decided to set aside money regularly so that, if the time came when he wanted to leave them, he would have a financial head-start. Cyrus made it clear that he appreciated the money but had no intention of departing, unless they wanted him to go. They made it clear that there was no danger of that.

In festive mood, James and Sarah met Richard in the foyer of the large Broadway house used by the 17th Light Dragoons as their headquarters and officers' mess. They arrived at six-thirty o'clock in what finery they could muster, Sarah looking rather more splendid than did James who was restricted to a cleaned up version of his ordinary infantry uniform, though he had managed with Cyrus's help to put a shine on his boots.

Sarah was led off by the colonel's wife into an ante-room which was furnished with various spirits, where she met the other ladies of the party. Accompanying Richard into a withdrawing room, James was served champagne and introduced to the regimental commander, Lieutenant Colonel Samuel Birch. "Ah, bless me, so this is the famous Ricketts about whom Lord Bassett waxes eloquent. I'm pleased to see you here and I hope it will be the first of many such occasions."

Various other introductions followed including a number of officers bearing titles; James noted they affected no side whatever but immediately put him at his ease. At ten past seven, a drummer and fifer marched in playing *The Roast Beef of Old England,* followed by the regimental chef carrying an enormous joint which he placed before the colonel to sample. Colonel Birch did not take long to do that and pronounced "this meat is fit for consumption".

Ten minutes later, a black cavalry trumpeter wearing a most ornate tri-cornered hat sounded a call and the guests were escorted from their different rooms into the dining room. To Sarah's surprise, she was escorted not by Richard but by the colonel, leaving Richard to usher in James. The normal custom of seating everybody at one long table was not observed, owing to the size of the room, so a number of smaller tables were laid.

At eight-thirty precisely, the colonel called for the grace, which was said nearly audibly by the chaplain, after which all sat down. A small number of musicians with fiddles, drum and hautboys played during a good bit of the meal, stationed in an adjoining room outside the dining room so as not to drown the conversation.

A succession of delicacies – turbot, herring, exquisitely grilled chicken with an egg sauce, hominy grits - which Sarah thought strange but had apparently been enthusiastically embraced by the colonel on a trip south – were in turn followed by generous helpings of roast beef, sliced thin, not thickly as in the American fashion, with roast potatoes, Yorkshire pudding, horseradish sauce, brussels sprouts and turnips.

A sumptuous pudding finished the meal. By that was meant several quarts of cream boiled and sweetened, put to two spoonfuls of rennet per quart of cream and the whole allowed to stand till it became like cheese – a version of the dessert of which Oliver Wendell Holmes would later write: "that most wonderful object of domestic art...with its charming confusion of cream and cake and almonds and jam and jelly and wine and cinnamon and froth".

Despite all the attention required by the seemingly endless procession of food, conversation was brisk. The colonel took a shine to Sarah and monopolized much of her conversation, his rank protecting him from challengers. On James's right hand was Major Oliver De Lancey, about whom almost everyone in New York knew, whose father was the leader of one of the two major factions in the politics of the province and raiser of three battalions of loyalists.

Major De Lancey pointed carefully to Richard, saying to James: "I don't know whether you've discovered it yet, but for all his hoity-toity dandy ways, that man there has one of the keenest brains in the whole army, let alone North America. It took me a long time to discover that – he manages to disguise it so cleverly. And I'm no mean judge of such things."

"Oh do stow it, Oliver," said Richard who, James was very surprised to see, was acutely embarrassed and flushing noticeably.

"That's all very well, Richard, but when it comes to the edge, there's no one I'd rather have at my side," De Lancey pressed on. "Why he wears that mask of London-society-incompetence when all his associates twig to his virtues – sooner or later, mostly later, I fear – I really don't know."

Fortunately, before Richard called him out or did some equally disastrous thing, a gorgeous woman to De Lancey's right broke in on the conversation, directing such flattering aspersions toward De Lancey that he was quite overcome and forgot the drift of his remarks.

"Ignore him, James, just ignore him, though these political chaps are pretty hard to ignore, I grant you."

At this, the colonel, who had an almost impenetrable north-of-England accent, burst out in a gale of mirth. "I've never been able to understand," he said when he had recovered himself sufficiently, "why these southern toff types make such a show of being totally incompetent when anybody might be looking." Someone aborted the pregnant moment by casually slipping in a new and unrelated question which the colonel felt he must turn his attention to, or risk being discourteous. The question was, naturally, unrelated to politics, the war or women.

At about ten o'clock, when they were finished, stewards removed the dishes and other items, leaving only a few items of regimental silver. Chairs were moved away from the end of the long rectangular high table which allowed servants to take hold of the white damask table cloth, whisking it away so smartly that none of the items on the table were upset. This stunt was always a highpoint for guests who had never seen it before and James wondered what horrible punishments would ensue for any servant who failed in this manoeuvre.

At that point, small glasses were distributed and decanters of port on elaborate coasters were placed on each table. Each table's host filled his own glass – the colonel even going so far as to utter that old hack "a woman by the waist, a bottle by the neck, m'dear," – and the bottle was passed from left to right.

Here there was no attempt to exclude the ladies as at civilian tables, but all filled their own glasses, even the one or two teetotallers for it would have been considered an insulting breach of etiquette not to have participated in the toasts that followed, by lifting the glass to the lips even if not drinking; water was not acceptable as a substitute. When the glasses had been filled, the Vice-president of the mess, who happened to be Richard, stood, saying "Mr President, the King", whereupon the colonel stood, inviting everyone else to stand for the loyal toast. Certain guests, naval officers and members of regiments which once served as marines and hence entitled to sit, did not rise. As soon as the murmurs of "God bless him" had died down, the adjutant called out "the Colonel", which turned out to be, not Birch, but the absent Lieutenant General Preston. Another officer toasted "our distinguished guests" at which all the guests quietly seated themselves. It was especially pleasant that no speeches followed, the evening being brought to an end by the singing of one verse of *God Save the King*.

Chapter 26

Sarah tried to be patient. She wrote her father at Basking Ridge forty miles beyond the river, across the lines separating the armies. Not for three years had she seen her family, nor had she heard from her father for four months. To her it was incredible that two sides were so busy tearing each other apart that they could not make room for family relations when everybody knew that family ties were the most enduring ones. How could such bonds be broken in the name of independence? Was that not a fatuous term, anyway? It was men who talked nonsense about independence. Women knew better. No one had independence. Everyone was dependent on others.

One day she turned to her husband. "I see my own family making allowances for each other. I mean, my father retired from active politics soon after independence was claimed. He'd been a strong supporter of colonial rights but when they tried to cut themselves off from Britain, he pulled back. Why would he do that? I'm sure it was because of the family.

"My brother Philip, who married Cornelia Van Horn, went to England, he felt so strongly, and just about the time Father pulled back. My brother William is a King's man. Mary and I are both British Army wives.

"On the other side, you might reckon Peter and Susannah. The others – James, Elizabeth, Ann – are too young to count. So my father's children are split in this war – but I don't hear of my father disowning any of them, not talking to them, not loving them. Nor are we children enemies. We don't hold each other at arm's length, except insofar as others make us do so. What a pretentious sham it is – as if anyone could be truly independent."

James was moved to look at his own recent past. He was independent, in a sense, witness his relations with Daphne Bainbridge. Yet he always knew that it wasn't true independence. He knew that true independence from his wife would appal him.

Finally, on the fourth of September, a letter did arrive. Her father's letter told her that in May he wrote his brother William, "the governor", explaining that James and Sarah were recently arrived from Jamaica, were in New York and ardently desired to visit their family. Since that entailed crossing into territory under his jurisdiction, he hoped his brother would see his way to letting Sarah pay such a visit. He realized that James could not make the trip but he hoped William would agree there was no reason to debar Sarah from such an entirely innocent and humane journey.

The governor replied that he had set a policy of allowing only wives of prisoners to leave and re-enter their lines, that he could admit of no exceptions and he much regretted to say that his closest relations must surely understand that he could not exempt his family from the rule or his whole policy would be morally undermined.

As James expected, Sarah had her own views of what Uncle William had said. "I can understand why he can't make exceptions for us – but why force *anyone* to obey such a vicious ruling?"

Her father and Uncle William clearly had different priorities over loyalty and what rules should be bent. Sarah's father redoubled his efforts to change his brother's mind. He enlisted the support of nearby relations and close friends. The governor's sister, Alida Hoffman, in whom William had enormous confidence and with whom he maintained a lively correspondence, wrote in the same vein as her brother-in-law. Her aunt, Lady Stirling, in Sarah's eyes saw reality like a woman even though her husband was one of Washington's top generals. Even her daughter, Lady Kitty, wrote her uncle on Sarah's behalf. The governor's two nieces, Sarah's younger sisters, might be too young to count for much in his eyes but even they wrote their uncle. The children of yet another sister, Mrs David Van Horne, wrote, and her husband had served in the Continental Army.

It was of no avail. The governor knew his enemies hovered above him like vultures hoping he would slip and they could attack him. He would later say of the family barrage directed against him: "The family at Baskenridge have in fact done more to injure my reputation and to furnish my personal enemies with weapons against me than perhaps twenty families in this State."

Whatever his reasons, he still came across as a hard man. Once an English friend had written to say what a terrible thing it was that fellow Britons were tearing at each other. The governor replied that he had not heard that Britons were attacking each other, and he was sorry to hear it.

"I think that it all comes down, Sarah," said James, "to whether you think of your kin as us - or them."

Sarah was nothing if not persistent. She knew her side would issue a pass on humanitarian grounds and, as for the rest, was prepared to take the risk. James was very uneasy, knowing of cases like Mark Prevost and James Moncrieff, the chief engineer at Savannah, whose wives the rebels kept under virtual house arrest. But the Livingston clan, even in the detached form of the New Jersey sept, could throw their weight around, and they did so.

Sarah slipped across the Hudson in a boat rowed by a seaman. Whatever theories Uncle William Livingston had on crossing lines, there was a brisk trade which the rebels had no ships to prevent and the British had no wish to.

On the other side, in a secluded cove, a carriage waited. In three hours the coach had covered the twenty-four miles to Basking Ridge. The coach had been sent by the family at Basking Ridge, even though it did not bear either the Livingston or Alexander coat-of-arms on its doors.

Apart from her blood relations, there was her step-mother, Mrs Elizabeth Livingston. That lady made no bones about how she felt: "My dearest Sarah, it seems so long, so long. I don't give a fig what your politics are – you are family and that's what matters to me."

Sarah warmed at once. "You are, as you always have been and what I expected you would be today: so gracious, ma'am." They clutched each other, tears fighting smiles.

"I have to say this to you, Sarah, and I'll not say it again. As far as politics go, I have no idea which side will beat. I have come more toward thinking we should rule our own affairs but I could live with either side's victory. And I can certainly respect those of my family who differ, either way. All right?" Once again they held each other closeley, sniveling disgracefully, thought Sarah's youngest sister Ann, aged thirteen.

James, somewhat to Sarah's chagrin, sympathized with his uncle-by-marriage. If he were in his shoes, he might well take the same view about issuing a pass to Sarah. True to the character of Livingston women, she did not let such a consideration deter her. Her trips behind enemy lines did not fulfil his fears but they caused him acute anxiety until she was again safe in his arms. His anxiety would have increased if he had known the governor was aware of her trips. William wrote two years later to Alida that Sarah Ricketts had illegally visited her father but, whether to his credit or not, he had made no move against her himself. The hard man, it seemed, did have weaknesses.

Chapter 27

The AGs customarily looked through the news that kept coming in to see what would be of particular use to their superiors. Occasionally, bits of news would arrive of interest to one of the department's members. One such item was passed on to James: the sad news that Colonel Mark Prevost, who had led the action at Brier Creek two years before, had died at Spanish Town in the island of Jamaica. It was not known why, only that he had been ill.

The next day, Richard introduced a topic rather abruptly, James thought: "James, there is something we ought to do." When Richard St Simon, Earl of Bassett laconically bestirred his lanky frame sufficiently to utter that anything was important, it was a signal to sit up and take notice. Lord Bassett's blueblood ennui-laden drawl might mislead one to assume nothing was so important to him as arranging the next glass of brandy, first-rate brandy, of course, and even that task did not merit so vulgar a demonstration as could be called "enthusiasm".

However, Sir Henry, his boss, was not hoodwinked by his penetrating, intuitive mind's camouflage. Nor was Lieutenant General Wilhelm von Knyphausen who in his long career had seen *hochdeutsch* imitators of the genuine English article. James, too, was not naïve in this respect.

"Yes, I'm afraid so" admitted Richard, much as if the admission was a year's ration of inconvenient misfortune. "Poor André – he was a most amiable fellow, so kind and considerate, so pleasant to have around, so affable. Ah well." James wondered if Richard was actually expressing some sort of tactful indirect criticism of André's replacement, but then he continued: "Splendid man, our new De Lancey, old New York family and all that," he rattled on with the true aristocrat's scorn of social pretence, "scion of the other political ilk from your Livingston lot," he said, fixing James with as fisheyed a glare as he could manage. "Being a colonial – no offence, ol' cock – he's not so inclined to take loyalists, or pretended ones, at face value the way his open-hearted predecessor was. After all, dear André's experience of them was mainly the fashionable ladies of

Philadelphia, an amiable, sophisticated crowd if ever there was one – sophisticated save only in their readiness to bestow amorous favours.

"At any rate, our new adjutant supremo is more curious than was John André about the loyalists of this city. There are, I think, about twenty-two thousand dwellers hereabouts of whom we might reckon a third are enthusiastic," – here he paused as if to savour this disreputable term suspiciously – "perhaps another third have royalist sentiments as long as it doesn't scupper them when all is over. Another third he takes to be 'politic', by which he means they wait to see what the future holds but hope for independence and are ready to cause us mischief whenever they may – a bit like the Jacobites, maybe."

It was clear to James that this vigorous demonstration had almost exhausted his friend's taciturn resources, so he thought he'd help:

"As a matter of fact, I have a slight acquaintance with Oliver De Lancey," interjected James. "When we were boys, he lived only half a mile south of my father's farm. I think his land was confiscated by the rebels and sold to Matthias Halsted"

"Love a duck!" observed Richard. "I always knew your were a blueblood at heart, however much you disguise it."

"Yes, well anyway what does the AG want?"

"Yes, well, ah, if you can contain yourself a little, I was just coming to that," said Richard with a mournful glance. "We have over twenty-six hundred men here, American civilians for the most part, enrolled in a score of companies of one sort or another. For over a year, the Board of Associated Loyalists under Governor Franklin has been allowed to control their own armed men. They're not soldiers and they don't belong to the army but they have commissioned officers and when they plan some expedition or other, they have to ask the AGs for weapons.

"Some could do us harm either wilfully or through incompetence, and Oliver would like us to go around detecting incompetents or, er, misfits. He's particularly keen that you, as an American, should have a look at your compatriots. Also, it's our job to do what we can to help the army run smoothly, so if we see anything glaringly amiss, we can pass it on to him."

At the risk of committing another faux-pas, James added: "Is not the Inspector General apt to resent this poaching?"

He was pleasantly surprised at Richard's response: "Good question, very astute, James. Just what I've come to expect from your penetrating intellect. It has all to be done in the name of security – it's under the umbrella of our intelligence-gathering – hush is the word."

"How do we set about it?" asked James.

"Yes, well I have a list here. It's divided into two classes – old companies and new "associated" companies, the latter so-called, I imagine, because they are sponsored by Governor Franklin's Associated Loyalists."

The first group included a company each of New York Rangers and New York Highlanders and seven companies of New York Volunteers, not to be confused, Richard pointed out, with the provincial regiment of the same name under Colonel Turnbull. These companies were virtually militia, committed solely to the defence of the city proper.

The association companies, under the Board, included an odd assortment: a company of New York Marine Artillery, companies of Ordnance Volunteers (one of artificers and three of seamen made up from the Royal Artillery Civil Branch), two companies of Commissariat Loyal Volunteers, a company of Engineer Volunteers, a company of Quartermaster General's Volunteers, one of Barrack Master General's Volunteers, three companies of King's Dock Yard Volunteers and four of City Militia. They all, as implied by their names, comprised civilian employees drilling on a voluntary basis. James noticed there were no Adjutant General's Volunteers as AG work must contain only tried and true, vetted, personnel.

These companies were parcelled out between Richard, James and two civilian assistants known as secretaries but whose opinions carried more weight with the AG department and with Sir Henry, than their job titles implied. It was arranged that James would cover the Ordnance Volunteers, the Commissariat Loyal Volunteers, Engineer Volunteers and Quartermaster General's Volunteers.

After a week's uneventful visiting other companies, James found the large warehouse on the west side where the Commissariat Loyal Volunteers drilled and worked. It was only a short distance from the Hudson River. He found that the small company undertook to guard the warehouse and two others not far away. Tuesday was their drill night but each night they provided eight sentries to mount guard at their main building, as well as sentinels on a rota basis for the other two warehouses. James chose to make his appearance on a drill night to get a feel for the companies and a chance to talk to their officers. He found them a mixed bunch – a very few were English civilian employees of the army commissary department but most were loyalists who had drifted into New York for refuge. Some were young but most were either elderly or were seasoned provincials who had been wounded or otherwise invalided out of the service. The volunteers' officers had all been recently appointed and were just becoming acquainted with each other and their motley rank-and-file.

"What can I do for you, sir?" asked a lieutenant who acted as adjutant for the companies, drawing up rosters, keeping the muster rolls and doing similar clerical duties. He was a short, fleshy man with a pockmarked face. Like the rest of his corps he wore the green tunic which were hand-me-downs from the provincials when they adopted the redcoat.

"I assume from the sign on the door, you must be Mr Masters. I'm Captain Ricketts, James Ricketts of the 3rd Battalion, 60th." James did not mention that only recently had he learned of his appointment as captain of the grenadiers of the 3rd Battalion, backdated to October of last year. "I'm attached to the Adjutant General's staff. We go round making a nuisance of ourselves, looking at security arrangements, but otherwise trying not to be too obnoxious."

"A pleasure, captain," said Masters in a manner that James felt more perfunctory than warm. His accent could be rural Pennsylvania. "See lots of action with the 60th, I guess. Haven't heard much about them – have they been in the garrison for a long time?"

It was surprising that this officer seemed to have no knowledge of the largest infantry regiment in the army. He seemed to think they were part of Sir Henry's command. James saw fit to reply: "No, not really – been behind a desk, mostly", some instinct urged him to play down his own experience and, in fact, any military details. He couldn't say why, but he did not warm to Mr Masters. "Have you been here long?" James continued, feeling he ought to do the questioning.

"I reckon I've been here since Colonel Cuyler's little battle at Bull's Ferry. We trounced the rebels good and plenty, we did."

"I take it you've been on our side for some time, then?" asked James, trying to draw him out.

"Oh, from the beginning, the very beginning. I've always said parliament can govern us a lot better than we can govern ourselves," affirmed the lieutenant.

James was uneasy. Masters seemed to have a reverence for parliament which James had never heard anyone express – British or colonial.

"What do you guard in this place, Mr Masters?" said he, changing the subject.

Masters indicated there was little of importance and showed him some items of army clothing, ordinary clothes for refugees entering the city and pieces of camp equipment. "No cannon or anything worth your while, I think."

James noted that several wooden crates almost hidden in a far corner were not included in the tour. He had taken the precaution, before leaving headquarters, of securing an inventory in which he saw only one item of interest – four crates of rifles, Ferguson rifles. James was no ordnance buff but he had heard of that weapon. He had always wondered how it handled and what it was like to fire it. He noticed the omission in his tour, did not understand it, and pressed the point.

"The commissary list I saw mentioned some firearms. I don't see them."

"They listed those, did they?" queried the officer with an unsmiling face. "Some old rejects, badly rusted, hardly worth mentioning."

At headquarters, James talked over his visit. "I've seen the Ordnance people and the Engineers so far. Everything looks as it should be. But I worry about the commissary people, at least about their adjutant or orderly officer or whatever he calls himself. He's a windbag, and he's devious. He did his best to play down the Ferguson rifles in their care. I wish I knew someone who could question him about Bull's Ferry – you remember that extraordinary affair with the Refugees a year ago – he claims he was there. Maybe he was, and maybe not."

"Of course I remember Bull's Ferry – I always recall such details," Richard remarked complacently. "Have you thought about using Captain Ward? You met him last week. He was at Bull's Ferry in a big way. Perhaps you remember that?"

James ignored the provocation.

Richard went on: "He comes into town now and then. In fact, I expect him tomorrow." James realized indulgently that this revelation had made Richard's entire morning worthwhile.

On the next day, James and Ward talked. Ward agreed to visit Masters at the warehouse to draw his own conclusions. "I suppose I should be overjoyed to meet another veteran of the battle, but to tell you the truth, it was such a bloody affair that I'd rather put it by. But I'll do it for you."

In a few days they conferred. Ward was now definitely interested: "I reckon you're on to something there, James. First – if I can get my thoughts into the sort of goose-pie logical order that Lord Bassett prefers – Masters: he didn't recognize me. Moreover, I didn't recognize him. There weren't all that many of us, so that's odd. Oh, he put on a show – comrades in arms and that sort of thing – when I said who I was."

"That sounds conclusive," said James rather prematurely, as Richard felt James was wont to do.

"But there's more," said Ward. "I casually threw in the names of three subalterns – fictitious ones who weren't there. He did not claim acquaintance with the first two but he changed tack on the third one. Perhaps he felt that if he didn't know any officers there, it would look odd. At any rate, he said he knew of him. Then I said it was a good thing we had so much ammunition that we didn't have to rely on the bayonet. He agreed. But we had almost exhausted our powder. It was the bayonet we routed them with. Then I said as how these Maryland troops did not seem much good in the fight and blow me, if he didn't correct me and say there were no Marylanders there, only Pennsylvanians. Now he was right about that and I was worried he might smoke me.

"There's more: he clearly did not know what we had in the fort because he agreed with my assertion that our swivel guns did great work – we had no swivel guns, only four-pounders. Curiously though, he did know the lie of the land outside the fort. He knew about the forty-foot rise four hundred yards from the fort. What do you think of that?"

James said it first: "It almost sounds as if he were there, but on the other side. I'll tell you what really made me wonder when I met him in the warehouse: it was that nonsense about parliament governing America better than anyone here could. I knew that didn't ring true. Have you ever heard the like from a loyalist?" Nobody said he had.

"Even old Joseph Galloway, whose loyalty is true blue, never said anything like that. He even came up with a plan in '74 for the colonies to unite under a president-general appointed by the King, with an elected grand council who'd have power to veto parliamentary acts affecting America. But this preposterous claim about parliament's wisdom – well, I ask you." James was getting quite carried away.

At this point, Richard, who had listened in silence, chuckled quietly: "Tsk, tsk, James, I've never heard the like, this seditious talk about parliament not being infallible." Richard added: "What do you think Masters is up to and what ought we to do about him?"

James had no reason to hesitate. "I can make a guess. What was he most devious about? Those rifles! He hoped I didn't know about them. When it was certain that I did, he pretended they were nothing but rusty scrap metal. No, gentlemen, it's the rifles. That's what he's after."

A plan was prepared in which Richard, James and Oliver De Lancey tried to cover all eventualities. James would go back on Tuesday to inform Masters that the AGs were not satisfied with the safety arrangements for the rifles and that on the following Monday a crew would arrive to move the crates to a better location. This was done. James noted that Masters did not spend any time protesting that his men could safely guard the rifles. Instead, he seemed to be thinking hard about something else.

From the Tuesday evening a discreet watch from a nearby building was placed over the warehouse. A company of marines was alerted so that, at short notice, they could prevent any movement from the warehouse.

Whether it was Masters' idea or from someone higher up, no one could tell, but on the Sunday night things took an unexpected turn threatening to undo the AGs' well-laid plans. Someone standing at the waterside could have heard the clunk and splash of muffled oars pulling a large rowing boat close up to shore.

But there was no one to hear. The boat was carefully rowed by men in dark clothes whose faces, hands and muskets were blackened to make them inconspicuous, and they pulled in about two furlongs from the warehouse which was receiving all the attention. As they pulled in near another commissary warehouse whose light guard was unaware of what was going on, they shipped their oars and stealthily moved ashore, making no sound. Two of them crept forward as the sentries disappeared from sight around the building. Using a slow-match they set alight a bundle of kindling they brought with them and from that set fire to the warehouse.

The marine detachment, now thoroughly alerted to danger along the waterfront, made its way quickly to the scene of the conflagration. There they engaged in a sharp bout of musketry with the invaders. Timed perfectly to coincide with the confusion a quarter of a mile upstream, another, more ungainly, flatboat pulled into the dock nearest the warehouse where the rifles were stored. The main door of the warehouse was undefended and unlocked, so they quickly set about the task of removing the four crates of rifles out of the warehouse and onto their flatboat.

The men who, on behalf of the AG department, had been watching the warehouse for several nights, fortunately had the sense not to be distracted by the diversion at the other warehouse. A messenger slipped out of their building and managed to race to the nearby naval station, unseen by the blackened team who were manhandling the crates.

In a matter of minutes, voices were bellowing and bo'sun's pipes were shrieking their messages to the sailors at the station. These had been alerted to the possibility of being needed and they responded at the double. Shouts echoed in the chill April air as, in a remarkably short time, a patrol gunboat hoisted its sails and moved out into the river. At the bows was a six-pounder gun and at the stern was a swivel-gun which could fire a mixture of nuts and bolts with deadly effect on the raiding crewmen. That crew took some time to put the heavy crates aboard their craft and they succeeded in getting off just ahead of the marines pouring toward the dockside.

As their boat got into midstream, the gunboat drew up with its bows toward their midships and it looked for a moment as if the gunboat would ram them. The gunboat skipper, however, was manoeuvring so that his six-pounder could hit the flatboat. "Ahoy, oarsmen there: ship oars and do not touch your arms. Surrender or suffer the consequences."

The effect of that demand was to produce an immediate scramble among the oarsmen to push the crates overboard, so that if they couldn't have the rifles, neither would their enemies. Seeing what was afoot, the captain of the gunboat ordered his gunner to fire and a sharp crack was instantly followed by a hideous tearing noise and the cries of two of the oarsmen as they collapsed into the cold and filthy river.

The remaining oarsmen, with intense effort, got three of the crates overboard, seeing them sink rapidly. The gunboat grappled the flatboat and its sailors rushed aboard coralling the oarsmen who by now were hoisting their hands into the air. The sailors did manage to save one of the crates, hoisting it aboard their own boat.

Next morning, the one chest not lost was opened and thirty-five of the rifles re-crated for transfer to a safer storage place. As a reward, the Adjutant General allowed James, Richard and Captain Ward each to retain one of the precious rifles. Though short of sleep and dishevelled, they received these weapons gratefully. They would be kept under lock and key.

"*Sic transit gloria mundi,*" proclaimed Richard – no one seemed startled by this as they assumed it was the sort of thing he might be expected to say. He added: "Poor Pattie Ferguson. I never had the pleasure of meeting you, but wherever you are I hope you realize that two of your lovely children are in our doting hands."

"At least we kept them out of the wrong hands. We kept them from being used against the people he invented them to serve," added James with feeling.

Chapter 28

In Elizabethtown, he met the Continental officer detailed to supervise his intelligence work. While the King's forces had Brigadier General Skinner, a native New Jersey man, who as a prisoner of the rebels had been part of the exchange for Lord Stirling in '76, Governor Livingston had Lieutenant Colonel Matthias Ogden. To see him, Cartwright had made his way safely to Elizabethtown. He was not sure what to make of Ogden. Ogden was lieutenant colonel of the 1st New Jersey Continentals – he'd been captured by the enemy in October 1780 and exchanged after six months. I suppose he got a taste for spying just looking round from his comfortable quarters, the spy conjectured. What bothered him was that Ogden came from Elizabethtown and moved easily in the blueblood circles which produced James Ricketts.

He met Ogden at a local tavern rather than at the house on the outskirts of Elizabethtown which was available for clandestine operations. Despite British raids, it was still worth using because it was so close to the city.

The colonel did not waste time: "What do you have in mind, Cartwright?"

The spy was genuinely curious what Ogden's attitude would be when he mentioned Elizabethtown aristocrats. He saw no point in beating about the bush with the colonel. "There's an officer in New York who has constantly interfered in my plans," he explained. "James Ricketts of the 60th Regiment, also on Clinton's staff."

Ogden's eyes widened. "What do you mean to do to him?"

I thought that would pique his interest, thought the spy. "Take him prisoner since his uncle the governor's kindly attempts to win him over have come to nought. Or perhaps take his wife prisoner so her husband will be forced to help us capture Sir Henry. You do not know him, do you?" he remarked, suddenly fearing some unforeseen complication.

"I'm well aware who he is." He forebore telling Cartwright they had been neighbours and he had known James since infancy and that his younger brother Jacob owed his life to the quick action of

James in the West Indies. As he suspected, there was something in this he did not like, something unworthy, and he had a good nose for that sort of thing. However, he let something slip out which he regretted as soon as he said it: "The governor is irked that Mrs Ricketts, his own niece, disobeys his orders and crosses the lines to visit her family at Basking Ridge. I doubt if James tries that, though." Cartwright knew that already.

Ogden, for all his displeasure at the direction Cartwright was taking, decided to let the matter rest till after he consulted the governor. He was in the habit of meeting with the governor perhaps twice a month.

A few days later at just such a meeting, Ogden brought him up to date. William Livingston looked at him thoughtfully, saying: "I can see you're not happy with Cartwright. Why is that?"

"It's the personal vindictiveness I sense in every pore. He's out to get Ricketts. He says he wants to make him a prisoner but I think he wants to do worse than that."

The governor groaned. "I knew Sarah would bring trouble by those visits of hers. The females of my family are such a headstrong lot."

"I can think of some other headstrong members, too," ventured Ogden, presuming on their long friendship.

"If what you say is true, Matthias," continued the governor without pause, "it fits the pattern of bestiality on both sides we've been seeing more and more of, lately."

"What do mean, your Excellency?"

"For instance, take Daniel Marsh, a commissioner of oyer and terminer whom we've both known for years – the patriot who was all fired up to try Tories at Rahway, which never came off, you recall perhaps. Two days ago, he appeared before me again wanting to be sure I'd got James down on my little list. What for, for God's sake? He used to be his neighbour. And James has no property in the town – it's his mother has it, the wife of my brother Peter. She's about as respected a woman as Lady Washington herself, and far less political. It's pure vindictiveness on his part, directed as much against his notion of gentry as against the King's friends.

"I remember Philadelphia in '76 when I went to the first Continental Congress. We had Tory prisoners jammed in, locked downstairs in disgraceful conditions. The stench was so appalling we could barely carry on. Or Bull's Ferry? You recall that, don't you? A mere seventy Tory refugees held a fort against Wayne's regulars, and routed them. How could that happen? Everyone asked that. Well, I'll tell you how. They'd been dispossessed of their homes and they fought with reckless abandon against those who'd done it. These aren't fights between disciplined troops any more, lined neatly up against each other."

"Civil war does bring the worst out," observed the colonel.

Turning again to the matter of Cartwright, the governor went on: "Not only do I love my niece, whatever her Tory highjinks, but can you not see what mischief the British would make of kidnapping or hurting her, and worse, through Cartwright's vindictiveness? We'd never hear the end of it Matthias, it must be stopped!"

"The man is really appalling," added Ogden. "I have my own personal reasons for keeping James Ricketts, and Sarah, out of harm's way. Leave it in my hands, sir."

While that conference took place, Cartwright's plans proceeded apace. Knowing of Sarah's trips across the lines, he had her closely watched. It was not such a difficult task to carry out, though he would be more cautious than that time he'd tried to set up the capture of Sir Henry Clinton. He did proceed more cautiously, sending one of his agents to watch her. He also had a menial of the headquarters house in his pay – Ricketts would have to notify his superiors when his wife planned to visit New Jersey, he felt sure. The plan to nab her as bait for her husband ought to work.

Just as his scheme was getting launched, the attention of the AGs was turned to another issue, entirely unrelated to that which at the time was preoccupying Cartwright. It was pure coincidence that another matter arose out of the blue, one which might have it's entertaining side but which, on the whole, the department would just as soon not have to deal with at present.

Oliver De Lancey called them together to alert the department to this matter. "In a few months, we are to have an important visitor, Prince William Henry, Duke of Gloucester." Looking round him he saw that that some heads were nodding sagely whilst others looked attentive, but perplexed. "I'm sure you all," he said with pointed emphasis, "know instantly who he is but just in case any of you is at all hazy on the peerage, I will be so bold as to remind you that he is the second son of King George the Second, of happy memory, and the eldest of the living brothers of our gracious sovereign, King George the Third. Admiral Digby is planning shortly to bring him over for a visit. Since it has never been possible for His present Majesty to visit his American dominions, we can only welcome this royal visitor with open arms even at this late time in the story of British rule in this place.

"I need not caution you that no one must know about this outside this room, for the present."

"Oliver, this only confirms the opinion I've had for some time," interjected Richard. "There are some pretty desperate men across the river, and with important things like this going on, we must keep a close eye on them. The fact is, one of the meanest of them is one Cartwright, of whom James and I know quite a lot. One of our people has risked his life to tell us Cartwright is in Elizabethtown, up to no good, I warrant, and since we already have foiled one kidnapping scheme, against our commander-in-chief, it is not inconceivable that, with even a bigger prize to tempt him, he may try it again. This time, he'll have the advantage of having had a dry run."

He went on: "The news that Cartwright, a man who will try anything and stop at nothing, is now across the river, means that we must use all our skill to arrange that His Royal Highness's visit goes without a hitch. If we do not take the need for this seriously, I am sure that the visit will not be easy and straightforward. Not by a long shot."

It was not often that the dapper light dragoon spoke so movingly and directly to the staff and they listened with the completest attention.

"What do you have in mind, Richard?" asked De Lancey. "Or is it too early to say at this point in your thinking?"

"It is never too early when Cartwright is about, sir. There is no way of discovering what Cartwright may get up to other than going to see him and find out," A number of coughs and sniffs were heard, indicating that this observation did not get them much farther. But Richard was not through yet.

"There is only one person who has experience in intelligence work in this room whom Cartwright is not likely to know, with the exception of the adjutant general himself. We would all agree that *he* cannot be expected to undertake such a mission. Apart from you, sir, there is only one person: myself. I should undertake to beard him in his den, pretending to be a deserter, and worm my way into his confidence."

"You realize, Richard, that I hold this post of adjutant general in North America because my predecessor was ill-advised enough to undertake just such a mission."

If De Lancey thought that would end the argument, he was wrong. Richard came back instantly: "Hoping you will not find me impertinent, I have to point out that John André was not advised by anyone to do what he did. Moreover, he enlisted no support so it all fell on his shoulders. If I go as a deserter, it should be after a well-publicized letter from me to Sir Henry, stating my high-principled reasons for deserting. There would also have to be a certain amount of huffing and puffing about what a scurrilous fellow I am – that shouldn't be hard for some of my acquaintance – about how I had been heard to breathe seditious remarks, and so forth. It should not be difficult for us to arrange a convincing pattern to deceive even Cartwright."

Discussion was hot and heavy and even James, who resisted the idea with passion, was in the end compelled to admit something like this must be done and Richard was the logical person to do so.

In a few days, an announcement had appeared in the *Royal Gazette* that Ensign D. Simon of the Royal Fusiliers had deserted. A description of the uniform he might have been wearing followed. The next issue carried a couple of letters to the editor bemoaning the failure to make sure personnel understood the righteousness of the cause they were fighting for.

Captain Richard St Simon clambered out of his rowing boat near Elizabethtown. Dressed in worn civilian clothes, he still retained a few accoutrements of the 7th Regiment, the Royal Fusiliers, from which he was supposed to be a deserter. Care had been exercised to ensure that not even AG staff knew details of the mission.

A voice out of sight behind some bushes challenged him outright: "Halt right there! Put things down and your hands in the air. If you try anything funny, you could be shot – I have you covered. Who are you and what is your business here?"

"All right, all right," said Richard, apprehensively, laying the satchel and the Ferguson rifle carefully on the round. "I'm Dick Simon, late of the 7th Regiment, seeking asylum amongst the patriots."

"And how would I know that?" asked the challenger.

"Look, why else would I take this awful risk – putting myself at your mercy? I can do nothing. I'm your prisoner. Perhaps you read about me in the *Royal Gazette*?"

"Hah! I don't get to see the newspapers. Why would you desert – you are obviously English?"

"I'm convinced we fight against a just cause. You seek independence – would any true Englishman do less? May I ask whom I have the honour of addressing?"

A militia private soldier emerged cautiously. "Willow is my name, Private Willow of the Jersey militia. Suppose you are genuine –I can't see why else you'd come, all on you own. What do you want?"

"Willow, I am tired of seeing people ill-treated – tired of the cruelties of this war."

Ten minutes was enough to relax the tension, and disclose that both men were appalled at the things decent men were doing to each other. Dick described in riveting detail a couple of orders he'd contrived to disobey rather than injure his fellow man, a fact which bought the complete attention and outright admiration of Willow. They sat comradely smoking their pipes.

"What about you, Willow? You strike me as a man of great sensitivity. You must see some rum behaviour in your official capacity."

"Oh, Dick. The things I could tell you."

Sympathy brought enlightenment: "This very day, or tomorrow, I sit here awaiting a lady, a perfectly innocent lady, coming to see her family on this side. But I have to whisk her away to Elizabethtown where she is to be used in God-knows-what dishonourable way, part of some plot which her tormentors dream up. War is war and I understand soldier against soldier, but this is filthy stuff. If there was something I could do, just something, to keep her out of it, I'd surely do it. I come from near where she lived and I remember her as a little girl, as pretty as could be. It ain't right, it ain't."

When Dick discovered that Sarah was the woman in question, he made Willow aware there was something he could do. He convinced Willow – at least he hoped he'd convinced him – that her husband was a decent sort who knew and approved his desertion. When finished with intercepting Sarah, Willow could take the letter Dick would give him – if Willow would describe where Sarah was to be kept – and it would guarantee Willow's safe conduct as well as earn her husband's undying gratitude.

High though Dick had risen in Willow's esteem, it took some minutes to bring him completely around. Dick cemented his reputation by saying, if Willow would allow him to proceed, he would go to – what did he say the man's name was: Cartwright? – and offer his services while, at the same time, doing what he could to protect Sarah until her husband arrived. "That way we can kill two birds with one stone: I need someone in authority to go to if I am to help the patriots, and I can prepare the way to rescue the lady from evil." This double appeal to patriotism and to chivalry overcame the last vestiges of Willow's hesitation.

In an hour, "Dick" appeared before Cartwright. He leaned his rifle up in the corner of the large room where Cartwright sat writing at a table, moving well away from the weapon to alleviate any anxiety Cartwright might have. Willow explained that he had discovered the man shortly after his arrival on the west side of the Hudson, ascertained who he was, thought he'd give the man a chance.

Cartwright sized up the man who stood before him. How might he best use him. "Why ever would you want to desert? You're clearly not a poorly-paid private soldier with nothing to lose."

"As one gentleman to another, can you not comprehend the compulsion of realizing that you work for an unjust cause? I take it you are a Briton and have the honourable instincts of a gentleman. You certainly sound like one. Why would *you* aid the Americans?"

Something in Richard's manner, his Englishness or his authority as a gentleman seemed to catch hold of Cartwright. "No Briton" – Cartwright thought of himself more as Scottish than English, despite his schooling – "should be brought up to toady to arbitrary authority, no matter how clothed in patriotic folderol. My motives, so far as it concerns you, are many. I sympathize with all who struggle against tyranny. Be that as it may" said Cartwright, collecting up his sense of mission, " why I work against the King is neither here nor there. The question is why you want to."

"I've already told you, it's a matter of principle. Surely, as I can see you are of gentle birth, you can understand what I am saying," said Richard in a direct appeal to the vanity he detected in his enemy.

"What am I to do with you?" the spy said, stroking his chin. "As one gentleman to another. What did you say your name is? Dick Simon? Truth, if I turn you in to my authorities, you'll either be hanged as a spy out of uniform, or locked up. In either case, you'll be no bloody good to us, will you?"

"Glad you're someone who sees things with imagination and clarity." Richard, felt he had nothing to lose. He hoped the imagination bit would appeal to the celtic, poetic side of the man, and his clarity bit to the educated part of him.

"Of course, I'll have to test you. I need time to think on that. Meanwhile, Dick, you're confined to your room." Cartwright's eyes again took in the unusual weapon Richard had brought with him. His eyes began to take on a look of outright cupidity. "I see you have one of those superb rifles. I'd appreciate it if you were able to leave it here, as I'd like to try it before long."

"If you like," replied Dick, with no discernible enthusiasm.

A day passed as Richard's apprehensions over Sarah's safety grew.

On the next day, the surveillance on Sarah produced results. In place of the family carriage she expected, an unfamiliar landau which Willow helped her into, in which she was rapidly conveyed to the purlieus of Elizabethtown. The only good thing about that journey was its brevity. When she was allowed to alight, it was to confront Peter Cartwright.

"Oh, no. I might have expected you to be behind this. Is there no place we can be free of your intrusions? What do you want now? Another letter asking my husband to rescue me?"

"To take your questions one at a time: no, there is nowhere you can hide from me, not after the inconvenience you have caused me. As to the other question: it is of no concern to me whether you write your husband a letter or not. He will soon hear of your plight and when he comes, he will be brought here under close guard. Unless he is too afraid to rescue you and prefers to leave you to me."

Sending Sarah to her room, he placed a sentry outside her door. He called Dick to come before him. "Just to illustrate the efficient way in which we work, should you actually join us, I will point out that we already have Mrs Ricketts, the wife of one of my most pestilent foes, in an upstairs bedroom. Does that not impress you?"

Richard answered: "I must agree, you certainly let no grass grow under your feet, Cartwright. My congratulations." Richard was returned to his room. That night, Richard found the sentry dozing and slipped a note under Sarah's door. It told of his presence and said that, under no circumstances, was she to recognize him in front of the spy.

A few hours later, James was accosted at his house by Willow, who had made his way from the docks with the aid of the pass Richard had given him, repeating "Captain Ricketts, I must find Captain Ricketts".

James was aghast at the news Willow brought him, being somewhat re-assured by the note from Richard saying the writer would be in the house shortly, certainly by the time James could reach it. He queried Willow and pressed some coins on him, wringing his hand for the risks he'd taken, saying: "Willow, I see you are an honest fellow and I thank you. Please take care in returning to the other side."

Willow did not feel his job was done. "Begging your pardon, Captain Ricketts, but I will go over with you and see you find the house without fail. But then, if I am not to get into trouble, I will resume my post at the river."

What Richard hoped would not happen, did happen. It seemed Cartwright could not resist showing off his prize. He had them both brought to him, scrutinizing them carefully. "See what I have here, 'the reward of mine adversaries'."

Richard spoke: "I'm sorry to see you are caught up in this affair, madam. I know not if you deserve to be, but the denial of liberty does always bring risk to the deniers."

"The less I hear from you, the better. I am not accustomed to taking lessons from traitors," she replied.

"I think, if you will excuse me, Cartwright," he said, turning away, "'It is better to dwell in the wilderness, than with a contentious and angry woman'".

"Well said, Mr Simon," remarked the spy, beaming with admiration. "Before you go, I have a task for you, Dick. You will take this note to her husband, telling him to come here without fanfare should he wish to see her again."

Richard looked aghast. "But I am a deserter. I will be walking right into their clutches."

"And so you should!" muttered Sarah.

Cartwright disregarded her and said: "If you are to work for us, you will have to be efficient and quick. I do not retain agents who are not up to the mark. You will have to find a way of getting the note to him, if you dare not do it yourself."

Chapter 29

"Meanwhile, Colonel Ogden had not been idle. Despite all the AGs' precautions, he caught wind of a projected visit by a member of the royal family and needed to consult Cartwright. While Sarah was locked in her room, Colonel Ogden, ignorant of what had occurred, arrived on horseback, searching for Cartwright.

"Good afternoon, colonel. To what do I owe this pleasure?" said the spy as he rocked slowly in a chair on the front porch, having only just sat down to smoke a cheroot.

The colonel hitched his mount to the porch railing and turned to face him. "What I have to say is for no one else's ears. Let us take a little walk, Cartwright."

A hundred yards from the dwelling, Ogden opened the matter of the Prince's visit to New York, advising Cartwright to make careful preparations well in advance. The spy felt he always made ample preparations, besides he had something more concrete than preparations to show the colonel. "Talking of abduction, colonel, I'm ahead of you there already. You'd never guess who is now my prisoner, locked upstairs."

"Your prisoner? I don't understand."

"The governor's niece, Sarah Ricketts, no less." He could scarcely contain himself for preening.

"But why, man? Why on earth hold *her*?"

"Set a sprat to catch a mackerel, I think the phrase goes."

After a moment's silence, Ogden burst forth: "You mean to force Captain Ricketts to come after her. But why? Indeed, sir, you are a blundering idiot. Don't you realize the harm you can do to our side by following some mad scheme of revenge, some pointless violence? What good is served by enticing a serving officer in this foul way? No good at all, sir. Except flattering your own vanity and and feeding your own vengefulness. The governor and I have discussed this tendency of yours. And we don't like it. No sir, we do not. Have you any idea what damage you could do to the cause of independence if we become associated with bloodthirsty abduction or assassination of civilians? I'll not stand for it an instant, d'ye hear? You will release her at once. Is that clear?"

Peter Cartwright's face had darkened more deeply at each phrase. "You talk of pointless violence, do ye? You pampered play-acting general's vassal!"

"How dare you talk to me like that, you traitor!" said Ogden.

"'What shall be done to thee, thou false tongue?' How can you call me a traitor, you hypocrite? You who have thrown off your oaths to German George – someone *I* have never sworn allegiance to. Traitor indeed!"

Some minutes before, Richard had met James hastening up from the river. James was now by himself, carrying his Ferguson rifle, as Willow was left behind at his usual post. Fearing an enemy was before him, James lifted the stock to his shoulder when the figure advancing cried out: "James, for God's sake, don't shoot. It's me, Richard." They quickly joined each other, making toward the house. On reaching the grounds, Richard decided to sneak into the house while James, fascinated by the contretemps going on in the garden, settled himself prone under a bush and brought the two men in the garden within his sights.

He recognized Cartwright who was menacing Ogden, himself also familiar but from the happier days of childhood in Elizabethtown. He saw the spy take a pistol from his belt and command the colonel to walk off a few yards. As the colonel moved off, with his back to Cartwright, the spy casually lowered his pistol. He's going to shoot him, realized James.

"I'll show you pointless violence," muttered Cartwright. He pulled the trigger carefully, but with some deliberation, so as to enjoy every moment of Ogden's discomfiture.

James aimed his rifle and squeezed the trigger. A loud crack sounded and James felt the strong recoil as the bullet sped to Cartwright, catching him in the back and passing through his heart. James rose up, running toward Ogden who stood still, dazed.

The sentry outside Sarah's room rushed downstairs at the noise and, seeing Richard's rifle propped up against the wall, grabbed it. He had envied "Dick" his rifle when newly-arrived and now saw his chance to use it. He broke the glass of a downstairs window and poked the rifle out, taking aim at James. Richard saw him take aim but was too far away to do anything. And, for some reason, he seemed oddly unperturbed.

When the sentry pulled the trigger, there was a slight hiss as the powder in the pan was ignited by the flint and almost instantaneously the rifle exploded, stripping off skin and hair - one eye smashed into his disfigured skull - taking away the right half of the sentry's face. He collapsed dead on the floor.

The rifle had virtually disintegrated, blowing up in the soldier's face. Birds twittered in panic as they shot out of the trees.

Richard smashed into Sarah's door. It flew open, almost unhinged by the blow. Sarah stood inside, her hands up to her face with anxiety. Before she could speak, he said to her, urgently: "Come on. No time." Grabbing her wrist, he led her as they shot down the stairs, where he unhitched the spy's horse and she mounted behind him, holding tight.

Richard wheeled the horse round the house, reaching the colonel and James, staring down at Cartwright's body. "James I know, and Sarah too, but who the devil are you?" the colonel blurted out, taking in Richard's tatty appearance.

"Captain the Earl of Bassett, of His Majesty's 17th Regiment of Light Dragoons, at your service, sir. I am returning Mrs Ricketts to her husband. Captain Ricketts seems to have made short work of Cartwright. Fellow aiming at James from the window, too. I thought he looked at my rifle greedily. Knew it was just a matter of time before one of them tried it, so I stuffed some mud in the muzzle. Never does to fire a dirty piece. Sorry about all the pother. I'm taking this horse off to the river and will make a gift of it to my good friend Private Willow. I suggest, James, you find another and follow with Sarah."

Ogden addressed James: "Someday I hope we'll have the chance to talk about all this, James. But, at the moment, you're an enemy officer behind our lines. Since you saved my life - and my old friend's - I can't do less than lend you my horse, so the sooner you're off, the better, for all of us, eh?" Turning to Richard, he said formally: "Your servant, sir." Seeing that Richard was still there, Ogden added: "I notice, young man, you're not in uniform. Unless King's Regulations have changed a lot since I knew them. If you hang about here much longer giving me fatuous excuses for your extraordinary conduct, I'll be obliged to arrest you as a spy." In a kindly tone, he added: "Now, off you go. Skedaddle out of here, fast, all of you."

"I will never forget this, dear Colonel," said Sarah to Ogden. Richard doffed his hat in his most meticulous salute-from-the-saddle style.

"Nor will I, nor will I," muttered Colonel Ogden, under his breath.

After they had galloped the mile to the rowing boat which Richard had hidden, they dismounted. Sarah kissed Richard lightly on the cheek and relieved his momentary confusion by adding: "Well, I just knew you must be good for something!"

Richard had to report to De Lancey that he had failed his assignment. They were no for'rarder in the matter of the princely visit. "My dear Richard, I think we can forgive you that as you have, in fact, helped to put an end to Cartwright."

"Yes, there is that," agreed Richard modestly.

"Now we must distribute reports about how Richard Simon met an untimely death, just to tie up loose ends" said the adjutant general. Funny how similar to your name that turncoat was."

James and Sarah rejoiced at first in the news of Cartwright's demise. Second thoughts proved less jubilant. James first put it into words: "Actually, I feel a bit sad over Cartwright. Oh, he was a villain, all right, but did he begin like that?" queried James. "I mean he was probably acting out of conviction and at cost to himself – he could have had few moments of ease and contentment in his kind of clandestine and adversarial life." They knew nothing of his murder of Healy.

Sarah knew what he meant. "Do you ever feel pulled down, morally I mean, tainted by war or the situations it puts you in, my sweet?"

"Yes, I do. Indeed, I do," said James. It was the closest he got to talking about his time in Savannah. He did admit to himself one duty that he could readily perform. The next day at his office, he took pen and paper to write:

October 8, 1781

My dear Daphne,

I entrust this letter to Mr Pierson of my regiment for safe delivery. He will be at Savannah for three months. If you are so inclined, you may reply without worry.

A few days ago, an event took place in New Jersey of benefit both to the service and to you. Our mutual acquaintance Cartwright died violently at my hand.

Unless something unforseen occurs, I expect the hold he had over you is now lifted. For this we can both rejoice. I cannot go into further details nor add to this letter as I would like to do, but end it by assuring you of my endless esteem.

James

Chapter 30

Unfairly, Sir Henry Clinton found himself to be the convenient scapegoat for the Yorktown defeat. Despite the endless meddling of Lord Germain, the Secretary of State for the Colonies, despite his disastrous grant of operational independence to Cornwallis, despite Sir Henry's attempts to prevent Cornwallis from entering Virginia and then, when that failed, to have Admiral Graves rescue him, Cornwallis remained the blue-eyed boy of Germain and all London. Clinton recognized his impossible position and, with a change of government in London imminent, resigned, planning to return to England. All this affected James, Richard and the other members of the staff of the adjutant general in New York.

Seeing his hopes go down the drain, one by one, De Lancey still strove to keep his staff up to date. "Now that Prince William Henry has safely come and gone, we can attend to other matters. You may not all of you yet know that in March, Lord North's government resigned, mostly owing to the failure of their policy over here. The Marquis of Rockingham has become prime minister. He has consistently said he would end the previous government's coercive policies and bring peace to America. Consequently, we look forward to a new commander-in-chief coming to us. He is Sir Guy Carleton, lately governor of Canada. He was appointed to command here in February and arrives the fifth of May. We'll all have to get used to him. And do whatever we can to assist him. Are there any questions?"

Apart from a few queries on administrative details to do with Sir Guy's expected arrival, nobody raised anything. Carleton alone could tell them his plans. They were preoccupied with digesting the fact that the attempt to quell the rebellion was a failure. They would have to contribute to the policy of making peace. They needed some sort of breather.

There was no breather. Sir Henry's peace of mind was plagued up to the moment he set sail by the violence of the struggle between rebels and loyalists. Driven frantic by the rebels' successful driving of loyalists from their homes, Governor Franklin and his Board of

Associated Loyalists embarked on a campaign of revenge and intimidation which reached its climax in the "execution" of Huddy, a rebel artillery officer, by Lippincott, an affair not directly involving James, but one which engaged the attentions of Governor Livingston, General Washington and the foreign minister and king and queen of France.

Clinton needed advice on how to deal with loyal Americans – they were turning out to be as much a problem as the rebels were. Where better to turn than the American on the AG staff that St Simon had talked so favourably about? James was startled to be summoned to the Commander-in-chief's office at the beginning of April.

The general told him: "I've sent for you, Ricketts, at the suggestion of St Simon who has a high opinion of you, and since I have a high regard for him, I will have the same opinion of you, I don't doubt. This bloody Lippincott affair. To be more precise, the entire matter of the Board of Associated Loyalists. It's a pandora's box. You are an American. I need your eyes to see clearly what is going on. The fact is – and what I say to you is in confidence – Governor Franklin and his board could well turn this war into a bandit's picnic. I want you to meet them and smoke them out for me."

James attended a number of Board and other legal meetings to observe the depth of enmity and duly reported his impressions of their implacable hostility to the general.

When Sir Guy arrived, he was thrown into the awkward matter. He quickly discovered that matter to be only one instance of an increasingly bitter and lawless feuding. It encouraged acrimonious pressure, both from British regulars and the rebels. He had no time to ease into his new position; he was being pressed to decide what to do about Lippincott. Sir Henry had already taken steps to curb the power of Franklin's Board of Associated Loyalists. That was some help. Much more would be required.

Sir Guy thus consulted the Chief Justice of New York and the Attorney General. In ten seconds the normally relaxed and affable, tall Irishman turned into a taut racquet, all stiff and explosive. "I am telling you straight, gentlemen, I have never before been in such an awkward and potentially dangerous situation. Irish protestants are known for hating Rome but I had less trouble winning the trust and

– yes, I'll say – affectionate friendship of the papish clergy of Quebec than I have coping with this loyalist board."

William Franklin was openly suspected of being behind his board's unprincipled behaviour and of duplicity toward Sir Henry Clinton. Sensing the increasing enmity which the British military authorities were feeling towards him and under the pretext of carrying a petition from the loyalists to the King, he left America, sailing to England the next month. What with both Clinton and Franklin gone, the guard was changing fast.

By summer's end, it was obvious that peace was coming. "It is not the peace I hoped for, with Britain and America united, but it will be peace, for all that," James commented to Sarah.

Sir Guy made a habit of looking in on his staff and on one occasion he asked James how, as an American, he felt. James tried to explain: "I am American. I've always thought of myself that way. It's odd. I don't think of myself often as a loyalist. Perhaps that's because I'm a regular officer, not in a provincial regiment. I'm not going to turn my back on New Jersey, not unless I am forced to. I suppose they – or do I say 'we' – will have independence. I don't regret that from any opposition to home rule. I regret it because it breaks our family ties to Britain. And I remember what both the Earl of Eglinton and our own Major John Brown said about our tendency to isolate ourselves, to turn inwards, to wallow in ignorance of the outside world, and even smugly enjoy that ignorance.

"I don't want my country to be self-centred like that and I don't want my children to, either. To me, Britain is our window to the outside. That's why I will always try to keep in touch, to be as much at home in one as in the other – if that's possible," he added wistfully.

Sir Guy looked at him hard and long but not unkindly. "You're not Irish, I suppose?" he remarked impishly, smiling. "Seriously though, I cannot say what is possible. As you know, I come from a country which is largely disaffected from the rest of Britain. My sort knows all the reasons for this and we share the blame for it, but we would still fight any lessening of the bonds with Britain. I come out of the "ascendancy" crowd, than which no lot is more bigoted. Yet I am the darling of the papists in Canada – some say I saved Canada for the Crown. Maybe. But what Canada did for me, a benighted Irish bigot, is wonderful. It taught me tolerance. Maybe some of that is true for your country, too. Unfortunately, those who teach us the value of toleration are not always themselves examples of it. At any rate, let's talk again."

"Thank you, sir,"

Sir Guy was not finished. "You've gained some insight into how courts martial work, I hear from De Lancey and St Simon. I'm going to put that to use and appoint you to one or two standing courts martial," said the general as he grabbed his tricornered hat with the gold piping, smiled and stooped cautiously, narrowly missing the door lintel as he made his way to the stairs, humming softly.

True to his word, Sir Guy put James on a general court martial constituted the third of August at ten o'clock at the City Hall under the presidency of Major Edward Eyre of the 40th Regiment. This detail took up a lot of James's time but the only trial was a private soldier of the 22nd Regiment, severely mauled at Elizabethtown during Knyphausen's expedition, who was convicted of desertion, having been captured by Associated Loyalists among whom was Captain Tilton - who had figured in the Lippincott trial and had later escaped the rebels or been exchanged. The defendant was sentenced to five hundred lashes. The court was dissolved at the end of the month.

Once more, James found himself on a court martial, from the nineteenth of October, exactly a year after Yorktown, sitting under Brigadier General Martin, the dispossessed governor of North Carolina, whom he had met during his prior introduction to the Board of Associated Loyalists. Two private men of the 3d Battalion New Jersey Volunteers were sentenced to death for assaulting Lieutenant Waller Locke of HMS *Warwick*. A drummer and five private men of General Skinner's New Jersey Volunteers were acquitted.

None of this registered with James as particularly significant for his life except that it reinforced his conviction that army life could be brutal and that with little to do but wait around to be withdrawn after a seven years' war it had not won, morale worsens and insubordination increases along with more and more extreme steps to maintain discipline. It was a fine thing when ex-governors of provinces were kept employed sitting on courts martial, like General Martin. The sooner it all ended, the better, thought James.

James's sense of living in a finale was increased when Lieutenant Pierson arrived back from Savannah, bearing a letter for James. It read:

20th June, 1782

> *My dear James,*
>
> *Your kind letter arrived without mishap. In times such as these, however, correspondence is always uncertain. In our situation, many details which beg to be stated must be left unsaid lest others derive aid and comfort to our cost. You will understand me if I stick close to the news you sent me and which, I assume, is in the public domain.*
>
> *Glad as I am that someone as hurtful to our interests as Mr C. has quitted our lives, my feelings of anger towards him are not assuaged by his failure to tell me, for reasons we can both imagine, of the death through fever of my dear brother a full year before the time when I informed you of his part in complicating my affairs.*
>
> *It brings home to me the hope that this hateful struggle of brother against brother will soon end – we hear that the King's troops will quit Savannah in July – and that the corrupting influences of clandestine activity – of which C. was so signal an example – will leave you untouched by them.*
>
> *I am so grateful that amidst the many demands on your time and attention, you nevertheless took pains to tell me the news of C. (whose name I cannot bear to write out). We both have reason for wanting peace to come and, more than that, being able to live in that heavenly state where hatred has no power and love can be shewn without inhibition or dissembling.*

D.B.

Breakfasting in their garden one cool November morning, Sarah noticed her husband in a particularly silent and uncommunicative mood. At last he broke the quiet: "I've been thinking a lot about our future."

"So have I, my sweet," she said, barely above a whisper.

"Of course you must have, my darling. Not right for me to be so self-absorbed – not to notice what you've been thinking," he admitted guiltily.

"Never mind. *What* do you think?" she asked him.

He paused to pour more tea. "In a few months, the war will be over and then, sooner or later, the army will be gone. That leaves us two alternatives: we follow the drum and make a career in England or the Caribbean or wherever. In that case, I have an uncertain prospect – uncertain as to promotion. For one thing, the regiment is always reduced in peacetime. It may go to one or two battalions and vacancies will be few. Even though we both feel at home in England, it would be uncertain, professionally, and we would be far away from all our connections here."

"And if, my sweet, we should have children – what then? They'll be reared entirely in England, I imagine, without those connections which in England, for better or worse, we know are necessary to get on comfortably in society, to be a mite crass," she added.

"But you're right," he cut in. "They always say women are the greatest realists, don't they?"

"What's the other alternative?" she said, putting their conversation back on a pragmatic track.

"Suppose I resign. I think Sir Guy would let me do that. It would not mean running out on anybody. There is little I can do now to have any effect on this country's future. We're all just marking time until someone else makes decisions. If I resign, we could go to England until everything quietens down. Before doing so, I'd like to have some idea if we can go back to Elizabethtown – I assume we'd go there, rather than Basking Ridge. Lord Stirling will want his place back and, besides, it's a little too close for comfort to Uncle William, I fancy."

There was not much more to be said. The latter choice was the one they both favoured. Sarah undertook to write, broaching the subject to her relations: their parents, still presumably at Basking Ridge, and some of James's family at Elizabethtown. After all, Sarah particularly had made every effort to keep in touch, to the annoyance of the hard man of the family.

Replies came back by the end of November; all agreed that while they were overjoyed at the prospect of reunion, it was too early to say anything definite. Perhaps a couple of years would suffice for things to settle. They might find it easier than they thought to make a life in England, in which case they would have a real choice when the right time came, though all hoped the choice would be Elizabethtown.

James and his wife looked at each other steadily. A few seconds later, they simultaneously burst into gales of mirth. They clasped hands. It always seemed that serious talk between them heightened their desire for each other. Knowing the house was momentarily empty of servants, they went inside. Even though it was morning, they abandoned themselves to one another as if it were the most natural thing in the world to do.

James decided to see Sir Guy. It was easier for him to do than he thought it would be – Sir Guy was one of those people who make it seem as if he had been waiting for his guest; James almost had to bite his tongue not to apologize for being late. He repeated what Sarah and he had discussed. Sir Guy agreed that peace was coming but pointed out that treatment of loyalists – and whatever James thought of himself, his neighbours would think of him as one – was going to vary from "province, er, state to state". He remarked that people in their social circles had advantages, especially since James had seen no fighting in his own state. Sir Guy had friends in London to whom he would be happy to recommend them and he was sure they would make out. As for the army, James had never joined the company of which he was captain. That was all right because Lieutenant Samuel DeVisme, paymaster to the 60th in New York and known to James and Sarah, professionally and socially, was anxious to buy a company – DeVisme would probably stay in the army and eventually settle in London.

"By the way," added the general, "a word of advice, if I may. You may not wish to use your rank on this side of the ocean when the peace does finally come, but life being as it is in England, you'll always want to be "Captain" Ricketts – it won't hurt. Irishmen like me are famous for being aware of such matters, you know." It was thus arranged for James to sell his captaincy to DeVisme for fifteen hundred pounds and resign eleven days before Christmas.

One person James hated to say goodbye to was Richard.

"My dear fellow, what you plan is eminently sensible. I'm not sure how long I'll stay in the army once this is over. One of these days, you'll find a penniless waif lounging on your London doorstep begging food and a bed for the night." The unlikelihood of such an event befalling the Earl of Bassett threw James into gales of laughter. He noticed that Richard's face did no more than hint at a smile, so he knew how emotionally trying the peer was finding the occasion. Sarah was not fooled for an instant and threw her arms round Richard, planting a noisy kiss on his cheek.

"When you come to see us, you unspeakable wretch" she said, "I'll scare up some London beauties to plague you, you rogue."

"Bless you," he said in a strained voice, turning quickly away to leave the room.

Not everyone was so buttoned up. Laurie, cleaning dishes in the kitchen, broke into floods of tears and was for a short while inconsolable until she remembered she was a Black Watch wife and dried her tears. Cyrus was in raptures over being given the option of going to England with them and leapt at the chance with both hands. "You never do know – I might be grabbed back into servitude in this country, but I know a black man is really free the minute he sets foot in ol' England."

Chapter 31

In April of 1785, London consented to bestow a balmy and sunny spring day on its inhabitants, an event unusual enough to bring citizens away from their fires and out into the streets. Among those strolling up and down St Mary Street in Marylebone were Captain and Mrs Ricketts. Other strollers were about too. One, a lanky man with dark hair, walked down to the end of the street and then turned about at the top. He turned down it again. At that moment, James and Sarah entered the street, arm in arm, moving toward the fields later known as Regents Park. They came up abreast to the dark-haired man who seemed about to pass them by when he suddenly halted, recognizing James. The man looked excited.

"Well, ah'm jiggered. Have we not met, sir?" asked the man in an unmistakeably southern American drawl. "Yes, ah'm certain we have. Do you not recall the circumstances, sir?"

James and Sarah were startled not only by the accent but by the exclamation which had not yet appeared on the English scene and which gave away the speaker's origins. James looked hard at the speaker, then broke into a smile as he extended his hand. "Temple, is it not?" said he, surprised at his own power of recall. Sarah was even more surprised at that uncharacteristic accomplishment. Faces, yes – names, no. "I believe it was at Brier Creek, was it not?" said James.

"Most assuredly! John Temple, late of the Georgia Continentals, at your service."

James hastily introduced him to Sarah but before he could say more, Temple cut in: "Your husband saved ma life, ma'am, a-shovin' that hie'lan' brute who was about to skewer me out of this world. A not inconsiderable thing to do, considering ma wife had just played him a trick – pretending our small boy had a pox – so she could ride south and warn us of the enemy's approach. But your husband was too sharp for her. When he spied our hoss in the field ready to carry her, he nipped the crittur. The horse did manage eventually to find his way home, so I reckon ya didn't take him too far off."

"Of course, it's true I didn't know you were her husband when we had our meeting at Brier Creek, did I?"

"That still doesn't detract from your credit in my eyes, or in her's," observed John Temple.

James recollected his manners and introduced John Temple to Sarah. However, the lanky Georgian was not to be derailed by this courtesy. Doffing his hat and almost making a leg to her, he resumed his account: "Your husband, ma'am, at some risk to himself, performed a most christian and charitable act. He did not know me from Adam. To him ah was nothin' but a two-bit Georgia cracker, and his enemy to boot. Yet he intervened and that, truly, is the only reason ah can stand afore ye now. It was a kindness the like of which I'd never seen and neither ma wife nor ah can forget - ever."

"I'm delighted we met in one of my more acceptable moments," replied James, wanting to lighten the occasion. "How is your charming and – if I may say so without offence – most plausible wife? Have you more family?" James was becoming more than a little embarrassed by being lauded as a hero in tones loud enough to be heard in Oxford Street.

"Jes' fine, sir. We have three young-uns now. They're with us in London and you must come and see them."

Thinking it would be more comfortable and noting James's squeamishness over being thrust noisily into the public eye, Sarah invited Temple to walk the few yards to their own house where the conversation continued. John Temple revealed that he was set up in business in the City as agent for some American financiers.

"After your experiences at our hands, it is perhaps surprising to find you here?" remarked James.

"Not at all. Not at all. Ah was exchanged pretty quick back in '80 and then had a chance to work for some northern financial men. Besides, I do love London. So does ma wife, despite the dirt and the smells – it is the most wonderful city in the whole world. Of course it helps if you grew up on a Georgia hog farm! But you and your good lady must come and meet ma family and ma colleagues. They'd be jes' delahted to meet the man about whom they've heard so many times."

It was arranged for James and Sarah to make a visit to a merchant's house on the western edge of the mile-square City. About a week later, Sarah and James went and were shown upstairs where Captain David Price was introduced to them.

"I can't believe it. Now it's my turn to be astonished" said James, beaming happily. "I remember David as a neighbour when we were both boys in Elizabethtown."

"Absolutely right. We grew up in the same place. I well recall your very imposing father, telling us not to sit around but do something useful.

"But come along," said Temple, as the handsome woman James recognized to be Mrs Temple, accompanied by a boy of about eleven years of age, entered the room. Amy Temple stopped just short of giving James a hug, saying: "Captain Ricketts – James, if ah may make so bold, whatever must you have thought of me, tellin' you that cock-and-bull stow-ry about Petey havin' the chickenpox? And all the tahm, you knew t'was but a fable."

James did not choose to enlighten her that it was later, through the regimental surgeon, that he learned of her deception. "Why, ma'am," she said, addressing a thoroughly amused Sarah, "all the tahm he was such a gallant gennaman, a-strivin' to reassure us no harm would befall. Ah declare, ma'am, and ah hope you'll take no offence, I was fair swep' off ma feet, and would have set ma cap for your husband but for ma dearest John havin' that role already!"

James and Sarah were relieved when she turned to introduce her son, The boy was apparently imbibing his London schooling with a vengeance as he spoke in the irritating, clipped cadence of Mayfair. Amy had not exhausted her fund of surprises, however. "Our second son is called Mark - after your colonel, such a kind man. This whole affair made us behold y'all in a new light, ya know – sorry we had to fight you," she averred.

"We have an even bigger surprise in store," continued Price, clearly relishing the aura of mystery that now settled on the room. "Indeed, I think I hear him on the stairs."

A man of middle age entered the room which he instantly dominated. He was Matthias Ogden. To add to the surprise, he was followed by his friend Jacob Hart. They stood back to examine James who was assailed by nostalgia.

"They say it's a small world, don't they, James? I believe them." He addressed them all: "I've known James and Sarah since they were youngsters. I recall you as a lad just before you went off to college – King's, it was then. Then there was the endless exorbitant praises your former fellow officer, my fellow officer Jacob here, keeps pouring over your name for saving his life and letting him obey his conscience when he decided to join us in '75. Sarah and I were able to renew our friendship, though only briefly, when she was kidnapped four years ago. Though I've always wondered about that gallant buck who swept you off on, er, *my* horse."

Sarah yelped, "There's no harm telling you now, he was Captain Richard St Simon, Earl of Bassett."

"Oh, I heard him give his name, and any fool can look up people in the Army List. What I had in mind is how he happened to be there?"

James explained: "In September of '81, Admiral Digby brought Prince William Henry to New York. We knew Cartwright might catch on and try one of his kidnapping stunts, so Richard took himself off to worm his way into the spy's confidence. It was pure chance he happened to be there when Sarah was brought in and, as Colonel Ogden knows, rescued her."

"How entertaining! Well, your account of Cartwright's part in the plot to capture the King's brother is not quite acurate. It was too high-level to impart to Cartwright, so it was given to me, if I say so modestly. In fact, I had a letter from General Washington telling me to safeguard the health of the Prince and Admiral Digby should we catch them, but something went wrong and the plan was compromised. It would have been quite a coup – nabbing a member of the royal family. Anyway, strange coincidences do happen, I've discovered. Sarah was fortunate to have him so alert and ready to act on her behalf. It also strikes me how oddly war throws people together. I felt little liking for the wretch Cartwright, and he for me, but there we were, having to work together. Isn't it strange what bedfellows, er, excuse me, what colleagues a nasty thing like a war can produce?"

Ogden was Temple's and Price's superior in the firm. The colonel, who no longer used his rank, went on: "Of course, Sarah, I well remember your family. Perhaps that's the gift of a happy marriage." Turning to James, he said: "What brings you to London, James?"

James took his time framing an answer. He felt that the question was not a casual one. "Well, Colonel,"

"Matthias," interposed Ogden, "please."

"Well," said James, trying to pick up his thread, "as you may know, I was commissioned into the 60th of Foot before the Revolution. By the end of the war, I was in New York, attached to the Adjutant General's staff, and I retired at the end of '82. Since our side lost, we left for London where we have been the last three years."

"For me, what's past is past. I can see nothing to be gained through being fettered to it. And how do you like London? I have worked in Paris but, for me, London is the place – I feel it's my second home."

"We love London, too" admitted James.

Sarah went out on a limb. "In truth, sir, much as we love this country, New Jersey has always been home in our eyes, and recently we have made overtures to discover if we are considered odious by our neighbours."

"Anyone considering you two to be odious must be either blind or a prisoner of obsolete passions," said Ogden comfortingly. "But talking of those days – and listening to you I feel confident we can do so candidly and *sans rancour* – were you in New York in September of '81 when Prince William Henry was there?"

"Yes. In fact, it was quite an exciting time for us. I wasn't directly involved but our department was."

"Yes, yes," chuckled Ogden. "I was to lead a party of men to seize him, but somehow they got on to us."

James concurred: "It certainly was a bold plan which at the time, I recall, evoked our anxiety, and our admiration. But tell me, sir, why do I see so many New Jersey people in London all at once?"

Ogden provided an answer: "Apart from the fact that we like the place, we represent Robert Morris – you may know his name. He practically financed the last few years of the Revolution personally, though he was Liverpool-born. But, may I ask, how would you both feel if you were living in the state of New Jersey?"

James saw no point in dissembling. "I cannot deny it, Matthias – the war did not come out as we hoped. But, as you say, what's done is done. We would like above all else to live in Elizabethtown, though we will always keep in touch with England. I hope that would not rule out our being useful citizens – people our neighbours could depend on. I don't know if these two things seem incompatible to you?"

Ogden spread his hands expressively. "But why should these things be at odds, now that peace is come? As far as affection for Great Britain goes, you can see that we are all here, and not against our wills either. Since self-governance is no longer an issue, why should wider interests be an embarrassment?"

As if to give substance to this, he added: "I hope you won't think me out of line if I say that when the time comes for your return home, I trust you will get in touch with me.

"Let me speak candidly. When Sir Guy Carleton evacuated New York in November of '83, he took seven thousand Americans with him. The population of New York was then about twenty-two thousand. That means the real diehards – begging your pardon – who followed the old flag and gave up virtually everything to do it, were about a third of the city. Think of – a third!

"There must have been more who were disappointed by the break with England yet managed to stay on, so at least half the people of the city were not exactly thrilled with the war's outcome. As you know, I was for independence as I am still. But I'm also a realist. Who knows what will become of our states? We might just need friends in all parts of the world, and people like you could be the very ones to help your Jersey neighbours."

Amplifying his remarks, Ogden pointed out something James had not thought of: "You'll probably find quite a number of former 60th people engaged in business in New York. Our lawyers, for a start - Asby and Hutchins. Just so" he added on seeing James's surprised look.

"I have wondered what happened to Thomas. I know about him as far as his being geographer of the United States."

"He became a lawyer after the war. Being such a skilled mapmaker, he was invaluable to his firm, especially as so many cases involved surveying. Even tried to recover land in Pennsylvania for his old colonel, General Haldimand – but that was hopeless. Nobody would enforce claims by the former power against squatters. And there's young Prevost who now lives in New York, formerly one of your captains. Perhaps these 60th names are a surprise?"

Before he could answer, Ogden continued: "What you ought to know is what Hutchins says about you." If possible, James looked even more surprised.

"Yes, indeed. He's mentioned you several times. Credits you with convincing him not to quit his regiment in an underhand way, but to do everything honourably."

James said: "We had a talk in London in '77 but I never realized the idea of resigning with honour was a contribution of mine."

"You clearly had some effect on him. Perhaps in contrast to all those people trying to get something out of him – either to fight Americans or spy on his employers. Perhaps he appreciated someone who didn't twist his arm to do something. I think he feels it clarified the ethical issues.

"But more to the point: he has a degree of acquaintanceship with Governor Livingston. He might be persuaded – considering his debt to you – to write saying you'd be a good man to have in the state. If you like, I'll sound him out. After all, what with Temple and me living to tell the tale, the governor can't be too negative about someone who provided invaluable maps to the Continental Army, can he?"

"It's strange – the possibility of returning arises from a chance meeting with John Temple in front of our house," said Sarah.

"Well, ma'am," said Temple, exchanging a glance with Ogden, "it might not have been completely by chance."

After the departure of the Rickettses, the American associates, including Amy Temple, poured themselves whisky and discussed the get-together.

"What think ye, my friends? Do you see them settling back in New Jersey?" asked Price.

The Temples saw no reason they shouldn't. "They'ah first-raters , whateva' their political history," volunteered Amy Temple. It seemed she spoke for all.

"Do you think they would come? They've got a rah't interestin' life hyar in London," observed her husband.

"Oh, I don't have much doubt about that. They made it quite plain, I think," remarked Matthias Ogden. "Well, how's about it? Shall we do what we can?"

"By all means," said Jacob, seconded by Price. "Personally, I think we can use people of integrity, people who take their allegiance seriously, however they see it, in our new republic," Jacob added.

"Good. Let's do what we can," summarized Ogden.

Two years later, a carriage drawn by a pair of greys, plain built but handsomely sprung, comfortable if hardly sumptuous, pulled up in front of a three-storey house in Bond Street. Assisted by the coachman, a handsome black man of impressive bearing, emerged first a trim man in a blue coat, buff breeches and white small-clothes, wearing not a wig but, in the newer fashion of the time, his own hair swept back in a queue. He waited as the footman adjusted the steps and handed down a girl of just over four years of age. She was pretty, with a pink chubby face but determined features, reddish-brown hair cut short, wearing a party dress with a pink sash.

In turn, she was followed by her stunning-looking mother in a full-skirted, low-bodiced ivory-coloured dress, her thin waist accentuated by the blue sash round it. The father of the family had a somewhat boyish demeanour with a prominent, retroussé nose, but his deportment spoke of self-confidence and an authority beyond his years. He supervised his family's descent from the carriage, gave instructions to the driver to await their return in what he said would not be a long time.

It was not the first time that the three had visited Daniel Gardner's studio. The servant who admitted them greeted them with the pleasant smile reserved for those he had seen before. In his opinion, they seemed to be unselfconsciously affable in that beneficent, easy-going, unobtrusive way persons of quality sometimes exhibited.

Upstairs, they were greeted by the artist in a paint-streaked smock exuding the faint odour of gum-arabic. "Good afternoon, ladies – Captain Ricketts, your servant, sir," he said robustly as befitted a man in his late thirties who had made a fair name for himself painting portraits of society patrons. Originally from Kendal in the very paintable northern lake district, he had taken lessons from the young Romney as a boy, moving to London at eighteen years of age. At twenty he entered the Royal Academy Schools, assisting briefy in Sir Joshua Reynolds's studio at age twenty-three.

In 1771 he ventured his chances at the annual Royal Academy exhibition and was so successful that he never needed to exhibit there again, contenting himself, not with notoriety or fame, but with a solid reputation amongst those who would patronize him because they could see that his work was good. That exhibition established him and he worked up a fashionable practice in rather small portraits in crayons or gouache, sometimes using a highly-loaded medium of uncertain composition, though perhaps of brandy or wine spirits with crayons scraped to dust with a knife – a formula he kept secret. Reynolds's influence was apparent in his work though he used such patterns in a rococo manner.

For the moment, the painter was seized with a fit of coughing which provoked Sarah to begin to recommend a doctor she knew. He interrupted: "Oh, my dear lady, I stay away from physics whenever I can; I much prefer to quack myself with medicines."

This sitting was the last of several, just to see that everything was as it should be. Sarah had been persuaded to wear a fantastical hat he kept for such portraits. She was unsure at first but when he pointed out that it was in keeping with the, to her rather exorbitant, background of an immense stone pillar and deep forest, she was emboldened to put it on.

They were less thrilled by the depiction of their daughter Maria: it struck them as a bit stereotypical – rather like other young girls whom Mr Gardner had painted. With that one hesitation, they thought the picture a grand one in the tradition of English family portraits, more lively and charming than the wooden-faced, amateurish efforts of so many earlier colonial paintings they had seen in New York.

Gardner himself seemed pleased, though he was modest enough not to say so, despite an inclination to extravagance of style. He was satisfied that some people had noted his children's portraits showed remarkable tenderness of feeling.

The artist was emboldened by their comments to ask "Will you be hanging it in your London house?" To be honest, he did not know if their residence near St Marylebone was permanent or not or whether they had a country seat – he fancied not since his frequent incursions into Debrett's *The New Peerage* and *Paterson's Roads* did not reveal one for them. He knew only that they were comfortably-off and had connections with America.

"We will take it with us back to Elizabethtown – New Jersey," James added when he noticed that, given the name of the town on its own, the artist was none the wiser, if better informed. "We often rent a place in London for long periods, usually in the winter, but our home is really at Elizabethtown."

"I see. You have been coming to the metropolis for a long time, then. How fortunate to know both the old world and the new."

Sarah could see he was discreetly fishing. Nevertheless, she was inclined to satisfy the curiosity of this talented young man. "My husband left the army a year before the peace of Paris and we came here, not knowing how our neighbours would feel about us since so many of them had been on the other side in that cruel, cruel war," Sarah explained.

"I see. Yes it must have been very hard. I hope it all worked out for the best," he ventured sympathetically. "No doubt America was very divided by the struggle. So was this country. I hail from the north of England where industrial towns are growing. These places know what "taxation without representation" means and they were hard hit when trade with the colonies was cut off. No, I think it fair to say, English merchants and men of trade in the newer industries were very put out by the war and consistently, if vainly, opposed the government's coercive policies."

Sarah continued: "Two years ago, we felt confident enough to return home where our parents have a farm."

James added: "We intend to keep up our connections with this country, though. And our daughter was born here. You don't remember being born here, I imagine, do you Maria?" said he to the young girl, his eyebrow lifted.

She looked at him pertly, muttering "Oh Papa. Really!" Gardner had the impression it was not her first need of that expression.

Curiosity plucked at the painter. "I imagine not everyone welcomed you back, though. No doubt you had to endure a few ugly scenes."

"There were," said James, seeing they were not going to get on with any painting until Gardner had been placated.

Sarah picked up the story: "There was a man named Marsh who was particularly venomous toward what he called Tories – though that name never really fitted. My family were firm Whigs, even though some of them were strongly loyal, too. At any rate, he came round to the house one day and ran into my father. That gave him pause, but I have to say he was a plucky fellow and told my father what he thought of opening his house to people who had tried to make America a nation of serfs, as he put it.

"Papa said that if the man really believed in freedom, including free speech, as his people were always claiming, then he ought to be able to tolerate people who didn't agree with him, or at least give them the benefit of the doubt and assume they were doing what they felt was for the best, even if it wasn't the way he would choose. My father had been pretty high in rebel circles, as we used to call them, and he had authority with staunch rebels like Marsh."

James added: "He rather clinched the argument, though, when he told him that my mother danced a cotillion with General Washington in the New York city assembly rooms, and the general knew all about the Ricketts family."

Sarah added: "Marsh then said something about it was all very well rich people being able to settle back into a nice house while poor people like him had to pay a mortgage."

Sarah chuckled. "What James hasn't told you is that he didn't just let others fight his battles for him, but took the trouble to go round and see Mr Marsh. He said that if this country was going to make its way in the world, it would have to show a largeness of spirit and put up with differences and not harbour grudges. Then James offered to help with the mortgage."

"That must have caused some confusion," remarked Gardner.

"Well, he knew James didn't have to do that – he could have relied on his powerful relatives to protect him and, after all, Marsh had been pretty vindictive over that Rahway hearing which never came about," added Sarah. "I think it did pull him up short and things really began to change. I can actually remember the moment the change occurred: Marsh's wife Sadie rounded on her husband for not offering hospitality. Then she asked James to have some tea."

"I was there for a couple of hours in all. And we ended with something stronger than tea," concluded James. "Mind you, there were other unpleasantnesses, but within a year the atmosphere had really changed. I suppose people had other things to think about than recent history. For one thing, having gone on and on about the evils of strong government, people began to see that the articles of confederation were not working and the threat of chaos put central government in an entirely different light. Time does move on."

"Talking of time moving on," said Gardner, whose curiosity had apparently been satisfied, "we'd better press on with our business." In the span of an hour, the sitting was concluded. A well-merited compliment was paid to the youngest sitter for her patience which earned the painter a quick bobbing curtsey and a smile.

Maria seized her opportunity: "If you please, sir, is George here with you today?" George was Gardner's first son and Maria had formed a solid admiration for the nine-year old on her last visit to the studio. Gardner's wife Anne had died six years ago giving birth to a second son who also perished.

"Ah no, me dear, George is up in Kendal with my old friend Mr Pennington."

Meanwhile, Gardner's man had been cultivating the acquaintance of Cyrus whom he had ushered into the kitchen where they shared a glass of porter. "It's been several years since I was in America," observed the painter's servant. "I'm always glad to meet someone from there. Do you know New York by chance? I was in garrison there in the 44th of Foot before we moved to Quebec, so we were out of it by the time the war ended."

"Yes, indeed, I know the city well. It's where I first was taken up by the Rickettses. They have always been so kind to me," said Cyrus, wondering if his experiences had enabled the old soldier to know what sorts of kindness a black man would need in a slave-holding society. He did not fail to notice that, whatever Cyrus's original pattern of speech had been, his master and mistress had seen to his education.

"I reckon redcoats like me and blackskins like you have some experiences in common. People don't always love us. We can't always foresee how they will treat us," reminisced the former corporal.

Cyrus was encouraged to talk. "Some time ago, my master and mistress said I was a free man and free to go anytime I wanted to. Oh, I know nobody is a slave in England – at least not from colour. But being free to go doesn't mean much if you don't know how to earn a living. That's where they are different. They saw that I could read and write and they've contributed over the years to my purse for the future."

"So, you don't want to remain their coachman, I guess."

"Well, sir, I was always more than that to them. But now I've decided I want to be apprenticed to the tailoring trade and they've looked into it with me so, 'ere long, I'll be staying in London when they go back home."

"I'm right glad to know that, Cyrus. I might be able to use a tailor me'self one of these days."

As was not unusual in both their professions, the conversation had to be cut off at short notice. Noises above indicated that the Ricketts family was about to leave. They made their way downstairs, bid the servant goodbye and rode off in their carriage.

As they disappeared round the corner, Gardner turned to his servant and remarked: "It can't have been easy making their peace in America, for all their money and social connections, I fancy."

"Quite true, sir," said the middle-aged servant. "I imagine some of their more live-and-let-live neighbours were happy to let bygones be bygones but some must have cut 'em – made them feel unwanted." He, too, had learned to read and write in the army and that had allowed him to carry on a correspondence with one or two old soldiers of his regiment. Clearly, he knew a thing or two. It was heart-warming to see even the smallest signs of reconciliation and peace.

-end-

AUTHOR'S NOTES

The adventures of James and Sarah are fiction, though they could have happened. They are my forebears, however, and the main points of their story are true: James had a commission in the British Army, though there is no evidence that he ever was in combat against Americans. That may help to account for his success in resettling in Elizabethtown.

On another level, I have highlighted their, and their families', posture toward the American Revolution, because the usual way of telling about the Revolution does distort history in the service of a national mythology. That mythology turns the war into a straight British v. American fight, ignoring it as America's first civil war. That strong bonds existed between the two countries, before, during and after the war, has been ignored or suppressed. One of the first blows in favour of real history rather than winners' propaganda, was the publication of Kenneth Roberts' *Oliver Wiswell*, which alerted me to a cursorily-explored area of American history, long before I knew anything about the Ricketts family. Remembering the indispensable contribution of the French to American independence – there were more French regulars at Yorktown than American - I have tried to redress their downplaying in favour of the truth.

The relations within the Ricketts and Livingston families are accurate, at least as far as the evidence allows. Major John Brown was James's brother-in-law and did escort Sarah to Scotland where the Montgomeries of Eglinton were hosts for the wedding. Daphne Bainbridge is fictional and there is no evidence that James was ever unfaithful to his wife.

Cartwright is completely fictional as is Mr Green.

There was, indeed, an abortive attempt to attaint James in Rahway as an enemy of the United States but no one has advanced an explanation as to why nothing ever came of it. The act of reconciliation in which James's mother danced a cotillion with George Washington is true, though it occurred at the inaugural ball in 1789.

History knows Governor Livingston as a committed patriot and that he was thoroughly put out by Sarah's crossing the lines, is a matter of record. There is no evidence that he ever tried to sway his future nephew. Colonel Ogden did have a distinguished career in the Continental Army and dabbled in espionage (there was an abortive plot to kidnap Prince William Henry) but Ogden's daughter was a bridesmaid at the marriage of James and Sarah's youngest daughter in 1818. The Ogden and Ricketts families remained on close terms. The painting with which the story ends exists and was by Daniel Gardner.

Close connection with Britain did not cease with the peace of 1783. James and Sarah's daughter Maria was married in London in 1808 to an English barrister. James and Sarah were there as was her brother Philip, newly commissioned in the 89th Foot. He transferred into the 62nd Regiment and served as aide-de-camp to Brigadier General Sir Charles Ashworth, commanding Portuguese troops during the Peninsular War, was also a captain in the Portuguese army and retired to Philadelphia on half-pay in the 44th Foot until his death in 1843.

Maria's other brother, James William Otto, joined the Royal Navy, was a lieutenant in 1815 and retired in 1819. Wracked with fever, he died young in New York. Maria's sister Julia married an ex-midshipman of HMS *Britannia* who appears on the Trafalgar Roll. James Ricketts's granddaughter married Thomas Turner of Kinloch – a Virginian who, like James, did not fit expectations regarding loyalties; as captain of the USS *Ironsides* he took part in the naval blockade of his home state. One could say that his family, having seen the breakup of one English-speaking Union, he was not about to participate in another.

Such connections persist to the present day – one of my sisters is married to an Irishman she met in London; my wife is English; one of our daughters is married to an Englishman. When I married, I knew nothing of this pattern's existence.

Along with that, there is another curious fact: all spouses in connection with the above marriages were brought back to America. Remembering that the United States has usually abjured blood and culture – the traditional European bases of identity - as its distinguishing national traits, it is perhaps surprising that a family like the Rickettses should insist on the maintenance of its ties to the mother country. The national melting-pot mythology discourages the recognition of such links. Today, it could be argued, we may need supranational bonds more than ever, whatever the sacred cow of American exceptionalism may demand.

James's regiment has also maintained such connections. The 60th Royal Americans bore that title until 1824. In the Second World War, eighteen Americans were officers in the 60th, then called The King's Royal Rifle Corps, being granted temporary British citizenship. Later, as the 1st Battalion of The Royal Green Jackets, I am told their title Royal Americans has surfaced as a nickname. Recently they have been merged into The Rifles, as their 2nd Battalion. Their exploits at the Spring Hill redoubt were indeed celebrated on the London stage. Serjeant Smith is fictional but other soldiers like the Prevosts, Glasier, Etherington, Fuser and Brehm, did serve.

Thomas Hutchins became Geographer to the United States but remained an opportunist. He was heavily into a scheme to develop Louisiana for Spain and it is said that he was preparing to renounce his American citizenship to become a Spanish subject but died before it happened. Though it would seem improbable after his defection, he too did keep up some of his old connections. As a member of the New York law firm of Asby and Hutchins, he did indeed try, unsuccessfully, to recover land in Pennsylvania for his old colonel, General Haldimand. There is no evidence James and he ever met. I'm afraid no one knows what happened to most of those rifles after Ferguson's death.

Nor do we know of any meeting between James and Lord Amherst, though the general took considerable care to nurture his regiment in North America and the Caribbean.

Beamsley Glasier was the hero of the Spring Hill redoubt and led the horrendous inner passage voyage back to St Augustine; he went on to carve out a land-speculation career in Canada, doubtless living alongside many of the Germans of the 60th who were disbanded and given land there. Their tale has been meticulously researched by Lieutenant Colonel Don Londahl-Scmidt, formerly of the United States Air Force. Much detailed information about the Associated Loyalist refugees can be found on the superb and ever-expanding On-line Institute for Advanced Loyalist Studies, pioneered by Todd Braisted and Nan Cole.

The plight of loyalists was as described. Some fared better than others. Stephen Kemble of the 60th, brother-in-law of General Gage, retired to New Jersey in 1805 and lived another sixteen years, having become a full colonel in the British Army and Deputy Judge Advocate in England.

Other characters were real: Valli Morris was the vindictive foe of George Etherington, the strange behaviour of Imbert de Traytorrens was recounted in a letter from Captain Brehm to General Haldimand. Lippincott's trial is a matter of public record which I have only alluded to but is well worth detailed study. Admiral Thornbrough was indeed wounded at Bunker Hill and was a humane officer who was fondly remembered by his foes for landing some shipwrecked rebel sailors near their home.

My impressions of New York were drawn largely from the account of the often disappointed and bitter loyalist Thomas Jones in his *History of New York during the Revolutionary War* and from the diaries of William Smith, Chief Justice of New York, a man profoundly respected by both sides.

I am conscious of a debt to the *Encyclopedia of the American Revolution* by Mark Mayo Boatner whose even-handed account never loses sight of the humanity of those whose doings are so meticulously related. Without the tireless help of the staff of the Public Record Office, Kew (now The National Archives of England), this book could not have been written – particularly useful were the Colonial Office series of volumes, especially No. 5, and the War Office series, No. 34. Technical and historical advice was unstintingly given by Lieutenant General Sir Christopher Wallace KBE, DL, Chairman of the Board of Trustees of The Royal Green Jackets Museum at Winchester. Finally, I am grateful to my wife, Jean, to my daughters Alexandra and Sarah, and to Colin Hill, formerly of ABC documentaries, and others who patiently bore the task of reviewing, commenting on and correcting the text.

Author Biography

John Frederick is a native of Manhattan but has spent most of his professional life in England. A holder of U.S. and British citizenship, he is an Anglican priest. While he has authored a theological study of liturgy, he is perhaps better known for two authoritative books on British Army lineage. *A Royal American* is his first venture into historical fiction, drawing heavily on his knowledge of the make-up and culture of Britain's military forces. He is married with two daughters and a step-daughter. He lives in Princeton, New Jersey.